Hugh Worthington
A novel

By

Mary Jane Holmes

Hugh Worthington
A novel
by Mary Jane Holmes

Copyright © 2024

All Rights reserved.

ISBN: 978-93-62767-30-1

Published by

DOUBLE 9 BOOKS

2/13-B, Ansari Road
Daryaganj, New Delhi – 110002
info@double9books.com
www.double9books.com
Tel. 011-40042856

ABOUT THE AUTHOR

American novelist Mary Jane Holmes is well known for her widely read novels and short tales from the 19th century. She was raised in a low-income household and was born in Brookfield, Massachusetts, in 1825. Her work was renowned for its emotional and romantic tone and often addressed issues of love, family, and social status. In her lifetime, she wrote more than 60 books, demonstrating her prodigious talent. Despite Holmes' writing being well-liked during her lifetime, it went out of favor in the years after her death in 1907. Scholars and readers alike, who value her contributions to the romance novel genre and her insights into 19th-century American life and society, have lately shown a renewed interest in her work.

CONTENTS

CHAPTER I
SPRING BANK

It was a large, old-fashioned, wooden building, with long, winding piazzas, and low, square porches, where the summer sunshine held many a fantastic dance, and where the winter storm piled up its drifts of snow, whistling merrily as it worked, and shaking the loosened casement, as it went whirling by. In front was a wide-spreading grassy lawn with the carriage road winding through it, over the running brook and onward beneath tall forest trees until it reached the main highway, a distance of nearly half a mile. In the rear was a spacious garden, with bordered walks, climbing roses and creeping vines showing that some where there was a ruling hand, which, while neglecting the sombre building and suffering it to decay, lavished due care upon the grounds, and not on these alone, but also on the well kept barns, and the white-washed dwellings of the negroes,— for ours is a Kentucky scene, and Spring Bank a Kentucky home.

As we have described it so it was on a drear December night, when a fearful storm, for that latitude, was raging, and the snow lay heaped against the fences, or sweeping down from the bending trees, drifted against the doors, and beat against the windows, whence a cheerful light was gleaming, telling of life and possible happiness within. There were no flowing curtains before the windows, no drapery sweeping to the floor—nothing save blinds without and simple shades within, neither of which were doing service now, for the master of the house would have it so in spite of his sister's remonstrances.

"Some one might lose their way on that terrible night," he said, "and the blaze of the fire on the hearth, which could be seen from afar, would be to them a beacon light to guide them on their way. Nobody would look in upon them, as Adaline, or 'Lina as she chose to be called seemed to think there might, and even if they did, why need she care? She was looking well enough, and she'd undone all those little braids which disfigured her so shockingly in the morning, but which, when brushed and carefully arranged, gave her hair that waving appearance she so much desired. As for himself, he never meant to do anything of which he was ashamed, so he did not care how many were watching him through the window," and stamping his heavy boots upon the rug, for he had just come in from the storm, Hugh Worthington piled fresh fuel upon the fire, and shaking back the mass of short brown curls which had fallen upon his forehead, strode across the room and arranged the shades to his liking, then, sitting down before the fire, he went off into a reverie, the nature of which his mother, who was watching him, could not guess; and when at last she asked of what he was thinking so intently, he made her no reply. He could hardly have told himself, so varied were the thoughts crowding upon his brain that wintry night. Now they were of the eccentric old man, from whom he had received Spring Bank, together with the many peculiar ideas which made him the strange, odd creature he was, a mystery to his own sex, and a kind of terror to the female portion of the neighborhood, who, looking upon him as a woman-hater, avoided or coveted his society, just as their fancy dictated. For years the old man and the boy had lived alone in that great house, enjoying the freedom from all restraint, the liberty of turning the parlors into kennels if they chose, and converting the upper rooms into a hay-loft, if they would. No white woman was ever seen upon the premises, unless she came as a beggar, when some new gown, or surplice, or organ, or chandelier, was needed for the pretty little church, lifting its modest spire so unobtrusively among the forest trees, not very far from Spring Bank. John Stanley didn't believe in churches, nor gowns nor organs, nor women, but he was proverbially liberal and so the fair ones of Glen's Creek neighborhood ventured into his den, finding it much pleasanter to do so after the handsome, dark-haired boy came to live with him for about Hugh there was then something very attractive to the little girls, while their mothers pitied him, wondering why he had been permitted to come there, and watching for the change in him, which was sure to ensue.

Not all at once did Hugh conform to the customs of his uncle's household, and at first there often came over him a longing for the refinements of his Northern home, and a wish to infuse into Chloe, the colored housekeeper, some of his mother's neatness. But a few attempts at reform had taught him how futile was the effort, Aunt Chloe always meeting him with the argument,

"'Tain't no use, Mas'r Hugh. A nigger's a nigger; and I spec' ef you're to talk to me till you was hoarse bout your Yankee ways of scrubbin', and sweepin', and moppin' with a broom, I shouldn't be an atomer white-folksey than I is now. Besides Mas'r John wouldn't bar no finery; he's only happy when the truck is mighty nigh a foot thick, and his things is lyin' round loose and handy."

To a certain extent this was true, for John Stanley would have felt sadly out of place in any spot where, as Chloe said, "his things were not lying round loose and handy," and as habit is everything, so Hugh soon grew accustomed to his surroundings, and became as careless of his external appearance as his uncle could desire. Only once had there come to him an awakening—a faint conception of the happiness there might arise from constant association with the pure and refined, such as his uncle had labored to make him believe did not exist. He was thinking of that incident now, and it was not strange that he did not heed his mother when she spoke, for Hugh was far away from Spring Bank, and the storm beating against its walls was to him like the sound of the waves dashing against the vessel's side, just as they did years ago on that night he remembered so well, shuddering as he heard again the murderous hiss of the devouring flames, covering the fated boat with one sheet of fire, and driving into the water as a safer friend the shrieking, frightened wretches who but an hour before had been so full of life and hope, dancing gayly above the red-tongued demon stealthily creeping upward from the hold below, where it had taken life. What a fearful scene that was, and the veins grew larger on Hugh's brow while his broad chest heaved with something like a stifled sob as he recalled the little childish form to which he had clung so madly until the cruel timber struck from him all consciousness, and he let that form go down—'neath the treacherous waters of Lake Erie never to come up again alive, for so his uncle told him when, weeks after the occurrence, he awoke from the delirious fever which ensued and listened to the sickening detail.

"Lost, my boy, lost with many others," was what his uncle had said.

"*Lost*"—there was a world of meaning in that word to Hugh and though it was but a child he lost, yet in the quiet night, when all else around Spring Bank was locked in sleep, he often lay thinking of her and of what he might perhaps have been had she been spared to him. He had talked with her scarcely an hour in all, but even in that time she had made upon him an impression which could never be effaced. He was thinking of her now, and as he thought, visions of a sweet, young face, shadowed with curls of golden hair, came up before his mind, and he saw again the look of surprise and pain which shone in the soft, blue eyes and illuminated every feature when in answer to some remark of hers he gave vent to the half infidel principles he had learned from his uncle. Her creed was different from his, and she explained it to him so earnestly, that he said to her at last he did but jest to hear what she would say, and though she seemed satisfied he felt there was a shadow between them which was not swept away, even after he promised to read the Bible she timidly offered him and which he had accepted wondering at her interest in one whose *name* she did not even know. *Hers* was written on the fly-leaf of the little book which he had yet hidden away where no curious eye could find it, while carefully folded between its leaves was a curl of golden hair. That tress and the Bible which enclosed it had made Hugh Worthington a better man. He did not often read the Bible, it is true, and his acquaintances were frequently startled with opinions which had so pained the little girl on board the St. Helena, but this was merely on the surface, for far below the rough exterior there was a world of goodness, a mine of gems kept bright by memories of the angel child who flitted for so brief a span across his pathway and then was lost forever. He had tried so hard to save her—had clasped her so fondly to his bosom when with extended arms she came to him for aid. He could save her, he said—he could swim to the shore with perfect ease; and so without a moment's hesitation she had leaped with him into the surging waves, and that was about the last he could remember, save that he clutched frantically at the long, golden hair streaming above the water, retaining in his grasp the lock which no one at Spring Bank had ever seen, for this one romance of Hugh's life was a secret with himself. No one save his uncle had witnessed his emotions when told that she was dead; no one else had seen his bitter tears or heard the vehement exclamation, "You've tried to teach me there was no hereafter, no Heaven for such as she, but I know better now, and I am glad there is, for she is safe forever."

These were not idle words, and the belief then expressed became with Hugh Worthington a fixed principle, which his skeptical uncle tried in vain to eradicate. "There was a Heaven, and she was there," comprised nearly the whole of Hugh's religious creed, if we except a vague, misty hope, that he, too, would some day find her, how or by what means he never seriously inquired; only this he knew, it would be through her influence, which even now followed him every where, producing its good effects. It had checked him many and many a time when his fierce temper was in the ascendant, forcing back the harsh words he would otherwise have spoken, and making him as gentle as a child; and when the temptations to which young men of his age are exposed were spread out alluringly before him, a single thought of her was sufficient to lead him from the forbidden ground.

Every incident connected with his brief acquaintance with Golden Hair seemed to be recalled to his mind this wintry night, and so absorbed was he in his reverie that until twice repeated he did not hear his mother's anxious inquiry,

"What is that noise? It sounds like some one in distress."

Hugh started at last, and after listening for a moment he, too, caught the sound which had alarmed his mother, and made 'Lina stop her reading. A moaning cry, as if for help, mingled with an infant's wail, now here, now there it seemed to be, just as the fierce north wind shifted its course and drove first at the window of the sitting-room, and then at the ponderous doors of the gloomy hall.

"It is some one in the storm," Hugh said, going to the window and peering out into the darkness.

"Lyd's child, most likely. Negro young ones are always squalling, and I heard her tell Aunt Chloe at supper time that Tommie had the colic," 'Lina remarked, opening again the book she was reading, and with a slight shiver drawing nearer to the fire.

"Where are you going, my son?" asked Mrs. Worthington, as Hugh arose to leave the room.

"Going to Lyd's cabin, for if Tommie is sick enough to make his screams heard above the storm, she may need some help," was Hugh's reply, and a moment after he was ploughing his way through the drifts which lay between the house and the negro quarters.

"How kind and thoughtful he is," the mother said, more to herself than to her daughter, who nevertheless quickly rejoined,

"Yes, kind to niggers, and horses, and dogs, I'll admit, but let me, or any other white woman come before him as an object of pity, and the tables are turned at once. I wonder what does make him hate women so."

"I don't believe he does," Mrs. Worthington replied. "His uncle, you know, was very unfortunate in his marriage, and had a way of judging all our sex by his wife. Living with him as long as Hugh did, it's natural he should imbibe a few of his ideas."

"A few," 'Lina repeated, "better say all, for John Stanley and Hugh Worthington are as near alike as an old and young man well could be. What an old codger he was, and how like a savage he lived here. I never shall forget how the house looked the day we came, or how satisfied Hugh seemed when he met us at the gate, and said, 'everything was in splendid order,'" and closing her book, the young lady laughed merrily as she recalled the time when she first crossed her brother's threshold, stepping, as she affirmed, over half a dozen dogs, and as many squirming kittens, catching her foot in some fishing tackle, finding tobacco in the china closet, and segars in the knife box, where they had been put to get them out of the way.

"But Hugh really did his best for us," mildly interposed the mother. "Don't you remember what the servants said about his cleaning one floor himself because he knew they were tired!"

"Did it more to save the lazy negroes' steps than from any regard for our comfort," retorted 'Lina. "At all events he's been mighty careful since, how he gratified my wishes. Sometimes I believe he perfectly hates me, and wishes I'd never been born," and tears which arose from anger, rather than any wounded sisterly feeling, glittered in 'Lina's black eyes.

"Hugh does not hate any one," said Mrs. Worthington, "much less his sister, though you must admit that you try him terribly."

"How, I'd like to know?" 'Lina asked, and her mother replied,

"He thinks you proud, and vain, and artificial, and you know he abhors deceit above all else. Why he'd cut off his right hand sooner than tell a lie."

"Pshaw!" was 'Lina's contemptuous response, then after a moment, she continued, "I wonder how we came to be so different. He must be like his father, and I like mine, that is, supposing I know who he is. Wouldn't it be funny if, just to be hateful, he had sent you back the wrong child!"

"What made you think of that?" Mrs. Worthington asked, quickly, and 'Lina replied,

"Oh, nothing, only the last time Hugh had one of his tantrums, and got so outrageously angry at me, he said he'd give all he owned if it were so, but I reckon he'll never have his wish. There's too much of old Sam about me to admit of a doubt," and, laughing spitefully, 'Lina returned to her book, just as Hugh re-entered the room.

"Have you heard that sound again?" he asked. "It wasn't Tommie, for I found him asleep, and I've been all round the house, but could discover nothing. The storm is beginning to abate, I think, and the moon is trying to break through the clouds," and going again to the window, Hugh looked out into the yard, where the shrubbery and trees were just discernible in the greyish light of the December moon. "That's a big drift by the lower gate," he continued "and queer shaped, too. Come see, mother. Isn't that a shawl, or an apron, or something blowing in the wind?"

Mrs. Worthington arose, and joining her son, looked in the direction indicated, where a garment of some kind was certainly fluttering in the gale.

"It's something from the wash, I guess," she said. "I thought all the time Hannah had better not hang out the clothes, as some of them were sure to be lost."

This explanation was quite satisfactory to Mrs. Worthington, but that strange drift by the gate troubled Hugh, and the signal above it seemed to him like a signal of distress. Why should the snow drift there more than elsewhere? He never knew it do so before. He had half a mind to turn out the dogs, and see what that would do.

"Rover," he called suddenly, as he advanced to the rear room, where, among his other pets, was a huge Newfoundland, of great sagacity. "Rover, Rover, I want you."

In an instant the whole pack were upon him, jumping and fawning, and licking the hands which had never dealt them aught save kindness. It was only Rover, however, who was this time needed, and leading him to the door, Hugh pointed toward the gate, and bade him see what was there. Snuffing slightly at the storm which was not over yet, Rover started down the walk, while Hugh stood waiting in the door. At first Rover's steps were slow and uncertain, but as he advanced they increased in rapidity, until, with a sudden bound and a cry, such as dogs are wont to give when they have caught their destined prey, he sprang upon the mysterious ridge, and commenced digging it down with his paws.

"Easy, Rover—be careful," Hugh called from the door, and instantly the half savage growl which the wind had brought to his ear was changed into a piteous cry, as if the faithful creature were answering back that other help than his was needed there.

Rover had found something in that pile of snow.

CHAPTER II
WHAT ROVER FOUND

Unmindful of the sleet beating upon his uncovered head, Hugh hastened to the spot, where the noble brute was licking a baby face, which he had ferreted out from beneath the shawl wrapped so carefully around it to shield it from the cold, for instead of *one* there were *two* in that drift of snow—a mother and her child! Dead the former seemed, for the white cheek which Hugh touched was cold as stone, and with a sickening feeling the young man leaned against the gate-post and tried to assure himself that what he saw was a mere fancy of the brain. But it was terribly real. That stiffened form lying there so still hugging that sleeping child so closely to its bosom, was no delusion, and his mother's voice, calling to know what he was doing, brought Hugh back at last to a consciousness that he must act immediately.

"Mother," he screamed, "send a servant here, quick, or let Ad come herself. There's a woman dead, I fear. I can carry her well enough, but Ad must come for the child."

"The what?" gasped Mrs. Worthington, who, terrified beyond measure at the mention of a dead woman, was doubly so at hearing of a child. "A child," she repeated, "whose child?" while 'Lina, shrinking back from the keen blast, refused to obey, and so the mother, throwing her cloak around her, joined the group by the gate.

Carefully Hugh lifted the light figure in his arms and bore it to the house, where 'Lina, whose curiosity had overcome her selfishness, met him on the piazza and led the way to the sitting-room, asking innumerable questions as to how he found her and who she was.

Hugh made no reply save an order that the lounge should be brought near the fire and a pillow from his mother's bed. "From mine, then," he added, as he saw the anxious look in his mother's face, and guessed that she shrank from having her own snowy pillow come in contact with the wet, limpid figure he was depositing upon the lounge. It was a slight, girlish form, and the long brown hair, loosened from its confinement, fell in rich profusion over the pillow which 'Lina brought half reluctantly, eyeing askance the insensible object before her, and daintily holding back her dress lest it should come in contact with the child her mother had deposited upon the floor, where it lay crying lustily, unnoticed save by Rover, who, quite as awkward as his master would have been in like circumstances, seemed trying to amuse and protect it, interposing his shaggy proportions between that and the fire when once it showed a disposition to creep that way.

"Do one of you *do something*," Hugh said, as he saw how indisposed both his mother and sister were to help, the former being too much frightened and the latter too indignant to act.

The idea of a strange woman being thrust upon them in this way was highly displeasing to Miss 'Lina, who haughtily drew back from the little one when it stretched its arms out toward her, while its pretty lip quivered and the tears dropped over its rounded cheek. To her it was nothing but an intruder, a brat, and so she steeled her heart against its touching appeal, and turned her back upon it, leaving for Rover the kindly office of soothing the infant.

Meantime Hugh, with all a woman's tenderness, had done for the now reviving stranger what he could, and as his mother began to collect her scattered senses and evince some interest in the matter, he withdrew to call the negroes, judging it prudent to remain away awhile, as his presence might be an intrusion. From the first he had felt sure that the individual thrown upon his charity was not a low, vulgar person, as his sister seemed to think. He had not yet seen her face distinctly, for it lay in the shadow, but the long, flowing hair, the delicate hands, the white neck, of which he had caught a glimpse as his mother unfastened the stiffened dress, all these had made an impression, and involuntarily repeating to himself, "Poor girl," he strode a second time across the drifts which lay in his back yard and was soon pounding at old Chloe's cabin door, bidding her and Hannah dress at once and come immediately to the house.

"They will need hot water most likely," he thought and returning to the kitchen he built the fire himself and then sat down to wait until such time as it was proper for him to appear again in the sitting-room, where a strange scene was enacting.

The change of atmosphere and the restoratives applied had done their work, and Mrs. Worthington saw that the long eyelashes began to tremble, while a faint color stole into the hitherto colorless cheeks, and at last the large, brown eyes unclosed and looked into hers with an expression so mournful, that a thrill of yearning tenderness for the desolate young creature shot through her heart, and bending down she said, kindly, "Are you better now?"

"Yes, thank you. Where is Willie?" was the low response, the tone of the voice thrilling Mrs. Worthington with an undefinable emotion. Even 'Lina started, it was so low, so sweet, so musical, and coming near she answered "If it's the baby you mean, he is here, playing with our dog, Rover."

There was a look of gratitude in the brown eyes, while the white lips moved slowly, and Mrs. Worthington caught the whispered words of thanksgiving that baby Willie was safe.

"Where am I?" she said next, "and is *he* here? Is this his house?"

"Whose house?" Mrs. Worthington asked. "Whom are you looking for?"

The girl did not answer at once, and when she did her mind seemed wandering.

"I waited so long," she said, "and watched from morning till dark, but he never came again, only the letter which broke my heart. Willie was a wee baby then, and I almost hated him for awhile, but he wasn't to blame. *I* wasn't to blame. Our Father in Heaven knew I wasn't and after I went to him and told him all about it, and asked him to care for *Adah*, the first terrible pain was over and love for Willie came back with a hope that the letter might be false. I'm glad God gave me Willie now, even if he did take his father from me."

Mrs. Worthington and her daughter exchanged curious glances of wonder, and the latter abruptly asked,

"Where is Willie's father?"

"I don't know," came in a wailing sob from the depths of the pillow where the face for a moment hid itself from view.

"Where did you come from?" was the next question, put in a tone so cold and harsh that the young girl looked up in some alarm, and answered meekly,

"From New York, ma'am. It's a great ways off, and I thought I'd never get here, but every body was so kind to me and Willie, and the driver said if 'twan't so late, and he so many passengers, he'd drive across the fields. He pointed out the way and I came on alone. I saw the light off on the hill and tried to hurry, but the snow blinded me so bad and Willie was so heavy, that I fell down by the gate, and guess I went to sleep, for I remember dreaming that the angels were watching over me, and covering Willie with the snow to keep him warm."

The color had faded now from Mrs. Worthington's face, for a terrible suspicion of she scarcely knew what had darted across her mind, and very timidly she asked again,

"Whom did you hope to find?"

"Mr. Worthington. Does he live here?" was the frank reply; whereupon 'Lina, with crimsoning cheek, drew herself up haughtily, exclaiming,

"I knew it. I've thought so ever since Hugh came home from New York."

In her joy at having, as she supposed, found something tangible against her provoking brother—some weapon with which to ward off his offensive attacks upon her own deceit and want of truth—'Lina forgot that she had never seen much of him until several months after his return from New York, at which time she had become, from necessity, a member of his household and dependent upon his bounty. 'Lina was unreasonable, and without stopping to consider the effect her remarks would have upon the young girl, she was about to commence a tirade of abuse, when the mother interposed, and with an air of greater authority than she generally assumed toward her imperious daughter, bade her keep silence while she questioned the stranger, gazing wonderingly from one to the other, as if uncertain what they meant.

Mrs. Worthington had no such feelings for the girl as 'Lina entertained. If she were anything to Hugh, and the circumstances thus far favored that belief, then she was something to Hugh's mother, and the kind heart of the matron went out toward her even more strongly than it had done at first.

"It will be easier to talk with you," she said leaning forward, "if I knew what to call you."

"Adah," was the response, and the brown eyes, swimming with tears, sought the face of the questioner with a wistful eagerness.

"Adah, you say. Well, then, Adah, why have you come to my son on such a night as this, and what is he to you?"

"Are you his mother?" and Adah started up. "I did not know he had one. Oh, I'm so glad. And you'll be kind to me, who never had a mother?"

A person who never had a mother was an anomaly to Mrs. Worthington, whose powers of comprehension were not the clearest imaginable.

"Never had a mother!" she repeated. "How can that be?"

A smile flitted for a moment across Adah's pale face, and then she answered,

"I never knew a mother's care, I mean. There is some mystery which I could not fathom, only sometimes there comes up visions of a cottage with water near, and there's a lady there with voice and eyes like yours, and somebody is teaching me to walk—somebody who calls me little sister, though I've never seen him since. Then there is confusion, a rolling of wheels, and a hum of some great city, and that's all I know of mother."

"But your father? What do you know of him?" said Mrs. Worthington, and instantly a shadow stole into the sweet young face, as Adah replied, "Nothing definite."

"And Hugh? Where did you meet him? And what is he to you?"

"The only friend I've got in the wide world. May I see him, please?"

"First tell what he is to you and to this child," 'Lina rejoined, her black eyes flashing with a gleam, before which the brown eyes for an instant quailed; then as if something of a like spirit were called to life in her bosom, Adah answered calmly,

"Your brother might not like me to tell. I must see him first—see him alone."

"One thing more," and 'Lina held back her mother who was starting in quest of Hugh, "are you a wife?"

"Don't, 'Lina," Mrs. Worthington whispered, as she saw the look of agony pass over Adah's face. "Don't worry her so; deal kindly by the fallen."

"I am not fallen!" came passionately from the quivering lips. "I'm as true a woman as either of you—look!" and she pointed to the golden band encircling the third finger.

'Lina was satisfied, and needed no further explanations. To her, it was plain as daylight. Two years before Hugh had gone to New York on business connected with his late uncle's affairs, and in an unguarded moment had married some poor girl, whose pretty face had pleased his fancy. Tiring of her, as of course he would, he had deserted her, keeping his marriage a secret, and she had followed him to Spring Bank. These were the facts as 'Lina read them, and though she despised her brother for it, she was more than half glad. Hugh could never taunt her again with double dealing, for wouldn't she pay him back if he did, with his neglected, disowned wife and child? She knew they were his, and it was a resemblance to Hugh, which she had noticed from the first in Willie's face. How glad 'Lina was to have this hold upon her brother, and how eagerly she went in quest of him, keeping back old Chloe and Hannah until she had witnessed his humiliation.

Somewhat impatient of the long delay, Hugh sat in the dingy kitchen, watching the tallow candle spluttering in its iron socket, and wondering who it was he had rescued from the snow, when 'Lina appeared, and with an air of injured dignity, bade him follow her.

"What's up now that Ad looks so solemn like?" was Hugh's mental comment as he took his way to the room where, in a half reclining position Adah lay, her large, bright eyes fixed eagerly upon the door through which he entered, and a bright flush upon her cheek called up by the suspicions to which she had been subjected.

Perhaps they might be true. She did not know. Nobody knew or could tell her unless it were Hugh, and she waited for him so anxiously, starting when she heard a manly step and knew that he was coming. For an instant she scanned his face curiously to assure herself that it was he, then with an imploring cry as if for him to save her from some dreaded evil she stretched her little hands toward him and sobbed, "Mr. Worthington, was it true? Was it a real thing, or only sheer mockery, as his letter said? George, George Hastings, you know," and shedding back from her white face the wealth of flowing hair, Adah waited for the answer, which did not come at once. In utter amazement Hugh gazed upon the stranger, and then with an interjection of astonishment, exclaimed,

"Adah, Adah Hastings, why are you here?"

In the tone of his voice surprise was mingled with disapprobation, the latter of which Adah, detected at once, and as if it had crushed out the last lingering hope, she covered her face with her hands and sobbed piteously,

"Don't you turn against me, or I'll surely die, and I've come so far to find you."

By this time Hugh was himself again. His rapid, quick-seeing mind had taken in both the past and the present, and turning to his mother and sister, he said,

"Leave us alone for a time. I will call you when you are needed and, Ad, remember, no listening by the door," he continued, as he saw how disappointed 'Lina seemed.

Rather reluctantly Mrs. Worthington and her daughter left the room, and Hugh was alone with Adah, whose face was still hidden in her hands, and whose body shook with strong emotion. Deliberately turning the key in the lock, Hugh advanced to her side, and kneeling by the couch, said, kindly, "I am more pained to see you here than I can well express. Why did you come, and where is— —?"

The name was lost to 'Lina, listening outside, in spite of her brother's injunction. Neither could she understand the passionate, inaudible response. She only knew that sobs and tears were mingled with it, that there was a rustling of paper, which Adah bade Hugh read, asking if it were true. This was all 'Lina could hear, and muttering to herself, "It does not sound much like man and wife," she rather unwillingly quitted her position, and Hugh was really alone with Adah.

Never was Hugh in so awkward a position before, or so uncertain how to act. The sight of that sobbing, trembling, wretched creature, had perfectly unmanned him, making him almost as much a woman as herself. Sitting down by her side, he laid her poor aching head upon his own broad bosom, and pushing back her long, bright hair, tried to soothe her into quiet, while he candidly confessed that he feared the letter was true. It had occurred to him at the time, he said, that all was not right, but he had no suspicion that it could be so bad as it now seemed or he would have felled to the floor every participant in the cruel farce, which had so darkened Adah's life. It was a dastardly act, he said, pressing closer to him the light form quivering with anguish. He knew how innocent she was, and he held her in his arms as he would once have held the Golden Haired had she come to him with a tale of woe.

"Let me see that letter again," he said, and taking the rumpled sheet, stained with Adah's tears, he turned it to the light and read once more the cruel lines, in which there was still much of love and pity for the poor helpless thing, to whom they were addressed.

"You will surely find friends who will care for you, until the time when I may come to really make you mine."

Hugh repeated these words twice, aloud, his lip curling with contempt for the man who could so coolly thrust upon others a charge which should have been so sacred; and his heart, throbbing with the noble resolve, that the confidence she had placed in him by coming there, should not be abused, for he would be true to the trust, and care for poor, little, half-crazed Adah, moaning so piteously beside him, and as he read the last line, saying eagerly,

"He speaks of coming back. Do you think he ever will? or could I find him if I should try? I thought of starting once, but it was so far; and there was Willie. Oh, if he could see Willie! Mr. Worthington, do you believe he loves me one bit?" and in the eyes there was a look as if the poor creature were famishing for the love whose existence she was questioning.

Hugh did not understand the nature of a love which could so deliberately abandon one like Adah. It was not such love as he had cherished for the Golden Haired, but men were not alike; and so he said, at last, that the letter contained many assurances of affection, and pleadings for forgiveness for the great wrong committed.

"It seems family pride has something to do with it. I wonder where his people live, or who they are? Did he never tell you?"

"No," and Adah shook her head mournfully. "There was something strange about it. He never gave me the slightest clue. He only told how proud they were, and how they would spurn a poor girl like me; and said, we must keep it a secret until he had won them over. If I could only find them!"

"Would you go to them?" Hugh asked quickly; and Adah answered,

"Sometimes I've thought I would. I'd brave his proud mother—I'd lay Willie in her lap. I'd tell her whose he was, and then I'd go away and die. They could not harm my Willie!" and the young girl mother glanced proudly at her sleeping boy. Then, after a pause, she continued, "Once, Mr. Worthington, when my brain was all on fire, I went down to the river, and said I'd end my wretched life, but God, who was watching me, held me back. He cooled my scorching head—he eased the pain, and on the very spot where I meant to jump, I kneeled down and said, 'Our Father.' No other words would come, only these, 'Lead us not into temptation.' Wasn't it kind in God to save me?"

There was a radiant expression in the sweet face as Adah said this, but it quickly passed away and was succeeded by one of deep concern, when Hugh abruptly asked,

"Do you believe in God?"

"Oh, Mr. Worthington. Don't you? You do, you must, you will," and Adah shrank away from him as from a monster.

The action reminded him of the Golden Haired, when on the deck of the St. Helena he had asked her a similar question, and anxious further to probe the opinion of the girl beside him, he continued,

"If, as you think, there is a God who knew and saw when you were about to drown yourself, why didn't he prevent the cruel wrong to you? Why did he suffer it?"

"What He does we know not now, but we shall know hereafter," Adah said, reverently, adding, "If George had feared God, he would not have left me so; but he didn't, and perhaps he says there is no God—but you don't, Mr. Worthington. Your face don't look like it. Tell me you believe," and in her eagerness Adah grasped his arm beseechingly.

"Yes, Adah, I believe," Hugh answered, half jestingly, "but it's such as you that make me believe, and as persons of your creed think every thing is ordered for good, so possibly you were permitted to suffer that you might come here and benefit me. I think I must keep you until he is found."

"No, no," and the tears flowed at once, "I cannot be a burthen to you. I have no claim."

"Why then did you come at all?" Hugh asked, and Adah answered,

"For a time after I received the letter every thing was so dark that I didn't realize, and couldn't think of any thing. But when the landlady hinted those terrible things, and finally told me I must leave to give place to a respectable woman, that's just what she said, a *respectable* woman, with a child who knew its own father, then I woke up and tried to think of something, but the more I tried, the more I couldn't, till at last I prayed so hard one night, that God would tell me what to do, and suddenly I remembered you and your good, kind, honest face, just as it looked when you spoke to me after it was over, and called me by the new name. Oh, dear, oh, dear," and gasping for breath, Adah leaned against Hugh's arm, sobbing bitterly.

After a moment she grew calm again, and continued,

"I wrote down your name, and where you lived, though why I did not know, and I forgot where I put it, but as if God really were helping me I found it in my old portfolio, and something bade me come, for you perhaps would know if it was true. It was sometime before I could fully decide to come, and in that time I hardly know how I lived, or where. George left me money, and sent more, but it's most gone now. But I must not stay. I can take care of myself.

"What can you do?" Hugh asked, and Adah replied, sadly,

"I don't know, but God will find me something. I never worked much, but I can learn, and I can already sew neatly, too; besides that, a few days before I decided to come here, I advertised in the Herald for some place as governess or ladies' waiting-maid. Perhaps I'll hear from that."

"It's hardly possible. Such advertisements are thick as blackberries," Hugh said, and then in a few brief words, he marked out Adah's future course.

George Hastings might or might not return to claim her, and whether he did or didn't, she must live meantime, and where so well as at Spring Bank.

"I do not like women much," he said, "but something makes me like you, pity, I reckon, and I'm going to take care of you until that scoundrel turns up; then, if you say so, I'll surrender you to his care, or better yet, I'll shoot him and keep you to myself. Not as a sweetheart, or anything of that kind," he hastened to add, as he saw the flush on Adah's cheek. "Hugh Worthington has nothing to do with that species of the animal kingdom, but as my sister Adah!" and as Hugh repeated that name, there arose in his great heart an undefinable wish that the gentle girl beside him had been his sister instead of the high tempered Adaline, who never tried to conciliate or understand him, and whom Hugh could not love as brothers should love sisters.

He knew how impatiently she was waiting now to know the result of that interview, and just how much opposition he should meet when he announced his intention of keeping Adah. But Hugh was master of Spring Bank; his will was all powerful, and not an entire world could move him when once he was determined. Still contention was not agreeable, and he oftentimes yielded a point rather than dispute. But this time he was firm. Without any intention of wronging Adah, he still felt as if in some way he had been instrumental to her ruin, and now when she came to him for help, he would not cast her off, though the keeping her would subject him to a multitude of unpleasant remarks, surmises and suspicions from the people of Glen's Creek, to say nothing of his mother's and 'Lina's displeasure. Added to this was another objection, a serious one, which most men would have weighed carefully before deciding to burden themselves with two additional individuals. Though the owner of Spring Bank, Hugh was far from being rich, and many were the shifts and self denials he was obliged to make to meet the increased expense entailed upon him by his mother and sister. John Stanley had been accounted wealthy, but at his death there was nothing left, save a few acres of nearly worn out land, the old dilapidated house, and a dozen or more negroes. With good management this was amply sufficient to supply Hugh's limited wants, and he was looking forward to a life of careless ease, when his mother from New England wrote, asking for a home. Hugh did not know then as well as he did now what it would cost to keep a young lady of his sister's habits. He only knew that his home was far different from the New England one he remembered so well, but such as it was he would share it with his mother and sister, and so he had bidden them welcome, concealing from them as far as possible the trouble he oftentimes had to meet the increased demand for money which their presence brought. This to a certain extent was the secret of his patched boots, his threadbare coat and coarse pants, with which 'Lina so often taunted him, saying he wore them just to be stingy and mortify her, when in fact necessity rather than choice was the cause of his shabby appearance. He had never told her so, however, never said that the unfashionable coat so offensive to her fastidious vision was worn that she might be the better clothed and fed. Yet such was the case, and now he was deliberately adding to his already heavy burden. But Hugh was capable of great self sacrifices. He could manage somehow, and Adah should stay. He would say that she was a friend whom he had known in New York; that her husband had deserted her, and in her distress she had come to him for aid; for the rest he trusted that time and her own appearance would wear away any unpleasant impressions which her presence might create.

All this he explained to Adah, who assented tacitly thinking within herself that she should not long remain at Spring Bank, a dependant upon one on whom she had no claim. She was too weak now, however, to oppose him, and merely nodding to his suggestions laid her head upon the arm of the lounge with a low cry that she was sick and warm. Stepping to the door Hugh turned the key and summoning the group waiting anxiously in the adjoining room, bade them come at once, as Mrs. Hastings appeared to be fainting. Great emphasis he laid upon the *Mrs.* and catching it up at once 'Lina repeated, "*Mrs. Hastings!* So am I just as much."

"Ad," and the eyes which shone so softly on poor Adah flashed with gleams of fire as Hugh said to his sister, "not another word against that girl if you wish to remain here longer. She has been unfortunate."

"I guessed as much," sneeringly interrupted 'Lina.

"Silence!" and Hugh's foot came down as it sometimes did when chiding a refractory negro. "She is as true, yes, truer than you. He who should have protected her has basely deserted her. And I shall care for her. See that a fire is kindled in the west chamber, and go up yourself when it is made and see that all is comfortable. Do you understand?" and he gazed sternly at 'Lina, who was too much astonished to answer, even if she had been so disposed.

That Hugh should take in a beggar from the streets was bad enough, but to keep her, and worse yet to put her in the best chamber, where ex-Governor Russ had slept; and where was nailed down the carpet, brought from New England—was preposterous, and Hugh was certainly crazy. But never was man more sane than Hugh; and seeing her apparently incapable of carrying out his orders he himself sent Hannah to build the fire, bidding her, with all a woman's forethought, be careful that the bed was aired, and clothes enough put on. "Take a blanket from my bed, if necessary," he added, as Hannah, bewildered with the "carryin's on," disappeared up the staircase, a long line of smoke streaming behind her.

When all was ready, Hugh went for Adah, and taking her in his arms carried her to the upper chamber, where, the fire was burning brightly, casting cheerful shadows upon the wall, and making Adah smile gratefully, as she looked up in his face, and murmured,

"God bless you, Mr. Worthington! Adah will pray for you to-night, when she is alone. It's all that she can do."

They laid her upon the bed. Hugh himself arranging her pillows, which no one else appeared inclined to touch.

Family opinion was against her, innocent and beautiful as she looked lying there—so helpless, so still, with her long-fringed lashes shading her colorless cheek, and her little hands folded upon her bosom, as if already she were breathing the promised prayer for Hugh. Only in Mrs. Worthington's heart was there a chord of sympathy. She couldn't help feeling for the desolate stranger; and when, at her own request, Hannah placed Willie in her lap, ere laying him by his mother, she gave him an involuntary hug, and touched her lips to his fat, round cheek. It was the first kiss given him at Spring Bank, and it was meet that it should come from her.

"He looks as you did, Hugh, when you were a baby," she said, while Chloe rejoined,

"De very spawn of Mar's Hugh, now. I 'tected it de fust minit. Can't cheat dis chile," and, with a chuckle which she meant to be very expressive, the fat old woman waddled from the room, followed by Hannah, who was to sleep there that night, and who must first return to her cabin to make the necessary preparations for her vigils.

Hugh and his mother were alone, and turning to her son, Mrs. Worthington said, gently,

"This is sad business, Hugh; worse than you imagine. Do you know how folks will talk?"

"Let them talk," Hugh growled. "It cannot be much worse than it is now. Nobody cares for Hugh Worthington; and why should they, when his own mother and sister are against him, in actions if not in words?—one sighing when his name is mentioned, as if he really were the most provoking son that ever was born, and the other openly berating him as a monster, a clown, a savage, a scarecrow, and all that. I tell you, mother, there is but little to encourage me in the kind of life I'm leading. Neither you nor Ad have tried to make anything of me or have done me any good; but somehow, I feel as if she would," and he pointed to the now sleeping Adah. "At all events, I know it's right to keep her, and I want you to help me, will you? That is, will you be kind to her; and when folks speak against her, as they may, will you stand for her as for your own daughter? She's more like you than Ad," and

Hugh gazed wonderingly from one to the other, struck, for the first time, with a resemblance, fancied or real, between the two.

Mrs. Worthington did not heed this last, so intent was she on the first of Hugh's remarks. Choking with tears she said,

"You wrong me, Hugh; I do try to make something of you. You are a dear child to me, dearer than the other; but I'm a weak woman, and 'Lina sways me at will."

A kind word unmanned Hugh at once, and kneeling by his mother, he put his arms around her, and begging forgiveness for his harsh words, asked again a mother's care for Adah.

"Hugh," and Mrs. Worthington looked him steadily in the face, "is Adah your wife, or Willie your child?"

"Great guns, mother!" and Hugh started to his feet as quick as if a bombshell had exploded at his side. "No by all that's sacred, no! Upon my word; you look sorry instead of glad! Are you sorry, mother, to find me better than you imagined it possible for a bad boy like me to be?"

"No, Hugh, not sorry. I was only thinking that I've sometimes fancied that, as a married man, you might be happier; and when this woman came so strangely, and you seemed so interested, I didn't know, I rather thought— —"

"I know," and Hugh interrupted her. "You thought maybe, I raised Ned when I was in New York; and, as a proof of said resurrection, Mrs. Ned and Ned junior, had come with their baggage. But it is not so, she does not belong to me," and going up to his mother he told her all he knew of Adah, adding, "Now will you be kind to her for my sake? and when Ad rides her highest horse, as she is sure to do, will you smooth her down? Tell her Adah has as good right here as she, if I choose to keep her."

There was a faint remonstrance on Mrs. Worthington's part, her argument being based upon what folks would say, and Hugh's inability to take care of many more.

Hugh did not care a picayune for *folks*, and as for Adah, if his mother did not wish her there, and he presumed she did not, he'd get her boarded for the present with Aunt Eunice, who, like himself, was invincible to public opinion, she needed just such a companion. She'd be a mother to Adah, and Adah a daughter to her, so they needn't spend further time in talking, for he was getting tired.

Mrs. Worthington was much more easily won over to Hugh's opinion than 'Lina, who, when told of the arrangement, raised a perfect hurricane of expostulations and tears. They'd be a county talk, she said; nobody would come near them, and she might as well enter a nunnery at once; besides, hadn't Hugh enough on his hands already without taking more?

"If my considerate sister really thinks so, hadn't she better try and help herself a little?" retorted Hugh in a blaze of anger. "I've only paid two hundred and fifty dollars for her since she came here, to say nothing of that bill at Harney's due in January."

'Lina began to cry, and Hugh, repenting of his harsh speech as soon as it was uttered, but far too proud to take it back, strode up and down the room, chafing like a young lion.

"Come, children, it's after midnight, let us adjourn until to-morrow," Mrs. Worthington said, by way of ending the painful interview, at the same time handing a candle to Hugh, who took it silently and withdrew, banging the door behind him with a force which made 'Lina start and burst into a fresh flood of tears.

"I'm a brute, a savage," was Hugh's not very self complimentary soliloquy, as he went up the stairs. "What did I want to twit Ad for? What good did it do, only to make her mad and bother mother? I wish I could do better, but I can't. Confound my badness!" and having by this time reached his own door, Hugh entered his room, and drawing a chair to the fire always kindled for him at night, sat down to think.

CHAPTER III
HUGH'S SOLILOQUY

"One, two, three, yes, as good as four women and a child," he began, "to say nothing of the negroes, who all must eat and drink. A goodly number for one whose income is hardly as much as some young men spend every year upon themselves; and the hardest of all is the having people call me stingy and mean, the seeing young girls lift their eyebrows and wink when young Hunks, as Ad says they call me, appears, and the knowing that this opinion of me is encouraged and kept alive by the remarks and insinuations of my own sister, for whom I've denied myself more than one new coat that she might have the dress she coveted," and in the red gleam of the firelight the bearded chin quivered for a moment as Hugh thought how unjust 'Lina was to him, and how hard was the lot imposed upon him.

Soon recovering his composure he continued, "There's that bill at Harney's, how in the world I'm to pay it when it comes due is more than I know. These duds," and he glanced ruefully at his coarse clothes, "will look a heap worse than they do now," and shifting the position of his feet, which had hitherto rested upon the hearth, to a more comfortable and suggestive one upon the mantel, Hugh tried to find a spot in which he could economize.

"I needn't have a fire in my room nights," he said, as a coal fell into the pan and thus reminded him of its existence, "and I won't, either. It's nonsense for a great hot-blooded clown like me to be babied with a fire. I've no tags to braid, no false switches to comb out and hide, only a few buttons to undo, a shake or so, and I'm all right. So there's one thing, the fire—quite an item, too, at the rate coal is selling. Then there's coffee. I can do without that, I suppose, though it will be perfect torment to smell it, and Hannah makes such splendid coffee, too; but will is everything. Fire, coffee—I'm getting on famously. What else?"

"*Tobacco*," something whispered, but Hugh answered promptly, "No, sir, I shan't! I'll sell my shirts, before I'll give up my best friend. It's all the comfort I have when I get a fit of the blues. Oh, you needn't try to come it!" and Hugh shook his head defiantly at his unseen interlocutor, urging that 'twas a filthy practice at best, and productive of no good. "You needn't try for I won't," and Hugh deliberately lighted a cigar and resumed his soliloquy, while he complacently watched the little blue rings curling so gracefully above his head. "Blamed if I can think of any thing else, but maybe I shall. I might sell something, I suppose. There's Harney wants to buy Bet, but Ad never rides any other horse, and she does ride uncommonly well, if she *is* Ad. There's the negroes, more than I need," but from this suggestion Hugh turned away quite as decidedly as from the one touching his tobacco. "He didn't believe much in negroes any way, surely not in selling them; besides that, nobody'd want them after they'd been spoiled as he had spoiled them," and he laughed aloud as he fancied a new master trying to break in old Chloe, who had ruled at Spring Bank so long that she almost fancied she owned it. No, Hugh wouldn't sell his servants, and the negroes sleeping so soundly in their cabins had nothing to fear from him.

Horses were suggested again. "You have other horses than Bet," and Hugh was conscious of a pang which wrung from him a groan, for his horses were his idols, and parting with them would be like severing a right hand. It was too terrible to think about, and Hugh dismissed it as an alternative which might have to be considered another time. Then hope made her voice heard above the little blue imps tormenting him so sadly.

He should get along somehow. Something would turn up. Ad might marry and go away. He knew it was wrong, and yet he could not help thinking it would be nice to come home some day and not find her there, with her fault-finding, and her sarcastic remarks. What made her so different from his mother—so different from the little sister he always remembered with a throb of delight? He had loved her, and he thought of her now as she used to look in her dainty white frocks, with the strings of coral he had bought with nuts picked on the New England hills.

He used to kiss her chubby arms—kiss the rosy cheeks, and the soft brown hair. But that hair had changed sadly since the days when its owner had first lisped his name, and called him "Ugh," for the bands and braids coiled around 'Lina's head were black as midnight. Not less changed than 'Lina's tresses was 'Lina herself, and Hugh had often felt like crying for the little baby sister, so lost and dead to him in her young womanhood. What had changed Ad so? To be sure he did not care much for females any way, but if Ad were half way decent, and would let him, he should love her, he presumed. Other young men loved their sisters. There was Bob Reynolds seemed to idolize his, crippled though she was, and he had mourned so bitterly, when she died, bending over her coffin, and kissing her white face. Would Hugh do so to Ad? He thought it very doubtful! though, he supposed, he should feel sorry and mourn some, but he'd bet he wouldn't wear a very wide band of crape around his hat; he couldn't afford it! Still he should remember all the harsh things he had said to her, and be so sorry.

There was many a tender spot in Hugh Worthington's heart, and shadow after shadow flitted across his face as he thought how cheerless was his life, and how little there was in his surroundings to make him happy. Poor Hugh! It was a dreary picture he drew as he sat alone that night, brooding over his troubles, and listening to the moan of the wintry wind—the only sound he heard, except the rattling of the shutters and the creaking of the timbers, as the old house rocked in the December gale.

Suddenly there crept into his mind Adah's words, "I shall pray for you to-night." Would she? Had she prayed for him, and did prayers do any good? Was any one bettered by them? Golden Hair had thought so, and he was sure she had talked with God of him, but since the waters closed over her dear head, no one had remembered Hugh Worthington in that way, he was sure. But Adah would, and Hugh's heart grew stronger as he thought of Adah praying for him. What would she say? How would she word it? He wished he knew, but prayer was strange to Hugh. He *never* prayed, and the Bible given by Golden Hair had not been opened this many a day, but he would do so now, and unlocking the trunk where it was hidden, he took it from its concealment and opened it reverently, half wondering what he should read first and if it would have any reference to his present position.

"Inasmuch as ye did it to the least of these ye did it unto me."

That was what Hugh read in the dim twilight, that, the passage on which the lock of hair lay, and the Bible dropped from his hands as he whispered,

"Golden Hair, are you here? Did you point that out to me? Does it mean Adah? Is the God you loved on earth pleased that I should care for her?"

To these queries, there came no answer, save the mournful wailing of the night wind roaring down the chimney and past the sleet-covered window, but Hugh was a happier man for reading that, and had there before existed a doubt as to his duty toward Adah, this would have swept it away. Bending closer to the fire, Hugh read the chapter through, wondering why he should feel so much better, and why the world looked brighter than it had an hour before. If it made folks feel so nice to read a little bit in the Bible, how would they feel to read it through? He meant to try and see, beginning at Genesis the very next night, and hiding his treasure away, Hugh sought his pillow just as the first greyish streak of daylight was beginning to show in the east.

CHAPTER IV
TERRACE HILL

The storm which visited Kentucky so wrathfully was far milder among the New England hills, and in the vicinity of Snowdon, whither our story now tends, was scarcely noticed, save as an ordinary winter's storm. There were no drifts against the fences, no driving sleet, no sheets of ice covering the valleys, nothing save a dark, sour, dreary day, when the grey December clouds seemed wading in the piles of snow, which, as the sun went down, began to fall in those small misty flakes, which betoken a storm of some duration. As yet it had been comparatively warmer in New England than in Kentucky; and Miss Anna Richards, confirmed invalid though she was, had decided not to take her usual trip to the South, so comfortable was she at home, in her accustomed chair, with her pretty crimson shawl wrapped around her. Besides that, they were expecting her brother John from Paris, where he had been for the last eighteen months, pursuing his medical profession, and she must be there to welcome him.

Anna was proud of her young, handsome brother, for on him and his success in life, all their future hopes were pending.

All were proud of John, and all had petted and spoiled him, from his precise lady mother, down to invalid Anna, who, more than any one else, was anxious for his return, and who had entered, with a good deal of interest into the preparations which, for a week or more, had kept Terrace Hill Mansion in a state of bustle and excitement, for John was so refined and fastidious in his tastes, that he was sure to notice if aught were amiss or out of place. Consequently great pains was taken with his room, while Anna, who had a private purse of her own, went into the extravagance of furnishing a new carpet of more modern style than the heavy, old-fashioned Brussels, which for years, had covered the floor.

John had never been very happy at home—and hence the efforts they were putting forth to make it attractive to him after his long absence. He could not help liking it now, the ladies said to each other, as, a few days before his arrival, they rode from the village, up the winding terraced hill, admiring the huge stone building embosomed in evergreens, and standing out so distinctly against the wintry sky. And Terrace Hill Mansion was a very handsome place, exciting the envy and admiration of the villagers, who could remember a time when it had looked better even than it did now—when the house was oftener full of city company, when high-born ladies rode up and down in carriages, or dashed on horseback through the park and off into leafy woods—when sounds of festivity were heard in the halls from year's end to year's end, and the lights in the parlors were rarely extinguished, or the fires on the hearth put out. This was during the lifetime of its former owner, whose covering had been the tall green grass of Snowdon cemetery for several years. With his death there had come a change to the inhabitants of Terrace Hill, a curtailing of expenses, a gradual dropping of the swarms of friends who had literally fed upon them during the summer and autumn months. In short it was whispered now that the ladies of Terrace Hill were restricted in their means, that there was less display of dress and style, fewer fires, and lights, and servants, and an apparent desire to be left to themselves.

This was what the village people whispered, and none knew the truth of the whisperings better than the ladies in question, or shrank more from having their affairs canvassed by those whom they looked down upon, even if the glory of their house was departed. Mrs. Richards and her elder daughters, Miss Asenath and Eudora, were very proud, very exclusive, and but for the existence of Anna, few of the villagers would ever have crossed their threshold. Anna was a favorite in the village, and when confined to her room for weeks, as she sometimes was, there were more anxious enquiries concerning her than would have been bestowed on Asenath and Eudora had they both been dying. And yet in her early girlhood she too had been cold and haughty, but since the morning when she had knelt at her father's feet, and begged him to revoke his cruel decision, and say she might be the bride of a poor missionary, Anna had greatly changed, and the father had sometimes questioned the propriety of separating the hearts which clung so tenaciously together. But it was then too late to remedy the mistake. The young missionary had married another, and neither the parents nor the sisters ever forgot the look of anguish which stole into Anna's face, when she heard the news. She had told him to do so, it is true, for she knew a missionary to be strictly useful must have a wife. She had thought herself prepared, but the news was just as crushing when it came, accompanied though it was with a few last lines from *him*, such as a husband might write to the woman he had loved so much, and only given up because he must. Anna kept this letter yet, reading it often to herself, and wondering, if through all the changes which fourteen years had wrought, the missionary remembered her yet, and if they would ever meet again. This was the secret of the numerous missionary papers and magazines scattered so profusely through the rooms at Terrace Hill. Anna was interested in everything pertaining to the work, though, it must be confessed, that her mind wandered oftenest to the city of mosques and minarets, where *he* was laboring; and once, when she heard of a little grave made with the Moslem dead, the grave of darling Anna, named for her, she wept bitterly, feeling as if she, too, had been bereaved as well as the parents, across the Eastern waters. This was sweet Anna Richards, who, on the day of her brother's expected arrival from Paris, dressed herself with unusual care and joined her mother and elder sisters in the parlor below. It was a raw, chilly evening, and a coal fire had been kindled in the grate, the bright blaze falling on Anna's cheek, and lighting it up with something like the youthful bloom for which she had once been celebrated. The harsh expression of Miss Asenath's face was softened down, while the mother and Eudora looked anxiously expectant, and Anna was the happiest of them all. Taken as a whole it was a very pleasant family group, which sat there waiting for the foreign lion, and for the whistle of the engine which was to herald his approach.

"I wonder if he has changed," said the mother, glancing at the opposite mirror and arranging the puffs of glossy false hair which shaded her aristocratic forehead.

"Of course he has," returned Miss Asenath. "Nearly two years of Paris society must have imparted to him that *air distingue* so desirable in a young man who has travelled."

"He'll hardly fail of making a good match now," Miss Eudora remarked. "I think we must manage to visit Saratoga or some of those places next summer. Mr. Gardner found his wife at Newport, and they say she's worth half a million."

"But horridly ugly," and Anna looked up from the reverie in which she had been indulging. "Lottie says she has tow hair and a face like a fish. John would never be happy with such a wife."

"Possibly you think he had better have married that sewing girl about whom he wrote us just before going to Europe," Miss Eudora suggested.

"No, I don't," Anna answered, mildly. "I am almost as anxious as yourselves for him to marry rich, for I know you need money sadly, and my income is not so large as for your sakes I wish it was, but poverty and love are better than riches and hatred, and I have always felt a strange interest in that young girl, whom I know John loved, or he would never have written to see how we would bear his taking a portionless bride."

"I told him plainly how *I* would bear it. She should never cross *my* threshold," and the face of Mrs. Richards, the mother, was highly indicative of the feeling she entertained for the young, penniless girl, whom it would seem John Richards M. D., had thought to marry.

"I trust he is over that fancy," she continued, "and ready to thank me for the strong letter I wrote him."

"Yes, but the girl," and Anna leaned her white cheek in her whiter hand. "None of us know the harm his leaving her may have done. Don't you remember he wrote how much she loved him—how gentle and confiding her nature was, how to leave her then might prove her ruin?"

"Our little Anna is growing very eloquent upon the subject of sewing girls," Miss Asenath said, rather scornfully, and Anna rejoined,

"I am not sure she was a sewing girl. He spoke of her as a school girl."

"But it is most likely he did that to mislead us," said the mother. "The only boarding school he knows anything about is the one where Lottie was. He often visited her, but I've questioned her closely, and she cannot think of a single young lady whom he fancied more than another. All were in love with him, she said, herself included. If he were not her uncle by marriage I should not object to Lottie as a daughter," was the next remark, whereupon there ensued a conversation touching the merits and demerits of a certain Lottie Gardner, whose father had taken for a second wife Miss Laura Richards.

During this discussion of Lottie, Anna had sat listlessly looking up and down the columns of an old Herald which Dick, Eudora's pet dog, had ferreted out from the table and deposited at her feet. She evidently was not thinking of Lottie, nor yet of the advertisements, until one struck her notice as being very singular from the fact that a name was appended to it, a thing she had never seen before. Holding it a little more to the light and bending forward she said, "Possibly this is the very person I want—one who will be either a companion or a waiting-maid, only the child might be an objection, though I do love the little things. Just listen," and Anna read as follows:

"Wanted—by an unfortunate young married woman, with a child a few months old, a situation in a private family either as governess, seamstress, or lady's maid. Country preferred. Address ——"

Anna was about to say whom, when a violent ringing of the bell and a heavy stamping of feet on the steps with out announced an arrival, and the next moment a tall, handsome young man, exceedingly Frenchified in his appearance, entered the room, and was soon in the arms of his mother, who, kissing his bearded cheek, welcomed him as her son.

John, or Dr. Richards, did not care particularly to be caressed by ladies unless he could choose them, and releasing himself as soon as practicable from his lady mother's embrace, he submitted himself a moment to his two elder sisters, and then, hastening to where Anna sat, wound his arms around her light figure, and lifting her as he would have lifted a little child, kissed her white lips and looked into her face with an expression which told that, however indifferent he might be to others, he was not so to Anna.

"You have not changed for the worse," he said, replacing her in her chair and sitting down beside her.

"And you are vastly improved," was Anna's answer, as she smoothed playfully the Parisian mustache, her brother's special pride.

Then commenced from mother and sisters a volley of questions. Had he been well? Did he like Paris? Was he glad to be home again? And why had he gone off without coming out to say good-bye?

This last was put by his mother, who continued, "I thought, perhaps, you were offended at my plain letter concerning that girl, and resented it by not coming, but of course you are glad now, and see that mother was right. What could you have done with a wife in Paris?"

"I should not have gone," John answered, moodily, a shadow stealing over his face.

It was not good taste for Mrs. Richards thus early to introduce a topic on which John was really so sore, and for a moment an awkward silence ensued, broken at last by the mother again, who, feeling that all was not right, and anxious to know if there was yet aught to fear from a poor, unknown daughter-in-law, asked, hesitatingly,

"Have you seen her since your return?"

She is *dead* was the reply, and then anxious to change the conversation, the Doctor began talking to Anna until the supper bell rang, and his mother led the way to the dining room where a most inviting supper was prepared in honor of *the Doctor's* return. How handsome he looked in his father's place at the head of the table. How gracefully he did the honors, and how proud all were of him as he repeated little incidents of Parisian life, speaking of the Emperor and Eugenie as if they had been every day sights to him. In figure and form the fair Empress reminded him of Anna, he said, except that Anna was the prettier of the two—a compliment which Anna acknowledged with a blush and a trembling of her long eyelashes. It was a very pleasant family reunion, for John did his best to be agreeable, and by the time they returned to the parlor his mother had quite forgiven him the flagrant act of loving an unknown girl.

"Oh, John, please be careful where you tear that paper. There's an advertisement I want to save," Anna exclaimed, as she saw her brother tearing a strip from the Herald with which to light his cigar, but as she spoke, the smoke and flame curled around the narrow strip, and Dr. Richards had lighted his cigar with the name and address appended to the advertisement which had so interested Anna.

How disturbed she was when she found that nought was left save the simple wants of the young girl who, with a breaking heart had penned the lines, and who now lay so still beneath a Kentucky rift of snow!

"Let's see," and taking the mutilated sheet, Dr. Richards read the "Wanted, by a young unfortunate married woman."

"That unfortunate may mean a great deal more than you imagine," he said, in order to quiet his sister, who quickly rejoined,

"Yes, but she distinctly says married. Don't you see, and I had really some idea of writing to her, or at least I think I had, now that 'tis too late."

"I'm sorry I was so careless, but there are a thousand unfortunate women who would gladly be your maid, little sister. I'll send you out a score, if you say so, either with or without babies," and John laughed, as with the utmost nonchalance he smoked the cigar lighted with the name of *Adah Hastings*!

"Has any thing of importance occurred in this slow old town?" he inquired, after Anna had become reconciled to her loss. "Has there been any desirable addition to Snowdon society?"

"Yes," returned Anna. "A Mrs. Johnson, who is every way cultivated and refined, while Alice is the sweetest girl I ever knew. You have a rare pleasure in store in forming their acquaintance.

"Whose, the old or the young lady's?" John asked, carelessly knocking the ashes from the end of his cigar.

"Both," was Anna's reply. "The mother is very youthful in her appearance. Why, she scarcely looks older than I do, and I, you know, am thirty-two."

As if fearful lest her own age should come next under consideration, Miss Eudora hastened to say,

"Yes, Mrs. Johnson does look very young, and Alice seems like a child, though I heard her say she was almost twenty. Such beautiful hair as she has. It used to be a bright yellow, or golden, so the old nurse says, but now it has a darker, richer shade, midway between golden and chestnut, while her eyes are the softest, handsomest blue."

Alice Johnson was evidently a favorite at Terrace Hill, and as this stamped her somebody John began to ask who the Johnsons were, and where they came from.

Mrs. Richard seemed disposed to answer these questions, which she did as follows:

"Mrs. Johnson used to live in Boston, and her husband was grandson of old Governor Johnson, one of the best families in that State."

"Ah, yes," and John began to laugh. "I see now what gives Miss Alice's hair that peculiar shade, and her eyes that heavenly blue, over which my staid sister Dora waxed so eloquent. Miss Alice is an ex-Governor's great grand daughter—but go on, mother, only come to Alice herself and give her *figure* as soon as may be."

"What do you mean?" asked Anna, who took things literally. "I should suppose you'd care more for her face than her form."

John smiled mischievously, while his mother continued.

"I fancy that Mrs. Johnson's family met with a reverse of fortune before her marriage, but know nothing certainly except that she was greatly beloved in Boston. Her husband has been dead some years, and recently she has bought and fitted up that pretty cottage down by the river. I do not see her as often as I would like to, for I am greatly pleased with her, although she has some habits of which I cannot approve, such as associating with the poor of the town to the extent she does. Why, I hear that Alice had a party the other day consisting wholly of ragged urchins."

"They were her Sunday school scholars," interposed Anna. "Alice has picked up a large class of children, who before her coming, used to run the streets on Sundays breaking up birds' nests and pilfering gardens. I am sure we ought to be much obliged to her, for our fruit and flowers are now comparatively safe."

"I vote that Anna goes on with Alice's history. She gives it best," said John, and so Anna continued,

"There is but little to tell. Mrs. Johnson and her daughter are both nice ladies, and I am sure you will like them—every body does; and rumor has already given Alice to our young clergyman, Mr. Howard."

"And she is worth fifty thousand dollars, too," rejoined Asenath, as if that were a powerful reason why a poor clergyman should not aspire to her hand.

"I have her *figure* at last," said John, winking slily at Anna, who only looked bewildered. And, the $50,000 did seem to make an impression on the young man, who made numerous inquiries concerning the heiress, asking how often she came to Terrace Hill, and where he would be most likely to see her.

"At church," was Anna's reply. "She is always there and their pew joins ours."

Dr. Richards did not much like going to church, unless it were where the music was grand and operatic. Still he had intended honoring the benighted Snowdonites with a sight of himself for one half day, though he knew he should be terribly bored; but now the case was different, for besides being, to a certain extent, a kind of *lion*, he should see Miss Alice, and he reflected with considerable satisfaction that as this was Friday night, only one day intervened ere his curiosity and that of the villagers would be gratified. He was glad there was something new and interesting in Snowdon in the shape of a pretty girl, for he did not care to return at once to New York, where he had intended practising his profession. There were too many sad memories clustering about that city to make it altogether desirable, but Dr. Richards was not yet a hardened wretch, and thoughts of another than Alice Johnson, crowded upon his mind as on that first evening of his return, he sat answering questions and asking others of his own.

It was late ere the family group broke up, and the storm beating so furiously upon Spring Bank, was just making its voice heard round Terrace Hill Mansion, when the doctor took the lamp the servant brought, and bidding his mother and sisters good night, ascended the stairs whither Anna, who kept early hours, had gone before him. She was not, however, in bed, and when she heard his step passing her door she called softly to him,

"John, brother John, come in a moment, please."

CHAPTER V
ANNA AND JOHN

He found her in a tasteful dressing gown, its heavy tassels almost sweeping the floor, while her long glossy hair loosened from its confinement of ribbon and comb, covered her neck and shoulders as she sat before the fire always kindled in her room.

"How picturesque you look," he said gaily, bending his knees in mock homage before her. Then seating himself upon the sofa at her side, he wound his arm around her and waited for her to speak.

"John," and Anna's voice was soft and pleading, "tell me more of that young girl. Did you love her very much?"

"Love her! yes," and John spoke excitedly while the flush deepened on his cheek when Anna continued, "why didn't you marry her then?"

"Why didn't I? yes, why didn't I?" and John started to his feet; then resuming his seat again he continued, "why didn't *you* marry that *Missionary* who used to be here so much? Anna, I tell you there's a heap of wrong for somebody to answer for, but it is not you, and it is not me—it's—it's mother!" and John whispered the word, as if fearful lest the proud, overbearing woman should hear.

"You are mistaken," Anna replied, "for as far as Charlie was concerned father had more to do with it than mother. He objected to Charlie because he was poor—because he was a missionary—because he was not an Episcopalian, and because he loved me. He turned Charlie from the house—he locked me in my room, lest I should get out to meet him, and from that window I watched him going from my sight. I've never seen him since, though I wrote to him once or twice, bidding him forget me and marry some one else. He did marry another, but I've never quite believed that he forgot me. I know, though, that as Hattie's husband he would do right and be true to her, for he was good, and when I was with him I was better; but I've forgotten most all he taught me, and the way he pointed out so clearly seems dark and hard to find, but I shall find it—yes, Charlie, I shall find it out at last, so we may meet in Heaven."

Anna was talking more to herself than to John, and Charlie, could he have seen her, would have said she was not far from the narrow way which leadeth unto life. To John her white face, irradiated with gleams of the soft firelight, was as the face of an angel, and for a time he kept silence before her, then suddenly exclaimed.

"Anna, you are good, and so was she, and that made it hard to leave her, to give her up. Anna do you know what my mother wrote me? Listen, while I tell, then see if she is not to blame. She cruelly reminded me that by my father's will all of us, save you, were wholly dependent upon her, and said the moment I threw myself away upon a low, vulgar, penniless girl, that moment she cast me off, and I might earn my bread and hers as best I could. She said, too, my sisters, Anna and all, sanctioned what she wrote, and your opinion had more weight than all the rest."

"Oh, John, mother could not have so misconstrued my words. I said I thought it would be best for you not to marry her, unless you were too far committed; at least you might wait awhile, and when you started for Europe so abruptly, I thought you had concluded to wait and see how absence would affect you. Surely my note explained—I sent one in mother's letter."

"It never reached me," John said bitterly, while Anna sighed at this proof of her mother's treachery.

Always conciliatory, however, she soon remarked,

"You are sole male heir to the Richards name. Mother's heart and pride are bound up in you. She wishes you to make a brilliant match, such as she is sure you can, and if she has erred, it was from her love to you and her wish for your success. A poor, unknown girl would only add to our expenses, and not help you in the least, so it's for the best that you left her, though I'm sorry for the girl. Did she suffer much? What was her name? I've never heard."

John hesitated a moment and then answered, "I called her Lily, she was so fair and pure."

Anna was never in the least suspicious, or on the watch for quibbles, but took all things for granted, so now she thought within herself, "Lillian, most likely. What a sweet name it is." Then she said aloud. "You were not engaged to her outright, were you?"

John started forward and gazed into his sister's face with an expression as if he wished she would question him more closely, for confession to such as she might ease his burdened conscience, but Anna never dreamed of a secret, and seeing him hesitate, she said,

"You need not tell me unless you like. I only thought maybe, you and Lilly were not engaged."

"We were;" and rising to his feet John leaned his forehead upon the marble mantel, which cooled its feverish throbbings. "Anna, I'm a wretch—a miserable wretch, and have scarcely known an hour's peace since I left her."

"Was there a scene?" Anna asked; and John replied,

"Worse than that. Worse for her. She did not know I was going till I was gone. I wrote to her from Paris, for I could not meet her face and tell her how mean I was. I've thought of her so much, and when I landed in New York I went at once to find her, or at least to inquire, hoping she'd forgotten me. The beldame who kept the place was not the same with whom I had left Lily, but she knew about her, and told me she died with cholera last September. She and—oh, Lily, Lily——" and hiding his face in Anna's lap, John Richards sobbed like a little child.

Had Anna been possessed of ordinary penetration, she would have guessed that behind all this there was something yet untold, but she had literally no penetration at all. In her nature there was no deceit, and she never suspected it in others, until it became too palpable not to be seen. Very caressingly her white hand smoothed the daintily perfumed hair resting on her dress, and her own tears mingled with her wayward brother's as she thought, "His burden is greater than mine. I will help him bear it if I can."

"John," she said at last, when the sobbing had ceased, "I do not think you so much to blame as others, and you must not reproach yourself so bitterly. You say Lily was good. Do you mean she was a Christian, like Charlie?"

"Yes, if there ever was one. Why, she used to make a villain like me kneel with her every night, and say the Lord's Prayer."

For an instant, a puzzling thought crossed Anna's brain as to the circumstances which could have brought her brother every night to Lily's side, but it passed away immediately as she rejoined,

"Then she is safe in Heaven, and there are no tears there; no broken hearts, or weary hours of watching. We'll try to meet her some day. You did right to seek her out. You could not help her dying. She might have died had she been your wife, so, I'd try to think it happened for the best, and you'll soon get to believing it did. That's my experience. You are young yet, only twenty-six, and life has much in store for you. You'll find some one to fill Lily's place; some one whom we shall all think worthy of you, and we'll be so happy together."

The Doctor did not reply to this but sat as if lost in painful thought, until he heard the clock strike the hour of midnight.

"I did not think it was so late," he exclaimed. "I must really leave you now."

Anna would not keep him longer, and with a kiss she sent him away, herself holding the door a little ajar to see what effect the new carpet would have upon him. It did not have any at first, so much was he absorbed in thinking of *Lily*, but he noticed it at last, admiring its pattern and having a pleasant consciousness that every thing in his room was in keeping, from the handsome drapery which shaded the windows to the marble hearth on which a fire was blazing. He could afford to have a fire, and he sat enjoying it, thinking far different thoughts from Hugh Worthington, who, in his scantily furnished room, sat, with a curl of golden hair upon the stand beside him, and a well worn Bible in his hand. Dr. Richards had no Bible of his own; he did not read it now—had never read it much, but somehow his talk with Anna had carried him back to the time when just to please his Lily he had said with her the Lord's Prayer, kneeling at her side with his arm around her girlish form. He had not said it since, and he never would again, he thought. It was sheer nonsense, asking not to be led into temptation, as if God delighted to lead us there. It was just fit for weak women to believe, though now that Lily was dead and gone he was glad that she had believed it, and he felt that she was better off for having said those prayers and acted up to what she said. "Poor Lily," he kept repeating to himself, while in his dreams that night there were visions of a lonely grave in a secluded part of Greenwood, and he heard again the startling words,

"Dead, both she and the child."

He did not know there was a child, and he staggered in his sleep, just as he staggered down the creaking stairs, repeating to himself,

"Lily's child—Lily's child! May Lily's God forgive me!"

CHAPTER VI
ALICE JOHNSON

The Sunday anticipated by Dr. Richards as the one which was to bless him with a sight of Snowdon's belle, dawned at last, a clear, cold, winter morning, when the air was full of frost, and the crispy snow creaked beneath the tread, and glittered like diamonds in the sunshine. The Doctor had not yet made his appearance in the village, for a hoarseness, to which he was subject, had confined him at home, and Saturday had been spent by him in rehearsing to his sisters and the servants the things he had seen abroad, and in wondering if Alice Johnson would meet his expectations. He did not believe her face would at all compare with the one which continually haunted his dreams, and over which the coffin-lid was shut weary months ago, but $50,000 had invested Miss Alice with that peculiar charm which will sometimes make an ugly face beautiful. The Doctor was beginning to feel the need of funds, and now that *Lily* was dead, the thought had more than once crossed his mind that to set himself to the task of finding a wealthy wife was a duty he owed himself and his family. Had poor, deserted Lily lived, he could not tell what he might have done, for the memory of her love was the one restraining influence which kept him from much sin. He never could forget her; never love another as he had once loved her, but she was dead and he was free to do his mother's will. Similar to these were the Doctor's cogitations, as, on that Sunday morning, he made his toilet for church, anticipating not a little satisfaction from the sensation he was sure to create among some of the worshippers at St. Paul's, for he remembered that the Terrace Hill gentry had always been people of much importance to a certain class of Snowdonites.

Anna was not with the party which at the usual hour entered the family carriage with Bibles and prayer-books in hand. She seldom went out except on warm, pleasant days; but she stood in the deep bay window watching the carriage as it wound down the hill and thinking, how handsome and stylish her young brother looked with his Parisian cloak and cap, which he wore so gracefully. Others than Anna thought so too; and at the church door there was quite a little stir, as he gallantly handed out first his mother and then his sisters, and followed them into the church.

Dr. Richards had never enjoyed a reputation for being very devotional, and the interval between his entrance and the commencement of the service was passed by him in a rather scornful survey of the timeworn house, which had not improved during his absence. With a sneer in his heart, he mentally compared the old-fashioned pulpit, with its steep flight of steps and faded trimmings, with the lofty cathedral he had been in the habit of attending in Paris, and a feeling of disgust and contempt for people who could be satisfied with a town like Snowdon, and a church like St. Paul's, was creeping over him, when a soft rustling of silk and a consciousness of a delicate perfume, which he at once recognized as aristocratic, warned him that somebody was coming; somebody entirely different from the score of females who had distributed themselves within range of his vision, their countrified bonnets, as he termed them, trimmed outside and in without the least regard to taste, or combination of color. But the little lady, moving so quietly up the aisle, her full skirt of dark blue silk trailing as she came, her handsome cloth cloak, falling so gracefully from the sloping shoulders, which the fur of Russian sable fitted so well, her plain, but fashionable hat tied beneath her chin, with broad, rich ribbon, the color of her dress, her dainty little muff, and, more than all, the tiny glove, fitting, without a wrinkle, the little hand which tried the pew door twice ere it yielded to her touch; she was different. She was worthy of respect, and the Paris beau felt an inclination to rise at once and acknowledge her superior presence.

Wholly unconscious of the interest she was exciting, the lady deposited her muff upon the cushions, and then kneeling reverently upon the well worn stool, covered her face with the hands which had so won the doctor's admiration. What a little creature she was, and how gloriously beautiful were the curls of indescribable hue, falling in such profusion from beneath the jaunty hat. All this Dr. Richards noted, marvelling that she knelt so long, and wondering what she could be saying. His mother and sisters did the same, it is true, but he always imagined it was merely to be fashionable; but in the attitude of this kneeler at his side there was something which precluded mockery. Was she sincere? Was there one hearing what she said—an ear which marked the faintest sigh and caught the weakest tone? He wished he knew; and a pang, keen as the cut of a dissector's knife, shot through his heart, as he remembered another maiden, almost as fair as this one, kneeling at her prayers. *Lily* had believed in Alice Johnson's God, and he was glad that she had so believed, for without God, poor Lily's short, sad life had been worse than vain!

Alice's devotions ended at last, and the view so coveted was obtained; for in adjusting her dress Alice turned toward him, or rather toward his mother, and the doctor drew a sudden breath as he met the brilliant flashing of those laughing sunny blue eyes, and caught the radiant expression of that face, slightly dimpled with a smile. Beautiful, wondrously beautiful was Alice Johnson, and yet the features were not wholly regular, for the piquant nose had a slight turn up, and the forehead was not very high; but for all this, the glossy hair, the dancing blue eyes, the apple-blossom complexion, and the rose-bud mouth made ample amend; and Dr. Richards saw no fault in that witching face, flashing its blue eyes for an instant upon him, and then modestly turning to the service just commencing. But few of the sacred words, we fear, took deep root in the doctor's heart that morning. He could scarcely have told the day, certainly not the text, and when the benediction was pronounced he was astonished that what he had dreaded as prosy and long had proved to be so short.

As if divining his wishes in the matter, his mother, after waiting a moment, till Alice arose from her knees, offered her hand to the young girl, inquired kindly for Mrs. Johnson, expressed extreme concern when told of a heavy cold, suggested one or two remedies, commented upon the weather, spoke of Mr. Howard's sermon, and then, as if all the while this had not been the chief object in stopping, she turned to the eagerly expectant doctor, whom she introduced as "My son, Dr. Richards."

With a smile which he felt even to his finger tips, Alice offered him her hand, welcoming him home, and making some trivial remark touching the contrast between their quiet town and the cities he had left.

"But you will help make it pleasanter for us this winter, I am sure," she continued, and the sweet blue eyes sought his for an answer as to whether he would desert Snowdon immediately.

"No," he replied, he should probably remain at home some time, he always found it pleasant at Snowdon though as a boy he had often chafed at its dullness; but it could not now be dull, with the acquisition it had received since he was there before; and he bowed toward the young lady, who acknowledged the compliment with a faint blush and then turned toward the group of noisy "ill-bred children," as Dr. Richards thought, who came thronging about her, one offering a penny lest it should be forgotten, a second whispering that Tommie couldn't come because he had no shoes, while a third climbed upon the seat for the kiss, which was promptly given, the giver all unconscious of the disgust felt by the foreign gentleman, who had a strong desire to take the kissed by the neck and thrust him out into the snow! What affinity was there between that sparkling, beautiful girl, and that pack of vulgar young ones, he'd like to know? What was she to them, or they to her, that they should cling to her so confidingly?

"My Sunday School scholars; I have a large class, you see," Alice said, as if in answer to these mental queries. "Ah, here comes my youngest—" and Alice stooped to caress a little rosy cheeked boy, with bright brown eyes and patches on both coat sleeves.

The doctor saw the patches, and with a gesture of impatience, turned to go, just as his ear caught another kiss, and he knew the patched boy received what he would have given much to have.

"Hanged if I don't half wish I was one of those ragged urchins," he said, after handing his mother and sisters to their carriage, and seating himself at their side. "But does not Miss Johnson display strange taste. Surely some other one less refined might be found to look after those brats, if they must be looked after, which I greatly doubt. Better leave them as you find them; can't elevate them if you try. It's trouble thrown away," and John Richards wrapped his Parisian cloak closer around him, and leaning back in his corner, wondered if Alice Johnson really was happy in her teaching, or did she do it for effect.

"It is like what Lily would have done," he thought, "had she possessed the power and means. Alice and Lily must be alike," and with a mental wish that Alice's fate might prove a happier one than poor Lily's had been, John relapsed into a silent mood, such as usually came over him when Lily was in his mind.

That afternoon, while his mother and elder sisters were taking their usual Sunday nap, and Anna was nodding in her chair, the Doctor sat watching the blazing fire and trying to decide upon his future course.

Should he return to New York, accept the offer of an old friend of his father's, an experienced practitioner, and earn his own bread honorably; or, should he remain at Snowdon and cultivate Alice Johnson? John wanted money sadly; the whole family wanted money, as every hour of his stay among them proved. They were growing poor so fast; and it showed plainly, in spite of their attempts to conceal it. John would almost as soon be dead as be poor. He never had denied himself; he never could, he said, though well he knew the time was coming when he must, unless, to use Micawber's expression, "something should turn up." And hadn't it turned up in the shape of a beautiful heiress? What was to hinder him from entering the lists and carrying off the prize? He had never yet failed when he chose to exert himself, and though he might, for a time, be compelled to adopt a different code of morality from that which he at present acknowledged, he would do it for once. He could be interested in those ragged children; he could encourage Sunday schools; he could attend church as regularly as Alice herself and, better yet, he could doctor the poor for nothing, as that was sure to tell, and he would do it, too, if necessary. This was the finale which he reached at last by a series of arguments pro and con, and when it was reached, he was anxious to commence the task at once. He presumed he could love Alice Johnson; she was so pretty, but even if he didn't, he would only be doing what thousands had done before him. He should be very proud of her, and would certainly try to make her happy. One long, almost sobbing sigh to the memory of poor Lily, who had loved so much and been so cruelly betrayed, one faint struggle with conscience, which said that Alice Johnson was too pure a gem for him to trifle with, and then the past, with its sad memories, was buried. Lily's sweet pleading face, asking that no other one should be wronged as she had been, was thrust aside, and Dr. Richards stood ready for his new career.

CHAPTER VII
RIVERSIDE COTTAGE

Mrs. Johnson did not like Dr. Richards when she came to know him, and yet he was an almost daily visitor at Riverside Cottage, where one face at least grew brighter when he came, and one pair of eyes beamed on him a welcome. His new code of morality worked admirably, and as weeks passed away he showed no signs of weariness in the course he had adopted. Mr. Howard himself was not more regular at church, or Alice more devout, than Dr. Richards. The children, whom he had denominated "ragged brats," were no longer spurned with contempt, but fed instead with pea-nuts and molasses candy, the doctor going frequently into the by-lanes where they lived, and where they began to expect him almost as much as Alice. He was popular with the children, but the parents, clearer sighted, treated him most shabbily at his back, accusing him of caring only for Miss Alice's good opinion, and of being at heart a most consummate knave!

This was what the poor said, and what many others thought. It could not be that John Richards, whom they had known from boyhood as proud, selfish, and overbearing, could so suddenly change his entire nature, becoming at once so amiable, so familiar, so generous, so much, in short, like Alice herself. As well might the leopard change its spots, and many were the insinuations thrown darkly at Alice, who smiled at them all and thought how little Dr. Richards was understood.

As the winter passed away and spring advanced, he showed no intentions of leaving Snowdon, but on the contrary opened an office in the village, greatly to the surprise of the inhabitants, and greatly to the dismay of old Dr. Rogers, who for years had blistered and bled the good people without a fear of rivalry.

"Does Dr. Richards intend locating permanently in Snowdon?" Mrs. Johnson asked of her daughter as they sat alone one evening.

"His sign would indicate as much," was Alice's reply.

There was a faint sigh in the direction of the sofa, on which Mrs. Johnson, who for several days had been suffering from a severe pain in her head, was lying, and the sigh smote painfully on Alice's ear, for well she guessed its import.

"Mother," she said gently, as leaving her chair she came and knelt by her mother's side, "you look pale and worried, as if something ailed you more than your head. You have looked so for some time past. What is it, mother? Are you very sick, or— —" and Alice hesitated, "are you troubled about me?"

"Is there any reason why I should be troubled about my darling?" asked the mother, smoothing fondly the bright curls almost touching her face.

Alice never had any secrets from her mother, and she answered frankly, "I don't know, unless—unless—mother, why don't you like Dr. Richards?"

The ice was fairly broken now, and very briefly but candidly Mrs. Johnson told why she did not like him. He was handsome, refined, educated and agreeable, she admitted, but there was something lacking. The mask he was wearing had not deceived her, and she would have liked him far better without it. This she said to Alice, adding gently, "He may be all he seems, but I doubt it. I distrust him greatly. I think he fancies you and loves your money."

"Oh, mother, you do him injustice, and he has been so kind to us, while Snowdon is so much pleasanter since he came."

"Are you engaged to him?" was Mrs. Johnson's next question.

"No," and Alice looked up wonderingly. "I do not like him well enough for that."

Alice Johnson was wholly ingenuous and would not for the world have concealed a thing from her mother, and very frankly she continued,

"I like Dr. Richards better than any gentleman I have ever met, and it seems to me that people here do him injustice, but I may be mistaken. I know he is unpopular, and that first made me sorry for him. I am sure he is pleased with me, but he has never asked me to be his wife. I should have told you, mother," and the beautiful eyes which had so charmed the doctor, looked up confidingly at the pale face bending over them.

"God bless my darling, and keep her as innocent as now," Mrs. Johnson murmured, bowing her head upon her daughter's, and kissing the rosy cheek. "I am glad there is no engagement. Will you promise there shall not be for one year at least?"

It was a hard thing to ask, for more than she guessed, till then, did Alice's heart incline toward Dr. Richards. Slily, adroitly, he had insinuated himself into her affections, boasting that he could sway her at will, only let him attend the Lenten services, week days and all, drop something in the plate every Sabbath, speak to all the ragamuffins he met, take old Mrs.

Snyder out for an airing every week, and he was all right with Alice Johnson. And this was the man from whom Mrs. Johnson would save her daughter, asking again for the promise.

"Yes, I will, I do," Alice said at last.

A second "God bless my darling," came from the mother's lips, and drawing her treasure nearer to her, she continued, "You have made me very happy, and by and by you'll be so glad. You may leave me now, for I am tired and faint."

It was long ere Alice forgot the expression of her mother's face or the sound of her voice, as she bade her good night on that last evening they ever spent together alone. The indisposition of which Mrs. Johnson had been complaining for several days, proved to be no light matter, and when next morning Dr. Rogers was summoned to her bedside, he decided it to be a fever which was then prevailing to some extent in the neighboring towns.

That afternoon it was told at Terrace Hill that Mrs. Johnson was very sick, and half an hour later the Richards carriage, containing the doctor and his sister Anna, wound down the hill, and passing through the park, turned in the direction of the cottage, where they found Mrs. Johnson worse than they had anticipated. The sight of distress roused Anna at once, and forgetting her own feebleness she kindly offered to stay until night if she could be of any service. Mrs. Johnson was fond of Anna, and she expressed her pleasure so eagerly that Anna decided to remain, and went with Alice to remove her wrappings.

"Oh, I forgot!" she exclaimed, as a sudden thought seemed to strike her. "I don't know as I can stay after all, though I might write it here, I suppose, as well as at home; and as John is going to New York to-night he will take it along."

"What is it?" Alice asked; and Anna replied,

"You'll think me very foolish, no doubt; they all do, especially John, and have tried to laugh me out of it, but I have thought about it, and dreamed about it, until it is impressed upon me that I must do it, and I had decided to attend to it this very day, when we heard of your mother's illness, and John persuaded me to come here with him, as he wished to say good-bye to you."

"I'll get you writing materials if you like," Alice said, "or you can go at once to the library. Your brother will wait, I am sure."

"Yes; but I want to know if you too think me foolish. I'm so dependent on others' opinions;" and, in a low tone, Anna told how long she had been wanting some nice young person to be constantly with her as companion or waiting-maid, and of the advertisement seen early last winter, how queerly it was expressed, and how careless John had been in tearing off the name and address, with which to light his cigar. "It seems to me," she continued, "that 'unfortunate married woman' is the very one I want. I cannot account for the interest I feel in her, and in spite of all my family can say, I've concluded to write, and let John take it to the *Herald*."

"Yes; but how will you find her? I understand that the address was burned," Alice rejoined quickly, feeling herself that Anna was hardly sane in her calculations.

"Oh, I've fixed that in the wording," Anna answered. "I do not know as it will ever reach her, it's been so long, but if it does, she'll be sure to know I mean her, or somebody like her."

It was not at all clear to Alice, but she made no objections, and taking her silence as a tacit approval of her project, Anna followed her to the library.

"I dislike writing very much," she said, as she saw the array of materials, "and I write so illegibly too. Please do it for me, that's a dear, good girl," and she gave the pen to Alice, who wrote the first word, "Wanted," and then waited for Anna to dictate.

"Wanted.—By an invalid lady, whose home is in the country, a young woman, who will be both useful and agreeable, either as a companion or waiting-maid. No objection will be raised if the woman is married, and unfortunate, or has a child a few months old.

"Address,

"A. E. R., Snowdon, Hampden Co., Mass"

"That is what will assure her, should she ever see it," Anna said, pointing to the lines,— —

"No objection raised if the young woman is married and unfortunate, or has a child a few months old."

Alice thought it the queerest advertisement she had ever seen, but Anna was privileged to do queer things, and folding the paper, she went out into the hall, where the doctor sat waiting for her. Handing him the note, she was about to explain its import, when Anna joined her, and explained herself, charging him to attend to it the very first thing.

John's mustached lip curled a little scornfully as he read it.

"Why, puss, that girl or woman is in Georgia by this time, and as the result of this, Terrace Hill will be thronged with unfortunate women and children, desiring situations. They'll stand three deep from the park gate to the house. Better let me burn this, as I did the other, and not be foolish. She will never see it," and John made a gesture as if he would put it in the stove, but Anna caught his hand, saying imploringly, "Please humor me this once. She may see it, and I'm so interested."

Anna was always humored, and so the doctor placed in his memorandum book the note, then turning to Alice he addressed her in so low a tone that Anna readily took the hint and left them together. Dr. Richards was not intending to be gone long, he said, though the time would seem a little eternity, so much was his heart now bound up in Snowdon.

Afraid lest he might say something more of the same nature, Alice hastened to ask if he had seen her mother and what he thought of her.

"I stepped in for a moment while you were in the library," he replied. "She seemed to have a high fever, and I fancied it increased while I stood by her. I am sorry to leave while she is so sick, but remember that if anything happens you will be dearer to me than ever," and the doctor pressed the little hand which he took in his to say good-bye, for now he must really go.

With a swelling heart Alice watched him as he left the house, and then running to her own room locked the door and throwing herself upon the bed sobbed bitterly. What did his words, "if anything happens" imply? Did he think her mother so very sick? Was she going to die? "Oh, mother, mother! I will not let her go!" was the cry of a heart which at first rebelled against the threatened blow, refusing to receive it. Anon, however, better, calmer thoughts succeeded, and though Alice could not yet say "Thy will be done," she was not so rebellious, and a pleading prayer went up, "Spare, oh, spare my mother," while hope whispered that this terrible calamity would not happen to her.

As the day and night wore on Mrs. Johnson grew worse so rapidly that at her request a telegram was forwarded to Mr. Liston, who had charge of her moneyed affairs, and who came at once, for the kind old man was deeply interested in the widow and her lovely daughter. As Mrs. Johnson could bear it, they talked alone together until he perfectly understood what her wishes were with regard to Alice, and how to deal with Dr. Richards. Then promising to return again in case the worst should happen, he took his leave, while Mrs. Johnson, now that a weight was lifted from her mind, seemed to rally, and the physician pronounced her better. But with that strange foreknowledge, which sometimes comes to people whose days are nearly numbered, she felt that she would die, and that in mercy this interval of rest and freedom from pain was granted her, in which she might talk with Alice concerning the arrangements for the future.

"Alice, darling," she said, when they were alone, "come sit by me here on the bed and listen to what I say."

Alice obeyed, and taking her mother's hot hand in hers she waited for what was to come.

"Alice, darling, are you willing to be left alone for a little while? It won't be long, and our Father in Heaven knows best what is for our good."

"Oh, mother, don't; you will not die," and Alice sobbed convulsively. "Last night, when I thought you were in danger, I prayed so hard to be willing, but I couldn't, oh, I couldn't, and God seemed a great ways off— seemed as if he did not hear. In all the wide world I can never find another mother, and I shall be so desolate."

Mrs. Johnson knew just how desolate her dying would leave her child, for she had felt the same, and for a few moments she strove to comfort the weeping girl, who hid her face in the pillows, by telling her of One who will surely care for the orphan; for he has said he would, and his word never fails.

"You have learned to trust him in prosperity, and He will be a thousand fold nearer to you in adversity. You'll miss me, I know, and be very lonely without me, but you are young, and life has many charms for you, besides God will never forget or forsake his covenant children."

Gradually as she talked the sobbing ceased, and when the white face lifted itself from its hiding place there was a look upon it as if the needed strength had been sought and to some extent imparted.

"My will was made some time ago," Mrs. Johnson continued, "and that with a few exceptions, such as legacies to your nurse Densie Densmore, and some charitable institutions, you are my sole heir. Mr. Liston is to be your guardian, and will look after your interests until you are of age, or longer if you choose. You know that as both your father and myself were only children, you have no near relatives on either side to whom you can look for protection. There is a kind of second cousin, it is true, the old gentleman who visited us just before we came here. But his family are gay, fashionable people, and I'd rather you should not go there, even if he were willing. Mr. Liston would give you a home with him, but I do not think that best and there is but one other alternative.

"You will remember having heard me speak occasionally of a friend now living in Kentucky, a Mrs. Worthington whose husband was a distant relative of ours. Ralph Worthington and your father were school boys together, and afterward college companions. They were more like brothers than friends; indeed, they were often likened to David and Jonathan, so strongly were they attached to each other.

"I was but sixteen when I became a bride, and, as you know, several years elapsed ere God blessed me with a living child. Your father was consumptive, and the chances were that I should early be left a widow. This it was, I think, which led to the agreement made by the two friends to the effect that if either died the living one should care for the widow and fatherless as for a brother's family. To see the two as they pledged themselves to keep this solemn compact, you would not have guessed that the tall, athletic, broad chested Ralph, would be the first to go, yet so it was. He died ere you were born."

"Then *he* is dead? Oh, I'm so sorry," Alice exclaimed.

"Yes, he's dead; and, as far as possible, your father fulfilled his promise to Ralph's widow and her child—a little boy, five years old, of whom Mrs. Worthington herself was appointed guardian. I never knew what spirit of evil possessed Eliza who had been my schoolmate and to whom I was greatly attached; but in less than a year after her husband's death, she made a second and most unfortunate marriage. We both opposed it, for we distrusted the man. As the result of our opposition, a coolness sprang up between us, and we saw but little of each other after that. Mr. Murdoch proved a greater scoundrel that we supposed, and when their little girl was nearly two years old, we heard of a divorce. Mr. Johnson's health was failing fast, and we were about to make the tour of Europe, in hopes a change would benefit him. Just before we sailed we visited poor Eliza, whom we found doubly heart-broken, for, in addition to the other outrages heaped upon her, the brutal wretch had managed to steal her beautiful daughter, and carried it no one knew whither. I never shall forget the distress of the brother. I've often thought of him since, and wondered what he had grown to be. We comforted Eliza as best we could, and left money to be used for her in case she needed it. Then we embarked with you and Densie for Europe. You know how for a while, your father seemed to regain his strength, how he at last grew worse and hastened home to die. In the sorrow and excitement which followed, it is not strange that Eliza was for a time forgotten, and when I remembered and enquired for her again, I heard that Hugh had been adopted by some relation in Kentucky, that the stolen child had been mysteriously returned, and was living with its mother in Elmswood—a quiet, out-of-the-way town, which I never visited until that summer when you went West with the Gilmores.

"At first Eliza appeared a little cool, but this soon wore off, and was mostly owing, I fancy, to the mortification she felt at my finding her in circumstances so changed from what they used to be, for, though managing to keep up a genteel exterior, she was really very poor. She did not talk much of Hugh. Indeed, she knew but little of him, as his letters were far apart, and only contained praises of his horses, his dogs, and the rare sport he had in hunting with his eccentric uncle, whose name I have forgotten. Neither did she say much of Adaline, who was then away at school. Still my visit was a sadly satisfactory one, as we recalled old times when we were girls together weeping over our great loss when our husbands were laid to rest. Then we spoke of their friendship, and lastly of the contract.

"'It sounds preposterous in me, I know,' Mrs. Worthington said, when we parted, 'you are so rich and I so poor, but if ever Alice should want a mother's care, I will gladly give it to her.'

"This was nearly eight years ago. And, as I failed to write her for a long, long time, while she was long in answering, the correspondence ceased till just before her removal to Kentucky, when she apprised me of the change. You have now the history of Mrs. Worthington, the only person who comes to mind as one to whose care I can entrust you."

"But, mother, I may not be wanted there," and Alice's lip quivered painfully. "Adaline is a young lady now, and Hugh, what of him, mother? What is he?"

Mrs. Johnson could not tell; neither did she know if her darling would be welcome, but money, she knew, had a charm, and she replied to Alice's queries,

"You will not go empty handed, nor be a burden to them. They are poor, and money will not come amiss. We can but try at all events, and if they object, Mr. Liston will do the best he can for you. For some weeks, it has been impressed upon me that my time was short, and fancying it could do no harm, I have written to Mrs. Worthington a letter which you will send when I am gone. I have asked her to receive you, to care for you as her own. I said that Mr. Liston would attend to all pecuniary matters, paying your allowance quarterly; and I am sure you will not object when I tell you that I think it right to leave Adaline the sum of one thousand dollars. It will not materially lessen your inheritance, and it will do her a world of good. Mr. Liston will arrange it for you. You will remain here until you hear from Mrs. Worthington, and then abide by her arrangements. She is a gentle, affectionate woman, and will be kind to you. I do not know that she is a Christian, but your influence may do her good, and make her bless the day when you were sent to her. Will you go, my daughter—go cheerfully?"

"Yes, mother, I'll go," came gaspingly from Alice's lips, "I'll go but, mother, oh, mother," and Alice's cry ended as it always did, "you will not, you must not die!"

But neither tears, nor prayers could avail to keep the mother longer. Her work on earth was done, and after this conversation she grew worse so rapidly that hope died out of Alice's heart, and she knew that soon she would be motherless. There were days and nights of pain and delirium in which the sick woman recognized none of those around her save Alice, whom she continually blessed as her darling, praying that God, too, would bless and keep his covenant child. At last there came a change, and one lovely Sunday morning, when the sunlight lay upon the springing grass and sparkled on the river, when the air was laden with the early flowers' perfume, and birds were singing by the door, the delirium passed away, and in the room so long kept dark and still, were heard whispered words of joy, of peace, of perfect rest, such as the dying Christian only feels. It was early morning then and ere the bell from St. Paul's tower sent forth its summons to the house of God, there rang from its belfry a solemn toll, and the villagers listening to it, said, as they counted forty-four, that Mrs. Johnson was dead.

CHAPTER VIII
MR. LISTON AND THE DOCTOR

Among Snowdon's poor that day, as well as among the wealthier class, there was many an aching heart, and many a prayer was breathed for the stricken Alice, not less beloved than the mother had been. At Terrace Hill Mansion, much sorrow was expressed, and among the older sisters a considerable anxiety felt as to whether this sudden death would postpone indefinitely the marriage they had looked upon as sure to take place between their brother and the youthful heiress. They hoped not, for money was greatly needed at Terrace Hill. In the familiar intercourse which latterly had existed between themselves and Alice they had seen enough to know how generous and free she was. Once their sister, and Terrace Hill would blossom again as the rose. On the whole it was very unfortunate that Mrs. Johnson should have died so unexpectedly, and they did wish John was there to comfort the young girl who, they heard, refused to see any one except the clergyman and Mr. Liston.

"Suppose we telegraph for John," Eudora said, and in less than two hours thereafter, Dr. Richards in New York read that Alice was an orphan.

There was a pang as he thought of her distress, a wish that he were with her, and then the thought arose, "What if she does not prove as wealthy as I have supposed. Will that make any difference?"

He knew it would, for though more interested in Alice than he supposed he could be in any one after poor Lily died, he was far too mercenary to let his affections run away with his judgment, and could the stricken Alice have looked into his heart and seen what his cogitations were that morning, when at the St. Nicholas he sat thinking, how her mother's loss might possibly affect him, she would have shrunk from him in horror. He had best go home at once, he said, and on the day appointed for the funeral he reached the station adjoining Snowdon, where he alighted, as the Express train did not stop in the next town. It was not more than two miles to Terrace Hill across the fields, and as he preferred walking to riding, he sauntered slowly on, thinking of Alice and wishing he did know just the amount left her by her mother.

"I must do something," he soliloquized, "or how can I ever pay those debts in New York, of which mother knows nothing? I wish that widow— —"

He did not finish his wishes, for a turn in the path brought him suddenly face to face with Mr. Liston, whom he had seen at a distance, and whom he recognized at once.

"I'll quiz the old codger," he thought. "He don't, of course, know me, and will never suspect my object."

Mistaken doctor! The old codger was fully prepared. He did know Dr. Richards by sight, and was rather glad than otherwise when the elegant dandy, taking a seat upon the gnarled roots of the tree under which he was sitting, made some trivial remark about the weather, which was very propitious for the crowd who were sure to attend Mrs. Johnson's funeral.

Yes, Mr. Liston presumed there would be a crowd. It was very natural there should be, particularly as the deceased was greatly beloved and was also reputed wealthy. "It beats all what a difference it makes, even after death, whether one is supposed to be rich or poor," and the *codger* worked away industriously at the pine stick he was whittling.

"But in this case the supposition of riches must be correct, though I know people are oftener over valued than otherwise," and with his gold-headed cane the doctor thrust at a dandelion growing near.

"Nothing truer than that," returned the whittler, brushing the litter from his lap. "Now I've no doubt that prig of a doctor, who they say is shining up to Alice, will be disappointed when he finds just how much she's worth. Let me see. What is his name? Lives up there," and with his jack-knife Mr. Liston pointed toward Terrace Hill.

Smothering his desire to throttle and then pitch into the river the old man, calling him a *a prig of a doctor*, so coolly and deliberately marring his golden visions, the doctor answered, naturally,

"The Richards family live there, sir. You mean their son, I presume."

"Yes, the chap that has travelled and come home so changed. They do say he's actually taken to visiting all the rheumatic old women in town, applying sticking plasters to their backs and administering *squills* to their children, all free gratis. Don't ask a red—does it for charity's sake: but I know he expects to get his pay out of Alice's purse, as he does it to please her and nothing else. He ought to be rewarded for all his philanthropy with a rich wife, that's a fact. It's too bad to have him so disappointed, and if he comes out to the funeral I believe I'll tell him as a friend that my advice is, not to marry for money—it won't pay," and from beneath the slouched hat drawn so closely over the comical face, the keen gray eyes looked curiously.

Poor doctor! How he fidgeted, moving so often that his tormenter demurely asked him if he were sitting on a *thistle!*

"Does Miss Johnson remain here?" the doctor asked at last, and Mr. Liston replied by telling what he knew of the arrangements.

At the mention of Worthington the doctor, looked up quickly. Whom had he known by that name, or where had he heard it before? "Mrs. Worthington, Mrs. Worthington," he repeated, unpleasant memories of something, he knew not what, rising to his mind. "Is she living in this vicinity?"

"In Kentucky. It's a widow and her daughter," Mr. Liston answered, wisely resolving to say nothing of a young man, lest the doctor should feel anxious.

"A widow and her daughter! I must be mistaken in thinking I ever knew any one by that name, though it seems familiar," said the doctor, and as by this time he had heard all he wished to hear, he arose, and bidding Mr. Liston good morning walked away in no enviable frame of mind.

"I didn't tell him a lie. He will be disappointed when he finds just how much she is worth, and my advice to him, or any other man, is not to marry for money," Mr. Liston chucklingly soliloquized as he watched the crestfallen doctor disappearing from view, muttering to himself, "The wretch! to talk so to my face! I wish I'd knocked him down. Rheumatic woman and squills, indeed! But it's all true, every word, and that's the worst of it. I have turned fool just to get a pretty girl, or rather to get her money. But I won't stay here to be laughed at. I'll go back this very day. I am glad no one has seen me except that old rat, who never guessed I was the chap he complimented so highly, the rascal!"

Looking at his watch the doctor found that it lacked several hours ere the express from Boston was due. But this did not discourage him. He would stay in the fields or anywhere, and turning backward he followed the course of the river winding under the hill until he reached the friendly woods which shielded him from observation. How he hated himself hiding there among the trees, and how he longed for the downward train, which came at last, and when the village bell tolled out its summons to the house of mourning, he sat in a corner of the car returning to New York even faster than he had come.

Gradually the Riverside cottage filled with people assembling to pay the last tribute of respect to the deceased, who during her short stay among them had endeared herself to many hearts.

Slowly, sadly, they bore her to the grave. Reverently they laid her down to rest, and from the carriage window Alice's white face looked wistfully out as "earth to earth, ashes to ashes," broke the solemn stillness. Oh, how she longed to lay there too, beside her mother! How the sunshine, flecking the bright June grass with gleams of gold, seemed to mock her misery as the gravelly earth rattled heavily down upon the coffin lid, and she knew they were covering up her mother. "If I too could die!" she murmured, sinking back in the carriage corner and covering her face with her veil. But not so easily could life be shaken off by her, the young and strong. She must live yet longer. She had a work to do—a work whose import she knew not; and the mother's death, for which she then could see no reason, though she knew well that one existed, was the entrance to that work. She must live and she must listen while Mr. Liston talked to her that night on business, arranging about the letter, which was forwarded immediately to Kentucky, and advising her what to do until an answer was received.

Not a word did he say of his interview with the doctor, nor did Alice know he had been there. She would not have cared if she had, so crushed and desolate was her young heart, and after Mr. Liston was gone and the house had become quiet again, a species of apathy settled upon her as with a feeling akin to despair she sat down to wait for the news from Kentucky, which was to decide her future course.

CHAPTER IX
MATTERS IN KENTUCKY

Backward now with our reader we turn, and take up the broken thread of our story at the point where we left Adah Hastings, sleeping, in that best chamber at Spring Bank; while around the timeworn building the winter wind howled dismally, and drove the sleet in gusts against the windows. There were piles of snow next morning upon the steps, huge drifts against the doors, and banks against the fences, while the bent-up negroes shivered and drew back from the cutting blast, so foreign to their temperaments.

It was a bitter morning in which to face the fierce north wind, and plow one's way to the Derby cornfield, where in a small, dilapidated building, Aunt Eunice Reynolds, widowed sister of John Stanley, had lived for many years, first as a pensioner upon her brothers bounty, and next as Hugh's incumbent. At the time of her brother's death Aunt Eunice had intended removing to Spring Bank, but when Hugh's mother wrote, asking for a home, she abandoned the plan, and for two seasons more lived alone, watching from her lonely door the tasselled corn ripening in the August sun. It was strange that a house should have been built there in the center of that cornfield, with woods enclosing it on every side save one, and stranger still, that Aunt Eunice should care to stay there, year after year, as she did. But she preferred it, she said "to having a paltry, lazy nigger under foot," and so her brother suffered her to have her way, while the neighbors marvelled at and admired the untiring energy and careful neatness which made the cottage in the corn field so cozy-like and cheerful. Hugh was Aunt Eunice's idol, the object which kept her old heart warm and young with human love. For him she would endure any want or encounter any difficulty, and in his dilemma regarding Adah Hastings, he intuitively turned to her, as the one who would lend a helping hand. He had not been to see her in two days, and when the grey December morning broke and he looked out upon the deep, untrodden snow, he frowned impatiently, as he thought how bad the path must be between Spring Bank and the cornfield, whither he intended going, as he would be the first to tell what had occurred. 'Lina's fierce opposition to, and his mother's apparent shrinking from Adah, had convinced him how hopeless was the idea that she could stay at Spring

Bank with any degree of comfort to herself or quiet to him. Aunt Eunice's house was the only refuge for Adah, and there she would be comparatively safe from censorious remarks.

"Inasmuch as ye did it to the least of these ye did it unto me," kept ringing in Hugh's ears, as he hastily dressed himself, striking his benumbed fingers together, and trying hard to keep his teeth from chattering, for Hugh was beginning his work of economy, and when at daylight Claib came as usual to build his master's fire, he had sent him back, saying he did not need one, and bidding him go, instead, to Mrs. Hastings' chamber.

It took more than a shake or two that morning ere Hugh's toilet was completed, for the stiff, heavy boots refused at first to go on, but with a kick and a jerk, and what would have been an oath if he had not thought of Golden Hair in time to prevent its utterance, Hugh prevailed at last and the refractory boots came to their proper place. Bounding down the stairs he hurried out to the kitchen, where only a few of his negroes were stirring.

"Ho, Claib!" he called, "saddle Rocket quick and bring him to the door. I'm going to the corn field."

"Lor' bless you, mas'r, it's done snow higher than Rocket's head. He'll never stand it nohow."

"Do as I bid you," was Hugh's reply, and indolent Claib went shivering to the stable where Hugh's best horses were kept.

A whinnying sound of welcome greeted him as he entered, but was soon succeeded by a spirited snort as he attempted to lead out a most beautiful dapple gray, Hugh's favorite steed, his pet of pets, and the horse most admired and coveted in all the country.

"None of yer *ars*," Claib said coaxingly, as the animal threw up his neck defiantly, "You've got to get along 'case Mas'r Hugh say so. You know Mas'r Hugh."

As if he really knew and understood, the proud head came down at once, and Rocket suffered himself to be led from the stall, but when the keen north wind struck full upon his face, the gleaming eyes flashed with stubborn fire, and planting his feet firmly in the snow, Rocket resisted all Claib's efforts to get him any further. Scolding did no good, coax him he could not, strike him he dared not, and alternately changing the halter from hand to hand poor Claib blew his stiffened fingers and called lustily for help.

"What is it?" Hugh asked, coming out upon the stoop, and comprehending the trouble at a glance. "Rocket Rocket," he cried, "Easy, my boy," and in an instant Rocket's defiant attitude changed to one of perfect obedience.

He knew and loved the voice calling so cheerily to him, and with a sudden plunge, which wrenched his halter from Claib's grasp and sent the poor negro headlong into the snow, he bounded to his master's side. Rubbing his head against Hugh's shoulder, he suffered himself to be caressed for a moment, and then, playful as a kitten, gambolled around him in circles, sometimes making a feint of coming near to him, and again leaping backward with the peculiarly graceful motion for which he was so famous. How Hugh loved that noble animal, and how Rocket loved him, licking his hands whenever he entered the stable, and crying piteously after him when he left. Five hundred dollars had been offered him for that horse, but though wanting money sadly, he had promptly refused the offer, determined that Rocket should know no master save himself.

"There, my beauty," he said, as the animal continued to prance around him. "There, you've showed off enough. Come, now, I've work for you to do."

Docile as a lamb when Hugh commanded, he stood quietly while Claib equipped him for his morning's task.

"Tell mother I shan't be back to breakfast," Hugh said, as he sprang into the saddle, and giving loose rein to Rocket went galloping through the snow.

Under ordinary circumstances that early ride would have been vastly exhilarating to Hugh, who enjoyed the bracing air, but there was too much now upon his mind to admit of his enjoying any thing. Thoughts of Adah, and the increased expense her presence would necessarily bring, flitted across his mind, while Harney's bill, put over once, and due again ere long, sat like a nightmare on him, for he saw no way in which to meet it. No way save one, and Rocket surely must have felt the throbbing of Hugh's heart as that one way flashed upon him, for he gave a kind of coaxing whine, and dashed on over the billowy drifts faster than before.

"No, Rocket, no," and Hugh patted his neck. He'd never part with Rocket, He'd sell Spring Bank first with all its incumbrances.

The cornfield was reached by this time, and with a single bound Rocket cleared the gate at the entrance. A six-rail fence was nothing for him to leap, and like a deer he sped across the field, and ere long stood before

Aunt Eunice's door. It was now three days since Hugh had gladdened Aunt Eunice's cottage with the sunshine of his presence, and when she awoke that morning, and saw how high the snow was piled around her door, she said to herself, "The boy'll be here directly to know if I'm alive," and this accounted for the round deal table drawn before the blazing fire, and looking so inviting with its two plates and cups, one a fanciful china affair, sacredly kept for Hugh, whose coffee always tasted better when sipped from its gilded side. The lightest of egg bread was steaming on the hearth, the tenderest of steak was broiling on the griddle, while the odor of the coffee boiling on the coals came tantalizingly to Hugh's olfactories as Aunt Eunice opened the door, saying pleasantly,

"I told 'em so. I felt it in my bones, and the breakfast is all but ready. Put Rocket up directly, and come in to the fire."

Fastening Rocket in his accustomed place in the outer shed, Hugh stamped the snow from his heavy boots, and then went in to Aunt Eunice's kitchen-parlor, as she called it, where the tempting breakfast stood upon the table. Nimble as a girl Aunt Eunice brought his chair, and placing it in the warmest part of the room, the one next to the wall and farthest from the door where the wind and snow crept in. But Hugh was not selfish enough to keep it, and he made Aunt Eunice change, for he knew the blood moved more slowly through her veins than his.

"No coffee! What new freak is that?" and Aunt Eunice gazed at him in astonishment as he declined the cup she had prepared with so much care, dropping in the whitest lumps of sugar, and stirring in the thickest cream.

It cost Hugh a terrible struggle to refuse that cup of coffee, but if he would retrench, he must begin at once and determining to meet it unflinchingly he replied that "he had concluded to drink water for a while, and see what that would do; much was said nowadays about coffee's being injurious, and he presumed it was."

In great distress the good old lady asked if "his dyspeptic was out of order," still insisting that he should take the cup, whose delicious odor well nigh overcame resolution. But Hugh was firm as a granite rock when once his mind was settled, and assuring Aunt Eunice that his "dyspeptic" was right, he betook himself to the gourd, standing in the pail of water within his reach. Poor Aunt Eunice did not half enjoy her breakfast, and she would not have enjoyed it at all had she known that Hugh was abstaining from what he loved so much only that she and others might be fed and warmed.

"There's something on your mind," she said, observing his abstraction. "Have you had another dunning letter, or what?"

Aunt Eunice had made a commencement, and in his usual impulsive way Hugh told the story of Adah and then asked if she would take her.

"But, Hugh," and Aunt Eunice spoke earnestly, "you cannot afford the expense. Think twice before you commit yourself."

"I have thought twice, the last time just as I did the first. Adah shall stay. You need some one these winter nights. There's the room you call mine. Give her that. Will you, Aunt Eunice?" and Hugh wound his arm around Aunt Eunice's ample waist, while he pleaded for Adah Hastings.

Aunt Eunice was soon won over as Hugh knew she would be, and it was settled that she should come that very day if possible.

"Look, the sky is clearing," and he pointed to the sunshine streaming through the window.

"We'll have her room fixed before I go," and with his own hands Hugh split and prepared the wood which was to kindle Adah's fire, then with Aunt Eunice's help sundry changes were made in the arrangement of the rather meagre furniture, which never seemed so meagre to Hugh as when he looked at it with Adah's eyes and wondered how she'd like it.

"Oh, I wish I were rich," he sighed mentally, and taking out his well worn purse he carefully counted its contents.

Twenty-five dollars. That was all, and this he had been so long in saving for the new coat he meant to buy. Hugh would like to dress better if he could, and was even anticipating his sister's surprise when he should appear before her some day habited in a coat of the latest style. To do this Adah's room must go unfurnished yet awhile and with another sigh the purse was returned to his pocket, just as Aunt Eunice, who had stepped out for a moment, reappeared, bringing a counterpane and towel, one of which was spread upon the bed, while the other covered the old pine stand, marred and stained with ink and tallow, the result of Hugh's own carelessness.

"What a heap of difference that table cloth and pocket-handkerchief do make," was Hugh's man-like remark, his face brightening with the improved appearance of things and his big heart growing warm with the thought that he might keep his twenty-five dollars and Adah be comfortable still.

With a merry laugh Aunt Eunice explained that the *table cloth* was a *bed-spread*, and the *handkerchief* a *towel*. It was all the same to Hugh so long as they improved the room, and glancing at his watch, he said it was time to be gone.

"*Ad* may pick Adah's eyes out before I get home," was his laughing remark as he vaulted into his saddle and dashed off across the fields, where, beneath the warm Kentucky sun, the snow was already beginning to soften.

Breakfast had been late at Spring Bank that morning, for the strangers had required some care, and Miss 'Lina was sipping her coffee rather ill-naturedly when a note was handed her, and instantly her mood was changed.

"Splendid, mother!" she exclaimed, glancing at the tiny, three-cornered thing; "an invitation to Ellen Tiffton's party. I was afraid she would leave me out after Hugh's refusal to attend the Ladies' fair, or buy a ticket for her lottery. It was only ten dollars either, and Mr. Harney spent all of forty, I'm sure, in the course of the evening."

"Hugh had no ten dollars to spare," Mrs. Worthington said, apologetically, "though, of course, he might have been more civil than to tell Ellen it was a regular swindle, and the getters-up ought to be indicted. I almost wonder at her inviting him, as she said she'd never speak to him again."

"Invited him! Who said she had? It's only one card for me," and with a most satisfied expression 'Lina presented the note to her mother, whose face flushed at the insult offered her son—an insult which even 'Lina felt, but would not acknowledge, lest it should interfere with her going. "There may be some mistake," she suggested. "Lulu may have dropped his," and ringing the bell she summoned to their presence a bright, handsome mulatto girl, who answered frankly that

"Only one invite was given her, and, and that for Miss 'Lina. I asked Jake," she said, "where was Master Hugh's, and he said, 'Oh. Miss Ellen's ravin' at him; called him no gentleman; and wouldn't invite him any way.' I think it's right mean in her, for Master Hugh is enough sight better gentleman than Bob Harney, that she's after. I told Jake to tell her so," and having thus vindicated her master's cause, Lulu tripped back to the kitchen, leaving her mistress and 'Lina to finish their party discussion.

"You won't go, of course," Mrs. Worthington said, quietly. "You'll resent her slighting Hugh."

"Indeed I shan't," the young lady retorted. "I hardly think it fair in Ellen, but I shall accept, and I must go to town to-day to see about having my pink silk fixed. I think I'll have some black lace festooned round the skirt. How I wish I could have a new one. Do you suppose Hugh has any money?"

"None for new dresses or lace flounces either," Mrs. Worthington replied. "I fancy he begins to look old and worn with this perpetual call for money from us. We must economize."

"Never mind, when I get Bob Harney I'll pay off old scores," 'Lina said, laughingly, as she arose from the table and went to look over her wardrobe, having first investigated the weather, and ascertained, from a consultation with Cæsar, that the roads would undoubtedly be passable by noon.

Meantime Hugh had returned, meeting in the kitchen with Lulu, who worshipping her young master with a species of adoration, resented any insults offered him far more keenly than his own sister did.

"Well, Lu, what is it? What's happened?" Hugh asked, as he saw she was full of some important matter.

In an instant the impetuous Lulu told him of the party to which he was not invited, together with the reason why, and the word she had sent back.

"I'll give 'em a piece of my mind!" she said, as she saw Hugh change color. "She may have old Harney. He's jes good enough for her! The hateful! His man John, told Claib how his master said he meant to get me and Rocket, too, some day; me for her waiting-maid, I reckon. You won't sell me, Master Hugh, will you?" and Lulu's eyes looked pleadingly up to Hugh.

"Never!" and Hugh's riding whip came down upon the table with a force which made Lulu start.

Satisfied that she was safe from Ellen Tiffton's whims, Lulu darted away, while Hugh entered the sitting-room, where 'Lina sat, surrounded by her party finery, and prepared to do the amiable to the utmost.

"That really is a handsome little boy upstairs," she said, as if she supposed it were her mother who came in; then an affected start she added, "Oh, it's you! I thought 'twas mother. Don't you think, Ellen has not invited you. Mean, isn't it?"

"Ellen can do as she likes," Hugh replied, adding, as he guessed the meaning of all that finery, "You surely are not going?"

"Why not?" and 'Lina's black eyes flashed full upon him.

"I thought perhaps you would decline for my sake," he replied.

An angry retort trembled on 'Lina's lip, but she had an object to attain, so she restrained herself and answered that "she had thought of it, but such a course would do no good, and she wanted to go so much, the Tifftons were so exclusive and aristocratic."

Hugh whistled contemptuously, but 'Lina kept her temper, and continued, coaxingly,

"Everybody is to be there, and you'd like to have your sister look decent, I know; and really, Hugh, I can't unless you give me a little money. Do, Hugh, be good for once."

"Ad, I can't," and Hugh spoke sorrowfully, for a kind word from 'Lina always touched his weaker side. "I would if I could, but honestly I've only twenty-five dollars in the world, and I've thought of a new coat. I don't like to look so shabby. It hurts me worse than it does you," and Hugh's voice trembled as he spoke.

Any but a heart of stone would have yielded, but, 'Lina was too supremely selfish. Hugh had twenty-five dollars. He might give her half, or even ten. She'd be satisfied with ten. He could soon make that up. The negro hire came due ere long. He must have forgotten that.

No, he had not; but with the negro hire came debts, thoughts of which gave him the old worn look his mother had observed. Only ten dollars! It did seem hard to refuse, and if 'Lina went, Hugh wished her to look well, for underneath his apparent harshness lurked a kind of pride in his sister, whose beauty was of the bold, dashing style.

"Take them," he said at last counting out the ten with regretful sigh. "Make them go as far as you can, and Ad, remember don't get into debt."

"I won't," and with a civil "Thank you," 'Lina rolled up her bills, while Hugh repaired to Adah's room telling her of Aunt Eunice, and his plan of taking her there.

With a burst of tears, Adah listened to him, and then insisted upon going away, as she had done the previous night. She had no claim on him, and she could not be a burden.

"You, madam, think it best, I'm sure," she said, appealing to Mrs. Worthington, who was present and who answered promptly,

"I do not. I am willing you should remain until your friends are found."

Adah offered no further remonstrance, but turning to Hugh, said hesitatingly,

"I may hear from my advertisement. Do you take the *Herald*?"

"Yes, though I can't say I think much of it," Hugh replied, and Adah continued,

"Then if you ever find anything for me, you'll tell me, and I can go away," I said, "Direct to Adah Hastings. Somebody will be sure to see it. Maybe *George*, and then he'll know of Willie."

With a muttered invective against the "villain," Hugh left the room to see that the carriage was ready, while his mother, following him into the hall, offered to go herself with Adah if he liked. Glad to be relieved, as he had business that afternoon in Versailles, and was anxious to set off as soon as possible, Hugh accepted at once, and half an hour later, the Spring Bank carriage, containing Mrs. Worthington, Adah and Willie, drove slowly from the door, 'Lina calling after her mother to send Cæsar back immediately, as she was going to Frankfort after dinner, and wanted the carriage herself.

CHAPTER X
'LINA'S PURCHASE AND HUGH'S

There were piles of handsome dress goods upon the counter at *Harney's* that afternoon, and *Harney* was anxious to sell. It was not often that he favored a customer with his own personal services, and 'Lina felt proportionably flattered when he came forward and asked what he could show her. "Of course, a dress for the party—he had sold at least a dozen that day, but fortunately he still had the most, elegant pattern of all, and he knew it would exactly suit her complexion and style. There would be nothing like it at the party, unless she wore it, as he hoped she would, for he knew how admirably she would become it, and he'd had her in his mind all the time." 'Lina was easily flattered, while the silk was beautiful, and as she thought how well the soft tinted rose with its single white velvety leaf, standing out so full and rich, would become her dark hair and eyes, an intense desire came over her to possess it. But ten dollars was all she had, and turning away from the tempting silk she answered faintly, that "it was superb, but she could not afford it, besides, she had not the money to-day."

"Not the slightest consequence," was Harney's quick rejoinder, as he thought of Hugh's already heavy bill, and alas, thought of Rocket too! "Not the slightest consequence. Your brother's credit is good, and I'm sure he'll be proud to see you in it. I should, were *I* your brother."

'Lina blushed, while the wish to possess the silk grew every moment stronger.

"If it were *only fifty dollars*, it would not seem so bad," she thought. Hugh could manage it some way, and Mr. Harney was so good natured; he could wait a year, she knew. But the making would cost ten dollars more, for that was the price Miss Allis charged, to say nothing of the trimmings. "No, I can't," she said, quite decidedly at last, asking for the lace with which she at first intended renovating her old pink silk. "She must see Miss Allis first to know how much she wanted," and she tripped over to Frankfort's fashionable dressmaker, whom she found surrounded with dresses for the party.

Such an array and such elegance too; the old pink faded into nothing. She should be quite in the shade, and feeling much like crying, 'Lina sat watching the nimble fingers around her, and waiting for Miss Allis' advice, when a new idea crossed her mind. She heard Adah say that morning when she was in her room, that she could sew neatly, that she always made her own dresses, and if hers, why not 'Lina's! She certainly looked as if she might have good taste, and she ought to do something by way of remuneration; besides that, if Adah made it, she could, from her mother's budgets pick up enough for linings, whereas nothing but new entire would answer the purpose of a fashionable artiste, like Miss Diana Allis. 'Lina was fast persuading herself to buy the coveted silk, and as some time would elapse ere Miss Allis could attend to her she went back to Harney's just for one more look at the lovely fabric. It was, if possible, more beautiful than before, and Harney was more polite, while the result of the whole was that, when 'Lina at four o'clock that afternoon entered her carriage to go home, the despised pink silk, still unpaid on Harney's books, was thrown down any where, while in her hands she carefully held the bundle Harney brought himself, complimenting her upon the sensation she was sure to create, and inviting her to dance the first set with him. Then with a smiling bow he closed the door upon her, and returning to his books wrote down Hugh Worthington his debtor to fifty dollars more.

"That makes three hundred and fifty," he said to himself. "I know he can't raise that amount of ready money, and as he is too infernal proud to be sued, I'm sure of Rocket or Lulu, it matters but little which," and with a look upon his face which made it positively hideous, the scheming Harney closed his books, and sat down to calculate the best means of managing the rather unmanageable Hugh!

It was dark when 'Lina reached home, but the silk looked well by firelight, and 'Lina would have been quite happy but for her mother's reproaches and an occasional twinge as she thought of Hugh who had not yet returned, and whose purchase that afternoon was widely different from her own.

It was the day when a number of negroes, whose master had failed to a large amount, were to be sold in the Court House, and Hugh, as he reined up a moment before it, saw them grouped together upon the steps. He had no fancy for such scenes, but the eager, wistful glances the wretched creatures cast upon the passers by awoke his sympathy, and after finishing his business he returned to the Court House just as the auctioneer was detailing the many virtues of the bright-looking lad first upon the block. There was no trouble in disposing of them all, save a white-haired old man, whom they called Uncle Sam, and who was rather famous for having been stolen from his late master and sold into Virginia. With tottering steps the old man took his place, while his dim eyes wandered over the faces congregated around him as if seeking for their owner. But none was found who cared for Uncle Sam. He was too old—his work was done, and like a worn out horse he must be turned off to die.

"Won't nobody bid for *Sam*? I fotched a thousand dollars onct," and the feeble voice trembled as it asked this question.

"What will become of him if he is not sold?" Hugh asked of a bystander, who replied, "Go back to the old place to be kicked and cuffed by the minions of the new proprietor, *Harney*. You know Harney, of Frankfort?"

Yes, Hugh did know Harney as one who was constantly adding to his already large possessions houses and lands and negroes without limit, caring little that they came to him laden with the widow's curse and the orphan's tears. The law was on his side. He did nothing illegally, and so there was no redress. This was Harney, and Hugh always felt exasperated when he thought of him. Advancing a step or two he came nearer to the negro, who took comfort at once from the expression of his face, and stretching out his shaking hand he said beseechingly,

"You, mas'r, you buy old Sam 'case it 'ill be lonesome and cold in de cabin at home when they all is gone. Please mas'r," and the tone was so pleading, that Hugh felt a great throb of pity for the desolate, forsaken negro.

"How old are you?" he asked, taking the quivering hand still extended toward him.

"Bless you, mas'r, longer than I can 'member. They was allus puttin' me back and back to make me young, till I couldn't go backuds no more, so I spec's I's mighty nigh a thousan'," was the negro's reply, whereupon cheers for Uncle Sam resounded long and loud among the amused spectators.

"What can you do?" was Hugh's next query, to which the truthful negro answered,

"Nothin' much, or, yes," and an expression of reverence and awe stole over the wrinkled face, as in a low tone he added, "I can pray for young mas'r, and I will, only buy me, please."

Hugh had not much faith in praying negroes, but something in old Sam struck him as sincere. His prayers might do good, and he needed somebody's, sadly. But what should he offer, when fifteen dollars was all he had in the world, and was it his duty to encumber himself with a piece of useless property? Visions of the Golden Haired and Adah both rose up before him. They would say it was right. They would tell him to buy old Sam, and that settled the point.

"Five dollars," he called out, and Sam's "God bless you," was sounding in his ears, when a voice from another part of the building doubled the bid, and with a moan Uncle Sam turned imploringly toward Hugh.

"A leetle more, mas'r, an' you fotches 'em; a leetle more," he whispered, coaxingly, and Hugh faltered out "Twelve."

"Thirteen," came from the corner, and Hugh caught sight of the bidder, a sour-grained fellow, whose wife had ten young children, and so could find use for Sam.

"Thirteen and a half," cried Hugh.

"Fourteen," responded his opponent.

"Leetle more, mas'r, berry leetle," whispered Uncle Sam.

"Fourteen and a quarter," said Hugh, the perspiration starting out about his lips, as he thought how fast his pile was diminishing, and that he could not go beyond it.

"Fourteen and a half," from the corner.

"Leetle more, mas'r," from Uncle Sam.

"Fourteen, seventy-five," from Hugh.

"Fifteen," from the man in the corner, and Hugh groaned aloud,

"That's every dime I've got."

Quick as thought an acquaintance beside him slipped a bill into his hand, whispering as he did so,

"It's a V. I'll double it if necessary. I'm sorry for the darky."

It was very exciting now, each bidder raising a quarter each time, while Sam's "a leetle more, mas'r," and the vociferous cheers of the croud, whenever Hugh's voice was heard, showed him to be the popular party.

"Nineteen, seventy-five," from the corner, and Hugh felt his courage giving way as he faintly called out,

"Twenty."

Only an instant did the auctioneer wait, and then his decisive, "Gone!" made Hugh the owner of Uncle Sam, who crouching down before him, blessed him with tears and prayers.

"I knows you're good," he said; "I knows it by yer face; and mebby, when the rheumatics gits out of my ole legs I kin work for mas'r a heap. Does you live fur from here?"

"Three miles or more," Hugh replied, bidding the negro follow him.

The snow was melting, but out upon the turnpike it was still so deep that Hugh had many misgivings as to the old man's ability to walk, but Sam, intent on proving that he was smarter than he seemed, declared himself perfectly competent to go with "Mars'r" to the world's end, if necessary.

"It's mighty cold, though," he said, as he emerged into the open air, and the chilly wind penetrated the thin rags which covered him. "It's mighty cold, and my knees is all a shakin', but I'll git over it bimeby."

It was not in Hugh's nature to see the old man shiver so, and taking off his own thick shawl he wrapped it round the negro's shoulders, saying to the bystanders,

"My blood is warmer than his."

Another cheer from the crowd, another, "God bless you, mas'r," and the strange pair started on their homeward tour, Hugh riding very slowly, and accommodating Rocket's steps to the hobbling old man, who wheezed and puffed, and sweat with the wondrous efforts he made, and at last when only a mile was gone, gave out entirely, and pitched headlong into the snow.

"It's my dumb knees. They allus was crooked and shaky," he gasped, becoming more and more entangled in the shawl, which he was not accustomed to wearing.

"Look here, Sam," and Hugh laughed heartily at the negro's forlorn appearance, as, regaining his feet, he assumed a most deprecating attitude, asking pardon for tumbling down, and charging it all to his shaky knees. "Look here, there's no other way, except for you to ride and me to walk. Rocket won't carry double," and ere Sam could remonstrate, Hugh had dismounted and placed him in the saddle.

Rocket did not fancy the exchange, as was manifest by an indignant snort, and an attempt to shake Sam off, but a word from Hugh quieted him, and the latter offered the reins to Sam, who was never a skillful horseman, and felt a mortal terror of the high-mettled steed beneath him. With a most frightened expression upon his face, he grasped the saddle pommel with both hands, and bending nearly double, gasped out,

"Sam ain't much use't to gemman's horses. Kind of hold me on, mas'r, till I gits de hang of de critter. He hists me round mightily."

So, leading Rocket with one hand, and steadying Sam with the other, Hugh got on but slowly, and 'Lina had looked for him many times ere she spied him from the window as he came up the lawn.

"In the name of wonder, what is that on Rocket!" she exclaimed, as she caught sight of Sam, whose rags were fluttering in the wind. "An old white-headed nigger, as I live!" and she hastened to the door, where the servants were assembling, all curious like herself to see the new arrival.

Very carefully Hugh assisted him to dismount, but Sam's knees, cramped up so long on Rocket, refused to straighten at once, and Lulu was not far out of the way when she likened him to a toad, while her mischievous brother Jim called out,

"How d'ye, old bow legs?"

"Jest tol'able, thankee," was Sam's meek reply, then spying 'Lina he lifted his hat politely, bowing so low that his knees gave out again, and he would have fallen had not Hugh held him up.

"Who is he, and what did you get him for?" Mrs. Worthington asked, as Hugh led him into the dining room.

Briefly Hugh explained to her why he had bought the negro.

"It was foolish, I suppose, but I'm not sorry yet," he added, glancing toward the corner, where the poor old man was sitting, warming his shriveled hands by the cheerful fire, and muttering to himself blessings on "young mas'r."

Supper had been delayed for Hugh, and as he took his seat at the table, he inquired after Adah.

"Pretty well when I left," said his mother, adding that Lulu had been there since, and reported her as looking pale and worn, while Aunt Eunice seemed worried with Willie, who was inclined to be fretful.

"They need some one," Hugh said. "Can't you spare Lulu?"

Mrs. Worthington did not know, but 'Lina, to whom Lulu was a kind of waiting-maid, took the matter up, and said,

"Indeed they couldn't. There was no one at Spring Bank more useful, and it was preposterous for Hugh to think of giving their best servant to Adah Hastings. Let her take care of her baby herself. She guessed it wouldn't hurt her. Any way, they couldn't afford to keep a servant for her."

With a long drawn sigh, Hugh finished his supper, and was about lighting his cigar when he felt some one touching him, and turning round he saw that Sam had grasped his coat. The negro had heard the conversation, and drawn correct conclusions. His new master was not rich. He could not afford to buy him, and having bought him could not afford to keep him. There was a sigh in the old man's heart, as he thought how useless he was, but when he heard about the baby, his spirits rose at once. In all the world there was nothing so precious to Sam as a little white child, with waxen hands to pat his old black face, and his work was found.

"Mas'r," he whispered, "Sam kin take keer that baby. He knows how, and the little childrens in Georgy, whar I comed from, used to be mighty fond of Sam. I'll tend to the young lady too. May I, Mas'r?"

Sam did not look much like Hugh's ideas of a child's nurse or a ladie's waiting-maid, but necessity knows no choice, and thinking the old man might answer for Willie until something better offered, he replied,

"Perhaps you may. I will see to-morrow."

Then, stepping to the door he called Claib, and bidding him show Sam where he was to sleep, repaired himself to his own cold chamber which seemed doubly comfortless and dreary from its contrast with the warm pleasant sitting-room where the selfish 'Lina, delighted at his absence, was again admiring the handsome silk, which Adah was to make.

CHAPTER XI
SAM AND ADAH

With heavy eyes and aching head Adah worked day after day upon the dress, which 'Lina had coaxed her to make, saying both to her and Aunt Eunice that, as she wished to surprise Hugh with a sight of herself in full array, they were not to tell him that the dress was new, but suffer him to think it the old pink silk which she was fixing.

"I hardly suppose he'd know the difference," she said, "but if you can arrange it not to work when he is here, I wish you would."

'Lina could be very gracious when she chose, and as she saw a way by which Adah might be useful to her, she chose to be so now, and treated the unsuspecting girl so kindly, that Adah promised to undertake the task, which proved a harder one than she had anticipated. Anxious to gratify 'Lina, and keep what she was doing a secret from Hugh, who came to the cottage often, she was obliged to work early and late, bending over the dress by the dim candle light, until her head seemed bursting with pain, and rings of fire danced before her eyes. She never would have succeeded but for Uncle Sam, who proved a most efficient member of the household, fitting in every niche and corner, until Aunt Eunice wondered how she had ever lived without him. Particularly did he attach himself to Willie, relieving Adah from all care, and thus enabling her to devote every spare moment to the party dress.

"You's workin' yourself to death," he said to her, as late on Saturday night she sat bending to the tallow candle, her hair brushed back from her forehead and a purplish glow upon her cheek.

"I know I'm working too hard," Adah replied, and leaning back in her chair she closed her eyes wearily, while Sam, gazing admiringly at her continued, "You 'minds me some of de young lady in Virginny. Has I ever tole you 'bout her?"

"No, who was she?" Adah said, and Sam replied,

"She's what teached me the way to God. She took my dried-up-hand in dem little soft ones of hern, white as cotton bats, and lead me up to de narrow gap. She push me in and say, 'Go on now, Sam. You've got in de right track, that leads to glory hallelujah.' Didn't word it just dem words, be sure, but that's the heft of the meaning. I tell you Sam was mighty nigh as shipwrecked as dat Pollo somebody what Miss *Ellis* read about in the good book."

"*Miss who?*" Adah asked, and Sam replied,

"Miss Ellis. I done forget de other name. *Ellis* they call her way down thar whar Sam was sold, when dat man with the big *splot* on his forerd steal me away and sell me in Virginny. Miss ever hearn tell o' dat?"

"Big *what?*" Adah asked, and Sam replied, "Big *scar* or *mark* kinder purple, on his forrid, right clus to the har."

Adah shuddered, for the one she knew as her guardian was marked in that way, and she asked Sam to tell her more of the man with the splot.

Delighted to tell the story which he never tired of telling, Sam, in his own peculiar dialect, related how four years before, a man calling himself Sullivan had appeared in the neighborhood of his former master's plantation ingratiating himself into the good graces of the negroes and secretly offering to conduct any to the land of freedom who would put themselves under his protection.

"I had an idee," Sam said, "that freedom was sweet as bumble bees' honey and I hankered to get a taste, so me and two more fools steal away from the old cabin one rainy night, and go with Mas'r Sullivan, who strut round mighty big, with his three niggers, tellin' us not to say one word ef we not want to be cotched. We thinks he's takin' a bee line for Canada, when fust we knows we's in ole Virginny, and de villain not freein' us at all. He sells us. *Me* he most give away, 'case I was old, and the mas'r who buy some like Mas'r Hugh, he sorry for ole shaky nigger. Sam tell him on his knees how he comed from Kaintuck, but Mas'r Sullivan say he bought 'em *far*, and that the right mas'r sell 'em sneakin like to save raisin a furse, and he show a bill of sale. They believe him spite of dis chile, and so Sam 'long to anodder mas'r.

"Mas'r Fitzhugh live on big plantation—and one day she comed, with great trunk, a visitin'. She'd been to school with Miss Mabel, Mas'r Fitzhugh's daughter.

"They all think heap of Miss Ellis, and I hear de blacks tellin' how she berry rich, and comed from way off thar whar white niggers live—Masser-something."

"Massachusetts," suggested Adah.

"Yes; that's the very mas'r. I'se got mizzable memory, and I disremembers her last name. The folks call her *Ellis*, and the blacks Miss Ellis."

"A queer name for a first one," Adah thought, while Sam continued,

"She jest like a bright angel, in her white gownds and dem long curls, and Sam like her so much. She talk to Sam, too, and her voice so sweet, just like falling water when the moon is shining on it. Sam very sick, want to go home so much, and lie all day in his little cabin, when she come in, holdin' up her skirts so dainty like, and set right down with me. Ki, wasn't her little hand soft though when she put it on my head and said, 'Poor Sam, Ellis is sorry.' Sam cry berry much then; cry so loud Miss Mabel hear, and come in, tellin' Miss Ellis, 'Pooh he's only homesick; says he was stole from Kentucky but papa don't believe him. Do come out of this hole,' but Miss Ellis not go. She say, 'Then he needs comforting,' and she do that very thing. She talk so good, she ax Sam all 'bout it, and Sam feel she b'lieve him. She promise to write to Mas'r Brown and tell him whar I is. I didn't cry loud then—heart too full. I cry whimperin' like, and she cry too. Then she tell me about *God*, and Sam listen, oh, listen so much, for that's what he want to hear so long. Miss Nancy, in Kentuck, be one of them that reads her pra'rs o' Sundays, and ole mas'r one that hollers 'em. Sam liked that way best, seemed like gettin' along and make de Lord hear, but it don't show Sam the way, and when the ministers come in, he listen, but them that reads and them that hollers only talk about *High and Low—Jack and the Game*, or something, Sam misremembers so bad; got mizzable memory. He only knows he not find the way, till Miss Ellis tell him of *Jesus*, once a man and always God. It's very queer, but Sam believe it and then she sing, 'Come unto me.'

"Oh, so fine, the very rafters hold their breff, and Sam find the way. Sam feel the hand she say was stretched out for him. He grasp it tight. He never let it go, never cease thankin' God that 'Come unto me' mean just such an ole nigger as Sam, or that Miss Ellis was sent to him. She teach me 'Our Father,' and I say it every day, and I 'members her, too, and now I puts her and Mas'r Hugh in de same words. Seems ef they make good span, only Mas'r Hugh not so fixed up as she, but he's good."

"Where is Miss Ellis now?" Adah asked, and Sam replied,

"Gone home. Gone to Masser—what you say once—but not till letter come to her from Mas'r Brown, sayin' Sam was stealed, and 'fore long Mas'r Brown come on hisself after me and the others. Miss Ellis so glad, and Mas'r Fitzhugh, too. Sam not much 'count, he say, and let me go easy, that's the way I come home. Miss Ellis gived me five dollars and then ask what else. I look at her and say, 'Sam wants a spear or two of yer shinin' har', and Miss

Mabel takes shears and cut a little curl. I'se got 'em now. I never spend the money," and from an old leathern wallet Sam drew a bill and a soft silken curl which he laid across Adah's hand.

"And where is Sullivan?" asked Adah, a chill creeping over her as she remembered how about four years ago the man she called her guardian was absent for some time, and came back to her with colored hair and whiskers.

"Oh, he gone long before, nobody know whar. Sam b'lieves, though, he hear they cotch him, but misremembers, got such mizzable memory."

"You said he had a mark?" Adah continued. And Sam replied, "Yes, queer mark,—must of been thar when he was borned, showd better when he's cussin mad. You ever seen him?"

"I do not know," and Adah half groaned aloud at the sad memories which Sam's story had awakened within her.

She could scarcely doubt that *Sullivan* the negro-stealer, and Redfield, her guardian, were the same, but where was he now, and why had he treated her so treacherously, when he had always seemed so kind? Why did everybody desert her? What had she done to deserve so sad a fate? All the old bitter anguish was welling up again, and desirous of being alone, she bade Sam leave her as it was growing late.

"Miss Adah prays," the old man answered, "Won't she say Our Father with Sam?"

Adah could not refuse, and falling on her knees she joined her voice with that of Sam's in that most beautiful of all prayers—the one our Saviour taught. Sam did not know it correctly, but God heard him all the same; heard too, the strangely-worded petition that "He would bless Mas'r Hugh, Miss Ellis, and Miss Adah, and fotch 'em all right some time."

Surely Hugh's sleep was sweeter that night for the prayer breathed by the lowly negro, and even the wild tumult in Adah's heart was hushed by Sam's simple childlike faith that God would bring all right at last.

Early on Monday afternoon 'Lina, taking advantage of Hugh's absence, came over for her dress, finding much fault, and requiring some of the work to be done twice ere it suited her. Without a murmur Adah obeyed, but when the last stitch was taken and the party dress was gone, her overtaxed frame gave way, and Sam himself helped her to her bed, where she lay moaning, with the blinding pain in her head, which increased so fast that she scarcely saw the tempting little supper which Aunt Eunice brought, asking her to eat. Of one thing, however, she was conscious, and that of the dark form bending over her pillow and whispering soothingly the passage which had once brought Heaven to him, "Come unto me, and I will give you rest."

Dear old Sam! there was a world of kindness in his breast, and if he could he would gladly have taken Adah's suffering upon himself.

The night had closed in dark and stormy, and the wintry rain beat against the windows; but for this he did not hesitate a moment when at midnight Aunt Eunice, alarmed at Adah's rapidly increasing fever, asked if he could find his way to Spring Bank, and in a few moments the old, shriveled form was out in the darkness, groping its way over the fences, and through the pitfalls, stumbling often, and losing his hat past recovery, so that the snowy hair was dripping wet when Spring Bank was reached and he stood upon the porch.

In much alarm Hugh dressed himself and hastened to the cottage. But Adah did not know him and only talked of dresses and parties, and *George*, whom she begged to come back and restore her good name. The dresses and the party were enigmas to Hugh, and as Aunt Eunice kept silent for fear of his wrath, he gathered nothing from Sam's muttered jumble about, "working herself blind for Miss 'Lina over dar." He knew she must have medical advice, and giving a few directions to Aunt Eunice he went himself for the family physician and then returned to Spring Bank in quest of his mother, who, he was sure, would not hesitate to brave the storm for Adah's sake.

CHAPTER XII
WHAT FOLLOWED

There was a bright light in the sitting-room, and through the half-closed shutters Hugh caught glimpses of a blazing fire. 'Lina had come home, and half wishing she had staid a little longer, Hugh entered the room, starting with an exclamation of surprise at the sight which met his view. Divested of her gorgeous apparel, her ample dimensions considerably reduced, and her face indicative of her feelings, 'Lina stood upon the hearth, wringing her long black hair, which hung loosely about her shoulders, while her mother bent with deep concern over the mud-bespattered, ruined dress, which had cost so much.

Poor 'Lina! The party had proved a most unsatisfactory affair. She had not made the sensation she expected to make. Harney had scarcely noticed her at all, having neither eyes nor ears for any one save Ellen Tiffton, who surely must have told that Hugh was not invited, for, in no other way could 'Lina account for the remark she heard touching her want of heart in failing to resent a brother's insult. Added to this, it was very annoying to be quizzed, as she was, concerning *Adah*, of whom everybody seemed resolved to talk. In the most unenviable of moods, 'Lina left at an early hour, and though Harney did accompany her to the carriage, saying something about being sorry that she should go so soon when he meant to see more of her, it did not atone for his past neglect or for his holding the umbrella so that the little greenish streams of water dripped directly down her back, making her fidget with terror lest her rose-colored dress should be soiled. Coolly bidding him good night, she bade Cæsar drive carefully, as it was very dark, and the rain was almost blinding, so rapidly it fell.

"Ye-es, Mis-s, Cæs—he—he done been to party 'fore now. Git 'long dar, Sorrel," hiccoughed the negro, who, in Colonel Tiffton's kitchen had indulged rather too freely to insure the safety of his mistress.

Still the horses knew the road, and kept it until they left the main highway and turned into the fields. Even then they would probably have made their way in safety, had not their drunken driver persisted in turning them into a road which led directly through the deepest part of the creek, swollen now by the melted snow and the vast amount of rain which had fallen since the sun-setting. Not knowing they were wrong, 'Lina did not dream of danger until she heard Cæsar's cry of "Who'a dar, Sorrel. Git up, Henry. Dat's nothin' but de creek," while a violent lurch of the carriage sent her to the opposite side from where she had been sitting.

"What is the matter, Cæsar? Where are we?" she screamed, as she heard the waters splashing almost against the windows.

"Lor', Miss, I do' know whar we is, 'cept we're in the river. I never seen no creek so high as this," was the frightened negro's answer as he tried to extricate the noble brutes floundering in the stream and struggling to reach the opposite bank.

A few mad plunges, another wrench, which pitched 'Lina headlong against the window, and the steep, shelving bank was reached, but in endeavoring to climb it the carriage was upset, and 'Lina found herself in pitchy darkness, her mouth and nostrils filled with the soft mud, which, at first, prevented her screaming, and herself wet to her neck with the rushing water. Perfectly sobered now, Cæsar extricated her as soon as possible, and carrying her up the bank placed her upon her feet beneath a tree, whose leafless branches but poorly shielded her from the rain. The carriage was broken—one wheel was off entirely, he said, and thus there was no alternative save for 'Lina to walk the remaining distance home. It was not far, for the scene of the disaster was within sight of Spring Bank, but to 'Lina, bedraggled with mud and wet to the skin, it seemed an interminable distance, and her strength was giving out just as she reached the piazza, and called on her mother for help, sobbing hysterically as she repeated her story, but dwelling most upon her ruined dress.

"What will Hugh say? It was not paid for either. Oh dear, I most wish I was dead!" she moaned, as her mother removed one by one the saturated garments.

The sight of Hugh called forth her grief afresh, and forgetful of her dishabille, she staggered toward him, and impulsively winding her arms around his neck sobbed out,

"Oh, Hugh, I've had such a doleful time. I've been in the creek, the carriage is broken, the horses are lamed, Cæsar is drunk, and—and—oh, Hugh, I've spoiled my dress!"

The last came gaspingly, as if this were the straw too many, the crowning climax of the whole, the loss which 'Lina most deplored. Surely here was a list of disasters for which Hugh, with his other trouble, was not prepared.

But amid it all there was a glimmer of light, and Hugh's great, warm heart seized it eagerly. 'Lina's arms were round his neck, 'Lina's tears were on his cheek, 'Lina herself had turned to him for comfort, and he would not withhold it. Laughing merrily he held her off at a little distance, likening her to a mermaid fresh from the sea, and succeeding at last in quieting her until she could give a more concise account of the catastrophe.

"Never mind the dress," he said, good humoredly, as she kept recurring to that. "It isn't as if it were new. An old thing is never so valuable."

"Yes; but, Hugh—you don't know—oh, dear, dear," and 'Lina, who had meant to tell the whole, broke down again, while Hugh rejoined,

"Of course I don't know—just how a girl feels to spoil a pretty dress, but I wouldn't cry so hard. You shall have another some time," and in his generous heart the thought arose, that the first money he got should be appropriated to the purchase of a new dress in place of the one whose loss 'Lina so loudly bewailed.

It was impossible now for Mrs. Worthington to accompany Hugh to the cottage, so he returned alone, while 'Lina, with aching head and shivering limbs, crept into bed, crying herself to sleep, and waking in the morning with a burning fever, scarcely less severe than that raging in Adah Hastings' veins.

During the gloomy weeks which followed, Hugh's heart and hands were full, inclination tempting him to stay by Adah, and stern duty, bidding him keep with 'Lina, who, strange to say, was always more quiet when he was near taking readily from him the medicine refused when offered by her mother. Day after day, week after week, Hugh watched alternately at their bedsides, and those who came to offer help felt their hearts glow with admiration for the worn, haggard man, whose character they had so mistaken, never dreaming what depths of patient, all-enduring tenderness were hidden beneath his rough exterior. Even Ellen Tiffton was softened, and forgetting the Ladies Fair, rode daily over to Spring Bank, ostensibly to inquire after 'Lina, but really to speak a kindly word to Hugh, to whom she felt she had done a wrong. How long these fevers ran, and Hugh began to fear that 'Lina's never would abate, sorrowing much for the harsh words which passed between them, wishing they had been unsaid, for he would rather than none but pleasant memories should be left to him of his only sister. But 'Lina did not die, and as her disease had from the first assumed a far more violent form than Adah's, so it was the first to yield, and February found her convalescent. With Adah it was different, and the neighbors grew tired of asking how she was and receiving always the same doubtful answer. But there came a change, a morning when she awoke from the deathlike stupor which had clouded her faculties so long, and the attending physician said to Hugh that his services would be needed but a little longer. There was joy at the cottage then, old Uncle Sam stealing away to his accustomed place of prayer down by the Willow Spring, where he so oft had asked that Miss Adah might be spared, and where now he knelt to thank the God who had restored her. Joy at Spring Bank, too, when Mrs. Worthington wept tears almost as joyful as any she had shed when told that 'Lina would live. Joy, too, unobtrusive joy in Hugh's heart, a joy which would not be clouded by thoughts of the heavy bills which he must meet ere long. Physicians' bills, together with that of Harney's yet unpaid, for Harney, villain though he was, would not present it when Hugh was full of trouble; but the hour was coming when it must be settled, and Hugh at last received a note, couched in courteous terms, but urging immediate payment.

"I'll see him to-day. I'll know the worst at once," he said, and mounting Rocket, he dashed down the Frankfort turnpike, and was soon closeted with Harney.

CHAPTER XIII
HOW HUGH PAID HIS DEBTS

The perspiration was standing in great drops about Hugh's quivering lips, and his face was white as ashes, as, near the close of that interview, he hoarsely asked,

"Do I understand you, sir, that *Rocket* will cancel this debt and leave you my debtor for one hundred dollars?"

"Yes, that was my offer, and a most generous one, too, considering how little horses are bringing," and Harney smiled villainously as he thought within himself, "Easier to manage than I supposed. I believe my soul I offered too much. I should have made it an even thing."

He did not know Hugh Worthington, or dream of the volcano pent up beneath that calm exterior. Hugh had demurred to the fifty-dollar silk as a mistake, and when convinced that it was not, his wrath had known no bounds. Forgetting Golden Hair he had sworn so roundly that even Harney cowered before the storm; but that was over now, and ashamed of his passion, Hugh was making a strong effort to meet his fate like a man. Step by step as he knew so well how to do, Harney had reached the point of which for more than a year he had never lost sight.

"If Mr. Worthington had not the ready money, and, in these hard times, it was natural to suppose he had not, why then he would, as an accommodation, take Rocket, paying one hundred dollars extra, and Hugh's debt would be cancelled."

Hugh knew how long this plan had been premeditated, and his blood boiled madly when he heard it suggested, as if that moment had given it birth. Still he restrained himself, and asked the question we have recorded, adding after Harney's reply,

"And suppose I do not care to part with Rocket?"

Harney winced a little, but answered carelessly,

"Money, of course, is just as good. You know how long I've waited. Few would have done as well."

Yes, Hugh knew that, but Rocket was as dear to him as his right eye, and he would almost as soon have plucked out the one as sold the other.

"I have not the money," he said frankly, "and I cannot part with Rocket. Is there nothing else? I'll give a mortgage on Spring Bank."

Harney did not care for a mortgage, but there was something else, and the rascally face brightened, as, stepping back, while he made the proposition, he faintly suggested "Lulu." He would give a thousand dollars for her, and Hugh could keep his horse. For a moment the two young men regarded each other intently, Hugh's eyes flashing gleams of fire, and his whole face expressive of the contempt he felt for the wretch who cowed at last beneath the look, and turned away muttering that "he saw nothing so very heinous in wishing to purchase a nigger wench."

Then, changing his tone to one of defiance, he added,

"You'll be obliged to part with her yet, Hugh Worthington. I know how you are straitened and how much you think of her. You may not have another so good a chance to provide her with a kind master. Surely, you should be satisfied with that fair-haired New York damsel, and let me have the nigger."

Harney tried to smile, but the laugh died on his lips, as, springing to his feet, Hugh, with one blow, felled him to the floor, exclaiming,

"Thus do I resent the insult offered to Adah Hastings, as pure and true a woman as your own sister. Villain!" and he shook fiercely his prostrate foe struggling to rise.

Some men are decidedly better for being knocked down, and Harney was one of them. Feminine in figure and cowardly in disposition, he knew he was no match for the broad, athletic Hugh, and shaking down his pants when permitted to stand upright, he muttered something about "hearing from him again." Then, as the sight of the unpaid bill brought back to his mind the cause of his present unpleasant predicament he returned to the attack, by saying,

"Since you are not inclined to part with either of your pets, you'll oblige me with the money, and before to-morrow night. You understand me, I presume?"

"I do," and bowing haughtily, Hugh passed through the open door.

In a kind of desperation he mounted Rocket, and dashed out of town at a speed which made more than one look after him, wondering what cause there was for his headlong haste. A few miles from the city he slacked his speed, and dismounting by a running brook, sat down to think. The price offered for Lulu would set him free from every pressing debt, and leave a large surplus, but not for a moment did he hesitate.

"I'd lead her out and shoot her through the heart, before I'd do that," he said.

Then turning to the noble animal cropping the grass beside him, he wound his arms around his neck, and tried to imagine how it would seem to know the stall at home was empty, and Rocket gone. He could not sell him, he said, as he looked into the creature's eyes, meeting there an expression almost human, as Rocket rubbed his nose against his sleeve, and uttered a peculiar sound.

"If I could pawn him," he thought, just as the sound of wheels was heard, and he saw old Colonel Tiffton driving down the turnpike.

Stopping suddenly as he caught sight of Hugh, the colonel called out cheerily, "How d'ye, young man? What are you doing there by the brook? Huggin' your horse, as I live! Well, I don't wonder. That's a fine nag of yours. My Nell is nigh about crazy for me to buy him. What'll you take?"

Hugh knew he could trust the colonel, and after a moment's hesitation told of his embarrassments, and asked the loan of five hundred dollars, offering Rocket as security, with the privilege of redeeming him in a year. Hugh's chin quivered, and the arm thrown across Rocket's neck pressed more tightly as he made this offer. Every change in the expression of his face was noted by the colonel, and interpreted with considerable accuracy. He had always liked Hugh. There was something in his straight-forward manner which pleased him, and when he learned why he was not at his daughter's birth-day party, he had raised a most uncomfortable breeze about the capricious Nellie's ears, declaring she should apologize, but forgetting to insist upon it as he at first meant to do.

"You ask a steep sum," he said, crossing one fat limb over the other and snapping his whip at Rocket, who eyed him askance. "Pretty steep sum, but I take it, you are in a tight spot and don't know what else to do. Got too many hangers on. There's Aunt Eunice—you can't help her, to be sure, nor your mother, nor your sister, though I'd break her neck before I'd let her run me into debt. Your bill at Harney's, I know, is most all of her contracting, though you don't tell me so, and I respect you for it. She's your sister—blood kin. But that girl in the snow bank—I'll be hanged if that was ever made quite clear to me."

"It is to me, and that is sufficient," Hugh answered haughtily, while the old colonel laughingly replied,

"Good grit, Hugh. I like you for that. In short, I like you for every thing, and that's why I was sorry about that New York lady. You see, it may stand in the way of your getting a wife by and by, that's all."

"I shall never marry," Hugh answered, moodily, kicking at a decaying stump, and involuntarily thinking of the Golden Haired.

"No?" the colonel replied, interrogatively. "Well there ain't many good enough for you, that's a fact; there ain't many girls good for any body. I never saw but one except my Nell, that was worth a picayune, and that was *Alice Johnson*."

"*Who? Who* did you say?" And Hugh grew white as marble, while a strange light gleamed in the dark eyes fastened so eagerly upon the colonel's face.

Fortunately for him the colonel was too much absorbed in dislodging a *fly* from the back of his horse to notice his agitation; but he heard the question and replied, "I said Alice Johnson, twentieth cousin of mine—blast that fly!—lives in Massachusetts; splendid girl—hang it all, can't I hit him?—I was there two years ago. Never saw a girl that made my mouth water as she did. Most too pious, though, to suit me. Wouldn't read a newspaper Sunday, when that's the very day I take to read 'em—there, I've killed him." And well satisfied with the achievement, the old colonel put up his whip, never dreaming of the effect that name had produced on Hugh, whose heart gave one great throb of hope, and then grew heavy and sad as he thought how impossible it was that the Alice Johnson the colonel knew, could be the Golden Haired.

"There are fifty by that name, no doubt," he said, "and if there were not, she is dead. But oh, if it could be that she were living, that somewhere I could find her."

There was a mist before Hugh's vision, and the arm encircling Rocket's neck clung there now for support, so weak and faint he grew. He dared not question the colonel farther, and was only too glad when the latter came back to their starting point and said, "If I understand you, I can have Rocket for five hundred dollars, provided I let you redeem him within a year. Now that's equivalent to my lending you five hundred dollars out and out. I see, but seeing it's you, I reckon I'll have to do it. As luck will have it, I was going down to Frankfort this very day to put some money in the bank, and if you say so, we'll clinch the bargain at once;" and taking out his leathern wallet, the colonel began to count the required amount.

Alice Johnson was forgotten in that moment of painful indecision, when Hugh felt as if his very life was dying out.

"Oh, I can't let Rocket go," he thought, bowing his face upon the animal's graceful neck. Then chiding himself as weak, he lifted up his head and said: "I'll take the money. Rocket is yours."

The last words were like a smothered sob; and the generous old man hesitated a moment. But Hugh was in earnest. His debts must be paid, and five hundred dollars would do it.

"I'll bring him round to-morrow. Will that be time enough?" he asked, as he rolled up the bills.

"Yes," the colonel replied, while Hugh continued entreatingly, "and, colonel, you'll be kind to Rocket. He's never been struck a blow since he was broken to the saddle. He wouldn't know what it meant."

"Oh, yes, I see—Rarey's method. Now I never could make that work. Have to lick 'em sometimes, but I'll remember Rocket. Good day," and gathering up his reins Col. Tiffton rode slowly away, leaving Hugh in a maze of bewilderment.

That name still rang in his ears, and he repeated it again and again, each time assuring himself how impossible it was that it should be she—the only she to him in all the world. And supposing it were, what did it matter? What good could her existence do him? She would despise him now—no position, no name, no money, no Rocket, and here he paused, for above all thoughts of the Golden Haired towered the terrible one that Rocket was his no longer—that the evil he most dreaded had come upon him. "But I'll meet it like a man," he said, and springing into his saddle he rode back to Frankfort and dismounted at Harney's door.

In dogged silence Harney received the money, gave his receipt, and then, without a word, watched Hugh as he rode again from town, muttering to himself, "I shall remember that he knocked me down, and some time I'll repay it."

It was dark when Hugh reach home, his lowering brow and flashing eyes indicating the fierce storm which was gathering, and which burst the moment he entered the room where 'Lina was sitting. In tones which made even her tremble he accused her of her treachery, pouring forth such a torrent of wrath that his mother urged him to stop, for her sake if no other. She could always quiet Hugh, and he calmed down at once, hurling but one more missile at his sister, and that in the shape of Rocket, who, he said, was sold for her extravagance.

'Lina was proud of Rocket, and the knowledge that he was sold touched her far more than all Hugh's angry words. But her tears were of no avail; the deed was done, and on the morrow Hugh, with an unflinching hand, led his idol from the stable and rode rapidly across the fields, leading another horse which was to bring him home.

Gloomily the next morning broke, and at rather a late hour for him, Hugh, with a heavy sigh, had raised himself upon his elbow, wondering if it were a dream, or if during the night he had really heard Rocket's familiar tramp upon the lawn, when Lulu came running up the stairs; exclaiming, joyfully,

"He's done come home, Rocket has. He's at the kitchen door."

It was as Lulu said, for the homesick brute, suspecting something wrong, had broken from his fastenings, and bursting the stable door had come back to Spring Bank, his halter dangling about his neck, and himself looking very defiant, as if he were not again to be coaxed away. At sight of Hugh he uttered a sound of joy, and bounding forward planted both feet within the door ere Hugh had time to reach it.

"Thar's the old colonel now," whispered Claib, just as the colonel appeared to claim his runaway.

But Rocket kept them all at bay, snapping, striking, and kicking at every one who ventured to approach him. With compressed lip and moody face Hugh watched the proceeding for a time, now laughing at the frightened negroes hiding behind the lye leach to escape the range of Rocket's heels, and again groaning mentally as he met the half human look of Rocket's eyes turned to him as if for aid. At last rising from the spot where he had been sitting he gave the whistle which Rocket always obeyed, and in an instant the sagacious animal was at his side, trying to lick the hands which would not suffer the caress lest his courage should give way.

"I'll take him home myself," he said to the old colonel, emerging from his hiding place behind the leach, and bidding Claib follow with another horse, Hugh went a second time to Colonel Tiffton's farm.

Leading Rocket into the stable he fastened him to the stall, and then with his arms around his neck talked to him as if he had been a refractory, disobedient child. We do not say he was understood, but after one long, despairing cry, which rang in Hugh's ears for many a day and night, Rocket submitted to his fate, and staid quietly with the colonel, who petted him if possible more than Hugh had done, without, however, receiving from him the slightest token of affection in return.

CHAPTER XIV
MRS. JOHNSON'S LETTER

The spring had passed away, and the warm June sun was shining over Spring Bank, whose mistress and servants were very lonely, for Hugh was absent, and with him the light of the house had departed. Business of his late uncle's had taken him to New Orleans, where he might possibly remain all summer. 'Lina was glad, for since the fatal dress affair there had been but little harmony between herself and her brother. The tenderness awakened by her long illness seemed to have been forgotten, and Hugh's manner toward her was cold and irritating to the last degree, so that the young lady rejoiced to be freed from his presence.

"I do hope he'll stay," she said one morning, when speaking of him to her mother. "I think it's a heap nicer without him, though dull enough at the best. I wish we could go to some watering place. There's the Tifftons just returned from New York, and I don't much believe they can afford it more than we, for I heard their place was mortgaged to Harney. Oh, bother, to be so poor," and the young lady gave a little angry jerk at the hair she was braiding.

"Whar's ole miss?" asked Claib, who had just returned from Versailles. "Thar's a letter for her," and depositing it upon the bureau, he left the room.

"Whose writing is that?" 'Lina said, catching it up and examining the postmark. "Ho, mother! here's a letter in a strange handwriting. Shall I open it?" she called, and ere her mother could reply, she had broken the seal, and held in her hand the draft which made her the heiress of one thousand dollars.

Had the fabled godmother of Cinderilla appeared to her suddenly, she would scarcely have been more bewildered.

"Mother," she screamed again, reading aloud the 'Pay to the order of Adaline Worthington,' etc. "What does it mean, and who could have sent it? Isn't it splendid! Who is Alice Johnson? Oh, I know, that old friend of yours, who came to see you once when I was gone. What does she say? 'My dear Eliza, feeling that I have not long to live—' What—dead? Well, I'm sorry for that, but, I must say, she did a very sensible thing sending me a thousand dollars. We'll go somewhere now, won't we?" and clutching fast the draft, the heartless girl yielded the letter to her mother, who with blanched cheek and quivering lip read the last message of her friend; then burying her face in her hands she sobbed as the past came back to her, when the Alice now forever at rest and herself were girls together.

'Lina stood a moment, wishing her mother had not cried, as it made it very awkward—then, for want of something better to do took up the letter her mother had dropped and read it through, commenting as she read. "Wants you to take her daughter Alice. Is the woman crazy? And her nurse, Densie Densmore. Say, mother, you've cried enough, let's talk the matter over. Shall you let Alice come? Ten dollars a week, they'll pay. Five hundred and twenty dollars a year. Whew! We are rich as Jews. It won't cost half that sum to keep them. Our ship is really coming in."

By this time Mrs. Worthington was able to talk of a matter which had apparently so delighted 'Lina. Her first remark, however, was not very pleasing to the young lady.

"As far as I am concerned I would willingly give Alice a home, but it's not for me to say. Hugh alone can decide it. We must write to him."

"You know he'll refuse," was 'Lina's angry reply. "He hates young ladies. So if it hangs on his decision, you may as well save your postage stamp to New Orleans, and write at once to Miss Johnson that she cannot come, on account of a boorish clown."

"'Lina," feebly interposed Mrs. Worthington, feeling how inefficient she was to cope with 'Lina's stronger will. "Lina, we must write to Hugh."

"Mother, you shall not," and 'Lina spoke determinedly. "I'll send an answer to this letter myself, this very day. I will not suffer the chance to be thrown away. Hugh may swear a little at first, but he'll get over it."

"Hugh never swears," and Mrs. Worthington spoke up at once.

"He don't, hey? Maybe you've forgotten when he came home from Frankfort, that time he heard about my dress. As old Sam says, 'I've got a mizzable memory, but I have a very distinct recollection that oaths were thick as hail stones. Didn't his eyes blaze though!'"

"I know he swore then; but he never has since, I'm sure, and I think he is better, gentler, more refined than he used to be, since—since—*Adah* came."

A contemptuous "pshaw!" came from 'Lina's lips, and then she proceeded to speak of Alice Johnson, asking for her family. Were they the F. F. V.'s of Boston? and so forth.

To this Mrs. Worthington gave a decided affirmative; repeating to her daughter many things which Mrs. Johnson had herself told Alice in that sad interview when she lay on her sick bed with Alice sobbing near.

So far as she was concerned, Alice Johnson was welcome to Spring Bank; but justice demanded that Hugh should be consulted ere an answer were returned. 'Lina, however, overruled her arguments as she always did, and with a sigh she yielded the point, hoping there would be some way by which Hugh might be appeased.

"Now let us talk a little about the thousand dollars," 'Lina said, for already the money was beginning to burn in her hands.

"I'm going to Saratoga, and you are going, too. We'll have heaps of dresses. We'll take *Lu*, for a waiting-maid. That will be sure to make a sensation at the North. 'Mrs. Worthington, daughter, and colored servant, Spring Bank, Kentucky.' I can almost see that on the clerk's books. Then I can manage to let it be known that I'm an heiress, as I am. We needn't tell that it's only a thousand dollars, most of which I have on my back, and maybe I'll come home *Adaline* somebody else. There are always splendid matches at Saratoga. We'll go north the middle of July, just three weeks from now."

'Lina had talked so fist that Mrs. Worthington had been unable to put in a word; but it did not matter. 'Lina was invulnerable to all she could say. She'd go to town that very day and make her purchases. Miss Allis, of course, must be consulted for some of her dresses, while *Adah* could make the rest. With regard to Miss Alice, they would write to her at once, telling her she was welcome to Spring Bank, and also informing her of their intentions to come north immediately. She could join them at Saratoga, or, if she preferred, could remain at Snowdon until they returned home in the autumn.

'Lina's decision with regard to their future movements had been made so rapidly and so determinedly, that Mrs. Worthington had scarcely ventured to expostulate, and the few remonstrances she did advance produced no impression. 'Lina wrote to Alice Johnson that morning, went to Frankfort that afternoon, to Versailles and Lexington the next day, and on the morning of the third, after the receipt of Mrs. Johnson's letter, Spring Bank presented the appearance of one vast show-room, so full of silks, and muslins, and tissues, and flowers, and ribbons, and laces, while amidst it all, in a maze of perplexity as to what was required of her, or where first to commence, sat Adah, who had come at 'Lina's bidding.

Womanlike, the sight of 'Lina's dresses awoke in Adah a thrill of delight, and she entered heartily into the matter without a single feeling of envy.

"I's goin', too. Did you know that?" Lulu said to her, as she sat bending over a cloud of lace and soft blue silk.

"You? For what?" and Adah lifted her brown eyes inquiringly.

"Oh, goin' to wait on 'em. It's grand to have a nigger and Miss 'Lina keeps trainin' me how to act and what to say. I ain't to tell how mean Spring Bank is furnished, nor how poor master Hugh is. Nothin' of the kind. We're to be fust cut. Oh, so nice, Miss 'Lina an, *Airey*, and when we get home, if I does well, I'm to hev that gownd, all mud, what Miss 'Lina wared to the Tiffton party, whew!" and in the mischievous glance of Lulu's saucy eyes, Adah read that the quick-witted negro was not in the least deceived with regard to the "Airey," as she called Miss 'Lina.

Half amused at Lulu's remarks and half sorry that she had listened to them, Adah resumed her work, just as 'Lina appeared, saying to her, "Here is Miss Tiffton's square-necked bertha. She's just got home from New York, and says they are all the fashion. You are to cut me a pattern. There's a paper, the Louisville Journal, I guess, but nobody reads it, now Hugh is gone," and with a few more general directions, 'Lina hurried away, having first tossed into Adah's lap the paper containing Anna Richards' advertisement.

In spite of the doctor's predictions and consignment of that girl to Georgia, or some warmer place, it had reached her at last. The compositor had wondered at its wording, a few casual readers had wondered at it, too—a western editor, laughing jocosely at its "married or unfortunate woman with a child a few months old," had copied it into his columns, thus attracting the attention of his more south-western neighbor, who had thought it too good to lose and so given it to his readers with sundry remarks of his own. But through all its many changes, Adah's God had watched it, and brought it around to her. She did not see it at first, but just as her scissors were raised to cut the pattern, her eyes fell on the spot headed, "A curious advertisement," and suspending her operations for a moment, she read it through, a feeling rising in her heart that it was surely an answer to her own advertisement sent forth months ago, with tearful prayers that it might be successful. She did not know that "A. E. R." meant it for her, and no one else. She only felt that at Terrace Hall there was a place for her, a home where she would no longer be dependent on Hugh, whose straits she understood perfectly well, knowing why Rocket was sold, and how it hurt his master to sell him. Oh, if she only could redeem him, no toil, no weariness would be too great; but she never could, even if "A. E. R." should take her—the pay would be so small that Rocket would be old and worthless ere she could earn five hundred dollars; but she could do something toward it, and her heart grew light and happy as she thought how surprised Hugh would be to receive a letter containing money earned by the feeble Adah, to whom he had been so kind.

Adah was a famous castle-builder, and she went on rearing castle after castle, until 'Lina came back again and taking a seat beside her, began to talk so familiarly and pleasantly that Adah felt emboldened to tell her of the advertisement and her intention to answer it. Averse as 'Lina had at first been to Adah's remaining at Spring Bank, she now saw a channel through which she could be made very useful, and would far rather that she should remain. So she opposed the plan, urging so many arguments against it that Adah began to think the idea a foolish one, and with a sigh dismissed it from her mind until another time, when she might give it more consideration.

That afternoon Ellen Tiffton rode over to see 'Lina, who told her of Alice Johnson, whom they were expecting.

"Alice Johnson," Ellen repeated; "why, that's the girl father says so much about. Fortieth or fiftieth cousin. He was at their house in Boston a few years ago, and when he came home he annoyed me terribly by quoting Alice continually, and comparing me with her. Of course I fell in the scale, for there was nothing like Alice, Alice—so beautiful, so refined, so sweet, so amiable, so *religious*."

"Religious!" and 'Lina laughed scornfully. "Adah pretends to be religious, too, and so does Sam, while Alice will make three. Pleasant prospects ahead. I wonder if she's the blue kind—thinks dancing wicked, and all that."

Ellen could not tell. She only knew what her father said; but she did not fancy Miss Alice to be more morose or gloomy—at all events she would gladly have her for a companion, and she thought it queer that Mrs. Johnson should send her to a stranger, as it were, when they would have been so glad to receive her. "Pa won't like it a bit, I know, and I quite envy you," she said, as she took her leave, her remarks raising Alice largely in 'Lina's estimation, and making her not a little proud that Spring Bank had been selected as Miss Johnson's home.

One week later, and there came a letter from Alice herself saying that at present she was stopping in Boston with her guardian, Mr. Liston, who had rented the cottage in Snowdon, but that she would meet Mrs. Worthington and daughter at Saratoga. Of course she did not now feel like mingling in gay society, and should consequently go to the Columbian, where she could be comparatively quiet but this need not interfere with their arrangements, as they could see each other often.

The same day also brought a letter from Hugh, making many kind inquiries after them all, saying his business was turning out better than he expected, and enclosing forty dollars, fifteen of which, he said, was for Adah, and the rest for Ad, as a peace offering for the harsh things he had said to her. Hugh's conscience when away was always troubling him with regard to 'Lina, and knowing that money with her would atone for a score of sins, he had felt so happy in sending it, giving her the most because he had sinned against her the most. Once the thought suggested itself that possibly she might keep the whole, but he repudiated it at once as a base slander upon 'Lina.

Alas, he little suspected the treachery of which she was capable. As a taste of blood makes wild beasts thirst for more, so Mrs. Johnson's legacy had made 'Lina greedy for gold, and the sight of the smooth paper bills sent to her by Hugh, awoke her avaricious passions. Forty dollars was just the price of a superb pearl bracelet in Lexington, and if Hugh had only sent it all to her instead of a part to Adah! What did Adah want of money, any way, living there in the cornfield, and seeing nobody? Besides that, hadn't she just paid her three dollars, and a muslin dress, and was that not enough for a girl in her circumstances? Nobody would be the wiser if she kept the whole, for her mother was not present when Claib brought the letter. She'd never know they'd heard from Hugh; and on the whole she believed she'd keep it, and so she went to Lexington next day in quest of the bracelet, which was pronounced beautiful by the unsuspecting Adah, who never dreamed that her money had helped to pay for it. Truly 'Lina was heaping up against herself a dark catalogue of sin to be avenged some day, but the time was not yet.

Thus far every thing went swimmingly. The dresses fitted admirably, and nothing could exceed the care with which they had been packed. Her mother no longer annoyed her about Hugh. Lulu was quite well posted with regard to her duty. Ellen Tiffton had lent her quizzing-glass and several ornaments, while Irving Stanley, grand-nephew like Hugh, to Uncle John, was to be at Saratoga, so 'Lina incidentally heard, and as there was a kind of relationship between them, he would of course notice her more or less, and from all accounts, to be noticed by him was a thing to be desired.

Thus it was in the best of humors that 'Lina tripped from Spring Bank door one pleasant July morning, and was driven with her mother and Lulu to Lexington, where they intended taking the evening train for Cincinnati.

CHAPTER XV
SARATOGA

"Mrs. Worthington, daughter, and, colored servant. Spring Bank, Ky."

"Dr. John Richards and mother, New York City."

"Irving Stanley, Esq., Baltimore."

These were the last entries made by the clerk at Union Hall, which was so crowded, that for the new comers no rooms were found except the small, uncomfortable ones far up in the fourth story of the Ainsworth block, and thither, in not the most amiable mood, 'Lina followed her trunks, and was followed in turn by her mother and Lulu, the crowd whom they passed deciphering the name upon the trunks and whispering to each other, "From Spring Bank, Kentucky. Haughty looking girl, wasn't she?"

From his little twelve by ten apartment, where the summer sun was pouring in a perfect blaze of heat, Dr. Richards saw them pass, and after wondering who they were, gave them no farther thought, but sat jamming his pen-knife into the old worm-eaten table, and thinking savage thoughts against that capricious lady, Fortune, who had compelled him to come to Saratoga, where rich wives were supposed to be had for the asking. Too late he had discovered the ruse imposed on him by Mr. Liston—had discovered that Alice was the heiress of more than $50,000, and following the discovery came the mortifying knowledge that not one dime of it would probably ever be used for defraying his personal expenses. Alice had learned how purely sordid and selfish was the man whom she had thought so misunderstood by the Snowdonites, and in Dr. Richard's vest pocket there lay at this very moment a note, the meaning of which was that Alice Johnson declined the honor of becoming his wife. They would still be friends, she said; would meet as if nothing had occurred, but she could not be his wife. This it was which had brought him to Saratoga, indignant, mortified and desperate. There were other heiresses beside Alice Johnson—others less fastidious; and he could find them, too. Love was out of the question, as that had died with poor Lily, so that now he was ready for the first chance that offered, provided that chance possessed a certain style, and was tolerably good-looking. He did not see 'Lina at all, for she had passed the door before he looked up, so he only saw the mother, with Lulu trudging obediently behind, and hearing them enter the room, returned to his cogitations.

From his pleasanter, airier apartment, on the other side of the narrow hall, Irving Stanley looked through his golden glasses, pitying the poor ladies condemned to that slow roast, thinking how, if he knew them, he would surely offer to exchange, as it did not matter so much where a man was stowed away, he was so seldom in his room, while ladies must necessarily spend half their time there at least in dressing; and with a sigh for unfortunate ladies in general, the kind-hearted Irving Stanley closed his door and proceeded to make his own toilet for dinner, then only an hour in the future.

How hot, and dusty, and cross 'Lina was, and what a look of dismay she cast around the room, with its two bedsteads, its bureaus, its table, its washstand, and its dozen pegs for her two dozen dresses, to say nothing of her mother's. She'd like to know if this was Saratoga, and these its accommodations. It was not fit to put the pigs in, and she wondered what the proprietor was thinking of when he sent her up there.

"I s'pects he didn't know how you was an *Airey*," Lulu said, demurely, her eyes brimming with mischief.

'Lina turned to box her ears, but the black face was so grave and solemn in its expression that she changed her mind, thinking she had been mistaken in Lulu's ironical tone.

How tired and faint poor Mrs. Worthington was, and how she wished she had staid at home, like a sensible woman, instead of coming here to be made so uncomfortable in this hot room. But it could not now be helped, 'Lina said; they must do the best they could; and with a forlorn glance at the luxuriant patch of weeds, the most prominent view from the window, 'Lina opened one of her trunks, and spreading a part of the contents upon the bed, began to dress for dinner, changing her mind three times, driving her mother and Lulu nearly distracted, and finally deciding upon a rich green silk, which, with its crimson trimmings, was very becoming to her dark style, but excessively hot-looking on that sultry day. But 'Lina meant to make a good first impression. Everything depended upon that, and as the green was the heaviest, richest thing she had, so she would first appear in it. Besides that, the two young men who had looked at her from the door had not escaped her observation. She had seen them both, deciding that Dr. Richards was the most distingue of the two, though Irving Stanley was very elegant, very refined, and very intellectual looking in those glasses, which gave him so scholarly an appearance. 'Lina never dreamed that this was Irving Stanley, or she would have occupied far more time in brushing her hair and coiling among its braids the bandeau of pearls borrowed of Ellen Tiffton. As it was, the dinner bell had long since ceased ringing, and the tread of feet ceased in the halls below ere she descended to the deserted parlor, followed by her mother, nervous and frightened at the prospect of this, her first appearance at Saratoga.

"Pray, rouse yourself," 'Lina whispered, as she saw how white she was, when she learned that their seats were at the extreme end of the dining room—that in order to reach it, nearly one thousand pair of eyes must be encountered, and one thousand glances braved. "Rouse yourself, do; and not let them guess you were never at a watering place before," and 'Lina thoughtfully smoothed her mother's cap by way of reassuring her.

But even 'Lina herself quailed when she reached the door and caught a glimpse of the busy life within, the terrible ordeal she must pass.

"Oh, for a pair of pantaloons to walk beside one, even if Hugh were in them," she thought, as her own and her mother's lonely condition rose before her.

But Hugh was watching a flat boat on the Mississippi that summer afternoon, and as there was no other person on whom she had a claim, she must meet her fate alone.

"Courage, mother," she whispered again, and then advanced into the room, growing bolder at every step, for with one rapid glance she had swept the hall, and felt that amid that bevy of beauty and fashion there were few more showy than 'Lina Worthington in her rustling dress of green, with Ellen Tiffton's bracelet on one arm and the one bought with Adah's money on the other.

"Here, madam," and their conductor pointed to chairs directly opposite Dr. Richards, watching them as they came up to the hall, and deciding that the young lady's arms were most too white for her dark skin, and her cheeks a trifle too red.

"It's put on skillfully, though," he thought, while the showily dressed old lady beside him whispered,

"What elegant bracelets, and handsome point lace collar!" just as 'Lina haughtily ordered the servant to move her chair a little farther from the table.

Bowing deferentially, the polite attendant quickly drew back her chair, while she spread out her flowing skirts to an extent which threatened to envelop her mother, sinking meekly into her seat, confused and flurried. But alas for 'Lina. The servant did not calculate the distance aright, and the lady, who had meant to do the thing so gracefully, who had intended showing the people that she had been to Saratoga before, suddenly found herself, prostrate upon the floor, her chair some way behind her, and the plate, which, in her descent, she had grasped unconsciously, flying off diagonally past her mother's head, and fortunately past the head of her mother's left-hand neighbor.

Poor 'Lina! How she wished she might never get up again. How she hoped the floor beneath would open and swallow her up, and how she mentally anathematized the careless negro, choking with suppressed laughter behind her. As she struggled to arise she was vaguely conscious that a white hand was stretched out to help her, that the same hand smoothed her dress and held her chair safely. Too much chagrined to think who it was rendering her these little attentions, she took her seat, glancing up and down the table to witness the effect of her mishap.

There was a look of consternation on Dr. Richards face, but he was too well bred to laugh, or even to smile, though there was a visible desire to do so, an expression, which 'Lina construed into contempt for her awkwardness, and then he went on with his previous occupation, that of crumbling his bread and scanning the ladies near, while waiting for the next course. There was also a look of surprise in the face of the lady next to him, and then she too occupied herself with something else.

At first, 'Lina thought nothing could keep her tears back, they gathered so fast in her eyes, and her voice trembled so that she could not answer the servant's question,

"Soup, madam, soup?"

But he of the white hand did it for her.

"Of course she'll take soup," then in an aside, he said to her gently, "Never mind, you are not the first lady who has been served in that way. It's quite a common occurrence." There was something reassuring in his voice, and turning toward him 'Lina caught the gleam of the golden glasses, and knew that her *vis-à-vis* up stairs was also her right-hand neighbor. How grateful she felt for his kind attentions, paid so delicately, and with an evident desire to shield her from remark, and how she wondered who he was, as he tried, by numberless unobtrusive acts, to quiet her.

Kind and gentle as a woman, Irving Stanley was sometimes laughed at by his own sex, as too gentle, too feminine in disposition; but those who knew him best loved him most, and loved him, too, just because he was not so stern, so harsh, so overbearing as men are wont to be. A woman was a sacred piece of mechanism to him—a something to be petted, humored and caressed, and still treated as an equal. The most considerate of sons, the most affectionate of brothers, he was idolized at home, while the society in which he mingled, knew no greater favorite, and 'Lina might well be thankful that her lot was cast so near him. He did not talk to her at the table further than a few commonplace remarks, but when after dinner was over, and his Havana smoked, he found her sitting with her mother out in the grove, apart from everybody, and knew that they were there alone, he went to them, and ere many minutes had elapsed discovered to his surprise that they were his so called cousins from Kentucky. Nothing could exceed 'Lina's delight. He was there unfettered by mother or sister or sweetheart, and of course would attach himself exclusively to her. 'Lina was very happy, and more than once her loud laugh rang out so loud that Irving, with all his charity, had a faint suspicion that round his Kentucky cousin, there might linger a species of coarseness, not altogether agreeable to one of his refinement. Still he sat chatting with her until the knowing dowagers, who year after year watch such things at Saratoga, whispered behind their fans of a flirtation between the elegant Mr. Stanley and that haughty looking girl from Kentucky.

"I never saw him so familiar with a stranger upon so short an acquaintance," said Mrs. Buford, whose three daughters would any one of them have exchanged their name for Stanley. "I wonder if he knew her before. Upon my word, that laugh of hers is rather coarse, let her be who she will."

"Yes, but that silk never cost less than three dollars a yard at Stewart's. See the lustre there is on it," and old Mrs. Richards, who had brought herself into the field by way of assisting her son in his campaign, levelled her glass at 'Lina's green silk, showing well in the bright sunlight "Here, John," she called to her son, who was passing "can you tell me who that young lady is—the one who so very awkwardly sat down upon the floor at dinner?"

"I do not know, and I cannot say that I wish to," was the *nonchalant* reply, as the doctor took the vacant chair his mother had so long been keeping for him. "I hardly fancy her style. She's too *brusque* to suit me, though Irving Stanley seems to find her agreeable."

"Is that Irving Stanley?" and Mrs. Richards levelled her glass again, for Irving Stanley was not unknown to her by reputation. "She must be somebody, John, or he would not notice her," and she spoke in an aside, adding in a louder tone, "I wonder who she is. There's their servant. I mean to question her," and as Lulu came near, she said, "Girl, who do you belong to?"

"'Longs to them," jerking her head toward 'Lina and Mrs. Worthington.

"Where do you live?" was the next query, and Lulu replied.

"Spring Bank, Kentucky. Missus live in big house, most as big as this." Then anxious to have the ordeal passed, and fearful that she might not acquit herself satisfactorily to 'Lina, who, without seeming to notice her, had drawn near enough to hear, she added, "Miss 'Lina is an airey, a very large *airey*, and has a heap of—of——" Lulu hardly knew what, but finally in desperation added, "a heap of ars," and then fled away ere another question could be asked her.

"*What* did she say she was?" Mrs. Richards asked, and the doctor replied,

"She said an *airey*. She meant an heiress."

"Oh, yes, an heiress. I don't doubt it, from her appearance, and Mr. Stanley's attentions. *Stylish looking* isn't she?"

"Rather, yes—magnificent eyes at all events," and the doctor stroked his mustache thoughtfully, while his mother, turning to Mrs. Buford, began to compliment 'Lina's form, and the fit of her dress.

Money, or the reputation of possessing money, is an all powerful charm, and in a few places does it show its power more plainly than at Saratoga, where it was soon known that the lady from Spring Bank was heiress to immense wealth in Kentucky, how immense nobody knew, and various were the estimates put upon it. Among Mrs. Buford's clique it was twenty thousand; farther away and in another hall it was fifty, while Mrs. Richards, ere the supper hour arrived, had heard that it was at least a hundred thousand dollars. How or where she heard it she hardly knew, but she endorsed the statement as correct, and at the tea table that night was exceedingly gracious to 'Lina and her mother, offering to divide a little private dish which she had ordered for herself, and into which poor Mrs.

Worthington inadvertently dipped, never dreaming that it was not common property.

"It was not of the slightest consequence, Mrs. Richards was delighted to share it with her," and that was the way the conversation commenced.

'Lina knew now that the proud man whose lip had curled so scornfully at dinner, was Dr. Richards, and Dr. Richards knew that the girl who sat on the floor was 'Lina Worthington, from Spring Bank, where Alice Johnson was going.

"I did not gather from Mr. Liston that these Worthingtons were wealthy," he said to himself, "but if the old codger would deceive me with regard to Miss Johnson, he would with regard to them," and mentally resolving to make an impression before they could see and talk with Alice, the doctor was so polite that 'Lina scarcely knew whose attentions to prefer, his or Irving Stanley's, who, rather glad of a co-worker, yielded the field without a struggle, and by the time tea was over the doctor's star was in the ascendant.

How 'Lina wanted to stay in the crowded parlors, but her mother had so set her heart upon seeing Alice Johnson, that she was forced to humor her, and repaired to her room to make a still more elaborate toilet, as she wished to impress Miss Johnson with a sense of her importance.

A pale blue silk, with white roses in her hair, was finally decided upon, and when, just as the gas was lighted; she descended with her mother to the parlor, her opera cloak thrown gracefully around her uncovered shoulders, and Ellen Tiffton's glass in her hand, she had the satisfaction of knowing that she created quite a sensation, and that others than Dr. Richards looked after her admiringly as she swept through the room, followed by her mother and *Lulu*, the latter of whom was answering no earthly purpose save to show that they had a servant.

CHAPTER XVI
THE COLUMBIAN

It was very quiet at the Columbian, and the few gentlemen seated upon the piazza seemed to be of a different stamp from those at the more fashionable houses, as there were none of them smoking, nor did they stare impertinently at the gayly dressed lady coming up the steps, and inquiring of the clerk if Miss Alice Johnson were there.

"Yes, she was, and her room was No. — —. Should he send up the lady's card? Miss Johnson had mostly kept to her room."

'Lina had brought no card, but she gave her name and passed on into the parlor, which afforded a striking contrast to the beehive down town. In a corner two or three were sitting; another group occupied a window while at the piano were two more, an old and a young lady; the latter of whom was seated upon the stool, and with her foot upon the soft pedal, was alternately striking a few sweet musical chords, and talking to her companion, who seemed to be a servant. Taking her seat near these last, 'Lina watched them curiously; a thought once crossing her mind that this might be *Alice Johnson.* But no; Alice, of course, would be habited in deepest black, while the dress this lady wore was a simple, pure white, unrelieved by any color save the jet bracelets upon the snowy arms and the jet pin at the throat. This was not Alice sure, and she felt glad to know it, for she would rather that Alice Johnson should be a shade less lovely than the young girl before her. How dazzling she was in her radiant beauty, with all that wealth of chestnut hair shading her fair brow and falling almost to her waist; but the soft, dreamy eyes of blue, with their long silken lashes, were to 'Lina the chief attraction. None could withstand those eyes, now cast down upon the keys as if heavy with unshed tears, and now upraised to the woman beside her who appeared to regard her with a species of adoration, occasionally laying her hand caressingly upon the sunny hair, and letting it slide down until it rested upon the shoulder.

As the minutes went by 'Lina grew very impatient at Alice's long delay.

"I mean to ring," she said, just as the servant to whom she had delivered her message appeared.

Very haughtily 'Lina asked if he had found Miss Johnson. "If she's not in, we don't care to stay here all night," she said, angrily, whereupon she became conscious that the blue eyes of the lady were fixed inquiringly upon her, as if wondering how a well bred person could betray so much ill nature.

"Miss Johnson? I beg pardon, I supposed you knew her and had found her, as she was in here. This is Miss Johnson," and the waiter bowed toward the musician, who, quick as thought seized upon the truth, and springing to Mrs. Worthington's side, exclaimed,

"It's Mrs. Worthington, I know. Why did you sit here so long without speaking to me? I am Alice Johnson," and overcome with emotions awakened by the sight of her mother's early friend, Alice hid her face with childlike confidence in Mrs. Worthington's bosom, and sobbed for a moment bitterly.

Then growing calm, she lifted up her head, and smiling through her tears, said,

"Forgive me for this introduction. It is not often I give way, for I know and am sure it was best and right that mother should die. I am not rebellious now, but the sight of you brought it back so vividly. You'll be my mother, won't you?" and the impulsive girl nestled closer to Mrs. Worthington, looking up into her face with a confiding affection which won a place for her at once in Mrs. Worthington's heart.

"My darling," she said, winding her arm around her waist, "as far as I can I will be to you a mother, and 'Lina shall be your sister. This is 'Lina," and she turned to 'Lina, who, piqued at having been so long unnoticed, was frowning gloomily.

But 'Lina never met a glance purer or more free from guile than that which Alice gave her and it disarmed her at once of all jealousy, making her return the orphan's kisses with as much apparent cordiality as they had been given.

Sitting down beside them Alice made many inquiries concerning Kentucky, startling them with the announcement that as she had that day received a letter from Col. Tiffton, who she believed was a friend of theirs, urging her to come on at once, and spend a few weeks with him, she had about decided to do so, and only waited for Mrs. Worthington's advice ere answering the colonel's friendly letter. "They heard from you what were mother's plans for my future, and also that I was to meet you here. They must be very thoughtful people, for they seem to know that I cannot be very happy here."

For a moment, 'Lina and her mother looked aghast, and neither knew what to say. 'Lina, as usual, was the first to rally and calculate results. Had Alice been less beautiful she would have opposed her going to Colonel Tiffton's where she might possibly hear something unfavorable of herself from Ellen, but, as it was, it might be well enough to get rid of her, as she was sure to prove a most formidable rival. Thus it was pure selfishness which prompted her to adopt the most politic course which presented itself to her mind.

"They were very intimate at Colonel Tiffton's. She and Ellen were fast friends. It was very pleasant there more so than at Spring Bank; and all the objection she could see to Alice's going was the fear lest she should become so much attached to Moss Side, the colonel's residence, as to be homesick at Spring Bank."

Against this Alice disclaimed at once. She was not apt to be homesick. She had made up her mind to be happy at Spring Bank, and presumed she should.

"I am so glad you approve my plan, for my heart is really set on going," and she turned to Mrs. Worthington, who had not spoken yet.

It was not what she had expected, and she hardly knew what to say, though, of course, "she should acquiesce in whatever Alice and 'Lina thought best."

"If she's going, I hope she'll go before Dr. Richards sees her, though perhaps he knows her already—his mother lives in Snowdon," 'Lina thought, and rather abruptly she asked if Alice knew Dr. Richards, who was staying at the Union.

Alice blushed crimson as she replied,

"Yes, I know him well, and his family, too.

"His mother is here," 'Lina continued, "and I like her so much. She is very familiar and friendly, don't you think so?"

Alice would not tell a lie, and she answered frankly,

"She does not bear that name in Snowdon. They consider her very haughty there. I think you must be a favorite."

"Are they very aristocratic and wealthy?" 'Lina asked, and Alice answered,

"Aristocratic, but not wealthy. They were very kind to me, and the doctor's sister Anna is one of the sweetest ladies I ever knew." Then as if anxious to change the conversation she spoke of *Hugh*. Where was he now? How did he look, and should she like him?

'Lina and her mother exchanged rapid glances, and then, in spite of the look of entreaty visible on Mrs. Worthington's face, 'Lina replied,

"To be candid with you, Miss Johnson, I'm afraid you won't like Hugh. He has many good traits, but I'm sorry to say we have never succeeded in cultivating him one particle, so that he is very rough and boorish in his manner, and will undoubtedly strike you unfavorably. I may as well tell you of this, as you will probably hear it from Ellen Tiffton, and must know it when you see him. He is not popular with the ladies; he hates them all, unless it is a Mrs. Hastings, whom he took in from the street."

Alice looked up inquiringly, while 'Lina began to tell her of Adah. She had not proceeded far, however, when with a cry of terror she sprang up as a large beetle, attracted by the light, fastened itself upon her hair.

Mrs. Worthington was the first to the rescue, while Lulu, who had listened with flashing eye when *Hugh* was the subject of remark, came haggardly, whispering slily to Alice,

"That's a lie she done tell you about Mas'r Hugh. He ain't rough nor bad, and we blacks would die for him any day."

Alice was confounded by this flat contradiction between mistress and servant, while a faint glimmer of the truth began to dawn upon her. The "horn-bug" being disposed of, 'Lina became quiet, and might, perhaps, have taken up Hugh again, but for a timely interruption in the shape of Irving Stanley, who had walked up to the Columbian, and seeing 'Lina and her mother through the window, sauntered leisurely into the parlor.

"Ah, Mr. Stanley," and 'Lina half rose from her chair thus intimating that he was to join them. "Miss Johnson, Mr. Stanley," and she watched jealously to see what effect Alice's beauty would have upon the young man.

He was evidently pleased, and this was a sufficient reason for 'Lina to speak of returning. She would not hasten Mr. Stanley, she said, but Irving arose at once and bidding Alice good night, accompanied the ladies back to Union hall, where Mrs. Richards sat fanning herself industriously, and watching John with motherly interest as he sauntered from one group of ladies to another, wondering what made Saratoga so dull, and where Miss Worthington had gone. It is not to be supposed that Dr. Richards cared a fig for Miss Worthington as *Miss Worthington*. It was simply her immense figure he admired, and as, during the evening, he had heard on good authority that said figure was made up mostly of cotton growing on some Southern field, the exact locality of which his informant did not know, he had decided that of course Miss 'Lina's fortune was over estimated. Such things always were, but still she must be wealthy. He had no doubt of that, and he might as well devote himself to her as to wait for some one else. Accordingly, the moment he spied her in the crowd he joined her, asking if they should not take a little turn up and down the piazza.

"Wait till I ask mamma's permission to stay up a little longer. She always insists upon my keeping such early hours," was 'Lina's very filial and childlike reply as she walked up to mamma, not to ask permission, but to whisper rather peremptorily, "Dr. Richards wishes me to walk with him, and as you are tired you may as well go to bed."

Mrs. Worthington was tired, but motherlike, she thought it would be pleasant to stay where she could see her daughter walking with Dr. Richards, and then, too, she wanted to hear the band playing in the court.

"Oh, I ain't very tired," she said. "I begin to feel rested, and I guess I'll set a little while with Mrs. Richards on the sofa yonder. She seems like one of our folks."

'Lina did not care to leave her truthful, matter-of-fact mother with Mrs. Richards, so she said, rather angrily,

"How do you know Mrs. Richards wants you to sit by her? She has her own set, and you are not much acquainted; besides, I shall feel easier to know you are up stairs. Go, do. He's waiting for me," and in the black eyes there was a gleam which Mrs. Worthington always obeyed.

With a sigh, and a lingering glance at the comfortable sofa, where Mrs. Richards sat in solemn state, she left the comparatively cool parlor, and climbing the weary flights of stairs, entered her hot, sultry room, and laying her head upon the table, cried a grieved kind of cry, as she recalled 'Lina's selfishness and evident desire to be rid of her.

"She's ashamed of me," and the chin quivered as the white lips whispered it. "She wants me out of the way for fear I'll do something to mortify her. Oh, 'Lina, 'Lina, I'm glad I've got one child who is not ashamed of his mother," and the tears dropped like rain upon the table, as Mrs. Worthington remembered Hugh, longing for him so much, and reproaching herself so bitterly for having consented to receive Alice Johnson without even consulting him. "I'll write to-night," she said. "I'll confess the whole," and glad of something to occupy her mind, Mrs. Worthington took out her writing materials, and commenced the letter, which should have been written long before.

Meantime the doctor and 'Lina were walking up and down the long piazza, chatting gayly, and attracting much attention from 'Lina's loud manner of talking and laughing.

"By the way, I've called on Miss Johnson, at the Columbian," she said. "Beautiful, isn't she?"

"Ra-ather pretty, some would think," and the doctor had an uncomfortable consciousness of the refusal, in his vest pocket.

If Alice had told; but no, he knew her better than that. He could trust her on that score, and so the dastardly coward affected to sneer at what he called her primness, charging 'Lina to be careful what she did, if she did not want a lecture, and asking if there were any ragged children in Kentucky, as she would not be happy unless she was running a Sunday school!

"She can teach the negroes! Capital!" and 'Lina laughed so loudly that Mrs. Richards joined them, laughing, too, at what she did not know, only "Miss Worthington had such spirits; it did one good; and she wished Anna was there to be enlivened. Write to her John, won't you?"

John mentally thought it doubtful. Anna and 'Lina would never assimilate, and he would rather not have his pet sister's opinion to combat until his own was fully made up.

As it was growing rather late Mrs. Richards ere long expressed a wish to retire, and hoping to see more of Miss Worthington to-morrow, she bowed good night, and left the doctor alone with 'Lina.

But, somehow, he did not get on well without his mother. There was nothing in common between himself and 'Lina, except deception. She had read but little, and only talked well on commonplace matters, of which he soon grew tired. But she was rich, and perfectly willing to be admired by him, so he put aside his weariness, and chatted with her until the parlors were deserted, and the servants came to extinguish some of the burners.

"She had no idea it was so late, or she would not have staid for anything. He must excuse her. What would mamma think?" and bidding him good night, 'Lina hurried up to where mamma sat waiting for her, the traces of tears still on her patient face, which looked white and worn.

"In the name of the people, what are you sitting up for?" was 'Lina's first remark, followed by a glowing account of what Dr. Richards had said, and the delightful time she'd had. "Only play our cards well, and I'm sure to go home the doctor's *fiancée*. The doctor thinks I'm very rich. So do all the people here. Lulu has told that I'm an heiress; now don't you upset it all with your squeamishness about the truth. Nobody will ask you how much I'm worth, so you won't be compelled to a lie direct. Just keep your own counsel, and leave the rest to me. Will you?"

There was, as usual, a feeble remonstrance, and then the weak woman yielded so far as promising to keep silent was concerned, but she asked timidly,

"What will you do if you succeed? He must then know how you've deceived him."

"Humph! so far, it will be an easy thing.

"He thinks I am rich, and I am supposed to think he is. It's no thanks to him that I know better. But they are very aristocratic, and family position is sometimes better than money. On the whole, I prefer it to wealth. It will be something in this wise," she continued; "after the honeymoon is past, and my lord hears nothing about bank stock, negroes or lands, he'll come straight out, and say, 'Mrs. Richards, I supposed you were rich!' while Mrs. Richards would retort, 'And I thought you were rich!' Don't you see, it will be an equal thing, and I shall take my chance."

Meantime the doctor sat in his own room near by, thinking of 'Lina Worthington, and wishing she were a little more refined.

"Where does she get that coarseness?" he thought. "Not from her mother, certainly. She seems very gentle and lady-like. It must be from the Worthingtons," and the doctor wondered where he had heard that name before, and why it affected him rather unpleasantly, bringing with it memories of Lily. "Poor Lily," he sighed mentally. "Your love would have made me a better man if I had not cast it from me. Dear Lily, the mother of my child," and a tear half trembled in his eye lashes, as he tried to fancy that child, tried to hear the patter of the little feet running to welcome him home, as they might have done had he been true to Lily; tried to hear the baby voice calling him "papa;" to feel the baby hands upon his face—his bearded face—where the great tears were standing now. "I *did* love Lily," he murmured; "and had I known of the child I never could have left her. Oh, Lily, come back to me, come!" and his arms were stretched out into empty space, as if he fain would encircle again the girlish form he had so often held in his embrace.

It was very late ere Dr. Richards slept that night, and the morning found him pale, haggard, and nearly desperate. Thoughts of Lily all were gone, and in their place was a fixed determination to follow on in the course he had marked out, to find him a rich wife, to cast remorse to the winds, and be as happy as he could. In this state of feeling 'Lina did not find it hard to keep him at her side, notwithstanding that *Alice* herself came down in the course of the day. Mrs. Richards had not quite given up all hopes of Alice, and she received her very cordially, watching closely when the doctor joined them. A casual observer would not have seen the flush on Alice's cheek or the pallor upon his, so soon both came and passed away, but they did not escape 'Lina's notice, and she felt glad when told that she intended starting for Kentucky on the morrow.

"So soon," she said faintly, feeling that something like remonstrance was expected from her, but Alice was not in the least suspicious, and when next day she stood at the depot with Mrs. Worthington and 'Lina she never dreamed how glad the latter was, in knowing that the coming train would take away one whom she dreaded as a rival.

CHAPTER XVII
HUGH

An unexpected turn in Hugh's affairs made it no longer necessary for him to remain in the sultry climate of New Orleans, and just one week from his mother's departure from Spring Bank he reached it, expressing unbounded surprise when he heard from Aunt Eunice where his mother had gone, and how she had gone.

"Fool and his money soon parted," Hugh said,

"But who is that woman,—the one who sent the money?"

"A Mrs. Johnson, an old friend of your mother," Aunt Eunice replied, while Hugh looked up quickly, wondering why the Johnsons should be so continually thrust upon him, when the only Johnson for whom he cared was dead years ago.

"And the young lady—what about her?" he asked, while Aunt Eunice told him the little she knew, which was that Mrs. Johnson wished her daughter to come to Spring Bank, but she did not know what they had concluded upon.

"That she should not come, of course," Hugh said. "They had no right to give her a home without my consent, and I've plenty of young ladies at Spring Bank now. Oh, it was such a relief when I was gone to know that in all New Orleans there was not a single hoop annoyed on my account. I had a glorious time doing as I pleased," and helping his aunt to mount the horse which had brought her to Spring Bank, Hugh returned to the house, which seemed rather lonely, notwithstanding that he had so often wished he could once more be alone, just as he was before his mother came.

On the whole, however, he enjoyed his freedom from restraint, and very rapidly fell back into his old loose way of living, bringing his dogs into the parlor, and making it a repository for both his hunting and fishing apparatus.

"It's splendid to do as I'm a mind to," he said, one hot August morning, nearly three weeks after his mother's departure, as with his box of worms upon the music stool, in the little room which 'Lina claimed as exclusively her own, he sat mending his long fish line, whistling merrily, and occasionally thrusting back from his forehead the mass of curling hair, which somewhat obstructed his vision.

Around him upon the floor lay half a dozen dogs, some asleep, and others eyeing his movements curiously, as if they knew and appreciated what he was doing.

"There isn't a finer lot of dogs in Kentucky," soliloquized the young man, as he ran his eye over them; "but wouldn't my lady at Saratoga rave if she knew I'd taken her *boudoir* for a kennel, and kept my bootjack, my blacking brush, and Sunday shirts all on her piano! Good place for them, so handy to get at, though I don't suppose it's quite the thing to live so like a savage. Halloo, Mug, what do *you* want?" he asked, as a little mulatto girl appeared in the door.

"Claib done *buy* you this yer," and the child handed him the letter from his mother, which had been to New Orleans and was forwarded from there.

The first of it was full of affection for her boy, and Hugh felt his heart growing very tender as he read, but when he reached the point where poor, timid Mrs. Worthington tried to explain about Alice, making a wretched bungle, and showing plainly how much she was swayed by 'Lina, it began to harden at once.

"What the plague!" he exclaimed as he read on, "Supposes I remember having heard her speak of her old school friend, *Alice Morton*? I don't remember any such thing. Her daughter's name's *Alice—Alice Johnson*," and Hugh for an instant turned white, so powerfully that name always affected him.

Soon rallying, however, he continued, "Heiress to fifty thousand dollars. Unfortunate Alice Johnson! better be lying beside the Golden Haired; but what! actually coming to Spring Bank, a girl worth fifty thousand, the most refined, most elegant, most beautiful creature that ever was born, coming where *I* am, without my consent, too! That's cool upon my word!" and for a moment Hugh went off in a towering passion, declaring "he wouldn't stand it," and bringing his foot down upon the little bare toes of Muggins, crouched upon the floor beside him.

Her loud outcry brought him to himself, and after quieting her as well as he could, he finished his mother's letter, chafing terribly at the thought of a strange young lady being thrust upon him whether he would have her or not.

"She is going to Colonel Tiffton's first, though they've all got the typhoid fever, I hear, and that's no place for her. That fever is terrible on Northerners—terrible on anybody. I'm afraid of it myself, and I wish this horrid throbbing I've felt for a few days would leave my head. It has a fever feel that I don't like," and the young man pressed his hand against his temples, trying to beat back the pain which so much annoyed him.

Just then Colonel Tiffton was announced, his face wearing an anxious look, and his voice trembling as he told how sick *his Nell* was, how sick they all were, and then spoke of Alice Johnson.

"She's the same girl I told you about the day I bought Rocket; some little kin to me, and that makes it queer why her mother should leave her to you. I knew she would not be happy at Saratoga, and so we wrote for her to visit us. She is on the road now, will be here day after to-morrow, and something must be done. She can't come to us, without great inconvenience to ourselves and serious danger to her. Hugh, my boy, there's no other way—she must come to Spring Bank," and the old colonel laid his hand on that of Hugh, who looked at him aghast, but made no immediate reply.

He saw at a glance that Alice could not go to Moss Side with impunity, and if not there she must, of course come to Spring Bank.

"What can I do with her? Oh, Colonel, it makes me sweat like rain just to think of it, and my head thumps like a mill-hopper, but, I suppose, there's no help for it. You'll meet her at the depot. You'll give her an inkling of what I am. You'll tell her what a savage she may expect to find, so she won't go into fits at sight of me."

"Yes, yes, I'll fix it; but, I thought, maybe, you'd have Aunt Eunice come over till your mother's return. Women are gossipping things, and they'd' talk if she was to live here alone with you. I tell you, she's handsome; and if I's you, I'd be a little good, that is, I wouldn't walk the lots Sundays, but go to church instead."

"I always do, sir," and Hugh spoke quickly, for slowly, surely, Adah Hastings was influencing him for good, and more changes than one were already apparent in him.

"That's right," rejoined the colonel. "Going to church is well enough for them that like it, which I can't say I do, but I'll see her, I'll meet her; I'll tell her. Good-bye, my boy. Now, I think of it, you look mighty nigh sick. Your face is as red as a beetle, and eyes kind of blood shot. The very way my wife looked. Are you sick?"

"No, not sick, but this hot weather affects my head which feels much as if there were a snare-drum inside."

"No, that ain't the symptom. My wife's felt like a bumble-bee's nest. You are all right if you'll take an emetic, a good big one, such as will turn your stomach inside out. Good-bye—Nelly's awful sick. Struck to her brain last night. Good-bye. I wouldn't lose Nell for a farm, if she is a little gritty," and wringing Hugh's hand, the colonel hurried off, leaving Hugh to his own reflections.

"A pretty state of things, and a pretty place to bring a young lady," he muttered, glancing ruefully round the room, and enumerating the different articles he knew were out of place. "Fish-worms, fish-hooks, fish-lines, bootjack, boot-blacking, and rifle, to say nothing of the dogs—and ME!"

The last was said in a tone as if the me were the most objectionable part of the whole, as, indeed, Hugh thought it was.

"I wonder how I do look to persons wholly unprejudiced!" Hugh said, and turning to Muggins he asked what she thought of him.

"I thinks you berry nice. I likes you berry much," the child replied, and Hugh continued, "Yes; but how do I look, I mean? What do I look like, a dandy or a scarecrow?"

Muggins regarded him for a moment curiously, and then replied, "I'se dunno what kind of thing that dandy is, but I 'members dat yer *scarecrow* what Claib make out of mars'r's trouses and coat, an' put up in de cherry tree. I thinks dat look like Mas'r Hugh—yes, very much like!"

Hugh laughed long and loud, pinching Mug's dusky cheek, and bidding her run away.

"Pretty good," he exclaimed, when he was left alone. "That's Mug's opinion. Look like a scarecrow. I mean to see for myself," and going into the sitting-room, where the largest mirror was hung, he scanned curiously the figure which met his view, even taking a smaller glass, and holding it so as to get a sight of his back. "Tall, broad-shouldered, straight, well built. My form is well enough," he said. "It's the clothes that bother. I mean to get some new ones. Then, as to my face," and Hugh turned himself around, "I never thought of it before; but my features are certainly regular, teeth can't be beaten, good brown skin, eyes to match, and a heap of curly hair.

I'll be hanged if I don't think I'm rather good-looking!" and with his spirits proportionably raised, Hugh whistled merrily as he went in quest of Aunt Chloe, to whom he imparted the startling information that on the next day but one, a young lady was coming to Spring Bank, and that, in the meantime, the house must be cleaned from garret to cellar, and everything put in order for the expected guest.

With growing years, Aunt Chloe had become rather cross and less inclined to work than formerly, frequently sighing for the days when "Mas'r John didn't want no clarin' up, but kep' things lyin' handy." With her hands on her fat hips she stood, coolly regarding Hugh, who was evidently too much in earnest to be opposed. Alice was coming, and the house must be put in order.

Accordingly, two hours afterwards, there was a strong smell of soap suds arising from one room, while from another a cloud of dust was issuing, as Hugh himself bent over the broom, wondering where all that dirt came from, inasmuch as his six dogs had only lain there for a few days!

Aunt Eunice, too, was pressed into the service, and greatly against her will, come to play the hostess for Hugh, who drove both herself and Aunt Chloe nearly distracted with his orders and counter orders.

Particularly was he interested in what was to be Alice's room, sending for Adah to see if it were right, and would be likely to strike a young lady favorably.

The cleaning and arranging was finished at last, and everything within the house was as neat and orderly as Aunt Eunice and Adah could make it, even Aunt Chloe acknowledging that "things was tip-top," but said "it was no use settin' 'em to rights when Mas'r Hugh done on-sot 'em so quick," but Hugh promised to do better. He would turn over a new leaf; so by way of commencement, on the morning of Alice's expected arrival he deliberately rolled up his towel and placed it under his pillow instead of his night-shirt, which was hung conspicuously over the washstand. His boots were put behind the fireboard, his every day hat jammed into the bandbox where 'Lina kept her winter bonnet, and then, satisfied that so far as his room was concerned, every thing was in order, he descended the stairs and went into the garden to gather fresh flowers with which to adorn Alice's room. Hugh was fond of flowers, and two beautiful bouquets were soon arranged and placed in the vases brought from the parlor mantel, while Muggins, who trotted beside him, watching his movements and sometimes making suggestions, was told to see that they were freshly watered, and not allowed to stand where the sun could shine on them, as they might fade before Miss Johnson came.

"You likes her?" and Mug looked inquiringly at him.

"I never saw her," he replied, "but I mean to like her yes," and Hugh spoke the truth.

He could not account for it, but now that it came so near, there was something enlivening in the prospect of Alice's coming. He meant to like her—meant that she should like him. Not as the Golden Haired might have done had she lived, but as a friend, a sister. He'd try his best to win her respect before 'Lina came to prejudice her against him, if indeed she had not done so already and a pang shot through his heart as he thought how possible it was that Alice Johnson was prepared already to dislike him. But no, Ad could not be so mean as that, and Hugh went down to the breakfast which Aunt Eunice had prepared, and of which he could scarcely taste a morsel.

During the excitement of the last few days, the pain in his head had in a measure been forgotten, but it had come back this morning with redoubled force, and the veins upon his forehead looked almost like bursting with their pressure of feverish blood. Hugh did not think it possible for him to be sick, and he tried hard to forget the giddy, half blinding pain warning him of danger, and after forcing himself to sip a little coffee in which he would indulge this morning, he ordered Claib to bring out the covered buggy, as he was going up to Lexington, hoping thus to obtain a sight of Alice without being himself seen, or at least known as Hugh Worthington.

CHAPTER XVIII
MEETING OF ALICE AND HUGH

Could 'Lina have seen Hugh that morning as he emerged from a fashionable tailor's shop, she would scarcely have recognized him, so greatly was he improved by the entire new suit in which he had been indulging, and which gave him so stylish an appearance that Hugh for a moment felt uncomfortable, and was glad that one whole hour must elapse before the cars from Cincinnati were due as he could thus become a little accustomed to himself and not be so painfully conscious. The hour passed rapidly away, and its close found Hugh waiting at the terminus of the Lexington and Cincinnati Railroad. A moment more, and the broad platform was swarming with passengers, conspicuous among whom were an old lady and a young, both dressed in black, both closely veiled and both entire strangers, as was evinced by their anxiety to know what they were next to do, or where to go.

"These are ours," the young lady said, pointing to a huge pile of trunks, distinctly marked "A. J.," and Hugh drew so near to her that her long black veil swept against his coat, as she held out her checks in her ungloved hand.

Hugh noticed the hand, saw that it was very small and white and fat, but the face he could not see, and he looked in vain for the magnificent hair about which even his mother had waxed eloquent, and which was now put plainly back, so that not a vestige of it was visible. Still Hugh felt sure that this was Alice Johnson, so sure that when he had ascertained the hotel where she would wait for the Frankfort train, he followed on, and entering the back parlor, the door of which was partly closed, sat down as if he too were a traveller, waiting for the train. It never occurred to Hugh that he was acting the part of an eaves-dropper, so anxious he was to see Alice without being seen, and taking up an old paper, he pretended to be greatly interested in its columns, which, for any information he gleaned from them, might as well have been bottom side up.

Meantime, in the room adjoining, Alice divested herself of her dusty wrappings, and taking out her combs and brushes, began to arrange her hair, talking the while to Densie, her nurse, reclining on the sofa. How the tones of that voice thrilled on Hugh's ear like some forgotten music, heard he knew not when or where, and how still he sat, when at last the conversation turned upon his mother and 'Lina, about whom Alice talked freely, never dreaming of Hugh's proximity.

It would seem that Alice's own luxuriant tresses suggested her first remark, for she said to Densie, "That Miss Worthington had beautiful hair, so glossy, and so wavy, too. I wonder she never curls it. It looks as if she might."

A smile fitted over Hugh's face as he thought of the tags, and wondered what Alice would say could she see Ad early in the morning, with a red silk handkerchief, tied round her head by way of covering what he called tags, "It would take a steam engine to make Ad's hair curl," he said to himself, while Alice continued, "I did not like her eyes; they were too much like coals of fire, when they flashed angrily on that poor Lulu, who evidently was not well posted in the duties of a waiting-maid. If mother had not so decided, I should shrink from being an inmate of Mrs. Worthington's family. I like her very much, but I am afraid I shall not get on with 'Lina."

"I know you won't. I honor your judgment," was Hugh's mental comment, while Alice went on.

"And what she told me of her brother was not calculated to impress me favorably."

Nervously Hugh's hands grasped each other, and he could distinctly hear the beating of his heart as he leaned forward so as not to lose a single word.

"She seemed trying to prepare me for him by telling how rough he was; how little he cared for etiquette; and how constantly he mortified her with his uncouth manners."

The perspiration fairly dripped from Hugh's flushed face, as with clenched fist and a muttered curse upon his white lips he listened while Alice went on.

"Mother never dreamed he was such a man. Indeed, he was prepossessed in his favor, remembering his distress when he lost his little sister, who was mysteriously abducted by her father, and as mysteriously returned. He was a fine, handsome boy, mother said, and she thought I would like him. Bad as he may be, he is evidently a favorite with his negroes, for Lulu resented what her mistress said of him, and, in her peculiar way, told me it was false."

"Heaven bless Lulu!" Hugh mentally exclaimed. "I'll set her free the day that she's eighteen; but Ad, oh, must it go on thus? Will she always be a thorn to me?"

Alice did not hear the sigh of pain or see the mournful look which stole over Hugh's face. She did not even suspect his presence, and she continued to speak of Spring Bank, wondering if Hugh would be there before his mother returned, half hoping he would not, as she rather dreaded meeting him, although she meant to like him if she could.

Poor Hugh! How he winced and trembled, and wished he was away. How madly the hot blood poured through his swollen veins, and how fast the pain increased about his temples, while little sparks of fire danced before his eyes. Alice should have her wish, he said bitterly. She should not find Spring Bank encumbered with its hateful owner. 'Lina should not find him there when she returned, she should never blush again for him, for he would go away. With a stifled, noiseless moan, Hugh rose to leave the room, glancing once toward the narrow opening in the folding-doors. Then, as if petrified with what he saw, he stood riveted to the spot, his quivering lips apart, his head bent forward, and his eyes almost black, so strangely bright they grew.

Alice's long, bright hair, was arranged at last, and the soft curls fell about her face, giving to it the same look it had worn in childhood—the look which was graven on Hugh's heart, as with a pencil of fire; the look he never had forgotten through all the years which had come and gone since first it shone on him; the look he had never hoped to see again, so sure was he that it had been quenched by the waters of Lake Erie. Alice's face was turned fully toward him. Through the open window at her back the August sunlight streamed, falling on her chestnut hair, and tinging it with the yellow gleam which Hugh remembered so well. For an instant the long lashes shaded the fair round cheek, and then were uplifted, disclosing the eyes of blue, which, seen but once, could never be mistaken, and Hugh was not mistaken. One look of piercing scrutiny at the face unconsciously confronting him, one mighty throb, which seemed to bear away his very life, and then Hugh knew the grave had given up its dead.

She was not lost for she stood there before him. She whose memory had saved him oftentimes from sin. She, for whom he would almost lay him down and die. *She, the Golden Haired.* Changed, it is true, from a lovely child of thirteen to a far more lovely woman, but not past his recognition. The golden locks his hands had touched but once, and that when the mad waves were dashing over them, had put on a richer, darker tinge, and fell in heavier masses about her brow and neck. The face, too, with its piquant nose, was more mature; only the eyes were wholly unchanged. In them, the same truthful loving light was shining, and the curve of the silken lashes was just the same as when they drooped coyly, beneath the compliment which the tall youth had paid them.

Golden Hair had come back, but, alas, prejudiced against him. She hoped he might be gone. She would be happier if he never crossed her path. "And I never, never will," Hugh thought, as he staggered from the room and sought a small outer court, whose locality he knew, and where he could be alone to think.

The throbbing in his head had increased in violence, and what before were gleams of fire dancing before his eyes, were now like rings of blood, of which the sultry air seemed full. How sick and faint he was sitting there in that dingy court, with his head upon his hands, half wishing he might die, and so trouble no one any more. He felt that the dearest treasure he had ever possessed was wrested from him—that in losing Golden Hair's good opinion he had lost all that made life desirable.

"Oh, Adaline," he murmured, "what made you so cruel to me? I would not have served you so."

There was a roll of wheels before the door, and Hugh knew by the sound that it was the carriage for the cars. She was going. They would never meet again, Hugh said, and she would never know that the youth who tried to save her life was the same for whose coming they would wait and watch in vain at Spring Bank—the Hugh for whom his mother would weep awhile; and for whose dark fate even Ad might feel a little sorry. She was not wholly depraved—she had some sisterly feeling, and his loss would waken it to life. They would appreciate him after he was gone, and the poor heart which had known so little love throbbed joyfully, as Hugh thought of being loved at last even by the selfish 'Lina.

Fiercely the August sun poured down into that pent up court, creating a drowsiness which Hugh did not care to shake off. Unconsciousness was welcome at any price, and leaning his aching head against the damp, mouldy wall, he fell at last into a heavy sleep.

Meantime Alice and Densie proceeded on their way to the Big Spring station, where Col. Tiffton was waiting for them, according to his promise. There was a shadow in the colonel's good-humored face, and a shadow in his heart. His idol, Nellie, was very sick, while added to this was the terrible certainty that he alone must pay a $10,000 note on which he had foolishly put his name, because Harney had preferred it. He was talking with Harney when the cars came up, and the villain, while expressing regret that the colonel should be compelled to pay so much for what he never had received, had said with a relentless smile, "But it's not my fault, you know I can't afford to lose it."

From that moment the colonel felt he was a ruined man, but he would not allow himself to appear at all discomposed.

"Wait awhile," he said; "do nothing till my Nell lives or dies," and with a sigh as he thought how much dearer to him was his youngest daughter than all the farms in Woodford, he went forward to meet Alice, just appearing upon the platform.

The colonel explained to Alice why she must go to Spring Bank, adding by way of consolation, that she would not be quite as lonely now Hugh was at home.

"*Hugh* at home!" and Alice shrank back in dismay, feeling for a moment that she could not go there.

But there was no alternative, and after a few tears which she could not repress, she said, timidly,

"What is this Hugh? What kind of a man, I mean?"

She could not expect the colonel to say anything bad of him, but she was not prepared for his frank response.

"The likeliest chap in Kentucky. Nothing dandified about him, to be sure. Wears his trouser legs in his boots as often as any way, and don't stand about the very latest cut of his coat, but he's got a heart bigger than an *ox*— yes, big as *ten* oxen! I'd trust him with my life, and know it was safe as his own. You'll like Hugh— Nell does."

The colonel never dreamed of the comfort his words gave Alice, or how they changed her feelings with regard to one whom she had so dreaded to meet.

"There 'tis; we're almost there," the colonel said at last, as they turned off from the highway, and leaning forward Alice caught sight of the roofs and dilapidated chimneys of Spring Bank. "'Tain't quite as fixey as Yankee houses, that's a fact, but we that own niggers never do have things so smarted up," the colonel said, guessing how the contrast must affect Alice, who felt so desolate and homesick as she drew up in front of what, for a time at least, was to be her home.

At a single glance she took in every peculiarity, from the mossy, decaying eaves, where the swallows were twittering their songs, to the group of negroes ranged upon the piazza, staring curiously at her as she alighted, followed by Densie Densmore. Where was Hugh? Surely he should be there to greet her, and with a return of something like the olden terror Alice looked nervously in all directions, as if expecting some vampyre to start out and seize her. But only Aunt Eunice, in trim white cap and black silk apron, appeared, welcoming the strangers with a motherly kindness, which went to Alice's heart.

Aunt Eunice saw that she looked very tired, and asked if she would not go at once to her room and lie down. Glad to be alone, Alice followed her through the hall and up the stairs to the pleasant chamber in which Hugh had been so interested.

"You are tired and homesick, too, I guess," Aunt Eunice said, "but you'll get over it by and by. Spring Bank is a pleasant place, and if Hugh could he'd make it a handsome one. He has the taste."

"Where is Hugh?" Alice asked.

Aunt Eunice would not say he had gone to Lexington for the sake, perhaps, of seeing her, so she replied,

"He went to town this morning, but he'll be back pretty soon. He has done his best to make it pleasant for you. *You'll like Hugh.* There, try to go to sleep," and kind Aunt Eunice bustled from the room just as Densie entered it, together with Aunt Chloe. The old negress was evidently playing the hostess to Densie, for she was talking quite loud, and all about "Mas'r Hugh." "Pity he wasn't thar, 'twould seem so different; 'tain't de same house without him. *You'll like Mas'r Hugh,*" and she, too glided from the room.

Was this the password at Spring Bank, "You'll like Mas'r Hugh?" It would seem so, for when at last Hannah brought up the waffles and tea, which Aunt Eunice had prepared, she sat down her tray, and after a few inquiries concerning Alice's head, which was now aching sadly, she, too, launched forth into a panegyric on Mas'r Hugh, ending, as the rest had done, "You'll like Mas'r Hugh."

Alice began to believe she should, and with a silent thanksgiving that the great bugbear of Spring Bank was likely to prove so harmless, she waited and listened for any sounds which might herald Hugh's approach. But the summer evening waned and the summer night closed quietly around Spring Bank, without bringing its master home. One by one the negroes went to their cabins, and when at last the clock struck twelve, Aunt Eunice, who had been waiting for her boy, lighted her tallow candle and stole noiselessly to her room, where by the open window she sat for a long, long time, listening to the howl of Rover, who, sat upon the steps and filled the air with his lonely cries. Aunt Eunice was not superstitious, but Rover's howl sounded painfully in her ear, and when at last she crept slowly to her pillow there was a dread fear at her heart lest something had befallen Hugh.

CHAPTER XIX
ALICE AND MUGGINS

Had an angel appeared suddenly to the blacks at Spring Bank they would not have been more surprised or delighted than they were with Alice when she came down to breakfast looking so beautifully in her muslin wrapper, with a simple white blossom and geranium leaf twined among her flowing curls, and an expression of content upon her childish face which said that she had resolved to make the best of the place to which Providence had so clearly led her for some wise purpose of his own. She had arisen early and explored the premises in quest of the spots of sunshine which she knew were there as well as elsewhere, and she had found them, too, in the grand old elms and maples which shaded the wooden building, in the clean, grassy lawn and the running brook, in the well kept garden of flowers, and in the few choice volumes arranged in the old bookcase at one end of the hall. Who read those books? Not 'Lina, most assuredly, for Alice' reminiscences of her were not of the literary kind; nor yet Mrs. Worthington, kind, gentle creature as she seemed to be. Who then but Hugh could have pored over those pages? And with a thrill of joy she was turning from the corner, when the patter of little naked feet was heard upon the stairs, and a bright mulatto child, apparently seven or eight years old, appeared, her face expressive of the admiration with which she regarded Alice, who asked her name.

Curtesying very low the child replied,

"I dunno, missus; Mas'r Hugh don nickname me *Muggins*, and every folks do that now. You know Mas'r Hugh? He done *rared* when he read you's comin'; do this way with his boot, 'By George, Ad will sell the old hut yet without 'sultin' me,'" and the little darkey's fist came down upon the window sill in apt imitation of her master.

A crimson flush overspread Alice's face as she wondered if it were possible that the arrangements concerning her coming there had been made without reference to Hugh's wishes.

"It may be; he was away," she sighed; then feeling an intense desire to know more, and being only a woman and mortal, she said to *Muggins*, walking round her in circles, with her fat arms folded upon her bosom, "Your master did not know I was coming till he returned from New Orleans and found his mother's letter?"

"Who tole you dat ar?" and Muggin's face was perfectly comical in its bewilderment at what she deemed Alice's foreknowledge. "But dat's so. I hear Aunt Chloe say so, and how't was right mean in Miss 'Lina. *I hate Miss 'Lina! Phew-ew!*" and Muggins' face screwed itself into a look of such perfect disgust that Alice could not forbear laughing outright.

"You should not hate any one, my child," she said, while Muggins rejoined,

"I can't help it—none of us can; she's so—mean—and so—low-flung, Claib says. She hain't any *bizzens* orderin' us round nuther, and I will hate her!"

"But, Muggins, the Bible teaches us to love those who treat us badly, who are *mean*, as you say."

"Who's he?" and Muggins looked up quickly. "I never hearn tell of him afore, or, yes, I has. Thar's an old wared out book in Mas'r Hugh's chest, what he reads in every night, and oncet when I axes him what was it, he say 'It's a Bible, Mug.' Dat's what he calls me for short, *Mug*."

There was a warm spot now in Alice's heart for Hugh. A man who read his Bible every night could not be very bad, and she blessed Mug for the cheering news, little dreaming whose Bible it was Hugh read, or whose curl of yellow hair served him for a book mark. Mug's prying eyes had ferreted that out, too, and delighted with so attentive a listener as Alice, she continued:

"Dat's the thing, then, what teaches us to love the hatefuls. Mug don't want to read him, though I reckon Mas'r Hugh done grow some better, for he hain't been hoppin' mad this good while, like he got at Miss 'Lina 'bout that dress and Miss Adah. He was awful then. He *swared*, he did."

"Muggins, you must not tell me these things of your master. It is not right," Alice interposed and Muggins replied,

"Well, then, I done took 'em back. He didn't swared, but he do read the Bible, and he do kiss dat curl of yaller har what he keeps in it. I see him through the do' and I hear him whisper 'bout Golden Har or somethin' mighty like him."

Alice was in a tremor of distress. She knew Muggins ought not to disclose Hugh's secrets, and she saw no way to stop her except by sending her away, and this she was about to do when a new idea was suggested to her. Possibly she could keep her from repeating the story to others, so she asked if "Muggins had ever told this about the curl to any one else."

"Nobody but Chloe, and she *boxt* my ears so that I done forgot till I see you, and that har of your'n makes me 'member the one Mas'r Hugh kissed—real smackin' loud, so," and Muggins illustrated on her own hand.

"Well, then," Alice said, "promise you will not. Your master would be very angry to know you watched him through the door, and then told what you saw. You must be a good girl, Muggins. God will love you if you do. Do you ever pray?"

"More times I do, and more times when I'se sleepy I don't," was Muggins' reply, her face brightening up as she continued, "But I can tell you who does—Miss Adah and Uncle Sam, over dar in the cornfield. They prays, both of 'em, and Sam, is powerful, I tell you. I hears him at the black folk's meetin'. *Hollers*—oh! oh!" and Muggins stopped her ears, as if even the memory of Sam's prayers were deafening; but if the ears stopped, the tongue was just as busy as the talkative child went on: "Sam prays for Mas'r Hugh, that God would fetch him right some day, and Miss Adah say God will, 'case she say he see and hear everyting. Mug don't believe dat; can't cheat dis chile, 'case if he hear and see, what made him hold still dat time Miss 'Lina *licked* me for telling Mas'r Harney how't she done up her har at night in fourteen little braids, and slep' in great big cap to make it look wavy like yourn. Does you twist yourn up in tails?" and as she had all along been aching to do, Muggins laid her hands on the luxuriant tresses, which Alice assured her were not done up in tails.

Here was a spot where Alice might do good; this half-heathen, but sprightly, African child needed her, and she began already to get an inkling of her mission to Kentucky. She was pleased with *Muggins*, and suffered the little dusky hands to caress her curls as long as they pleased, while she questioned her of the bookcase and its contents, whose was it, 'Lina's or Hugh's?

"Mas'r Hugh's in course. Miss 'Lina *can't read!*" was Muggins' reply, which Alice fully understood.

'Lina was no reader, while Hugh was, it might be, and she continued to speak of him. Did he read evenings to his mother, or did 'Lina play to them?

Hugh Worthington | 129

"More'n we wants, a heap!" and Muggins spoke scornfully. "We can't bar them things she thumps out. Now we likes Mas'r Hugh's the best—got good voice, sing Dixie, oh, splendid! Mas'r Hugh loves flowers, too. Tend all them in the garden."

"Did he?" and Alice spoke with great animation, for she had supposed that 'Lina's or at least Mrs. Worthington's hands had been there.

But it was all Hugh, and in spite of what Muggins had said concerning his aversion to her coming there she felt a great desire to see him. She could understand in part why he should be angry at not having been consulted, but he was over that, she was sure from what Aunt Eunice said, and if he were not, it behooved her to try her best to remove any wrong impression he might have formed of her. "He shall like me," she thought; "not as he must like that golden haired maiden, whose existence this sprite of a negro has discovered, but as a friend, or sister," and a softer light shone in Alice's blue eyes, as she foresaw in fancy Hugh gradually coming to like her, to be glad that she was there, and to miss her when she was gone.

"What time did he come home last night?" she asked, feeling more disappointed than she cared to confess at Muggin's answer that, "he hadn't come at all!"

Alice was but human, and it must be confessed that she had made her toilet that morning with a slight reference to Hugh's eyes, wondering if he liked white, and wondering, too, if he liked flowers, when she placed the wax ball in her hair.

"You are sorry?" Mug said, interpreting her looks aright.

"Yes, I am sorry. I want to see your master, Hugh. I mean to like him very much."

"I'll tell him dat ar," thought Muggins. "I 'members how't he say oncet that nobody done love him," and, spying Claib in the distance, the little tattler ran off to tell him how beautiful the new missus was, and how she let her smooth her *har*, all she wanted to.

CHAPTER XX
POOR HUGH

Could Hugh have known the feelings with which Alice Johnson already regarded him, and the opinion she had expressed to Muggins, it would perhaps have stilled the fierce throbbings of his heart, which sent the hot blood so swiftly through his veins, and made him from the first delirious. They had found him in the quiet court just after the sun setting, and his uncovered head was already wet with the falling dew, and the profuse perspiration induced by his long, heavy sleep. He was well known at the hotel, and measures were immediately taken for apprising his family of the sudden illness, and for removing him to Spring Bank as soon as possible.

Breakfast was not yet over at Spring Bank, and Aunt Eunice was wondering what could have become of Hugh, when from her position near the window she discovered a horseman riding across the lawn at a rate which betokened some important errand. Alice spied him too, and the same thought flashed over both herself and Aunt Eunice. "Something had befallen Hugh."

Alice was the first upon the piazza, where she stood waiting till the rider came up,

"Are you Miss Worthington?" he asked, doffing his soil hat, and feeling a thrill of wonder at sight of her marvellous beauty.

"Miss Worthington is not at home," she said, going down the steps and advancing closer to him, "but I can take your message. Is any thing the matter with Mr. Worthington?"

Aunt Eunice had now joined her, and listened breathlessly while the young man told of Hugh's illness, which threatened to be the prevailing fever.

"They were bringing him home," he said—"were now on the way, and he had ridden in advance to prepare them for his coming."

Aunt Eunice seemed literally stunned and wholly incapable of action, while the negroes howled dismally for Mas'r Hugh, who, Chloe said, was sure to die.

Alice alone was calm and capable of acting. A room must be prepared, and somebody must direct, but to find the somebody was a most difficult matter. Chloe couldn't, Hannah couldn't, Aunt Eunice couldn't, and consequently it all devolved upon herself. Throwing aside the feelings of a stranger she summoned Densie to her aid, and then went quietly to work. By dint of questioning Muggins, who hovered near her constantly, she ascertained which was Hugh's sleeping room, and entered it to reconnoiter.

It was the most uncomfortable room in the house, for during two thirds of the day the hot sun poured down upon the low roof, heating the walls like an oven, and rendering it wholly unfit for a sick man. Hugh must not be put there, and after satisfying herself that her own chamber was the coolest and most convenient in the house, Alice came to a decision, and regardless of her own personal comfort, set to work to remove, with Densie's help, her various articles of luggage.

By this time Aunt Eunice had rallied a little, and hearing what Alice was doing, offered a faint remonstrance. Hugh would never be reconciled to taking Miss Johnson's room, she said, but Alice silenced every objection, and Aunt Eunice yielded the point, feeling intuitively that the sceptre had passed from her hand into a far more efficient one. The pleasant chamber, in which only yesterday morning Hugh himself had been so interested, was ready at last. The wide north windows were open, and the soft summer air came stealing in, lifting the muslin curtains which Alice had looped back, blowing across the snowy pillows which Alice's hands had arranged, and kissing the half withered flowers which Hugh had picked for Alice.

"I'll done get some fresher ones. Mas'r Hugh love the posies," Muggins said, as she saw Alice bending over the vase.

"Poor Hugh!" Alice sighed, as Muggins ran off for the flowers, which she brought to Miss Johnson, who arranged them into beautiful bouquets for the sick man now just at the gate. Alice saw the carriage as it stopped, and saw the tall form which the men were helping up the walk; and that was all she saw, so busily was she occupied in hushing the outcries of the excitable negroes, while Hugh was carried to the room designated by Densie, and into which he went unwillingly. "It was not his den," he said, drawing back with a bewildered look; "his was hot, and close, and dingy, while this was nice and cool—a room such as women had; there must be a mistake," and he begged of them to take him away.

"No, ho, my poor boy. This is right; Miss Johnson said you must come here just because it is cool and nice. You'll get well so must faster," and Aunt Eunice's tears dropped on Hugh's flushed face.

"Miss Johnson!" and the wild eyes looked up eagerly at her. "Who is she? Oh, yes, I know, I know," and a moan came from his lips as he whispered, "Does she know I've come? Does it make her hate me worse to see me in such a plight? Ho, Aunt Eunice, put your ear down close while I tell you something. Ad said—you know Ad—she said I was—I was—I can't tell you what she said for this buzzing in my head. Am I very sick, Aunt Eunice?" and about the chin there was a quivering motion, which betokened a ray of consciousness, as the brown eyes scanned the kind, motherly face bending over him.

"Yes, Hugh, you are very sick," and Aunt Eunice's tears dropped upon the face of her boy, so fearfully changed since yesterday.

He wiped them away himself, and looked inquiringly at her.

"Am I so sick that it makes you cry? Is it the fever I've got?"

"Yes, Hugh, the fever," and Aunt Eunice bowed her face upon his burning hands.

For a moment he lay unconscious, then raising himself up, he fixed his eyes piercingly upon her, and whispered hoarsely,

"Aunt Eunice, I shall die! I have never been sick in my life; and the fever goes hard with such. I shall surely die. It's been days in coming on, and I thought to fight it off, I don't want to die. I'm not prepared," and in the once strong man's voice there was a note of fear, such as only the dread of death could have wrung from him. "Aunt Eunice," and the voice was now a kind of sob, "tell Adah and Sam to pray. I shall lose my senses soon, they go and come so fast; and tell Miss Johnson, (I've heard that she too prays) tell her when she watches by me, as perhaps she will, tell her to pray, though I do not hear it, pray that I need not die, not yet, not yet. Oh if I had prayed sooner, prayed before," and the white lips moved as if uttering now the petitions too long left unsaid.

Then the mind wandered again, and Hugh talked of Alice and Golden Hair, not as one and the same, but as two distinct individuals, and then he spoke of his mother.

"You'll send for her; and if I'm dead when she comes, tell her I tried to be a dutiful son, and was always sorry when I failed. Tell her I love my mother more than she ever dreamed; and tell Ad——" Here he paused, and the forehead knit itself into great wrinkles, so intense were his thoughts. "Tell Ad—no, not tell her anything. She'll be glad when I'm dead, and trip back from my grave so gaily!"

Hugh Worthington | 133

He was growing terribly excited now, and Aunt Eunice hailed the coming of the doctor with delight. Hugh knew him, offering his pulse and putting out his tongue of his own accord. The doctor counted the rapid pulse, numbering even then 130 per minute, noted the rolling eyeballs and the dilation of the pupils, felt the fierce throbbing of the swollen veins upon the temple, and then shook his head. Half conscious, half delirious, Hugh watched him nervously, until the great fear at his heart found utterance in words,

"Must I die?"

"We hope not. We'll do what we can to save you. Don't think of dying, my boy," was the physician's reply, as he turned to Aunt Eunice, and gave out the medicine, which must be most carefully administered.

Too much agitated to know just what he said, Aunt Eunice listened as one who heard not, noticing which the doctor said,

"You are not the right one to take these directions. Is there nobody here less nervous than yourself? Who was that young lady standing by the door when I came in. The one in white, I mean, with such a quantity of curls."

"Miss Johnson—our visitor. She can't do anything," Aunt Eunice replied, trying to compose herself enough to know what she was doing.

But the doctor thought differently. Something of a physiognomist, he had been struck with the expression of Alice's face, and felt sure that she would be a more efficient aid than Aunt Eunice herself. "I'll speak to her," he said, stepping to the hall. But Alice was gone. She had stood by the sick room door long enough to hear Hugh's impassioned words concerning his probable death—long enough to hear him ask that she might pray for him; and then she stole away to where no ear, save that of God, could hear the earnest prayer that Hugh Worthington might live—or that dying, there might be given him a space in which to grasp the faith, without which the grave is dark and terrible indeed.

"I'm glad I came here now," she whispered, as she rose from her knees. "I know my work in part, and may God give me strength to do it."

"Is you talkin' to God, Miss Alice?" said a little voice, and Mug's round black face looked cautiously in.

"Yes, Muggins, I was talking to God."

"I'd mighty well like to know what you done say," was Mug's next remark, as she ventured across the threshold.

"I asked him to make your Master Hugh well again, or else take him to heaven," was Alice's reply; whereupon the great tears gathered in the eyes of the awe-struck child, who continued,

"I wish I could ax God, too. Would he hear a black nigger like me?"

"Yes, Muggins, God hears everybody, black as well as white."

"Then I jest go down in the woods whar Claib can't see me, and ax Him to cure Mas'r Hugh, not take him to heaven. I don't like dat ar."

It was in vain that Alice tried to explain. Muggins' mind grasped but one idea. Master Hugh must live; and she started to leave the room, turning back to ask, "if God could hear all the same if she got down by the brook where the bushes were so thick that Claib nor nobody could find her if they tried." Assured that he would, she stole from the house, and seeking out the hiding place kneeled down upon the tall, rank grass, and with her face hidden in the roots of the alder bushes, she asked in her peculiar way, that "God would not take Mas'r Hugh to heaven, but give him a heap of doctor's stuff, and make him well again," promising, if he did, that "She would not steal any more jam from the jars in the cellar, or any more sugar from the bowl in the closet." She could not remember for whose sake Alice had bidden her pray, so she said, "for the sake of him what miss done tell me," adding quickly, "Miss Alice, I mean, not Miss 'Lina! Bah!"

Muggins intended no irreverence, nor did she dream that she was guilty of any. She only felt that she had done her best, and into her childish heart there crept a trusting faith that God had surely heard, and Mas'r Hugh would live.

And who shall say that He did not hear and answer Muggin's prayer, made by the running brook, where none but Him could hear?

Meantime, the Hugh for whom the prayer was made had fallen into a heavy sleep, and Aunt Eunice noiselessly left the room, meeting in the hall with Alice, who asked permission to go in and sit by him until he awoke. Aunt Eunice consented, and with noiseless footsteps Alice advanced into the darkened room, and after standing still for a moment to assure herself that Hugh was really sleeping, stole softly to his bedside and bent down to look at him, starting quickly at the resemblance to somebody seen before. Who was it? Where was it? she asked herself, her brain a labyrinth of bewilderment as she tried in vain to recall the time or place a face like this reposing upon the pillow had met her view. But her efforts were all in vain to bring the past to mind, and thinking she was mistaken in supposing she had ever seen him before, she sat softly down beside him.

How disappointed Alice was in him, asking herself if it could be the dreaded Hugh. There was surely nothing to be dreaded from him now, and as if she had been his sister she wiped the sweat drops from his face.

There was a tremulous motion of the lids, a contracting of the muscles about the mouth, and then the eyes opened for a moment, but the stare he gave to Alice was wholly meaningless. He evidently had no thought of her presence, though he murmured the name "Golden Hair," and then fell away again into the heavy stupor which continued all the day. Alice would not leave him. She had heard him say, "When she watches by me as perhaps she will, though I may not know her," and that was sufficient to keep her at his side. She was accustomed to sickness, she said, and in spite of Aunt Eunice's entreaties, she sat by his pillow, bathing his burning hands, holding the cooling ice upon his head, putting it to his lips, and doing those thousand little acts which only a kind womanly heart can prompt, and silently praying almost constantly as Hugh had said she must.

There were others than Alice praying for Hugh that summer afternoon, for Muggins had gone from the brook to the cornfield, startling Adah with the story of Hugh's sickness, and then launching out into a glowing description of the new miss, "with her white gownd and curls as long as Rocket's tail."

"She talked with God, too," she said, "like what you does, Miss Adah. She axes him to make Mas'r Hugh well, and He will, won't He?"

"I trust so," Adah answered, her own heart going silently up to the Giver of life and health, asking, if it were possible, that her noble friend might be spared.

Old Sam, too, with streaming eyes stole out to his bethel by the spring, and prayed for the dear "Massah Hugh" lying so still at Spring Bank, and insensible to all the prayers going up in his behalf.

How terrible that deathlike stupor was, and the physician, when later in the afternoon he came again, shook his head sadly.

"I'd rather see him rave till it took ten men to hold him," he said, feeling the wiry pulse which were now beyond his count.

"Is there nothing that will rouse him?" Alice asked, "no name of one he loves more than another?"

The doctor answered "no; love for woman-kind, save as he feels it for his mother or his sister, is unknown to Hugh Worthington."

But Alice did not think so. The only words he had whispered since she sat there, together with Muggins' story of the Bible and the curl, would indicate that far down in Hugh's heart, where the world had never seen, there was hidden a mighty, undying love for some one. How she wished they were alone, that she might whisper, that name in his ear, but with the doctor there, and Aunt Eunice and Densie close at hand, she dared not, lest she should betray the secret she had no right to possess.

"I'll speak to him of his mother," she said, and moistening with ice the lips which were now of a purple hue she said to him softly,

"Mr. Worthington."

"Call him Hugh," Aunt Eunice whispered, and Alice continued,

"Hugh, do you know I'm speaking to you?"

She bent so low that her breath lifted the rings of hair from his forehead, and her auburn curls swept his cheek. There was a quivering of the lids, a scarcely perceptible moan, and thus encouraged, Alice continued,

"Hugh, shall I write to your mother? She's gone, you know, with 'Lina."

To this there was no response, and taking advantage of something outside which had suddenly attracted her three auditors to the window, Alice said again softly, lest she should be heard,

"Hugh, shall I call *Golden Haired*?"

"Yes, yes, oh yes," and the heavy lids unclosed at once, while the eyes, in which there was no ray of consciousness, looked wistfully at Alice.

"Are you the Golden Haired?" and he laid his hand caressingly over the shining tresses just within his reach.

Alice was about to reply, when an exclamation from those near the window, and the heavy tramp of horse's feet, arrested her attention, and drew her also to the window, just as a beautiful grey, saddled but riderless, came dashing over the gate, and tearing across the yard until he stood panting at the door. *Rocket* had come home for the first time since his master had lead him away!

Hearing of Hugh's illness, the old colonel had ridden over to inquire how he was, and fearing lest it might be difficult to get Rocket away if once he stood in the familiar yard, he had dismounted in the woods, and fastening him to a tree, walked the remaining distance. But Rocket was not thus to be cheated. Ever since turning into the well-remembered lane he had seemed like a new creature, pricking up his ears, and dancing and curvetting daintily along, as he had been wont to do on public occasions when Hugh was his rider instead of the fat colonel. In this state of feeling it was quite natural that he should resent being tied to a tree, and as if divining why it was done, he broke his halter the moment the colonel was out of sight, and went galloping through the woods like lightning, never for an instant slackening his speed until he stood at Spring Bank door, calling, as well as he could call, for Hugh, who heard and recognized that call.

Throwing his arms wildly over his head, he raised himself in bed, and exclaimed joyfully,

"That's he! that's Rocket! I knew he'd come. I've only been waiting for him to start on that long journey. Ho! Aunt Eunice! Pack my clothes. I'm going away where I shan't mortify *Ad* any more. Hurry up. Rocket is growing impatient. Don't you hear him pawing the turf? I'm coming, my boy, I'm coming!" and he attempted to leap upon the floor, but the doctor's strong arm held him down, while Alice, whose voice alone he heeded, strove to quiet him.

"I wouldn't go away to-day," she said soothingly. "Some other time will do as well, and Rocket can wait."

"Will you stay with me?" Hugh asked.

"Yes, I'll stay," was Alice's reply.

"All right, all right. Tell Claib to put up Rocket, till another day, and then we'll go together, you and I," and Hugh sank back upon his pillow, just as the wheezy colonel come in, greatly alarmed and surprised to find the young man so ill.

"It beats all," he said, "how symptoms differ. That buzzing he complained of wasn't an atom like my wife's—beats all;" then turning to Alice he delivered a message from Ellen who was better, and had expressed a wish to see Miss Johnson, hoping she might be induced to return with her father.

But Alice would not leave Hugh, and she declined the colonel's invitation.

"That's right. Stick to him," the colonel said. "He's a noble fellow, odd as Dick's hat band, but got the right kind of spirit. Poor boy. It makes me feel to see him some as I felt when my Hal lay ravin' mad with the dumb fever in his head. Poor Hal! He is up in the grave-yard now. Good day to you all. I've got a pesky job on hand getting that Rocket home."

And the colonel was right, for Rocket stubbornly refused to move, kicking and biting as he had done once before when any one approached him. He had taken his stand near by the block where Hugh had been accustomed to mount him, and there he staid, evidently waiting for his master, sometimes glancing toward the house and uttering a low whinny.

"I reckon I'll have to leave him here for a spell," the colonel said at last when every stratagem had been resorted to in vain.

"Yes, I 'specs mas'r will," returned the delighted Claib, who, had let one or two good opportunities pass for seizing Rocket's bridle. "I'll get Mas'r Tiffton anodder nag," and with great alacrity the negro saddled a handsome bay, on which the colonel was soon riding away from Spring Bank, leaving Rocket standing patiently by the block, and waiting for the master who might never come to him again.

"I'm glad he's roused up," the doctor said of Hugh, "though I don't like the way his fever increases," and Alice knew by the expression of his face, that there was but little hope, determining not to leave him during the night.

Aunt Eunice might sleep on the lounge, she said, but the care, the responsibility should be hers. To this the doctor willingly acceded, thinking that Hugh was safer with her than any one else. Exchanging the white wrapper she had worn through the day for one more suitable, Alice, after an hour's rest in her own room, returned to Hugh, who had missed her and who knew the moment she came back to him, even though, he seemed to be half asleep.

Softly the summer twilight faded and the stars came out one by one, while the dark night closed over Spring Bank, which held many anxious hearts. Never had a cloud so black as this fallen upon the household. There had been noisy, clamorous mourning when John Stanley died, but amid that storm of grief there was one great comfort still, Hugh was spared to them, but now he, too, was leaving them they feared, and the sorrow which at first had manifested itself in loud outcries had settled down into a grief too deep, too heart-felt for noisy demonstrations. In the kitchen where a light was burning casting fitful, ghastly glances over the dusky forms congregated there, old Chloe, as the patriarchess of the flock, sat with folded arms, talking to those about her of her master's probable death, counting the few who had ever survived that form of fever, and speculating as to who would be their next owner. Would they be sold at auction? Would they be parted one from the other, and sent they knew not whither? The Lord only knew, old Chloe said, as the hot tears rained over her black face,

"Mas'r Hugh won't die," and Muggins' faith came to the rescue, throwing a ray of hope into the darkness. "Miss Alice axed God to spar him, and so did I; now he will, won't he, miss?" and she turned to Adah, who with Sam, had just come up to Spring Bank, and hearing voices in the kitchen had entered there first. "Say, Miss Adah, won't God cure Mas'r Hugh—case I axed him oncet?"

"You must pray more than once, child; pray many, many times," was Adah's reply; whereupon Mug looked aghast, for the idea of praying a second time had never entered her brain.

Still, if she must, why, she must, and she stole quietly from the kitchen. But it was now too dark to go down in the woods by the running brook, and remembering Alice had said that God was every where, she first cast around her a timid glance, as if fearful she should see him, and then kneeling in the grass, wet with the heavy night dew, the little negro girl prayed again for Master Hugh, starting as she prayed at the sound which met her ear and which came from the spot where Rocket was standing by the block, waiting for his master.

Claib had offered him food and drink, but both had been refused, and opening the stable door so that he could go in whenever he chose, Claib had left him there alone.

Muggins knew that it was Rocket, and stole up to him, whispering as she laid her hand on his neck,

"Poor Rocket, I'm sory too for Mas'r Hugh, but he won't die, 'case I've prayed for him. I has prayed twicet, and I knows now he'll live. If you could only pray—I wonder if horses can!" and thinking she would ask the new miss, Mug continued to stroke the horse, who suffered her caress, and even rubbed his face against her arm, eating the tuft of grass she plucked for him. Once Mug thought of trying to lead him to the stall, but he looked so tall and formidable, towering up above her, that she dared not, and after a few more assurances that Mas'r Hugh would live, she left him to himself, with the very sensible advice, that if she's he, she wouldn't *ac* so, but would go to bed, in the stable like a good boy.

Returning to the house Mug stole up stairs to the door of the sick room, where Alice was now alone with Hugh.

He was awake, and for an instant seemed to know her, for he attempted to speak, but the rational words died on his lips, and he only moaned, as if in distress.

"What is it?" Alice said, bending over him.

"Are you the Golden Haired?" he asked again as her curls swept his face.

"No, I'm not Golden Hair," she answered, soothingly. "I'm Alice, come to nurse you. You have heard of Alice Johnson. 'Lina told you of her."

"*Ad!*" he almost screamed. "Do you know Ad? I am sorry for you. Who are you?" and as if determined to solve the mystery he raised himself upon his elbow and stretching out his hand, pushed her flowing curls back from her sunny face, muttering as he did so, "'There angels do always behold his face.' That's in her Bible. I'm reading it through. I began last winter, when Adah came. Have you heard of Adah?"

Alice had heard of Adah and suggested sending for her, asking "if he would not like to have her come."

"And you go away?" he said, grasping her hand and holding it fast. "No, you must not go. There's something in your face that makes me happy, something like hers. When I say her or she, I mean Golden Hair. There's only one *her* to me."

"Who is Golden Hair?" Alice asked, and instantly the great tears gathered in Hugh's dark eyes as he replied.

"Don't say who is she, but who was she. I've never told a living being before. Golden Hair was a bright angel who crossed my path one day, and then disappeared forever, leaving behind the sweetest memory a mortal man ever possessed. It's weak for men to cry, but I have cried many a night for her, when the clouds were crying, too, and I heard against my window the rain which I knew was falling upon her little grave."

He was growing excited, and thinking he had talked too much, Alice was trying to quiet him, when the door opened softly and Adah herself came in. Bowing politely to Alice she advanced to Hugh's bedside, and bending over him spoke his name. He knew her, and turning to Alice, said, "This is Adah; you will like each other; I am sure."

And they did like each other at once, Alice recognizing readily a refinement of feeling and manner, which showed that however unfortunate Adah might have been, she was still the true-born lady, while Adah felt intuitively that in Alice she had found a friend in whom she could trust. For a few moments they talked together, and then in the hall without there was a shuffling sound and Adah knew that Sam was coming. With hobbling steps the old man came in, scarcely noticing either of the ladies so intent was he upon the figure lying so still and helpless, before him.

"Massah Hugh, my poor, dear Massah Hugh," he cried, bending over his young master.

"You may disturb him," Adah said, putting from her lap little Willie, who had come in with Sam, and at whom Alice had looked with wonder, marvelling at the striking resemblance between him and Hugh.

"Could it be?" and Alice grew dizzy with that dreadful thought. "*Could it be?* No, no, oh, no. Adah was too pure, too good, while Hugh was too honorable," and Alice felt a pang at this injustice to both.

Taking the child in her lap while Adah spoke with Sam she smoothed his soft, brown hair, and scanned his infantile features closely, tracing now another look than Hugh's, a look which made her start as if smitten suddenly. The eyes, the brow, the hair were Hugh's, but for the rest; the dedicate mouth, with its dimpled corners, the curve of the lip, the nose, the whole lower part of the face was like, oh, so like, sweet *Anna Richards*, and *she* was like *her brother*. Alice had heard from 'Lina that Adah professed to have had a husband who deserted her and as she held Willie in her lap, there were all sorts of fancies in her bewildered brain nor was it until a loud outcry from Sam, fell on her ear that she roused herself from the castle she was building as to what might be if Willie were indeed of the Richard's line. Sam had turned away from Hugh, and with his usual politeness was about making his obeisance to Alice, when the words, "Your servant, Miss," were changed into a howl of joy, and falling upon his knees, he clutched at Alice's dress, exclaiming,

"Now de Lord be praised, I'se found her again. I'se found Miss Ellis, an' I feels like singin' 'Glory Hallelujah.' Does ye know me, lady? Does you 'member shaky ole darkey, way down in Virginny? You teach him de way, an' he's tried to walk dar ever sence. Say, does you know ole Sam?" and the dim eyes looked eagerly into Alice's face.

She did remember him, and for a moment seemed speechless with surprise, then, stooping. beside him, she took his shrivelled hand and pressed it between her own, asking how he came there, and if Hugh had always been his master.

"You 'splain, Miss Adah. You speaks de dictionary better than Sam," the old man said, and thus appealed to, Adah told what she knew of Sam's coming into Hugh's possession.

"He buy me just for kindness, nothing else, for Sam aint wo'th a dime, but Massa Hugh so good. I prays for him every night, and I asks God to bring you and him together. Oh, I'se happy chile to-night. I prays wid a big heart, 'case I sees Miss Ellis again," and in his great joy Sam kissed the hem of Alice's dress, crouching at her feet and regarding her with a look almost idolatrous.

At sight of his nurse Willie had slid from Alice's lap and with his arm around Sam's neck, was lisping the only words he as yet could speak, "Up, up, Tam, Willie up," meaning that he must be taken. Struggling to his feet Sam took Willie on his shoulder, then with another blessing on Miss Ellis and a pitying glance at Hugh, he left the room, Willie looking down from his elevated position triumphant as a young lord, and crowing in childish glee as he buried his hands in Uncle Sam's white wool.

In every move which Willie made there was a decidedly Richards' air, a manner such as would have been expected from John Richards' son playing in the halls of Terrace Hill.

"Is Willie like his father?" Alice asked as the door closed after Sam.

"Yes," and a shadow flitted over Adah's face.

She did not like to talk of Willie's father and was glad when Hugh at last claimed their attention. They watched together that night, tending Hugh so carefully that when the morning broke and the physician came, he pronounced the symptoms so much better that there was hope, he said, if the faithful nursing were continued. Still Hugh remained delirious, lying often in a kind of stupor from which nothing had power to arouse him unless it were Alice's voice, whispering in his ear the name of "Golden Hair," or the cry of Rocket, who for an entire week waited patiently by the block, his face turned towards the door whence he expected his master to appear. During the day he would neither eat nor drink, but Claib always found the food and drink gone, which was left in the stall at night, showing that Rocket must have passed the hours of darkness in his old, accustomed place. With the dawn of day, however, he returned to his post by the block, and more than one eye filled with tears at sight of the noble brute waiting so patiently and calling so pitifully for one who never came. But Rocket grew tired at last, and they missed him one morning at Spring Bank, while Col. Tiffton on that same morning was surprised and delighted to find him standing demurely by the gate and offering no resistance when they led him to the stable which he never tried to leave again. He seemed to have given Hugh up and a part of the affection felt for his young master was transferred to the colonel, who petted and caressed the beautiful animal, sighing the while as he thought how improbable it was that Hugh ever could redeem him, and how if he did not, the time was coming soon when Rocket must again change masters, and when *Harney's* long cherished wish to possess him would undoubtedly be gratified.

CHAPTER XXI
ALICE AND ADAH

At Alice's request, Adah and Sam staid altogether at Spring Bank, but Alice was the ruling power—Alice, the one whom Chloe and Claib consulted; Alice to whom Aunt Eunice looked for counsel, Alice, who remembered all the doctor's directions, taking the entire charge of Hugh's medicines herself—and Alice, who wrote to Mrs. Worthington, apprising her of Hugh's illness. They hoped he was not dangerous, she said, but he was very sick, and Mrs. Worthington would do well to come at once. She did not mention 'Lina, but the idea never crossed her mind that a sister *could* stay away from choice when a brother was so ill; and it was with unfeigned surprise that she one morning saw Mrs. Worthington and Lulu alighting at the gate, but no 'Lina with them.

"She was so happy at Saratoga," Mrs. Worthington said, when a little over the first flurry of her arrival. "So happy, too, with Mrs. Richards that she could not tear herself away, unless her mother should find Hugh positively dangerous, in which case she should, of course, come at once."

This was the mother's charitable explanation, made with a bitter sigh as she recalled 'Lina's heartless anger when the letter was received, as if Hugh were to blame, as indeed, 'Lina seemed to think he was.

"What business had he to come home so quick? If he'd staid in New Orleans, he might not have had the fever. Any way, she wasn't going home. Alice had said he was not dangerous yet, so if her mother went, that was enough;" and utterly forgetful of the many weary hours and days when Hugh had watched by her, the heartless girl had stifled every feeling of self reproach, and hurried her mother off, entrusting to her care a note for Alice, who, she felt, would wonder at her singular conduct.

Giving the note to Alice, Mrs. Worthington hastened to her child, with whom Adah and Sam were sitting. He had just awakened from a quiet sleep, and knew his mother at once. Winding his arms around her, he kissed her forehead and lips, and then his eyes wandered past her towards the door through which she had entered, as if in quest of some one else. His mother did not observe the glance, or know for whom he was looking so wistfully until the white lips whispered, "'Lina, mother, where is she?"

It was strange for him to call her 'Lina. Indeed, the mother could remember no other time when he had done so, but he called her 'Lina now, speaking it tenderly, as if her presence would be very welcome to him. There was a hesitancy on the part of the mother, and then she said, "'Lina staid in Saratoga. She is very happy there. She will come if you grow worse. She sent her love."

Poor Mrs. Worthington! She mentally asked forgiveness for this fabrication. 'Lina had sent no love, and the mother only said so because she must say something. Wistfully, eagerly, Hugh's eyes sought hers for a moment, and then filled with tears which dropped upon the pillow.

"Did you want 'Lina to come?" Mrs. Worthington asked.

"Yes," and Hugh's lip quivered like a grieved child. "I'm going to die, and I wanted to tell her how sorry I am for the harsh things I've said to her. I've been crazy some, I guess, for nothing was clear in my mind— nothing but the words 'Forgive as ye would be forgiven.' They were the last I ever read in that little Bible you never saw. It's in my trunk, and when I'm gone you'll give it to Miss Johnson. I think she's here; and you'll tell 'Lina I was sorry, and if—if—if she's ever sorry, tell her I forgive her, and wanted her to come so much. I thought, maybe, she'd kiss me; she never has since she was a little child. If she comes before you put me out of sight, ask her to kiss me in the coffin, because I was her brother. I shall be sure to know it. Will you, mother?"

Mrs. Worthington could only sob as she pressed the hands she held between her own and tried to quiet him.

Meantime Alice, in her own room, was reading 'Lina's note, containing a most glowing description of the delightful time she was having at Saratoga, and how hard it would be to leave.

"I know *dear Hugh* is in good hands," she wrote, "and it is so pleasant here that I really do want to stay a little longer. What a delightful lady that Mrs. Richards is—not one bit stiff as I can see. I don't know what people mean, to call her proud. She has promised, if mamma will leave me here, to be my chaperon, and it's possible we may visit New York together, so as to be there when the Prince arrives. Won't that be grand? She talks so much of you that sometimes I'm really jealous. Perhaps I may go to Terrace Hill before I return, but I rather hope not, it makes me fidgetty to think of meeting the Misses Richards, though, of course, I know I shall like them, particularly Anna."

Not a word was there in this letter of the doctor, but Alice understood it all the same. *He* was the attraction which kept the selfish girl from her brother's side. "May she be happy with him," was Alice's mental comment, shuddering as she recalled the time when she was pleased with the handsome doctor, and silently thanking God who had saved her from much sorrow.

Just then Adah came in, and sitting down by the window seemed to be looking at something far away, something, which brought to her face the sad hopeless expression, which Alice had often observed before. Drawing near to her Alice said softly, "Of what are you thinking, Adah?"

There were no reserves now between the two girls, and laying her head in Alice's lap, Adah sobbed, "I'm thinking of Willie's father. Will he never come back? Can it be he meant to deceive me, Miss Johnson?" and Adah lifted up her head, disclosing a face which Alice scarcely recognized, for the strange expression there. "Miss Johnson, if I knew that George deliberately planned my ruin under the guise of a mock marriage, and then when it suited him deserted me as a toy of which he was tired, *I should hate him!*"

She hissed the words between her shut teeth, and Alice involuntarily shuddered at the hard, relentless look, which only a deceived, deserted woman can wear. She did not dream that Adah, who had seemed so gentle, so good, could put on such a look, and she gazed at her in astonishment, as in clear, determined tones she repeated the words, "Yes, *I should hate him!*

"I know it's wrong," she continued, "and I've asked God many a time to take the feeling away, but it's in me yet, and sometimes, when I get to thinking of the time before he came, when I was a happy, innocent school girl, without a care for anything, my heart turns into stone, and the prayer I would say will not come. Miss Johnson, you don't know what it is to love with your whole soul one who, to all appearance, was worthy of your love, and who, the world would say, was above you in position—to trust him implicitly, to worship the very earth he trod, to feel 'twas Heaven where he was, to have no shadow of suspicion, to believe yourself his lawful wife, and then some dreadful morning wake up and find him gone, you know not where—to wait and watch through weary weeks and months of agonizing pain, and then to hear at last, in his own handwriting, that you were not a wife that the whole was a mockery, a marriage of convenience, which circumstances rendered it necessary for him to break, that his proud family would not receive you, that though he loved you still, his bride must be rich to please his aristocratic mother, and then to end with the hope thrown out that sometime he might come back and make you truly his. But for that I should have died, and, as it was, I felt my heart-strings snapping, one by one, felt the blood freezing in my veins, felt that I was going mad. I frighten you, Miss Johnson," she said, as she saw how Alice shrunk away from the dark eyes in which there was a fierce, resentful gleam, unlike sweet Adah Hastings. "I used to frighten myself when I saw in my eyes the demon which whispered suicide."

"Oh, Adah, Mrs. Hastings," and Alice involuntarily wound her arm around the young girl-woman as if to shield her from sin. "You could not have dreamed of that!"

"I did," and Adah spoke sadly now. "I forgot God awhile, and He left me to myself, but followed me still, going with me all through those crowded streets, close at my side, though I did not know it, and holding me back at the last moment, when the tempter was about to triumph, and the river rolling at my feet looked so invitingly to poor, half-crazed me, He put other thoughts in my head, and where I went to throw my life away, I knelt down and prayed. It was kind in God to save me, and I've tried to love Him better since, to thank Him for His great goodness in leading me to Hugh, as He surely did; but there's something savage in my nature, which has not been all subdued, and sometimes I'm rebellious, just as you see me now, and my heart, which at first was full of love for George, goes out against him for his base treachery."

"And yet you love him still?" Alice said, inquiringly as she smoothed the beautiful brown hair.

"I suppose I do. A kind word from him would bring me back, but will it ever be spoken? Shall we ever meet again?"

She was silent a moment, and then Alice said, "I do not seek your confidence unless you are willing to give it. As you have told me your story in part, will you tell me the whole?"

There was no vindictiveness now in Adah's face, and the soft brown eyes drooped mournfully beneath the heavy lashes as she told the story of her wrongs. Told of a young girl at Madam Dupont's school, of the elegant stranger present at one examination, and who watched her with unfeigned interest as she worked out upon the board a most difficult problem in Euclid, standing so near to her that once when she accidentally dropped her crayon he picked it up and offered it to her with a few whispered words of commendation for her skill in mathematics. Of a chance meeting in the street. Of walks and rides, and blissful interviews at her own cozy little room in the boarding-house, where she had lived for years. Of marriage proposed at last, and sanctioned by her guardian. Of the necessity urged upon her why it should be kept a secret until the proud relatives were reconciled. Of going one night with her lover, her guardian and another witness, far out into the suburbs of the city to the house of a justice, who made her George's wife. Of her guardian's sudden departure, she knew not whither. Of a removal to another boarding-house more obscure, and in a part of the city where she never met again with any whom she had known before. Of months of perfect happiness. Of the hope growing within her that she was gradually, leading George to God. Of letters from home which made him blue, and which she never saw. Of his leaving her at last without a word or sign that he was going or had grown weary of her. Of the terrible suspense, the cruel letter, the attempt to take her life, of Willie's birth, of her being turned from the house as a disreputable character, and coming at last to Spring Bank in quest of Hugh, and of the gradual dying out, as she sometimes feared, of her love for George Hastings.

"And Hugh?" Alice said, when Adah paused. "Why did you come to him? Had you known him before?"

"Hugh was that other witness. I never saw him till that night, neither, I think, did George. My guardian planned the whole."

"Hugh Worthington is not the man I took him for," and Alice spoke bitterly, a look of horror on her face which Adah quickly detected.

"You mistake him," she cried eagerly. "He is all you imagine him to be, the noblest, truest man, and the best friend I ever had. My guardian possessed a most singular power over all young men, and Hugh was fresh from the country. I don't know where or how they met, but at a hotel, I think. He did not know it was a farce. He went in perfect good faith, although he says since that it did once occur to him that something might be wrong.

"And your guardian," interrupted Alice, "is it not strange that he should have acted so cruel a part, particularly if, as you sometimes fancied, he was your father?"

"Yes, that's the strangest part of all. I cannot understand it, or where he is, though I sometimes imagined he must be dead, or in prison," and Adah thought of what Sam had said concerning Sullivan, the negro-stealer.

"What do you mean; why should he be in prison?" Alice asked in some surprise, and Adah replied by telling her what Sam had said, and the reason she had for thinking Sullivan and her guardian, Redfield, one and the same.

Just then Willie's voice was heard in the hall, and hastening to the door Alice admitted him into the room. Taking him in her lap she kissed his rosy cheek, and pushing back his soft curls said to Adah, "Do you know I think he looks like *Hugh*?"

"Yes," and Adah spoke sadly. "I know he does, and I am sorry for Hugh's sake, as it must annoy him. Neither can I account for it, for I am certainly nothing to Hugh. But there's another look in Willie's face, his father's. Oh, Miss Johnson, George was handsome, and 'twas his face which first attracted me."

"Can you describe him, or will it be too painful?" Alice asked, and forcing back her tears, Adah told how George Hastings looked, while Alice's hands worked nervously together, and her heart beat almost audibly, for, save the absence of moustache and whiskers, which might have been grown since, Adah was describing *Dr. Richards.*

"And you've never seen him since, nor heard from him, nor guessed where his mother lived?"

"Never, and when only the wrong is remembered, I think I never care to see or hear from him again; but when the love I bore him comes surging back, as it sometimes does, I'd crawl to the end of the world for one more tender look from him. I'd lay his boy at his feet and die there myself so willingly. I used to form all sorts of castles about his coming after me, but they are all blown down, and I've learned to look the future in the face, to know that I must meet it alone. I wish there was something I could do to relieve Hugh of the expense I am to him. I did not know till after I was sick last spring how very poor he was, and how many self denials he had to make for his family. I heard his mother talking with Aunt Eunice when they thought I was asleep, and it almost broke my heart. He goes without decent clothes, without a fire in his room on wintry nights, goes without every thing, and then 'Lina calls him mean and stingy. The noble, self-denying Hugh! I would almost die for him; and I ask God every day to bring him some good fortune at last."

"I never knew that Mr. Worthington was so straightened," said Alice. "Was Rocket sold to Col. Tiffton for debt?"

"Yes, for 'Lina's debts, contracted at Harney's and for my sick bills, too. I've cried the hardest over that, for I know how Hugh loved that horse, but the worst of it is that Col. Tiffton has in some way become indebted to Harney for an immense sum of money. I don't understand it, but the colonel signed a note for ten thousand dollars with somebody and for somebody, both of which somebodys have failed, and the colonel has to pay. It will take his home, they say, and his personal property, including Rocket, whom Harney is determined to secure. I've heard of his boasting that Hugh should yet be compelled to see him galloping down the pike upon his idol."

"He never shall!" and Alice spoke under her breath, asking further questions concerning the sale of Colonel Tiffton's house, and how much Mosside was worth.

Adah could not tell. She only knew that Rocket was pawned for five hundred dollars. "Once I insanely hoped that I might help redeem him—that God would find a work for me to do—and my heart was so happy for a moment."

"What did you think of doing?" Alice asked, glancing at the delicate young girl, who looked so unaccustomed to toil of any kind.

"I thought to be a governess or waiting-maid," and Adah's lip began to quiver as she told how, before coming to Spring Bank, she had advertised for such a situation; how she had waited and watched for an answer, and how at last it came, or at least the words seemed addressed *to her*, and she had thought to answer it, but had been discouraged by 'Lina.

"Do you remember the address?" and Alice waited curiously for the answer.

"Yes, 'A. E. R., Snowdon.' You came from Snowdon, Miss Johnson, and I've wanted so much to ask if you knew 'A. E. R.'"

Alice was confounded. Surely the leadings of Providence were too plainly evident to be unnoticed. There was a reason why Adah Hastings must go to Anna Richards, and Alice hastened to explain who the Richards family were.

"Oh, I can't go there. They are too proud. They would hate me for Willie, and ask me for his father," Adah cried, the tears breaking through the fingers she pressed before her eyes.

Very gently Alice talked to her of Anna, so lovely in disposition, so beautiful in her mature womanhood. Adah would be happy with her, she said, and Anna would be a second mother to her child. She did not hint of her suspicions that at Terrace Hill Adah would find *George* for fear she might be mistaken, but she talked of Snowdon and Anna Richards, whom Adah was sure to like.

"I'm so glad for your sake that it has come round at last," she said. "Will you write to her to-day, or shall I for you? Perhaps I had better."

"No, no, oh, no—" and Adah's voice trembled, for she shrank nervously from the thought of meeting the Richards family.

If 'Lina liked the old lady, she certainly could not, and the very thought of these elder sisters, in all their primness, dismayed and disheartened her.

"There's a young man, is there not—a Dr. Richards?" she asked.

"Yes; but he is not often at home. He need be no bugbear. He is practicing in New York, when practicing at all. At present he is at Saratoga."

Adah looked up quickly, guessing, in a moment, what was keeping 'Lina there, and feeling more averse than ever to Terrace Hill.

Gradually, however, as Alice continued to talk of Anna, her feelings changed and she said at last, "I will go to Miss Richards, but not till Hugh is better, not till he knows and approves. Do you think it will be long before be regains his reason!"

Alice could not tell. She hoped for the best, and thought with Adah that she ought to stay until he could be consulted.

"Do you correspond with Miss Richards?" Adah suddenly asked, after a long reverie.

"No, she dreads writing letters above all things else, while I am a wretchedly negligent correspondent. I will send a note of introduction by you, though."

"Please don't," and Adah spoke pleadingly, "I should have to give it if you did, and I'd rather go by myself. I know it would be better to have your influence, but it is a fancy of mine not to say that I ever knew you or any one at Spring Bank. I imagine this Dr. likes 'Lina, and they might question me of her. I could not say much that was good, and I should not like to say bad things of Hugh's sister. Then, too, Miss Richards never need know of my past life unless I choose to let her, as I should have to do in telling her how I came at Spring Bank."

Alice could understand Adah's motives in part, and feeling sure that whatever she might say would be the truth, she did not press the matter, but suffered her to proceed in her own way. Now it was settled that Adah should go, she felt a restless, impatient desire to be gone, questioning the doctor closely with regard to Hugh, who it seemed to her, would never waken from the state of unconsciousness into which he had fallen, and from which he only rallied for an instant, just long enough to recognize his mother, but never Alice or herself, both of whom watched over him day and night, waiting anxiously for the first symptom which should herald his return to reason.

CHAPTER XXII
WAKING TO CONSCIOUSNESS

The warm still days of September were gone and a wild October storm was dying out in a gentle shower, when Hugh awoke from the sleep which had so long hung over him, and listened, with a vague kind of delicious happiness, to the lulling music of the rain falling so softly upon the window sill, and sifting through the long boughs of the trees, visible from where he lay. Gazing about him in a maze of perplexity, he wondered what had happened, or where he could be.

"I must have been sick," he whispered, and pressing his hand to his head, he tried to recall and form into some definite shape the events which had seemed, and which seemed to him still, like so many phantoms of the brain.

Was it a dream—his mother's tears, upon his face, his mother's sobs beside him? Was it a dream that *Adah* had bent over him with words of tenderness, praying for him that he might not die, as he was sure he had heard her? And,—oh how Hugh started as he thought this;—Was it all a dream that the Golden Haired had been with him constantly?

No, that was not a dream, and Hugh lay panting on his pillow, as gleam after gleam flashed across his mind, bringing remembrance of the many times when another voice than Adah's had asked that he might live, had pleaded as only Golden Hair could plead with God for him. She did not hate him, else she had not prayed, and words of thanksgiving were going up to Golden Hair's God, when a footstep in the hall announced the approach of some one. Alice perhaps, and Hugh lay very still, with half shut eyes, until Muggins, instead of Alice, appeared. She had been deputed to watch by her master while the family were at dinner, pleased with the confidence reposed in her, determined strictly to obey Alice's injunction to be very quiet, and not wake him if he were sleeping.

He was asleep, she said, as, standing on tiptoe, she scanned his face, in her own dialect, Muggins talked to herself about him as he lay there so still, not a muscle moving, save those about the corners of his mouth, where a smile was struggling for life, as Hugh listened to Mug's remarks.

"Nice Mas'r Hugh—most as white as Miss Alice. De sweat has washed de dirt all off. Pretty Mas'r Hugh!" and Mug's little black hand was laid caressingly on the face she admired so much. "I mean to ask God about him, just like I see Miss Alice do," she continued, and stealing to the opposite side of the room, Muggins kneeled down, and with her face turned towards Hugh, she said, first, the prayer taught by Alice after an immense amount of labor and patience, after which she continued, "If God is hearin' me, will he please do all dat Miss Alice ax him 'bout curin' Mas'r Hugh, only not take him to heaven as she say, and scuse Mug, who is nothin' but poor little lazy nigger, all-us round under foot."

This was too much for Hugh. The sight of that ignorant negro child, kneeling by the window, with her hands clasped supplicatingly together, as she prayed for him in imitation of the Golden Haired, unmanned him entirely, and hiding his head beneath the sheets, he sobbed aloud. With a nervous start, Mug arose from her knees, and coming towards him, stood for an instant gazing in mute terror at the trembling of the bed-clothes which hid her master from sight.

"I'll bet he's in a fit. I mean to screech for Miss Alice," and Muggins was about darting away, when Hugh's long arm caught and held her fast. "Oh, de gracious, Mas'r Hugh," she cried, "you skeers me so. Does you know me, Mas'r Hugh?" and somewhat relieved by the expression of his face, she took a step towards him.

"Yes, I know you, and I want to talk a little. Where am I, Mug? What room, I mean?"

"Why, Miss Alice's in course. She 'sisted, and 'sisted till 'em brung you in here, 'case she say it cool and nice. Oh, Miss Alice so fine."

"In Miss Johnson's room," and Hugh looked perfectly bewildered, while Mug explained how Miss Alice "had prayed for Mas'r Hugh, and cried for Mas'r Hugh, and she didn't know but she had actually kissed Mas'r Hugh; any way, she got mighty clus to him sometimes. "Where is she now?" Hugh asked, and Mug replied, "Eatin her dinner, she watched las' night and bimeby she's gwine to lie down. I hearn her say so, an' old Miss comin' to set long of you!"

Hugh felt a pang of disappointment that he should not probably see Alice that afternoon. But she needed sleep, he knew, and he was mentally chiding himself for his selfishness, when his mother stepped into the room. She looked so pale and thin that Hugh involuntarily groaned as he thought how she had grown weary and worn for him who had sometimes accused her of indifference. The groan caught Mrs. Worthington's ear, and bending over him she said,

"What is it, Hugh?" "Are you worse? Do you want anything?"

"No, I'm better—the cobwebs are gone. I am myself again—dear, darling mother," and Hugh stretched his hands towards her.

"Oh, my boy, I am so glad, so glad! God is good to give you back, when I've never served Him all my life, but I'm trying to now. Oh, Hugh, my heart is so full," and Mrs. Worthington's tears dropped fast, as like a weary child, which wanted to be soothed, she laid her head upon his bosom, crying quietly.

And Hugh, stronger now than she, held the poor, tired head there, and kissed the white forehead, where there were more wrinkles than when he last observed it.

Folding his weak arms about her, mother and son wept together in that moment of perfect understanding and union with each other. Hugh was the first to rally. It seemed so pleasant to lean on him, to know that he cared so much for her, that Mrs. Worthington would gladly have rested on his bosom longer, but Hugh who noticed that she held an open letter in her hand brought her back to something of the old, sad life, by asking.

"If the letter were from 'Lina?"

"Yes, and I can't make it all out you know she writes so blind."

"It never troubles me, and I feel perfectly able to read it," Hugh said, and taking the letter from her unresisting hand, he asked that another pillow should be placed beneath his head, while he read it aloud.

The pillow was arranged, and then Mrs. Worthington sat down upon the bed to hear the letter, which read as follows:

"Fifth Avenue Hotel, New York,

"October, 1860:

"Dear Mother,—

"What a little eternity it is since I heard from you, and how am I to know that you are not all dead and buried. Were it not that no news is good news, I should sometimes fancy that Hugh was worse, and feel terribly for not having gone home when you did. But of course if he were worse, you would write, and so I settle down upon that, and quiet my troublesome conscience.

"Now, then, to business, I want Hugh to send me some money, or all is lost. Let me explain.

"Here I am at Fifth Avenue Hotel, as good as any lady, if my purse is almost empty. Plague on it, why didn't that Mrs. Johnson send me two thousand instead of one? It would not hurt her, and then I should get through nicely."

"You see that thousand is almost gone and as board is two and a half dollars per day, I can't stay long and shop in Broadway with old Mrs. Richards as I am expected to do in my capacity of heiress. There never was so lucky a hit as that, or anything that took so well, just think—I, Adeline Worthington, *nee* Adeline Murdoch, who used to help wash her own clothes in Elmwood, and who once talked of learning a vulgar trade, and did sew a week for old Aunt Jerusha Tubbs, here am I, metamorphosed into a Kentucky heiress, who can say and do anything she pleases on the strength of being an heiress, and hailing from a State where folks own niggers. I tell you, *Spring Bank, Kentucky*—has done wonders for me in the way of getting me noticed.

"You see I am a pure Southern woman here; nobody but Mrs. Richards knows that I was born, mercy knows where. But for you, she never need have known it either, but you must tell that we had not always lived in Kentucky. Honestly, I was glad when you left.

"But to do Mrs. Richards justice, she never alludes to my birth, and you ought to hear her introduce me to some of her friends, 'Mrs. So and So, Miss Worthington from Spring Bank, Kentucky,' then in an aside, which I am not supposed to hear, she adds, 'A great heiress of a very respectable family. You may have heard of them.' Somehow, this always makes me uncomfortable, as it brings up certain cogitations touching that scamp you were silly enough to marry, thereby giving me to the world, which my delectable brother no doubt thinks would have been better off without me. But to proceed—

"We left Saratoga a week ago—old lady Richards wanted to go to Terrace Hill awhile and show me to Anna who it seems is a kind of family oracle. If she approve *Johnny's* choice, it is all right."

"Who is *Johnny*?" Hugh asked, his face a purplish hue and contrasting strangely with the ashen one resting on his shoulder.

Mrs. Worthington explained to him what she knew of Dr. Richards, and Hugh went on:

"After counting the little gold eagles in my purse, I said perhaps I'd go for a few days, though I dreaded it terribly, for the doctor had not yet bound himself fast, and I did not know what the result of those three old maid sisters, sitting on me, would be. Old lady was quite happy in prospect of going home, when one day a letter come from Anna. I happened to have a headache, and was lying on madam's bed, when the dinner bell rang. Of course I insisted that madam should go down without me, and of course she went. It was tedious lying there alone, and to pass away the time I just peeped into the letter, feeling amply rewarded by the insight I obtained into the family secrets.

"They are poorer than I supposed, but that does not matter, position is what I want. Anna has an income of her own, and, generous soul that she is, gives it out to her mother. You see there had been some talk of her coming to Saratoga, and in referring to it, said, 'Much as I might enjoy it, I cannot afford to come, I can pay your bills for some time longer, if you really think the water a benefit, but my presence would just double the expense. Then, if brother does marry, I wish to surprise him with a handsome set of pearls for his bride, and I am economizing to do so.' (Note by 'Lina)—Isn't she a clever old soul? Don't she deserve a better sister-in-law than I shall make her, and won't I find the way to her purse often?"

Hugh groaned aloud, and the letter dropped from his hand.

"Mother," he gasped, "it must not be. 'Lina shall not thrust herself upon them. This Anna shall not be so cruelly deceived. I don't care a picayune for the doctor or the old lady. They are much like 'Lina, I reckon, but this Anna awakens my sympathy. I mean to warn her."

"Hugh," and in the mother's voice there was a tone which startled him, "Hugh, let her alone. Let Dr. Richards marry her if he will. You and I shall be——"

The trembling voice faltered, for it could not say "happier without her," but Hugh understood it, and smoothing the soft, thin hair of the head nestling close to him, he replied,

"Yes we should be happier with 'Lina gone, but there's a right and there's a wrong, which is it best to choose?"

"I don't know. Oh, I don't know. The right, I suppose. We'll decide by and by. Read on."

And Hugh did read on, feeling as if he, too were guilty, thus to know what Anna Richards had intended only for her mother's eye.

"'From some words you have dropped, I fancy that Miss Worthington does not suit you in all respects, and you wish me to see her. Dear mother, John marries for himself, not for us, and though I could wish my new sister to be every way congenial, I shall try to like her, even if there are certain little coarse points about her. These may result from education rather than bad blood, and if so, they can easily be rubbed off. If she is bright and observing she will soon learn that slang phrases together with loud talking and laughing, are not lady-like or marks of cultivation. But we must be very cautious not to let her know what we are doing. Extreme kindness and affection must mark every action, and in the end we shall succeed. If John is satisfied and happy, that is all I ask. Asenath and Eudora think you had better persuade her to come home with you for a few days before going to New York and I concur in their wishes. The house will seem dull to her, no doubt, after Saratoga gayeties but we will make it as pleasant as possible.

"'When will you come? Asenath has sent the curtains in the north chamber to the laundress, but will go no farther until we hear for certain that Miss Worthington is to be our guest. Write immediately.

"'Yours, affectionately, Anna.'

"'Remember me to John and Miss W——'

"There then, this is what I read, lying on madam's bed, and it decided my future course. Do you suppose I'm going to Terrace Hill to be watched by that trio of old maids? No, ma'am, not by a ——, I was going to say 'jug full,' but remembered slang phrases just in time. Anna would be delighted with that improvement.

"I am resolved now to win Dr. Richards at all hazards. Only let me keep up the appearance of wealth, and the thing is easily accomplished; but I can't go to Terrace Hill yet, cannot meet this Anna, for, I dread her decision more than all the rest, inasmuch as I know it would have more weight with the doctor.

"But to come back to madam. I was fast asleep when she returned. Had not read Anna's letter, nor anything! You should have seen her face when I told her I had changed my mind, that I could not go to Terrace Hill, that *mamma* (that's you!) did not think it would be proper, inasmuch as I had no claim upon them. You see, I made her believe I had written to you on the subject, receiving a reply that you disapproved of my going, and brother Hugh, too, I quote him a heap, making madam laugh till she cries with repeating his odd speeches, she does so want to see that eccentric Hugh, she says."

Hugh Worthington | 157

Another groan from Mrs. Worthington—something sounding like an oath from Hugh, and he went on:

"I said, brother was afraid it was improper under the circumstances for me to go, afraid lest people should talk; that I preferred going at once to New York. So it was finally decided, to the doctor's relief, I fancied, that we come here, and here we are—hotel just like a beehive, and my room is in the fifth story.

"It is very expensive staying here at two dollars and a half per day, and I want so much to see England's future king. Then, too, I am determined to bring the doctor to terms, and so rid you and Hugh of myself, but to do this, I must have more money, and you must manage some way to get it. Beg, borrow, pawn, or *steal*, any thing to get it at once.

"Your distracted

"Lina."

"P. S. One day later. Rejoice, oh, rejoice! and give ear. The doctor has actually asked the question, and I blushingly referred him to mamma, but he seemed to think this unnecessary, took alarm at once, and pressed the matter until I said yes. Aren't you glad? But one thing is sure—Hugh must sell a nigger to get me a handsome outfit. There's Mug, always under foot, doing no one any good. She'll bring six hundred any day, she's so bright and healthy. Nobody will think of abusing her either, she's so cunning, and thus Hugh can swallow his Abolition principles for once, and bestir himself to find a buyer for Muggins. Lulu he must give me out and out for a waiting-maid. There's no other alternative."

So absorbed were Hugh and his mother, as not to hear the low howl of fear echoing through the hall, as Mug fled in terror from the dreaded new owner to whom Master Hugh was to sell her. Neither did they hear the cat-like tread with which Lulu glided past the door, taking the same direction Mug had gone, namely, to Alice Johnson's room.

Lulu had been sitting by the open window at the end of the hall, and had heard every word of this letter, while Mug, sent by Chloe on some errand to Mrs. Worthington, had reached the threshold in time to hear all that was said about selling her. Instinctively both turned for protection to Alice, but Mug was the first to reach her. Throwing herself upon her knees and hiding her face in Alice's dress she sobbed frantically,

"You buys me, Miss Alice. You give Mas'r Hugh six hundred dollars for me, so't he can get Miss 'Lina's weddin' finery. I'll be good, I will. I'll learn de Lord's prar, ebery word on't; will you, Miss Alice, say?"

In amazement Alice tried to wrest her muslin dress from the child's grasp, asking what she meant.

"I know, I'll tell," and Lulu scarcely less excited, but more capable of restraining herself, advanced into the room, and ere the bewildered Alice could well understand what it all meant, or make more than a feeble attempt to stop her, she had repeated rapidly the entire contents of 'Lina's letter, omitting nothing of any consequence, but, as was quite natural, dwelling longest upon the engagement, as that was the point which particularly concerned herself and Muggins.

Too much amazed at first to speak, Alice sat motionless, then rallying her scattered senses, she said to Lulu,

"I am sorry that you told me this, sorry you knew it to tell. It was wrong in you to listen, and you must not repeat it to any one else. Will you promise?"

Lulu would do anything which Alice asked, and she gave the required promise, then with terror in every lineament of her face she said,

"But, Miss Alice, must I be Miss 'Lina's waiting-maid? Will Master Hugh permit it?"

Alice did not know Hugh as well as we do, and in her heart there was a fear lest for the sake of peace he might be overruled, resolving in her mind that Lulu and Muggins should change owners ere the capricious 'Lina's return, and endeavoring as far as she could to quiet both. It was no easy task, however, to soothe Muggins, and only Alice's direct avowal that if possible she would herself become her purchaser, checked her cries at all, but the moment this was said her sobbing ceased, and Alice was able to question Lulu as to whether it was really Hugh who had read the letter.

Lulu assured her that it was, and feeling that he must be better, Alice dismissed both Lulu and Mug, and then sat down to reflect as to her next best course of action.

Adah must go to Terrace Hill, and if Alice's suspicions were correct the projected marriage would be prevented without further interference, for 'Lina was not bad enough deliberately to take for a husband one who had so cruelly wronged another, and even if she were, *Anna* had power to stop it. Adah must go, and Alice's must be the purse which defrayed all the expense of fitting her up. If ever Alice felt thankful to God for having made her rich in this world's goods, it was that morning when so many calls for money seemed crowding on her at once. Only the previous night she had heard from Col. Tiffton that the day was fixed for the sale of his house, that he had no hope of redeeming it, and that *Nell* had nearly cried herself into a second fever at the thoughts of leaving Mosside. "Then there's *Rocket*," the colonel had said, "Hugh cannot buy him back, and he's so bound up in him too, poor Hugh," and with quivering lip the colonel had wrung Alice's hand, hurrying off ere she had time to suggest what all along had been in her mind.

"It does not matter," she thought. "A surprise will be quite as pleasant, and then Mr. Liston may object to it as a silly girl's fancy."

This was the previous night, and now this morning another demand had come in the shape of Muggins weeping in her lap, and Lulu begging to be saved from 'Lina Worthington.

Meantime in the sick room there was a consultation between mother and son, touching the money for which 'Lina had asked, and which Hugh declined sending to her. She had shown herself too heartless for any thing, he said, and were it not for *Anna*, who was too good to be so terribly duped, he should be glad when that Dr. took her off his hands; then he spoke of Alice asking many questions concerning her, and at last expressing a wish to see, and talk with her. This wish Mrs. Worthington at once communicated to Alice, who rather reluctantly went to his room, feeling that it was to all intents and purposes her first meeting with Hugh.

"This is Miss Johnson," Mrs. Worthington said, as Alice drew near, a bright flush spreading over her face as she met Hugh's look, expressive of more than gratitude.

"I fancy I am to a certain degree indebted to Miss Johnson for my life," Hugh said, offering her his hand, while he thanked her for her kindness to him during the long weeks of his illness.

"I was not wholly unconscious of your presence," he continued, still holding her hand. "There were moments when I had a vague idea of somebody different from those I have always known bending over me, and I fancied, too, that this somebody was sent to save me from some great evil. I am glad you were here, Miss Johnson; I shall not forget your kindness."

He dropped her hand then, while Alice attempted to stammer out some reply.

"Adah, too, had been kind," she said, "quite as kind as herself."

"Yes, Adah is a dear, good girl," Hugh replied. "She is to me all a sister could be. Do you like Adah?"

"Yes, very much."

"I'm glad, for she is worthy of your love. She has been terribly wronged, sometime she may tell you."

"She has told me," Alice replied, while Hugh continued, "I am sure you will respect her just the same."

Alice had not intended to talk with him of Adah then, but he had introduced the subject and so she said to him,

"I had thought to tell you of a plan which Mrs. Hastings has in view, but perhaps, I had better wait till you are stronger."

"I am strong enough now—stronger than you think. Tell me of the plan," and Hugh urged the request until Alice told him of Terrace Hill and Adah's wish to go there.

For a few minutes Hugh lay perfectly still. Once he would have spurned the idea, for Spring Bank would be so lonely without Adah and the little boy, but Alice was there now; Alice was worth a dozen Adahs, and so he said at last, "I have heard of the Richards family before. You know the Dr. I believe. Do you like him? Is he a man to be trusted?"

"Yes, I know Dr. Richards," Alice replied, half resolving to tell Hugh all she feared, but feeling that possibly she might be wrong in her suspicions, she concluded not to do so, Adah's presence at Terrace Hill would settle that matter, and she asked again if he did not think it well for her to go.

"Yes, on some accounts," Hugh answered, thinking of 'Lina. "But it looks too much like sending her out alone into the world. Does she wish to go? Is she anxious? Call her please. I would hear from her what she has to say."

Adah came at once, advancing so many reasons why she should go that Hugh consented at last, and it was finally settled that she should leave as soon as the necessary additions could be made to her own and Willie's wardrobe.

This being arranged, Alice and Adah withdrew, and Hugh was left alone to think over the incidents of his interview with Alice. He had not expected her to recognize him by his name, because she had not learned it when on board the steamer, neither did he really expect her to recognize his features, for he knew he had changed materially since that time, still he was conscious of a feeling of disappointment that she did not remember him, and once he thought to tell her who he was, but he would rather she should find that out herself; and while wondering what she would do and say when it did come to her knowledge that he was the lad who tried to save her life, he fell away to sleep.

Three weeks later there came another letter from 'Lina, and with his mother sitting beside him, Hugh read it aloud, learning "that Irving Stanley's widowed sister, Mrs. Carrie Ellsworth, was in New York and had come to the hotel with her brother, that having an object in view 'Lina had done her best to *cultivate* Mrs. Ellsworth, presuming a great deal on their relationship, and making herself so agreeable to her child, a most ugly piece of deformity, that *cousin Carrie*, who had hired a furnished house for the winter, had invited her to spend the season with her, and she was now snugly ensconced in most delightful quarters on Twenty-second street, between Fifth and Sixth avenues. Sometimes," she wrote, "I half suspect Mrs. Ellsworth did not think I would jump at her invitation so quick, but I don't care. The doctor, for some reason or other, has deferred our marriage until spring, and dear knows I am not coming to Spring Bank any sooner than I can help. The doctor, of course, would insist upon accompanying me, and that would explode my bubble at once. When I am ready to return, Hugh must do the brotherly, and come for me, so that the first inkling the doctor gets of Spring Bank will be when he comes to have tied the nuptial knot. I'm half sorry to think how disappointed he will be, for I begin to like him, and mean to make up in goodness what I lack in gold.

"By the way, Adah must *not* go to Terrace Hill as you wrote she thought of doing. You are crazy to think of it, of course they would quiz her to death about me and Spring Bank. So tie her up, or throttle her, or do some thing if she persists in going.

"I shall buy my bridal trousseau under Mrs. Ellsworth's supervision. She has exquisite taste, and Hugh must send the money. As I told him before, he can sell Mug. Harney will buy her. He likes pretty darkies."

"Oh, horror! can Ad be a woman, with womanly feelings!" Hugh exclaimed, as he deliberately tore the letter in fragments, and scattered them over the floor, feeling for a moment as if he hated his sister.

But he struggled hard to cast the bitterness away, and after a moment was able to listen and answer calmly, while his mother asked if it would not be better to persuade Adah not to go to Terrace Hill.

"It may interfere with 'Lina's plans," she said, "and now it's gone so far, it seems a pity to have it broken up. I know it is not right to deceive him so, but—but—I don't know what. It's—it's very pleasant with 'Lina gone," and with a choking sob, Mrs. Worthington laid her face upon the pillow, ashamed and sorry that the real sentiments of her heart were thus laid bare.

It was terrible for a mother to feel that her home would be happier for the absence of an only daughter, but she did feel so, and it made her half willing that Dr. Richards should be deceived. But Hugh shrank from the dishonorable proceeding. He would not interfere himself, but if Adah could be the agent through whose instrumentality the fraud was prevented, he would be glad, and he answered decidedly that "She must go."

Mrs. Worthington always yielded to Hugh, and she did so now, mentally resolving, however, to say a few words to Adah, relative to her not divulging anything which could possibly harm 'Lina, such as telling how poor they were, or anything like that. This done, Mrs. Worthington felt easier, and as Hugh looked tired and worried, she left him for a time, having first called Muggins to gather up the fragments of 'Lina's letter which Hugh had thrown upon the carpet.

"Yes, burn every trace of it," Hugh said, watching the child as she picked up piece by piece, and threw them into the grate.

"I means to save dat ar. I'll play I has a letter for Miss Alice," Mug thought, as she came upon a bit larger than the others, and when she left the room there was hidden in her bosom that part of 'Lina's letter relating to herself and Harney.

CHAPTER XXIII
THE SALE

Col. Tiffton could not pay the $10,000 note which he had foolishly endorsed, and as Harney knew no mercy where his interest was concerned. Mosside must be sold; and the day of the sale had come. There was a crowd of people out and they waited anxiously for the shrill voice and hammer of the auctioneer, a portly little man, who felt more for the family than his appearance would indicate.

There had been a long talk that morning between him self and a young lady, whose beauty had thrilled his heart just as it did every heart beating beneath a male's attire. The lady had seemed a little nervous, as she talked, casting anxious glances up the Lexington turnpike, and asking several times when the Lexington cars were due.

"It shan't make no difference. I'll take your word," the auctioneer had said in reply to some doubts expressed by her. "I'd trust your face for a million," and with a profound bow by way of emphasising his compliment, the well meaning Skinner went out to the group assembled in the yard, while the lady returned to the upper chamber where Mrs. Tiffton and Ellen were weeping bitterly and refusing to be comforted.

From Ellen's chamber a small glass door opened out upon an open balcony, where the Colonel sat leaning on his cane, and watching the movements in the yard below. To this balcony, and the glass door communicating with it, many eyes were directed, for it was known the family were in that vicinity, and it was also whispered that Miss Johnson, the beautiful young lady from Spring Bank was there, and great was the anxiety of some for a sight of her. But neither Ellen nor Alice were visible for the first hour, and only the white-haired colonel kept watch while one after another of his household goods were sold.

The crowd grew weary at last—they must have brisker sport, if they would keep warm in that chilly November wind, and cries for the "horses" were heard.

"Your crack ones, too. I'm tired of this," growled Harney, and Ellen's riding pony was led out, the one she loved and petted almost as much as Hugh had petted Rocket. The Colonel saw the playful animal, and with a moan tottered to Ellen's chamber, saying,

"They are going to sell Beauty, Nell. Poor Nellie, don't cry," and the old man laid his hand on his weeping daughter's head.

"Colonel Tiffton, this way please," and Alice spoke in a whisper. "I want Beauty, and I expected—I thought—" here she glanced again up the turnpike, but seeing no one continued, "Couldn't you bid for me, bid all you would be willing to give if you were bidding for Ellen?"

The colonel looked at her in a kind of dazed, bewildered way, as if not fully comprehending her, till she repeated her request; then mechanically he went back to his post on the balcony, and just as Harney's last bid was about to receive the final *gone*, he raised it twenty dollars and ere Harney had time to recover his astonishment, Beauty was disposed of, and the Colonel's servant Ham led her in triumph back to the stable.

With a fierce scowl of defiance Harney called for Rocket. He had not forgotten that knock-down months before, when Hugh resented the insult offered to Adah Hastings. He had hated him ever since—had sworn to have revenge, and as one mode of taking it, he would secure Rocket at all hazards. Even that morning as he rode past Spring Bank, he had thought with a fiendish exultation, how he would seek the opportunity to provoke to restlessness and then cowhide Rocket in Hugh's presence as a means of repaying the knock-down! And this was the savage, who, with eager, expectant look upon his visage, stood waiting for Rocket.

Suspecting something wrong the animal refused to come out, and planting his fore feet firmly upon the floor of his stable, kept them all at bay. With a fierce oath, the brutal Harney gave him a stinging blow, which made the tender flesh quiver with pain, but the fiery gleam in the animal's eye warned him not to repeat it. Suddenly among the excited group of dusky faces he spied that of *Claib*, and bade him lead out the horse.

"I can't. Oh, mars'r, for the dear — —" Claib began, but Harney's riding whip silenced him and he went submissively in to Rocket, who became as gentle beneath his touch as a lamb.

Loud were the cries of admiration which hailed his appearance; and Alice would have known that something important was pending without the colonel's groan,

"Oh, Rocket! Poor Hugh! It hurts me for the boy more than anything else!"

With one last despairing glance up the still lonely 'pike Alice hurried to the door, and looked out upon the eager throng. Gathered in a knot around Rocket were all the noted horse-dealers of the country, and conspicuous among them was Harney, his face wearing a most disagreeable expression, as in reply to some remark of one of his companions he said, by way of depreciating Rocket, and thus preventing bids.

"Yes, quite a fancy piece, but ain't worth a row of pins. Been fed with sugar plums too much. Why, it will take all the gads in Kentucky to break him in."

The bids were very rapid, for Rocket was popular, but Harney bided his time, standing silently by, with a look on his face of cool contempt for those who presumed to think they could be the fortunate ones. He was prepared to give more than any one else. Nobody would go above his figure, he had set it so high—higher even than Rocket was really worth. Five hundred and fifty, if necessary. No one would rise above that, Harney was sure, and he quietly waited until the bids were far between, and the auctioneer still dwelling upon the last, seemed waiting expectantly for something.

"I believe my soul the fellow knows I mean to have that horse," thought Harney, and with an air which said, "that settles it," he called out in loud, clear tones, "Four Hundred," thus adding fifty at one bid.

There was a slight movement then in the upper balcony, an opening of the glass door, and a suppressed whisper ran through the crowd, as *Alice* came out and stood by the colonel's side.

The bidding went on briskly now, each bidder raising a few dollars, till $450 were reached, and then there came a pause, broken at last by a silvery half-tremulous voice, which passed like an electric shock through the eager crowd, and roused Harney to a perfect fury.

"Five Hundred."

There was no mistaking the words, and with a muttered curse Harney yelled out his price, all he had meant to give. Again that girlish voice was heard, this time clear and decisive as it added ten to Harney's five hundred and fifty. Harney knew now who it was that bid against him, for, following the eyes of those around him, he saw her where she stood, her long curls blowing about her fair, flushed face, one little hand resting on the colonel's shoulder, the other holding together Ellen Tiffton's crimson scarf, which she had thrown over her black dress to shield her from the cold. There was nothing immodest or unmaidenly in her position, and no one felt that there was. Profound respect and admiration were the only feelings she elicited from the spectators, unless we except the villain Harney, and even he stood gazing at her for a moment, struck with her marvellous beauty, and the look of quiet resolution upon her childish face. Had Alice been told six months before that she would one day mingle conspicuously in a Kentucky horse-sale as the competitor of such a man as Harney, she would have scoffed at the idea, and even now she had no distinct consciousness of what she was doing.

Up to the latest possible moment she had watched the distant highway, and when there was no longer hope, had stolen to the colonel's side, and whispered in his ear what he must say.

"It will not do for me," he replied. "Say it yourself. There's no impropriety," and, almost ere she was aware of it, Alice's voice joined itself with the din which ceased as her distinct "Five Hundred" came ringing through the air.

Harney was mad with rage for he knew well for whom that fair Northern girl was interested. He had heard that she was rich—how rich he did not know—but fancied she might possibly be worth a few paltry thousands, and so, of course she was not prepared to compete with him, who counted his gold by hundreds of thousands. Five hundred was all she would give for Rocket. How, then, was he surprised and chagrined when, with a coolness equal to his own, she kept steadily on, scarcely allowing the auctioneer to repeat his bid before she increased it and once, womanlike, raising on her own.

"Fie, Harney! Shame to go against a girl! Better give it up, for don't you see she's resolved to have him? She's worth half Massachusetts, too, they say."

These and like expressions met Harney on every side until at last, as he paused to answer some of them, growing heated in the altercation, and for the instant forgetting Rocket, the auctioneer brought the hammer down with a click which made Harney leap from the ground, for by that sound he knew that Rocket was sold to Alice Johnson for six hundred dollars! There was a horrid oath, a fierce scowl at Alice passing from his view, and then, with the muttered sneer, "I wonder if she intends to buy the farm and niggers?" Harney tried to hide his discomfiture by saying, "he was glad on the whole, for he did not really want the horse, and had only bidden from spite!"

Meantime Alice had sought the friendly shelter of Ellen's room, where the tension of nerve endured so long gave way, and sinking upon the sofa she fainted just as down the Lexington turnpike came the man looked for so long in the earlier part of the day. Alice had written to Mr. Liston a few weeks previous to the sale, and indulgent almost to a fault to his beautiful ward, he had replied that he would surely be at Mosside in time.

He had kept his word, and it was his familiar voice which brought Alice back to consciousness; and pressing his hand, she told him what she had done, and asked if it were unmaidenly. She could not err, in Mr. Liston's estimation, and with his assurance that all was right, Alice grew calm, and in a hurried consultation explained to him more definitely than her letter had done, what her wishes were—Colonel Tiffton must not be homeless in his old age. There were 10,000 dollars lying in the — — Bank in Massachusetts, and she would have Mosside purchased in her name for Colonel Tiffton, not as a gift, for he would not accept it, but as a loan, to be paid at his convenience. This was Alice's plan, and Mr. Liston acted upon it at once. Taking his place in the motley assemblage, he bid quietly, steadily, until the whisper ran round, "Who is that man in that butternut-colored coat?"

None knew who he was though all came to the conclusion that Harney's hope of securing Mosside was as futile as had been his hope of getting Rocket. There were others disappointed, too—the fair matrons who coveted Mrs. Tiffton's carpets, mirrors, and cut-glass, all of which passed to the stranger. When it came to the negroes he winced a little, wondering what his abolition friends would say to see him bidding off his own flesh and blood, but the end answered the means, he thought, and so he kept on until at last Mosside, with its appurtenances, belonged ostensibly to him, and the half glad, half disappointed people wondered greatly who *Mr. Jacob Liston* could be, or from what quarter of the globe he had suddenly dropped into their midst.

Col. Tiffton knew that nearly every thing had been purchased by him, and felt glad that a stranger rather than a neighbor was to occupy what had been so dear to him, and that his servants would not be separated. With Ellen it was different. A neighbor might allow them to remain there a time, she said, while a stranger would not, and she was weeping bitterly, when, as the sound of voices and the tread of feet gradually died away from the yard below, Alice came to her side, and bending over her said softly, "Could you bear some good news now;—bear to know who is to inhabit Mosside?"

"Good news?" and Ellen looked up wonderingly.

"Yes, good news, I think you will call it," and then as delicately as possible Alice told what had been done, and that the colonel was still to occupy his old home. "As my tenant, if you like," she said to him, when he began to demur. "You will not find me a hard landlady," and with playful raillery she succeeded in bringing a smile to his face, where tears also were visible.

When at last it was clear to the old man, he laid his hand upon the head of the young girl and whispered huskily, "I cannot thank you as I would, or tell you what's in my heart. God bless you, Alice Johnson. I wish I too, had found him early as you have, for I know it's He that put this into your mind. God bless you, God bless my child."

CHAPTER XXIV
THE RIDE

That night after her return from Mosside, Alice had playfully remarked to Hugh, "The Doctor says you stay too closely in the house. You need more exercise, and to-morrow I am going to coax you to ride with me, I am getting quite proud of my horsemanship, and want your opinion, I shall not take an excuse. You are mine for a part of to-morrow," she added, as she saw him about to speak, and casting upon him her most bewildering smile, he hastily quitted the room, but not until she heard his muttered sigh and guessed that he was thinking of Rocket. He had not asked a question concerning Mosside, and only knew that a stranger had bought it with all its appurtenances. Rocket he had not mentioned, though his pet was really uppermost in his mind, and when he woke next morning from his feverish sleep and remembered Alice's proposal to ride, he said to himself, "I cannot go, much as I might enjoy it. No other horse would carry me as gently as Rocket. Oh, Rocket!"

This was always the despairing cry with which Hugh ended his cogitation of Rocket, and he said it now bitterly, without the shadow of a hope.

It was a bright, balmy morning, unlike the chilly one of the previous day, and Hugh, as he walked slowly to the window and inhaled the fragrant air, felt that it would do him good. "But I shan't go," he said, and when, after breakfast was over, Alice came, reminding him of the ride, telling him she was going then to get herself in readiness, and should expect to find him waiting when she came back, he began an excuse, but his resolution quickly gave way before her sprightly arguments, and he finally assented, saying, however, by way of apology, "You must not expect a gay cavalier, for I am still too weak, and I have no horse fit to ride."

"Yes, I know," and Alice ran gaily to her room and donned her riding dress, while not less eager than herself, Mrs. Worthington, Aunt Eunice, and Adah stood by, wondering what Hugh would say and how Rocket would act.

He was out in the back yard now, pawing and curvetting, and rubbing his nose against all who came near him, while Claib, never so happy in his life, was holding him by his bridle and talking to him of Mars'r Hugh, which name the animal was supposed to recognize.

"There, I'm ready," Alice said, running down to Hugh, who was so pale, that but for the surprise in store for him, Alice's kind heart would at once have prompted he do give up the project.

With a sigh Hugh rose and followed her to the door where Dido, held by Lulu, stood waiting for them.

"Where's Jim?" Hugh asked, glancing round in quest of the huge animal he expected to mount.

"Claib has your horse. He's coming," and with great apparent unconcern Alice worked industriously at one of her gauntlets, which obstinately refused to be buttoned, while the entire household including Mr. Liston, who had come to Spring Bank with Alice, congregated upon the piazza, waiting anxiously for Rocket.

Suddenly Adah flew to Hugh's side, and said, eagerly, "Hugh, please whistle as you used to do for Rocket—just once, and let Miss Johnson hear you."

Hugh felt as if she were mocking him, and answered no, but when Alice added her entreaties to Adah's, and even laid her hand coaxingly on his arm, he yielded, while like a gleam of lightning the shadow of a suspicion flitted across his mind. It was a loud, shrill whistle, penetrating even to the woods, and as it had never yet failed of its object, so it did not now, for the instant the old familiar sound fell on Rocket's ear he started as if a shell had exploded beneath his feet, and breaking away from Claib went tearing round the house, answering that call with the neigh he had been wont to give when summoned by his master. Utterly speechless Hugh stood gazing at him as he came up, his neck arched proudly, and his silken mane flowing as gracefully as on the day when he was led away to Col. Tiffton's stall.

"Mother, what does it mean—oh, mother!" and leaning himself against the pillar of the piazza for support, Hugh turned to his mother for an explanation, but she did not heed him, so intent was she in watching Rocket, who had reached his master, and seemed to be regarding him in some perplexity, as if puzzled at his changed appearance.

Possibly pity is an emotion unknown to the brute creation, but surely if pity can be felt by them, it was expressed by Rocket, as he stood eyeing his pale, wasted young master; then, with a low cry of joy, he lifted his head to Hugh's face, and rubbed against it, trying in various ways to evince his delight at seeing him again.

"Won't anybody tell me what it means?" Hugh gasped, stretching out his hands towards Rocket, who even attempted to lick them.

At this point Alice stepped forward, and taking Rocket's bridle, laid it across Hugh's lap, saying, softly —

"It means that Rocket is yours, purchased by a friend, saved from Harney, for you. Mount him, and see if he rides as easily as ever. I am impatient to be off."

But had Hugh's life depended upon it, he could not have mounted Rocket then. He knew the friend was Alice, and the magnitude of the act overpowered him.

"Oh, Miss Johnson," he cried, "what made you do it? It must not be. I cannot suffer it."

"Not to please me?" and Alice's face wore its most winning look. "It's been my fixed determination ever since I heard of Rocket, and knew how much you loved him. I was never so happy doing an act in my life, and you must not spoil it all by refusing. Mr. Liston knew and approved of my doing it," and she turned to her guardian, who advanced towards Hugh, and in a few low-spoken words told him how Alice's heart had been set upon redeeming Rocket, and how hurt she would be if Hugh did not accept him.

"As a loan then, not as a gift," Hugh whispered. "It shall not be a gift."

"It need not," Alice rejoined, "You shall pay for Rocket if you like, and I'll tell you how on our ride. Shall we go?"

There was no longer an excuse for lingering, and with Claib's help Hugh was once more seated in his saddle while Rocket's whole frame quivered with apparent joy at bearing his young master again. They made a splendid looking couple on horseback, and the family watched them admiringly until Hugh, feeling stronger with every breath he drew, struck into a gentle canter, and the hill hid them from view.

Once out upon the highway where there were no mud holes to shun, no gates to open and shut, Hugh broached the subject of Rocket again, when

Alice told him unhesitatingly how he could, if he would, pay for him and leave her greatly his debtor. The scrap of paper, which Muggins had saved from the letter thrown by Hugh upon the carpet, had been placed by the queer little child in an old envelope, which she called her letter to Miss Alice. Handing it to her with the utmost gravity she had asked her to read "Mug's letter," and Alice had read the brief lines written by 'Lina, "Hugh must send the money, as I told him before. He can sell Mug, Harney likes pretty darkies." There was a cold, sick feeling at Alice's heart, a shrinking with horror from 'Lina Worthington, and then she came to a decision. Mug should be hers, and so, as skillfully as she could she brought it round, that having taken a great fancy both to Lulu and Muggins, she wished to buy them both, giving whatever Hugh honestly thought they were worth. Rocket, if he pleased, should be taken as part or whole payment for Mug, and so cease to be a gift.

Hugh was confounded. Could Alice know what 'Lina had written? It did not seem possible, and yet she had laid her hand upon the very dilemma which was troubling him so much. If *Ad* should marry that doctor, she would want money as she had said, and money Hugh could not get unless he sold his negroes. He had said he never would part with them; but selling them to Alice was virtually setting them at liberty, and Hugh felt his own heart throb as he thought of Mug's delight when told that she was free. A slave master can love his bond servant, and Hugh loved the little Mug so much that the idea of parting with her as he surely must at some future time if he assented to Alice's plan, made him hesitate, and Alice's best arguments were called into requisition ere he came to a decision. But he decided at last, influenced not so much by need of money as by knowing how much real good the exchange of ownership would do to the two young girls. In return for Rocket Alice should have Muggins, while for Lulu she might give what she liked. Seven hundred, he had been offered, but he would take less.

"Heaven knows," he added, as he saw by the expression of Alice's face how distasteful to her was the whole idea of bargaining for human flesh and blood, "Heaven knows it is not my nature to hold any one in bondage, and I shall gladly hail the day which sees the negro free. But I cannot now help myself more than others around me. Our slaves are our property. Take them from us and we are ruined wholly. Miss Johnson, do you honestly believe that one in forty of those northern abolitionists would deliberately give up ten—twenty—fifty thousand dollars as the case might be, just because the thing valued at that was man and not beast? No, indeed. It's very easy for them to tell what must be done, but hard finding one to do it. Southern people, born and brought up in the midst of slavery can't see it as the North do, and there's where the mischief lies. Neither understands the other, and I greatly fear the day is not far distant when our fair Union shall be torn in tatters by enraged and furious brothers."

He had wandered from Lulu and Muggins to the subject which then, far more than the North believed, was agitating the Southern mind, but Alice, more interested in her purchases than in Secession, of which she had no fears, brought him back to the point, by suggesting that the necessary papers be made out at once, so there could be no mistake.

They had ridden far enough by this time, for Hugh was beginning to look tired, and so they turned their horses homeward, talking pleasantly of whatever presented itself to Alice's mind. Once as Hugh gave her a look which had often puzzled and mystified her, she said, "Do you know it seems to me I must have seen you before I came to Kentucky, for at times there is something very familiar in your face."

For a moment Hugh was tempted to tell her where they had met before, but feeling that he was not quite ready yet to do so, he refrained, and making her some evasive reply, relapsed into a thoughtful mood which continued until Spring Bank was reached.

CHAPTER XXV
HUGH AND ALICE

Three weeks had passed away since that memorable ride. Mr. Liston after paying to the proper recipients the money due for Mosside, had returned to Boston, leaving the neighborhood to gossip of Alice's generosity, and to wonder how much she was worth. It was a secret yet that Lulu and Muggins were hers, but the story of Rocket was known, and numerous were the surmises as to what would be the result of her familiar intercourse with Hugh. Already was the effect of her presence visible in his gentleness of manner, his care to observe all the little points of etiquette never practiced by him before, and his attention to his own personal appearance. His trousers were no longer worn inside his boots, or his soft hat jammed into every conceivable shape, while Ellen Tiffton, who came often to Spring Bank, and was supposed to be good authority, pronounced him almost as stylish looking as any man in Woodford.

It is strange how much dress and a little care as to its adjustment can do for one. It certainly did wonders for Hugh, who knew how much he was improved, and to whose influence he owed it, just as he knew of the mighty love he bore this gentle girl, working so great a good at Spring Bank.

To Hugh, Alice was every thing, and sometimes the thought crossed his mind that possibly he might win her for himself, but it was repudiated as soon as formed, for it could not be, he said, that one like Alice Johnson should ever care for him; and so, between hope and a kind of blissful despair, Hugh lived on until the evening of the day when Adah left Spring Bank for Terrace Hill. She had intended going immediately after the sale at Mosside, but Willie had been ailing ever since, and that had detained her. But now she was really gone; Hugh had accompanied her to Frankfort, seeing her safely off, and spending the entire day in town, so that it was rather late when he returned to Spring Bank. Being unusually fatigued Mrs. Worthington had already retired and as Alice was not in sight, Hugh sat down alone by the parlor fire.

He was sorry Adah was gone and he missed her sadly, but it was not so much of her he was thinking as of Alice. During the last few days she had puzzled him greatly. Her manner had been unusually kind, her voice unusually soft and low when she addressed him, while several times he had met her eyes fixed upon him with an expression he could not fathom, and which had made his heart beat high as hope whispered of what might perhaps be, in spite of all his fears. Poor Hugh! he never dreamed that Alice's real feelings towards him during those few days were those of pity, as she saw how silent and moody he grew, and attributed it to his grief at parting with Adah. She was of course very dear to him, she supposed, and Alice's kind heart went out toward him with a strong desire to comfort him, to tell him how she, as far as possible, would fill Adah's place. Had she dreamed of his real feelings, she never would have done what she did, but she was wholly unconscious of it, and so when, late that night, she returned to the parlor in quest of something she had left, and found him sitting there alone, she paused a moment on the threshold, wondering if she had better join him or go away. His back was toward her, and he did not hear her light step, so intently was he gazing into the burning grate, and trying to frame the words he should say if ever he dared tell Alice Johnson of his love.

There was much girlish playfulness in Alice's nature, and gliding across the carpet, she clasped both her hands before his eyes, and exclaimed—

"A penny for your thoughts."

Hugh started as suddenly as if some apparition had appeared before him, and blushing guiltily, clasped and held upon his face the little soft, warm hands which did not tremble, but lay still beneath his own. It was Providence which sent her there, he thought; Providence indicating that he might speak, and he would.

"I am glad you have come. I wish to talk with you," he said, drawing her down into a chair beside him, and placing his arm lightly across its back. "What sent you here, Alice? I supposed you had retired," he continued, bending upon her a look which made her slightly uncomfortable.

But she soon recovered, and answered laughingly—

"I came for my scissors, and finding you here alone, thought I would startle you, but you have not told me yet of what you were thinking."

"Of the present, past and future," he replied; then letting his hand drop from the back of the chair upon her shoulder, he continued, "May I talk freely with you? May I tell you of myself, what I was, what I am, what I hope to be?"

His hand upon her shoulder made Alice a little uneasy but he had put it there in such a quiet, matter of course way, that he might think her prudish if she objected. Still her cheeks burned, and her voice was not quite steady, as, rising from her seat, she said,

"I like a stool better than this chair. I'll bring it and sit at your feet. There, now I am ready;" and seating herself at a safe distance from him, Alice waited for him to commence.

But Hugh was in no hurry then; that little act of hers had chilled him somewhat. Perhaps she did not like his arm around her, perhaps she never would, and that was the saddest thought of all. She had never looked to him as she did to-night, sitting there beside him with the firelight falling upon her bright fair hair curling so gracefully about her forehead and neck.

On the high mantel a large mirror was standing, and glancing towards it, Hugh caught the reflection of both their figures, and with his usual depreciation of himself; felt the contrast bitterly. This beautiful young girl could not care for him; it were folly to think of it, and he sat for a moment silent, forgetting that Alice was waiting for him to speak. She grew tired of waiting at last, and turning her eyes upon him, said gently,

"You seem unhappy about something. Is it because Adah has gone? I am sorry, too; but, Hugh, I will do what I can to fill her place. I will be the sister you need so much. Don't look so wretched; it makes me feel badly to see you."

Alice's sympathy was getting the better of her again, and she moved her stool nearer to Hugh, while she involuntarily laid her hand upon his knee. That decided him; and while his heart throbbed almost to bursting, he began by saying,

"I am in rather a gloomy mood to-night, I'll admit. I do feel Adah's leaving us very much; but that is not all. I have wished to talk with you a long time—wished to tell you how I feel. May I, Alice?—may I open to you my whole heart, and show you what is there?"

For a moment Alice felt a thrill of fear—a dread of what the opening of his heart to her might disclose. Then she remembered Golden Hair, whose name she had never heard him breathe, save as it passed his delirious lips. It was of her he would talk; he would tell her of that hidden love whose existence she felt sure was not known at Spring Bank. Alice would rather not have had this confidence, for the deep love-life of such as, Hugh Worthington seemed to her a sacred thing; but he looked so white, so care-worn, so much as if it would be a relief, that Alice answered at last:

Hugh Worthington | 177

"Yes, Hugh, you may tell, and I will listen."

She moved her stool still nearer to him, beginning now to feel anxious herself to hear of one whose very memory had influenced Hugh for good.

So sure was Alice that it was Golden Hair of whom he would talk, that when, by way of a commencement, he said to her, "Can you guess what I would tell you?" she answered involuntarily:

"I guess it is of somebody you have loved, or do love still."

There was no tremor in her voice, no flush in her cheek, no drooping of the long lashes to cover her confusion; and yet deluded Hugh believed she knew his secret, and alas! believed his love reciprocated; else why should she thus encourage him to go on! It was the happiest moment Hugh had ever known, and for a time he could not speak, as he thought how strange it was that a joy so perfect as this should come to be his lot. Poor, poor Hugh!

He began at last by telling Alice of his early boyhood, uncheered by a single word of sympathy save as it came from dear Aunt Eunice, who alone understood the wayward boy whom people thought so bad.

"Then mother and Ad came to Spring Bank, and that opened to me a new era. In my odd way, I loved my mother so much—but *Ad*—say, Alice, is it wicked in me if I can't love Ad?"

"She is your sister," was Alice's reply; and Hugh rejoined:

"Yes—my sister. I'm sorry for it, even if it's wicked to be sorry. I tried to do my best with her—tried to be as gentle as I could; but she did not understand me. She gave me back only scorn and bitter words, until my heart closed up against her, and I harshly judged all others by her—all but one"; and Hugh's voice grew very low and tender in its tone, while Alice felt that now he was nearing the Golden Hair.

"Away off in New England there was a pure white blossom growing, a blossom so pure, so fair, that very few were worthy even so much as to look upon it, as day by day it unfolded some new beauty. There was nothing to support this flower but a single parent stalk, which snapped asunder one day, and Blossom was left alone. It was a strange idea, transplanting it to another soil; for the atmosphere of Spring Bank was not suited to such as she. But she came, and, as by magic, the whole atmosphere was changed—changed at least to one—the bad, wayward Hugh, who dared to love this fair young girl with a love stronger than his life. For her he would do anything, and beneath her influence he did improve rapidly. He was conscious of it himself—conscious of a greater degree of self-respect—a desire to be what she would like to have him.

"She was very, very beautiful; more so than anything Hugh had ever looked upon. Her face was like an angel's face, and her hair—much like yours, Alice;" and he laid his hand on the bright head, now bent down, so that he could not see that face so like an angel's.

The little hand, too, had slidden from his knee, and, fast-locked within the other, was buried in Alice's lap, as she listened with throbbing heart to the story Hugh was telling.

"In all the world there was nothing so dear to Hugh as this young girl. He thought of her by day and dreamed of her by night, seeing always in the darkness her face, with its eyes of blue bending over him—hearing the music of her voice, like the falling of distant water, and even feeling the soft touch of her hands as he fancied them laid upon his brow. She was good, too, as beautiful; and it was this very goodness which won on Hugh so fast, making him pray often that he might be worthy of her—for, Alice, he came at last to dream that he could win her; she was so kind to him—she spoke to him so softly and, by a thousand little acts, endeared herself to him more and more.

"Heaven forgive her if she misled him all this while; but she did not. It were worse than death to think she did—to know I've told her this in vain—have offered her my heart only to have it thrust back upon me as something she does not want. Speak, Alice! in mercy, speak! Can it be that I'm mistaken?"

Something in her manner had wrung out this cry of fear and now, bending over her as she sat with her face buried in her lap he waited for her answer. It had come like a thunderbolt to Alice, that she, and not Golden Hair, was the subject of his story—she the fair blossom growing among the New England hills. She did not guess that they were one and the same, for Hugh would not have her swayed ever so slightly by gratitude.

Alice saw how she had led him on, and her white lips quivered with pain, for, alas! she did not love him as he should be loved, and she could not deceive him, though every fibre of her heart bled and ached for him. Lifting up her head at last she exclaimed,

"You don't mean me, Hugh? Oh, you don't mean me?"

"Yes, darling," and he clasped in his own the hand raised imploringly toward him. "Yes, darling, I mean you. I love you and you must be mine. I shall die without you. You can mould me at your will. You can teach me the narrow way I want to find, Alice, more than you guess. We will walk it hand in hand, yours the stronger one at first, mine the stronger last, when I've been taught by you. Will you, Alice, will you be my wife, my darling, my idol? I know I have no money, just as I know you do not care for that. You will not prize me less for daring to ask you, an heiress, to be mine. I have no money, no position, but I have willing hands and a loving heart, which will answer in their stead. Will you be my wife?"

Alice had never before heard a voice so earnest, so full of meaning, as the one now pleading with her to be what she could not be, and a pang keener than any she had ever felt, or believed it possible for her to feel, shot through her heart as the dread conviction was forced upon her that she was to blame for all this. She had misled him, unwittingly, it is true, but that did not help him now; the harm, the wrong were just the same, and they loomed up before her in all their appalling magnitude. What could she do to atone? Alas! there was nothing except to be what he asked, and that she could not do. She could not be Hugh's wife. She would as soon have married her brother, if she had one. But she must do something, and sliding from her stool she sank upon her knees—her proper attitude—upon her knees before Hugh, whom she had wronged so terribly, and burying her face in Hugh's own hands, she sobbed,

"Oh, Hugh, Hugh, you don't know what you ask. I love you dearly, but only as my brother—believe me, Hugh, only as a brother. I wanted one so much—one of my own, I mean; but God denied that wish, and gave me you instead. I did not like you at first—that is, before I saw you. I was sorry you were here, but I got over that. I pitied first, and then I came to like or love you so much, but only as my brother; and if I let you see that love, it was because it is my nature to caress those whom I love—because I thought you understood that 'twas only as my brother. I cannot be your wife. I—oh, Hugh, forgive me for making you so unhappy. I'm sorry I ever came here, but I cannot go away. I've learned to love my Kentucky home. Let me stay just the same. Let me really be what I thought I was, your sister. You will not send me away?"

She looked up at him now, but quickly turned away, for the expression of his white, haggard face was more than she could bear, and she knew there was a pain, keener than any she had felt, a pang which must be terrible, to crush a strong man as Hugh was crushed.

"Forgive me, Hugh," she said, as he did not speak, but sat gazing at her in a kind of stunned bewilderment. "You would not have me for your wife, if I did not love you?"

"Never, Alice, never!" he answered; "but it is not any easier to bear. I don't know why I asked you, why I dared hope that you could think of me. I might have known you could not. Nobody does. I cannot win their love. I don't know how."

He put her gently from him, and arose to leave the room, but something mastered his will, and brought him back again to where she knelt, her face upon his chair, as she silently prayed to know just what was right. Something she had said about his sending her away rang in his ears, and he felt that the knowing she was gone would be the bitterest dreg in all the bitter cup, so he said to her, entreatingly—

"Alice, I know you cannot be my wife—I do not expect it now, but I want you here all the same. Promise that you will stay, at least until my rival claims you."

Alice neither looked up nor moved, only sobbed piteously, and this more than aught else helped Hugh to choke down his own sorrow for the sake of comforting her. The sight of her distress moved him greatly, for he knew it was grief that she had so cruelly misled him.

"Alice, darling," he said again, this time as a mother would soothe her child. "It hurts me more to see you thus than your refusal did. I am not wholly selfish in my love. I'd rather you should be happy than to be happy myself. I would not for the world take to my bosom an unwilling wife. I should be jealous even of my own caresses, jealous lest the very act disgusted her more and more. You did not mean to deceive me. It was I that deceived myself. I forgive you fully, and ask you to forget that to-night has ever been. It cut me sorely at first, Alice, to hear you tell me so, but I shall get over it; the wound will heal."

He said this falteringly, for the wound bled and throbbed at every pore, but he would comfort her. She should not know how much he suffered. "The wound will heal. Even now I am feeling better, can almost see my way through the darkness."

Poor Hugh! He mentally asked forgiveness for that falsehood told for her. He could *not* see his way through,—his brain was giddy, and his soul sick with that dull dreadful pain which is so hard to be borne, but he could hide his misery, for her sake, and he would.

"Please, don't cry," he said, stooping over her, and lifting her tenderly up. "I shall get over it. A man can bear better than a woman, and even if I should not, I would rather have loved and lost you, than not to have known and loved you at all. The memory of what might have been will keep me from much sin. There, darling, let me wipe the tears away, let me hear you say you are better."

"Oh, Hugh, don't, you break my heart. I'd rather you should scorn or even hate me for the sorrow I have brought. Such unselfish kindness will kill me," Alice sobbed, for never had she been so touched as by this insight into the real character of the man she had refused.

He would not hold her long in his arms, though it were bliss to do so, and putting her gently in the chair, he leaned his own poor sick head upon the mantel, while Alice watched him with streaming eyes and an aching heart which even then half longed to give itself into his keeping. She did not love him with a wife-like love, she knew but she might in time, and she pitied him so much. And Hugh had need for pity. He had tried to quiet her; had said it was no matter, that he should get over it, that he need not care, but the agony it cost him to say all this was visible in every feature, and Alice looked at him with wondering awe as he stood there silently battling with the blow he would not permit to smite him down.

At last it was Alice's turn to speak, hers the task to comfort. The prayer she had inwardly breathed for guidance to act aright had not been unheard, and with a strange calmness she arose, and laying her hand on Hugh's arm, bade him be seated, while she told him what she had to say. He obeyed her, sinking into the offered chair, and then standing before him, she began,

"You do not wish me to go away, you say. I have no desire to go, except it should be better for you. Even though I may not be your wife, I can, perhaps, minister to your happiness; and, Hugh, we will forget to-night, and be to each other what we were before, brother and sister. There must be no particular perceptible change of manner, lest others should suspect what has passed between us. Do you agree to this?"

He bowed his head, and Alice drew a step nearer to him, hesitating a moment ere she continued.

"You speak of a rival. But believe me, Hugh, you have none, there is not a man in the wide world whom I like as much as I do you, and Hugh——" the little hand pressed more closely on Hugh's shoulder, while Alice's breath came heavily, "And, Hugh, it may be, that in time I can conscientiously give you a different answer from what I did to-night. I may love you as your wife should love you; and—and, if I do, I'll tell you so at the proper time."

There was a gleam of sunshine now to illumine the thick darkness, and, in the first moments of his joy Hugh wound his arm around the slight form, and tried to bring it nearer to him. But Alice stepped back and answered,

"No, Hugh, that would be wrong. It may be I shall never come to love you save as I love you now, but I'll try—I will try," and unmindful of her charge to him Alice parted the damp curls clustering around his forehead, and looked into his face with an expression which made his heart bound and throb with the sudden hope, that even now she loved him better than she supposed.

It was growing very late, and the clock in the adjoining room struck one ere Alice bade Hugh good night, saying to him,

"No one must know of this. We'll be just the same to each other as we have been."

"Yes, just the same, if that can be," Hugh answered, and so they parted, Alice to her room, where, in the solitude, she could pray for that guidance without which she was nothing, and Hugh to his, where he, too, prayed, this night with a greater earnestness than ever he had done before—not for Golden Hair to come back, as of old, but that he might be led into the path she trod, and so be worthy of her, should the glad time ever come when she might be his.

Hugh had not yet learned the faith which asks for good, that God shall be glorified rather than our own desires fulfilled; but he who prays, ever so imperfectly, is better for it, because the very act of praying implies a faith in somebody to hear; and so soothed into comparative quiet by the petition offered, Hugh fell into a quiet slumber, and slept on undisturbed until Muggins came to wake him.

CHAPTER XXVI
ADAH'S JOURNEY

The night express from Rochester to Albany was crowded. Every car was full, and the clamorous bell rang out its first summons for all to get on board, just as a frightened-looking woman, bearing in her arms a sleeping boy, stepped upon the platform of the rear carriage, and looked wistfully in at the long, dark line of passengers filling every seat. Wearily, anxiously, she had passed through every car, beginning at the first, her tired eyes scanning each occupant, as if mutely begging some one to have pity on her ere exhausted nature failed entirely, and she sank fainting to the floor. None had heeded that silent appeal, though many had marked the pallor of her girlish face, and the extreme beauty of the baby features nestling in her bosom. She could not hold out much longer, and when she reached the last car and saw that too was full, the chin quivered, and a tear glistened in the long eyelashes, sweeping the colorless cheek.

Slowly she passed up the aisle until she came to where there was a vacant seat, only a gentleman's shawl was piled upon it, and the gentleman looking so unconcernedly from the window, and apparently oblivious of her close proximity to him, would not surely object to her sitting there. How the tired woman did wish he would turn toward her and give some token that she was welcome. But no, his eyes were only intent on the darkness without; he had no care for her, though he knew she was there. He had seen the shrinking figure with its sleeping burden, as it came in, and the selfishness which was so much a part of his whole being, prompted him to cover the seat as far as possible with his long limbs, while leaning his elbow upon the window stool, he seemed absorbed in something outside, peering into the foggy darkness, for it was a rainy winter's night, as persistently as if there were standing before him no half-fainting form, ready to sink down at his feet.

The oil lamp was burning dimly, and the girl's white face was lost in the shadow, when the young man first glanced at her, so he had no suspicion of the truth, though a most undefinable sensation crept over him when he heard the timid footfall, and the rustling of female garments as *Adah Hastings* drew near with her boy in her arms.

He heard its faint breathings, and half turned his head just as Adah passed on, her weary sigh falling distinctly on his ear, but failing to awaken a feeling of remorse for his unmanly conduct.

"I'm glad she's gone. I can't be bothered," was his mental comment as he settled himself more comfortably, feeling a glow of satisfaction when the train began to move, and he knew no more women with their babies would be likely to trouble him.

With that first heavy strain of the machinery Adah lost her balance, and would have fallen headlong but for the friendly hand put forth to save the fall.

"Take my seat, miss. It is not very convenient, but it is better than none. I can find another."

It was the friendliest voice imaginable which said these words to Adah, and the kind tone in which they were uttered wrung the hot tears from her eyes. She did not look up at him. She only knew that a gentleman had risen and was bending over her; that a hand, was laid upon her shoulder, putting her gently into the narrow seat next the saloon; that the same hand took from her and hung above her head the little satchel which was so much in her way, and that the manly voice, so sympathetic in its tone, asked if she would be too warm, so near the fire.

She did not know there was a fire. She only knew that she had found a friend, and with the delicious feeling of safety which the knowledge brought, the tension of her nerves gave way, and burying her head on Willie's face she wept for a moment silently. Then lifting it up she tried to thank her benefactor, looking now at him for the first time, and feeling half overawed to find him so tall, so stylish, so exceedingly refined in every look and action. Why had he cared for her? What was there about her to win attention from such as he? Nothing; his kindness was natural; it sprang from the great warm heart, shining out from the eyes, seen beneath the *glasses* which he wore!

Irving Stanley was a passenger on that train, bound for Albany. Like Dr. Richards, he had hoped to enjoy a whole seat, even though it were not a very comfortable one, but he would not resort to meanness for the sake of his own ease; so when he saw how pale and tired Adah was, he rose at once to offer his seat. He did not then observe her face, or dress, or manner. He only saw she was a delicate woman, travelling alone, and that was enough to elicit his attention. He heard her sweet, low voice as she tried to thank him, and felt intuitively that she was neither coarse nor vulgar. He saw, too, the little, soft, white hands, holding so fast to Willie. Was he her brother or her son? She was young to be his mother; but, there was no mistaking the mother-love shining out from the brown eyes turned so quickly upon the boy when he moaned, as if in pain, and seemed about to waken.

"He's been sick most all the way," she said, holding him closer to her bosom. "There's something the matter with his ear. Do children ever die with the ear-ache?" and the eyes, swimming in tears, sought the face of Irving Stanley as eagerly as if on his decision hung little Willie's life.

Irving Stanley hardly thought they did. At all events he never heard of such a case, and then, after suggesting a remedy, should the pain return, he left his new acquaintance and walked down the car in quest of another seat.

"A part of your seat, sir, if you please," and Irving's voice was rather authoritative than otherwise, as he claimed the half of what the doctor was monopolizing.

It was of no use for Dr. Richards to pretend he was asleep, for Irving spoke so quietly, so like a man who knew what he was doing, that the doctor was compelled to yield, and turning about, recognized his Saratoga acquaintance. The recognition was mutual, and after a few natural remarks, Irving explained how he had given his seat to a lady whose little child was suffering from the ear-ache.

"By the way, doctor," he added, "you ought to know the remedy for such ailments. Suppose you prescribe in case it returns."

"I know but little about babies or their aches" the Dr. answered, just as a scream of pain reached his ear, accompanied by a suppressed effort on the mother's part to soothe her suffering child.

Irving Stanley felt the sneer implied in the doctor's words, and it kept him silent for a time, while scream after scream filled the car, and roused every sleeping occupant to ask what was the matter. Some, and among them the doctor, *cursed* the child thus disturbing their slumbers; some wished it anything but complimentary wishes; some felt and evinced real sympathy, while nearly all glanced backward at the dark corner where the poor mother sat bending over her infant, unmindful of the many curious looks cast upon her. The pain must have been intolerable, for the little fellow, in his agony, writhed from Adah's lap and sank upon the floor, his whole form quivering with anguish as he cried, "Oh, ma! ma! ma ma!"

The hardest heart could scarce withstand that scene and many now gathered near, offering advice and help while even Dr. Richards experienced a most unaccountable sensation as that baby cry smote on his ear. Foremost among those who offered aid was Irving Stanley. His was the voice which breathed comfort to the weeping Adah, his the hand extended to take up little Willie, his the arms which held and soothed the struggling boy, his the mind which thought of everything available that could possibly bring ease, until at last the outcries ceased and Willie lay quietly in his arms.

"I'll take him now," and Adah put out her hands; but Willie refused to go, and clung closer to Mr. Stanley, who said, laughingly, "You see that I am preferred. He is too heavy for you to hold. Please trust him to me, awhile."

And Adah yielded to that voice, and leaning against the window, rested her tired head upon her hand, while Irving carried Willie to his seat beside the doctor. There was a slight sneer on the doctor's face as he saw the little boy, but Irving Stanley he knew was not one whose acts could be questioned by him; so he contented himself with saying, "You must be fond of young ones."

"Fond of children," Irving replied, laying great stress on the word *children*. "Yes, I am, very; and even if I were not, pity would prompt me to take this one from his mother, who is so tired, besides being very pretty, and that you knows goes far with us men.

"You don't like children, I reckon," Irving continued, as the doctor drew back from the little feet which unconsciously touched his lap.

"No, I hate them," was the answer, spoken half savagely, for at that moment a tiny hand was deliberately laid on his, as Willie showed a disposition to be friendly. "I hate them," and the little hand was pushed rudely off.

Wonderingly the soft, large eyes of the child looked up to his. Something in their expression riveted the doctor's gaze as by a spell. There were tears in the baby's eyes, and the pretty lip began to quiver. The doctor's finer feelings, if he had any, were touched, and muttering to himself, "I'm a brute," he slouched his riding cap still lower down upon his forehead, and turning away to the window, relapsed into a gloomy reverie, in which thoughts of *Lily* were strangely mingled with thoughts of the dark-haired 'Lina, his bride elect, waiting for him in New York. The Dr. was more than half tired of his engagement, and ere returning to the city, he was going to Terrace Hill to have a long talk with *Anna*, to tell her frankly of his fears that 'Lina never could be congenial to them, and perhaps he would tell her the *whole* of Lily's story.

But how should he commence a tale which would shock his gentle sister so terribly? He did not know, and while devising the best method, he forgot the two little feet which in their bright-colored hose were stretched out until they rested entirely upon his lap, while the tiny face was nestled against Irving Stanley's fatherly bosom, where it lay for hours, until Adah, waking from her refreshing slumber, came forward to relieve him.

"You had better not go on this morning. You ought to rest," Irving said to Adah, when at last the train stopped in Albany. "I have a few moments to spare. I will see that you are comfortable. You are going to Snowdon, I think you said," and taking Willie in his arms he conducted Adah to the nearest hotel.

There were but a few moments ere he must leave, and standing by her side, he said, "The meeting with you has been to me a pleasant incident, and I shall not soon forget it. I trust we may meet again. There is my card," and he placed it in her hand.

At a glance Adah read the name, knowing now who had befriended her. It was Irving Stanley, second cousin to Hugh, and 'Lina was with his sister in New York. He was going there, he might speak of her, and if she told her name, her miserable story would be known to more than it was already. It was a false pride which kept Adah silent when she knew that Irving Stanley was waiting for her to speak, and while she was struggling to overcome it, Irving's time expired and he must go if he would not be left. Taking her hand he said good-bye, while she tried again to thank him for his great kindness to her; but she did not tell her name, and as Irving would not ask it, he left her without the knowledge, thinking of her often as he went his way to New York, and wondering if they would ever meet again.

In the office below, Dr. Richards, who had purposely stopped for the day in Albany, smoked his expensive cigars, ordered oysters and wine sent to his room—wrote an explanatory note to 'Lina—feeling half tempted to leave out the "Dear," with which he felt constrained to preface it—thought again of Lily—thought once of the strange woman and the little boy, in whom Irving Stanley had been so interested, wondered where they were going, and who it was the boy looked a little like—thought of *Anna* in connection with that boy; and then, late in the afternoon, sauntered down to the Boston depot, and took his seat in the car which, at about 10 o'clock that night, would deposit him at Snowdon. There were no children to disturb him, for Adah, unconscious of his proximity, was in the rear car—weary, and nervous with the dread which her near approach to Terrace Hill inspired. What if, after all, Anna should not want her? And this was a possible contingency, notwithstanding Alice had been so sanguine.

"I can find employment somewhere—God will direct me," she whispered softly, drawing her veil over her tired face, and thinking, she scarcely knew why, of Irving Stanley.

Darkly the December night closed in, and still the train kept on, until at last Danville was reached, and she must alight, as the express did not stop again until it reached Worcester. With a chill sense of loneliness, and a vague, confused wish for the one cheering voice which had greeted her ear since leaving Spring Bank, Adah stood upon the snow-covered platform, holding Willie in her arms, and pointing out her trunk to the civil baggage man, who, in answer to her inquiries as to the best means of reaching Terrace Hill, replied, "You can't go there to-night; it is too late. You'll have to stay in the tavern kept right over the depot, though if you'd kept on the train there might have been a chance, for I see the young Dr. Richards aboard; and as he didn't get out, I guess he's coaxed or hired the conductor to leave him at Snowdon."

The baggage man was right in his conjecture, for the doctor had persuaded the polite conductor, whom he knew personally, to stop the train at Snowdon; and while Adah, shivering with cold, found her way up the narrow stairs into the rather comfortless quarters where she must spend the night, the doctor was kicking the snow from his feet and talking to Jim, the coachman from Terrace Hill.

CHAPTER XXVII
ADAH AT TERRACE HILL

The next morning was cold and frosty, as winter mornings in New England are wont to be, and Adah, shivered involuntarily as from her uncurtained window she looked out upon the bare woods and the frozen fields covered with the snow of yesterday. Oh, how cold and dreary and desolate everything seemed on that December morning; and only Adah's trust in Him who she knew would not forsake her kept her heart from fainting. Even this could not keep back her tears as she watched the coming of the eastern train, and wished that she could take it and go back to Spring Bank. Wistfully she watched the train which paused for a single moment and then sped on its way, just as there came a knock at the door, and the baggage man appeared.

"If you please, ma'am," he began, "the Terrace Hill carriage is here— brung over the doctor, who has took the train for New York. I told the driver how't you wanted to go there. Shall I give him your trunk?"

Adah answered in the affirmative, and then hastened to wrap up Willie. She was ready in a moment and descended to the room where Jim, the driver, stood waiting for her, eyeing her sharply, as if making up his mind with regard to her position.

"A lady," was his mental comment, and with as much politeness as if she had been Madam Richards herself, he opened the carriage door and held Willie while she entered, asking if she were comfortable, and peering a little curiously in Willie's face, which puzzled him somewhat. "A near connection, I guess, and mighty pretty, too. I'm most sorry she's come visiting just now, when old madam and the others is so cross. Them old maids will raise hob with the boy—nice little shaver," thought the kind hearted Jim, as he hurried up his horses, looking back occasionally, and smiling at Willie, who had forgotten the ache of yesterday, and was crowing with delight as the carriage moved swiftly on.

Once, as Adah caught his good-humored eye, she ventured to say to him, "Has Miss Anna procured a waiting-maid yet?"

There was a comical gleam in Jim's eye now, for Adah was not the first applicant he had taken up to Terrace Hill, and it was the memory of madam's reception of them which made him laugh. He never suspected that this was Adah's business, she was so unlike the others, and he answered frankly, "No, that's about played out. They don't come as thick as they did. Madam turned the last one out doors."

"Turned her out doors?" and Adah's face was as white as the snow rifts they were passing.

The driver felt that he had gossiped too much, and relapsed into silence, while Adah, in a paroxysm of terror sat with clasped hands and closed eyes, unmindful of Willie's attempt to make her look at the huge building, just in sight. In her dread of Mrs. Richards she scarcely knew what she was doing, and leaning forward, at last she said, huskily, "Driver, driver, do you think she'll turn me off too?"

"Turn you off!" and in his surprise at the sudden suspicion which for the first time darted across his mind, Jim brought his horses to a full stop, while he held a parley with the pale, frightened creature, asking so eagerly if Mrs. Richards would turn her off. "Why should she? You ain't going there for that, be you?"

"Not to be turned out of doors, no," Adah answered, "but I—I—I want that place so much. I read Miss Anna's advertisement; but please turn back, or let me get out and walk. I can't go there now. Is Miss Anna like the rest?"

Jim had recovered himself a little, and though he could not have been more astonished had Adah proved to be a washerwoman, than he was to find her a waiting-maid, it did not abate his respect for her one whit. She had been a lady sure, and as such he should treat her. She had also appealed to him for sympathy, and he would not withhold it.

"Miss Anna's an angel," he answered. "If you get her ear, you're all right; the plague is to get it with them two she cats ready to tear your eyes out. If I'se you, I'd ask to see her. I wouldn't tell my arrent either, till I did. She's sick up stairs; but I'll see if Pamely can't manage it. That's my woman—Pamely; been mine for four years, and we've had two pair of twins, all dead; so I feel tender towards the little ones," and Jim glanced at Willie, who had succeeded in making Adah notice the house standing out so prominently against the winter sky, and looking to the poor girl more like a prison than a home.

Only one part of it seemed inviting—the two crimson-curtained windows opening upon a verandah, from which a flight of steps led down into what must be a flower-garden.

"Miss Anna's room," the driver said, pointing towards it; and Adah looked out, vainly hoping for a glimpse of the sweet face she had in her mind as Anna's.

But Anna was sick in bed with a headache, induced by the excitement of her brother's visit and the harsh words which passed between him and his sisters, he telling them, jokingly at first, that he was tired of getting married, and half resolved to give it up; while they, in return, abused him for fickleness, taunted him with their poverty, and sharply reproached him for his unwillingness to lighten their burden, by taking a rich wife when he could get one.

All this John had repeated to Anna in the dim twilight of the morning, as he stood by her bedside to bid her good-bye; and she, as usual, had soothed him into quiet, speaking kindly of his bride-elect, and saying she should like her.

He had not told her Lily's story, as he meant to do. There was no necessity for that, for the matter was fixed. 'Lina should be his wife, and he need not trouble Anna further; so he had bidden her adieu, and was gone again, the carriage which bore him away bringing back Adah and her boy.

Jim opened the wide door for her, and ushered her into a little reception room, where the Misses Richards received their morning calls. Drawing a deep arm chair to the fire, Adah sat down before the cheerful blaze, and looked around her with that strange feeling one experiences where everything is new.

Willie seemed perfectly at home, seating himself upon a little stool, covered with some of Miss Eudora's choicest worsted embroidery, a piece of work of which she was very proud, never allowing anything to touch it lest the roses should be jammed, or the raised leaves defaced. But Willie cared neither for leaves not roses, nor yet for Miss Eudora, and drawing the stool to his mother's side, he sat kicking his little heels into a worn place of the carpet, which no child had kicked since the doctor's days of babyhood. The tender threads were fast giving way to the vigorous strokes, when two doors opposite each other opened simultaneously, and both Mrs. Richards and Eudora appeared.

They had heard from Jim that a stranger was there, and as all the cross questionings concerning Adah elicited only the assertion, that "she *was* a lady," both had made a slight change in their toilet ere starting for the room which they reached together, Mrs. Richards taking in at once the fit and material of Adah's traveling dress, deciding that the collar, unbuttoned and shoved back from the throat, was real mink, as were the wristlets on which a pair of small white hands were folded together. She noticed, too, the tiny linen cuffs, with the neat gold buttons which Alice had made Adah wear. Everything was in keeping, and their visitor was a lady. This was her decision, while Eudora noticed only Willie on the bouquet which had cost her so much labor, and the alarming size of that worn spot in the carpet where the little high heeled slipper still was busy. Her first impulse was to seize him by the arm and transfer him to some other locality, but the beauty of his face diverted her attention, and she involuntarily drew a step nearer to the child, fascinated by him, just as her mother was attracted towards Adah.

"Are you—ah, yes—you are the lady who Jim said wished to see me," the latter began, bowing politely to Adah, who had not yet dared to look up, and who when at last she did raise her eyes, withdrew them at once, more abashed, more frightened, more bewildered than ever, for the face she saw fully warranted her ideas of a woman who could turn a waiting-maid from her door just because she was a waiting-maid.

Something seemed choking Adah and preventing her utterance, for she did not speak until Mrs. Richards said again, this time with a little less suavity and a little more hauteur of manner, "Have I had the honor of meeting you before?"—then with a low gasp, a mental petition for help, Adah rose up and lifting to Mrs. Richards' cold, haughty face, her soft, brown eyes, where tears were almost visible, answered faintly, "We have not met before. Excuse me, madam, but my business is with Miss Anna, can I see her please?"

There was something supplicating in the tone with which Adah made this request, and it struck Mrs. Richards unpleasantly, making her answer haughtily, "My daughter is sick. She does not see visitors, but I will take your name and your errand."

Too much confused to remember anything distinctly Adah forgot Jim's injunction; forgot that Pamelia was to arrange it somehow; forgot everything, except that Mrs. Richards was waiting for her to speak. An ominous cough from Eudora decided her, and then her reason for being there came out. She had seen Miss Anna's advertisement, she wanted a place, and she had come so far to get it; had left a happy home that she might not be dependent but earn her bread for herself and her little boy. Would they take her message to Anna? Would they let her stay? and Adah's voice took a tone of wild entreaty as she marked the lowering of madam's brow, and the perceptible change in her manner when she ascertained that, according to her creed, not a lady but a menial stood before her.

"You say you left a happy home," and the thin, sneering lips of Eudora were pressed so tightly together that the words could scarcely find egress. "May I ask, if it was so happy, why you left it?"

There was a flush on Adah's cheek as she replied, "Because it was a home granted at first from charity. It was not mine. The people were poor, and I would not longer be a burden to them."

"And your husband—where is he?"

This was the hardest question of all, and Adah's distress was visible as she replied. "Willie's father left me, and I don't know where he is."

An incredulous, provoking smile flitted over Eudora's face as she returned, "We hardly care to have a deserted wife in our family—it might be unpleasant."

"Yes," and the old lady took up the argument, "Anna is well enough without a maid. I don't know why she put that foolish advertisement in the paper, in answer, I believe, to one equally foolish which she saw about an unfortunate woman with a child."

"I am that woman. I wrote that advertisement when my heart was heavier than it is now, and God took care of it. He pointed it out to Miss Anna. He caused her to answer it. He sent me here, and you will let me see her. Think if it were your own daughter, pleading thus with some one."

"That is impossible. Neither my daughter, nor my daughter-in-law, if I had one, could ever come to a servant's position," Mrs. Richards replied, not harshly, for there was something in Adah's manner which rode down her resentful pride; and she might have yielded, but for Eudora, whose hands had so ached to shake the little child, now innocently picking at a bud.

How she did long to box his ears, and while her mother talked, she had taken a step forward more than once, but stopped as often, held in check by the little face and soft blue eyes turned so trustingly upon her, the pretty lips once actually putting themselves toward her, as if expecting a kiss. Eudora could not harm that child sitting on her embroidery as coolly as if he had a right: but she could prevent her mother from granting the stranger's request; so when she saw signs of yielding, she said, decidedly, "She cannot see Anna, mother. You know how foolish she is, and there's no telling what fancy she might take."

"Eudora," said Mrs. Richards in a low tone, "it might be well for Anna to have a maid, and this one is certainly different from the others who have applied."

"But we can't be bothered with a child. It would drive us crazy."

"Yes, certainly, I did not think of that. A child would be very troublesome," Mrs. Richards rejoined.

"So madam, you see how impossible it is for us to keep you, but you can of course stay till car-time, when Jim will carry you back to the depot."

She said this so decidedly that all hope died out of Adah's heart and she felt as if she were going to faint with the crushing disappointment.

Just then the door bell rang. It was the doctor, come to visit Anna, and both Mrs. Richards and Eudora left the room.

"Oh, why did I come here, and where shall I go?" Adah moaned, as a sense of her lonely condition came over her.

She knew she would be welcome in Kentucky, but Hugh could not afford to have her back, and she had so counted on helping him with her first wages.

"Will my Father in Heaven direct me? will he tell me what to do?" she murmured brokenly, praying softly to herself that a way might be opened for her, a path which she could tread. She could not help herself. All her dependence now was in her God, and in trusting him she found rest at last.

She could not tell how it was, but a quiet peace stole over her, a feeling which had no thought or care for the future, and it had been many nights since she had slept as sweetly or soundly as she did for one-half hour with her head upon the table in that little room at Terrace Hill, Dr. Richard's home and Anna's. She did not see the good-humored face which looked in at her a moment, nor hear the whispering in the hall; neither did she know when Willie was coaxed from the room and carried up the stairs into the upper hall, where he was purposely left to himself, while Pamelia went to Anna's room, where she was to sit for an hour or so, while the ladies had their lunch. Anna's head was better; the paroxysms of pain were less frequent than in the morning, and she lay upon her pillow, so nearly asleep that she did not hear that unusual sound for Terrace Hill, the patter of little feet in the hall without. Tired of staying by himself and spying the open door, Willie hastened toward it, pausing a moment on the threshold as if to reconnoiter. Something in Anna's attitude, as she lay with her long fair hair falling over the pillow, must have reminded him of Alice, for with a cry of delight, he ran forward, and patting the white cheek with his soft baby hand, lisped out the word "Arn-tee, Arn-tee," making Anna start suddenly and gaze at him in wondering surprise.

"Who is he?" she said, drawing him to her at once and pressing a kiss upon his rosy face.

Pamelia told her what she knew of the stranger waiting in the reception room, adding in conclusion, "I believe they said you did not want her, and Jim is to take her to the depot when it's time. She's very young and pretty, and looks so sorry, Jim told me."

"Said I did not want her! How did they know?" and something of the Richards' spirit flashed from Anna's eyes. "The child is so beautiful, and he called me, *Auntie*, too! He must have an auntie somewhere. Little dear! how she must love him! Lift him up, Pamelia!"

The woman obeyed, and Willie was soon nestled close to Anna, who kissed him again, smoothed his curls, pinched his cheek, squeezed his soft hands, and then asked whom he so much resembled.

Pamelia could not tell. The likeness had puzzled her, but she never thought of finding it in her young mistress' face.

"I must see his mother," Anna said, as she continued to caress and fondle him. "Perhaps I should like her. At any events I will hear what she has to say. Show her up, Pamelia; but first smooth my hair a little and arrange my pillows," she added, feeling intuitively that the stranger was not like the others who had come to her on similar errands.

Pamelia complied with her request, brushing back the long, loose locks, and making the bed more smooth and tidy in its appearance; then leaving Willie with Anna, she repaired to the reception room, and rousing the sleeping Adah, said to her hurriedly,

"Please, miss, come quick; Miss Anna wants to see you. The little boy is up there with her."

CHAPTER XXVIII
ANNA AND ADAH

For a moment Anna was inclined to think that Pamelia had made a mistake and brought her the wrong individual, but Willie set her right by patting her cheek again, while he called out, "Mamma, arntee."

The look of interest which Anna cast upon him emboldened Adah to say,

"Excuse him, Miss Richards; he must have mistaken you for a dear friend at home, whom he calls *Auntie*. I'll take him down; he troubles you."

"No, no, please not," and Anna passed her arm around him. "I love children so much. I ought to have been a wife and mother, my brother says, instead of a useless old maid."

Adah was too much a stranger to disclaim against Anna's calling herself old, so she paid no attention to the remark, but plunged at once into the matter which had brought her there. Presuming they would rather be alone, Pamelia had purposely left the room, meeting in the lower hall with lady Richards, who, in much affright, was searching for the recent occupants of the reception room. She had ordered Dixson to carry them some lunch, and Dixson had returned with the news that there was no woman or child to be seen. Where were they then? Had they decamped, taking with them anything valuable which chanced to be in their way? Of course they had, and Eudora in the parlor, and Asenath in the dining room, and Mrs. Richards in the hall, were hunting for missing articles, when Pamelia quieted them by saying, "The lady was in Miss Anna's room."

At any other time Mrs. Richards would have corrected her domestic for calling a servant a lady, but she did not mind it now in her surprise.

"How came she there?" she said, angrily, while Pamelia replied, evasively,

"The little boy got up stairs, and, as children will, walked right into Miss Anna's room. She was taken with him at once, and asked who he was. I told her and she sent for the lady. That's how it happened."

It could not now be helped, and Mrs. Richards hurried up to Anna's chamber, where Willie still was perched by Anna's pillow, playing with the rings upon her fingers, while Adah, with her bonnet in her lap, sat a little apart, traces of tears and agitation upon her cheeks, but a look of happiness in the eyes fixed so wistfully on Anna's fair, sweet face.

"Please, mother," said Anna, motioning her away, "leave us alone awhile. Shut the door, and see that no one comes near."

Mrs. Richards obeyed, and Anna, waiting until she was out of hearing, resumed the conversation just where it had been interrupted.

"And so you are the one who wrote that advertisement which I read. Let me see—the very night my brother came home from Europe. I remember he laughed because I was so interested, and he accidentally tore off the name to light his cigar so I forgot it entirely. What shall I call you, please?"

Adah was silent a moment and then she answered, "Adah, Adah Hastings, but please do not ask *where* I came from now. I will tell you of the past, though I did not even mean to do that, but something about you makes me know I can trust you." And then, amid a shower of tears, in which Anna's, too, were mingled, Adah told her sad story—told of the mock marriage, the cruel desertion, of Willie's birth, her utter wretchedness, her attempt at suicide, her final trust in God, her going at last to one who gave her a home, even when he could not afford it; of her accidentally finding Anna's advertisement, and its result. No names were given, not even that of New York. It was merely the city and the country, and forgetful of the medium through which she first heard of Adah, Anna fancied Boston to have been the scene of her trials.

"But why do you wish to conceal your recent home?" she asked, after Adah had finished. "Is there any reason?"

For a moment Adah was tempted to tell the whole, but when she remembered how on the day of her departure from Spring Bank Mrs. Worthington had asked her not to say any thing disparaging of 'Lina, and admitted that it would be a great relief if the Richards family should not know for the present at least that she came from Spring Bank, she replied,

"At first there was none in particular, save a fancy I had, but there came one afterwards—the request of one who had been kind to me as a dear mother. Is it wrong not to tell the whole?"

"I think not. You have dealt honestly with me so far, and I am sure I can trust you."

She meant to keep her then. She was not going to send her away, and Adah's face lighted up with a joy which made it so beautiful that Anna gazed at her in surprise, marveling that any heart could be so hard as to desert that gentle girl.

"Oh, may I stay?" Adah asked eagerly.

"Of course you may. Did you think I would turn you away?" was Anna's reply; and laying her head upon the white counterpane of the bed, Adah cried passionately; not a wild, bitter cry, but a delicious kind of cry which did her good, even though her whole frame quivered and her low, choking sobs fell distinctly on Anna's ear.

"Poor child!" the latter said, laying her soft hand on the bowed head. "You have suffered much, but with me you shall find rest. I want you for a companion, rather than a maid. You are better suited for it, and we shall be very happy together, I am sure, though I am so much an invalid. I, too, have had my heart trouble; not like yours, but heavy enough to make me wish I could die. I was young and wayward then. I had not learned patience where alone it is to be found."

It was seldom that Anna alluded to herself in this way, and to do so to a stranger was utterly foreign to the Richards' nature. But Anna could not help it. There was something about Adah which interested her greatly. She knew she was above a waiting-maid's position, that in point of refinement and cultivation she was fully equal to herself; and when she decided to keep her, it was with the determination that she should be made to feel the degradation of her position as little as possible. She could not wholly shield her from her mother's and sisters' pride, but she would do what she could, and perhaps some day the recreant lover would be found and brought back to a sense of his duty.

Blessed Anna Richards,—the world has few like her, so gentle, so kind, so lovely, and as no one could long be with her and not feel her influence, so Adah grew calm, at last, and at Anna's request laid aside her cloak and hat in which she had been sitting.

"Touch that bell, if you please, and ring Pamelia up," Anna said. "There's a little room adjoining this, opening into the hall, and also in here—that's the door, with the bureau against it. I mean to give you that. You will be so near me, and so retired, too, when you like. John—that's my brother—occupied it when a boy, but as he grew larger he said it was too small. Still, I think it will answer nicely for you."

Obedient to the ring, Pamelia came, manifesting no surprise when told by Anna to move the dressing bureau back to the corner where it used to stand, to unlock the door and see if the little room was in order. "I know it is," she said, "I put it so this morning. There's a fire, too. Miss Anna has forgot that Dr. John slept here last night, because it did not take so long to warm up as his big chamber."

"I do remember now," Anna replied. "Mrs. Hastings can go in at once. She must be tired; and, Pamelia, send lunch to her room, and tell your husband to bring up her trunk."

Again Pamelia bowed and departed to do her young mistress' bidding, while Adah entered the pleasant room where Dr. Richards had slept the previous night, leaving behind him, as he always did, an odor of cigars. Adah detected the perfume, but it was not disagreeable—on the contrary, it reminded her of George, and for a brief moment there stole over her a feeling as if in some way she were brought very near to him by being in Dr. Richards' room! What a cosy place it was, and how she wished the people at Spring Bank could know all about it. How thankful they would be, and how thankful she was for this resting place in the protection of sweet Anna Richards. It was better than she had ever dared to hope for, and sinking down by the snowy-covered bed, she murmured inaudibly the prayer of thanksgiving to Him who had led her to Terrace Hill.

There were dark frowns on the faces of the mother and elder sisters when they learned of Anna's decision with regard to Adah, but Anna's income, received from the Aunt for whom she was named, gave her a right to act as she pleased, so they contented themselves with a few ill natured remarks concerning her foolishness, and the *airs* the waiting-maid put on. Adah, or Hastings as they called her, was not their idea of a waiting-maid, and they watched her curiously whenever she came in their sight, wondering at her cultivated manners and how Anna would ever manage one apparently so much her equal. Anna wondered so too, for it was an awkward business, requiring a menial's service of that lady-like creature, with language so pure and manner so refined, and she would have been exceedingly perplexed had not Adah's good sense come to the rescue, prompting her to do things unasked, and to do them in such a way that Anna was at once relieved from all embarrassment, and felt that she had found a treasure indeed. She did not join the family in the evening, but kept her room instead, talking with Adah, and caressing and playing with little Willie, who persisted in calling her "Arn-tee," in spite of all Adah could say.

"Never mind," Anna answered, laughingly; "I rather like to hear him. No one has ever called me by that name, and maybe never will, though my brother is engaged to be married in the spring. I have a picture of his betrothed there on my bureau. Would you like to see it?"

Adah nodded, and was soon gazing on the dark, haughty face she knew so well, and which even from the casing, seemed to smile disdainfully, upon her, just as the original had often done. There was Ellen Tiffton's bracelet upon the rounded arm, Ellen's chain upon the bare neck, while twined among the braids of her hair was something which looked like a bandeau of pearls, and which had been borrowed for the occasion of Mrs. Ellsworth, Irving's sister.

"What do you think of her?" Anna asked, wondering a little at the expression of Adah's face.

Adah must say something, and she replied,

"I dare say people think her pretty."

"Yes; but what do you think? I asked your opinion," persisted Anna, and thus beset Adah replied at last,

"I think her too showily dressed for a picture. She displays too much jewelry."

Feeling a little piqued that a stranger should have seized upon the very point which had seriously annoyed herself, Anna began to defend her future sister, never dreaming how much more than herself Adah knew of 'Lina Worthington.

It seemed to Adah like a miserable deceit, sitting there and listening while Anna talked of 'Lina, and she was glad when at last she showed signs of weariness, and expressed a desire to retire for the night.

"Would you mind reading to me from the Bible?" Anna asked, as Adah was about to leave her.

"Oh, no, I'd like it so much," and bringing her own little Bible to Anna's bedside, Adah read her favorite chapter, the one which had comforted her so often when life was at its darkest.

And Anna, listening to the sweet, silvery tones reading, "Let not your heart be troubled," felt her own sorrow grow less, while there went silently up a prayer of thanksgiving to heaven who had sent her such a comfort as Adah Hastings.

The chapter was ended, the little Testament closed, and then for a moment Adah sat as if waiting for Anna to speak. But Anna continued silent, her thoughts intent upon those mansions her elder brother had gone home before her to prepare.

"If you please," Adah said timidly, bending over the sweet face resting on the pillow, "if you please, may I say the Lord's Prayer here with you? I shall sleep better for it. I used to say it with— —"

She stopped suddenly ere the loved name of *Alice* had passed her lips, but Anna was kindly unconscious of the almost mistake, and only answered by grasping Adah's hand, and whispering to her,

"Yes, say it, do."

Then Adah knelt beside her, and Anna's fair hand rested, as if in blessing, on her head, as they said together, "Our Father."

It was a lovely sight, those two girls as it were, the one mistress, the other the maid, yet both forgetting the inequality in that expression of a common faith which made them truly equals; and Eudora, awed at the sight paused a moment on the threshold, and then moved silently away, lest they should know she had been there.

At first Adah's position at Terrace Hill was a very trying one, but Anna's unfailing kindness and thoughtfulness shielded her from much that was unpleasant, while the fact that Willie was finding favor in the eyes of those who had considered him an intruder, helped to make her burden easy.

Accustomed to the free range of Spring Bank, Willie asserted the same right at Terrace Hill, going where he pleased, and putting himself so often in Mrs. Richards way, that she began at last to notice him, and if no one was near, to caress the handsome boy. Asenath and Eudora held out longer, but even they were not proof against Willie's winning ways. His innocent prattle, and the patter of his little feet, heard from day dawn till night, thawed the ice from their hearts, until Asenath, the softer of the two, was once caught by Adah in the very undignified act of playing she was coach horse, while Willie's whip, given to him by Anna, was snapped in close proximity to her ears; Eudora, too, no longer hid her worsted stool, and as the weeks went on, there gradually came to be prints of little, soiled, dirty fingers—on the sideboard in the dining room, on the hat-stand in the hall, on the table in the parlor, and even on the dressing bureau in Madame's bed chamber, where the busy, active child had forced an entrance.

It was some weeks ere Adah wrote to Alice Johnson, and when at last she did, she said of Terrace Hill,

"I am happier here than I at first supposed it possible. The older ladies were so proud, that it made me very wretched, in spite of sweet Anna's kindness. But there has come a perceptible change, and they now treat me civilly, if nothing more, while I do believe they are fond of Willie, and would miss him if he were gone."

Adah was right in this conjecture; for had it now been optional with the Misses Richards whether Willie should go or stay, they would have kept him there from choice so cheery and pleasant he made the house. Adah was still too pretty, too stylish, to suit their ideas of a servant; but when they found she did not presume at all on her good looks, but meekly kept her place, they dropped the haughty manner they had at first assumed, and treated her with civility if not with kindness.

With Anna it was different. Won by Adah's gentleness, and purity, she came at last to love her almost as much as if she had been a younger sister. Adah was not a servant to her, but a companion, a friend, with whom she daily held familiar converse, learning from her much that was good, and prizing her more and more as the winter weeks went swiftly by.

She had also grown very confidential, telling Adah much of her past life, talking freely of Charlie Millbrook whose wife she had heard was dead, and for whose return to America she was hoping. She was talking of him one afternoon and blushing like a girl as Adah playfully suggested what might possibly ensue from his coming home, when her mother came in evidently annoyed and disturbed at something.

"I have a letter from John," she said. "They are to be married the — — day of April, which leaves us only five weeks more, as they will start at once for Terrace Hill. I am so bothered. I want to see you alone," and she cast a furtive glance at Adah, who left the room, while madam plunged at once into the matter agitating her so much.

She had fully intended going to Kentucky with her son. It would be a good opportunity for seeing the country, besides showing proper respect to her daughter-in-law, but 'Lina had objected, not in words, but in manner, objected, and the doctor had written, saying she must not go, at the same time urging upon her the necessity of having everything in perfect order, and in as good style as possible for his bride.

"I have not the money myself," he wrote, "and I'll have to get trusted for my wedding suit, so you must appeal to Anna's good nature for the wherewithal with which to fix the rooms. It's downright mean, I know, but she's the only one of the firm who has money. Do, pray, re-paper them; that chocolate color is enough to give one the blues; and get a carpet too, something lively and cheerful. She may stay with you longer than you anticipate. It is too expensive living here as she would expect to live. Nothing but Fifth Avenue Hotel would suit her, and I cannot ask her for funds at once. I'd rather come to it gradually."

And this it was which so disturbed Mrs. Richards' peace of mind. She could not go to Kentucky, and she might as well have saved the money she had expended in getting her black silk velvet dress fixed for the occasion, while worst of all she must have John's wife there for months, perhaps, whether she liked it or not, and she must also fit up the rooms with paper and paint and carpets, notwithstanding that she'd nothing to do it with, unless Anna generously gave the necessary sum from her own yearly income. This Anna promised to do, suggesting that Adah should make the carpet, as that would save a little.

"I wish, mother," she added, "that you would let her arrange the rooms altogether. She has exquisite taste, besides the faculty of making the most of things." Mrs. Richards, too, had confidence in Adah's taste, and so it was finally arranged that Adah should superintend the bridal rooms, subject of course to the dictation of Madame and her daughters.

At first Eudora and Asenath demurred, but when they saw how competent Adah was, and how modest withal in giving her opinions, they yielded the point, so far as actual overseeing was concerned, contenting themselves with suggestions which Adah followed or not just as she liked.

Frequently doubts crossed her mind as to the future when it might be known that *she* came from Spring Bank, and knew the expected bride. Would she not be blamed as a party in the deception? Did God think it right for her to keep silent concerning the past? Ought she not to tell Anna frankly that she knew her brother's betrothed? She did not know, and the harassing anxiety wore upon her faster than all the work she had to do.

The Dr. was expected home for a day before starting for Kentucky, and Adah frequently caught herself wondering if she should see him. She presumed she should not unless it were by accident, neither did she care particularly if she did not, and so on the morning of his expected arrival, when the other members of the household were anxious and watchful, she alone was quiet and self-possessed, doing her duties as usual, and feeling no presentiment of the shock awaiting her. She was in the dining room when the door bell rang, and she heard the tramp of horses' feet as Jim drove round to the stable. The doctor had come and she must go, but where was Willie? He was with her a moment ago, but she could not see him now. She hoped he was not in the parlor, for she knew it would annoy Eudora, who had more than once said something in her hearing about that "child forever under foot."

"Willie, Willie," she called, in a tremor of distress, as she heard his little feet pattering through the hall, together with the rush of other feet as madame, Asenath and Eudora, all came down together to admit their son and brother.

But Willie paid no heed, and as Eudora had said, was directly under foot, when she unlocked the door; his the first form distinctly seen, his the first face which met the doctor's view, and his fearless baby laugh the first sound which welcomed the doctor home!

CHAPTER XXIX
THE RESULT

It was not a disagreeable picture—that chubby, rosy cheeked little boy, his white fat shoulders peeping out from the dress of crimson and black, his fair curls blowing around his forehead, and his eyes raised curiously to the doctor's face. Willie had not expected to see a stranger, and at sight of the tall figure, muffled above the chin, he drew back timidly and half hid himself behind Mrs. Richards, whom he intuitively knew to be the warmest ally he had among the three ladies gathered in the hall.

As the doctor had said to Irving Stanley he disliked children, but he could not help noticing Willie, and after the first greetings were over he asked, "Whom have we here? whose child is this?"

Eudora and Asenath tried to frown, but the expression of their faces softened as they glanced at Willie, who had followed them into the parlor, and who, with one little foot thrown forward, and his fat hands pressed together, stood upon the hearth rug, gazing at the doctor with that strange look which had so often puzzled, bewildered, and fascinated the entire Richards family.

"Anna wrote you that the maid she so much wanted had come to her at last—a very lady-like person, who has evidently seen better days, and this is her boy, Willie. He is such a queer little fellow, that we allow him more liberties than we ought."

It was Mrs. Richards who volunteered this explanation, while her son stood looking down at Willie, wondering what it was about the child which seemed familiar. Anna had mentioned Mrs. Hastings in her letter—had said how much she liked her, had spoken of her boy, but the *Hastings* had been badly blotted, and as the Doctor was too much absorbed in his own affairs to care for Anna's waiting-maid, he had not thought of her since, notwithstanding that 'Lina had tried many times to make him speak of Anna's maid, so as to calculate her own safety.

"So you've taken to petting a servant's child, for want of something better," he said in answer to Mrs. Richards' rather long speech concerning Willie.

Ere Mrs. Richards could reply Anna made her appearance, and the fastidious Doctor forgot the little fellow, who was coaxed from the room by Pamelia, and taken to his mother.

The doctor was not in as good humor as men are supposed to be on the eve of their marriage with heiresses. He had offered to accompany 'Lina to Kentucky, but she had peremptorily declined his escort, and rather, as it seemed to him, thrust herself upon a gentleman and lady who were returning to Louisville. Several little things which she had done at the last had displeased him, as showing less refinement than he had given her credit for possessing, besides which he could not conceal from himself the suspicion that Mrs. Ellsworth was heartily glad to be rid of her, and had perhaps talked of going to Europe with her little girl as a ruse, and that she was not a favorite with any one of his particular friends. Still he meant to marry her, and after the late dinner was over he went with Anna to inspect the rooms which Adah had fitted for his bride. They were very pleasant, and he could find fault with nothing. The carpet, the curtains, the new light furniture, the arm chair by the window where 'Lina was expected to sit, the fanciful work basket standing near, and his chair not far away, all were in perfect taste, but still there was a load upon his heart, making him so silent and moody, that Anna forebore talking to him much and did not even mention *Adah*, though she had meant to tell him just what a treasure she was and perhaps have him see her too. But the doctor was in no frame of mind to talk of strangers, for thoughts of Lily were particularly haunting him to-day.

It was a great mistake he made when he cast her off but it could not now be helped. No tears, no regrets could bring back the dear little form laid away beneath the grassy sod, and so he would not waste his time in idle mourning. He would do the best he could with 'Lina. He did believe she loved him. He was almost sure of it, and as a means of redressing Lily's wrongs he would be kind to her. Lily would bid him do so if she could speak. She surely knew what he was doing; perhaps she was very near to him; he somehow felt that she was, and more than once, he caught himself turning suddenly with the fancy that Lily was behind him. The doctor was not superstitious, but he began at last to feel that it would be a relief to be freed from the Lily-laden atmosphere pervading Terrace Hill, and rather joyfully he watched the sun as it passed the meridian, and sank lower and lower in the west, for by that token he knew he had not a much longer time to stay at home, as he would take the evening train bound for Albany.

Slowly the twilight shadows crept over Terrace Hill and into the little room where Adah was preparing for her accustomed walk to the office. Willie was down with Pamelia, who, when she came up for him, had told Adah as something of which she should be proud, that the doctor had actually thrown Willie into the air and pronounced him a splendid-looking child, "considering."

That "considering" wounded Adah, for she felt the sneer at her position which it implied, and with a faint smile, she dismissed Pamelia, and then went to the closet for the over-shoes she would need in her damp walk. But what was it which fell like a thunderbolt on her ear, riveting her to the spot where she stood, rigid and immovable. Between the closet and Anna's room there was only a thin partition, and when the door was open every sound was distinctly heard. The doctor had just come in, and it was his voice, heard for the first time, which sent the blood throbbing so madly through Adah's veins, and made the sparks of fire dance before her eyes. She was not deceived—the tones were too distinct, too full, too well remembered to be mistaken, and stretching out her hands in the dim darkness, she moaned faintly: "George! 'tis George!" then sank upon the floor, powerless but not fainting, nor yet unconscious of the terrible certainty that *George* was so near to her that but for the partition she might almost have touched him! She could hear him now saying to Anna, "Are we alone? I wish to speak my farewell words in private."

"Yes, all alone," Anna replied. "Mrs. Hastings has gone to the Post-office. Was it any thing particular you wished to tell me?"

The Doctor either did not hear the name "Mrs. Hastings," or did not notice it, and again the familiar tones thrilled on Adah's ear as he replied, "Nothing very particular. I only wished to say a few words of 'Lina. I want you to like her, to make up, if possible, for the love I ought to give her."

"Ought to give her! Oh, brother, are you taking 'Lina without love? Better never make the vow than break it after it is made."

Anna spoke earnestly, and the doctor, who always tried to retain her good opinion, replied evasively, "I suppose I do love her as well as half the world love their wives before marriage, but she is different from any ladies I have known; so different from, what poor Lily was. Anna, let me talk with you again of Lily. I never told you all—but what *is* that?" he continued, as he indistinctly heard the choking, gasping, stifled sob, which Adah gave at the sound of the dear pet name, which used to make the blood thrill so ecstatically through her veins, and which now, for a single moment, made her heart bound with sudden joy; but only for a moment.

"Poor Lily," said a hundred times, with a hundred fold more tenderness than he was wont to say it, could not atone for the past; for the cruel desertion, for the deception even of the *name*; and so the poor, wounded heart grew still again as lead, while Anna answered, "It's only the rising wind. It sounds so always when it's in the east. What of Lily? Do you wish you were going after her instead of 'Lina?"

Could Anna have seen then into the darkness of the adjoining room, she would have shrunk in terror from the figure, which, as she asked *that* question, struggled to its knees, and creeping nearer to the door, turned its white, spectral face toward her, listening eagerly for the answer. Oh, why did the doctor hesitate a moment? Why did he suffer his dread of losing Anna's respect to triumph over every other feeling? He had meant to tell her all, how he did love the gentle girl, who confided herself to him—how he loved even her memory now far more than he loved 'Lina, but something kept the full confession back, and he answered,

"*I don't know.* We must have money, and 'Lina is rich, while Lily was very poor, and the only friend or relation she knew was one with whom I would not dare have you come in contact, he was so wicked and reckless."

This was what the doctor said, and into the brown eyes, now bloodshot and dim with anguish, there came the hard, fierce look, before which Alice Johnson once had shuddered, when Adah Hastings said,

"I should hate him!"

And in that dark hour of agony Adah felt that she did hate him. She knew now that what she before would not believe was true. He had not made her a lawful wife, else he had never dared to take another. She was a degraded creature, Willie a child of sin, and he had made them so. It was the bitterest dreg she had been forced to take, and for an instant, she forgot the God she served, forgot every thing save the desire to curse the man talking so calmly of her, as if her ruin were nought to him. But anon, the still small voice she always obeyed spoke to her tumultuous spirit, and the curse on her lips died away in the faint whisper, "Forgive me, Father, and forgive him, too."

She did not hear him now, for with that prayer, all consciousness forsook her, and she lay on her face insensible, while at the very last he did confess to Anna that *Lily was his wife*. He did not say unlawfully so. He could not tell her that. He said,

"I married her privately. I kept it from you all until she died. I would bring her back if I could, but I cannot, and I shall marry 'Lina."

"But," and Anna grasped his hand nervously, "I thought you told me once, that you won her love, and then, when mother's harsh letters came, left her without a word. Was that story false?"

The doctor was wading out in deep waters, and in desperation he added lie to lie, saying, huskily—

"Yes, that was false. I tell you I married her, and she died. Was I to blame for that?"

"No, no, oh, no. I'd far rather it were so. I respect you more than if you had left her. I am glad, so glad not that she died, but that you are not so bad as I feared. Sweet Lily," and Anna's tears flowed fast to the memory of the poor girl whose early grave she saw in fancy some where in a beautiful Greenwood.

There was a knock at the door, and Jim appeared, inquiring if the doctor would have the carriage brought round. It was nearly time to go, and with the whispered words to Anna, "I have told you what no one else must ever know," the doctor descended with his sister to the parlor, where his mother was waiting for him. The opening and shutting of the door caused a draught of air, which, falling on the fainting Adah, restored her to consciousness, and struggling to her feet, she tried to think what it was that had happened. She remembered it soon, and with a shudder listened to know if George was still in the adjoining chamber. All was quiet there. He had gone, and tottering into the room, she knelt by the chair where she knew he had sat. Then, as the last expiring throe of her love for him swept over her, she essayed to wind her trembling arms around the chair, as she would once have twined them about him.

"Oh, George! George!" she gasped, calling him still George, for, she almost hated that other name.

"Oh, George, I did love you so much," and she laid her poor, tired head upon the chair as if it had been his lap. "I loved you so much, but it is over now, or it soon will be. I feel its death struggles at my heart. You are worse than I believed. You have made me an outcast, and Willie — —" The sentence ended with the wailing cry—"My boy, my boy! that such a heritage should be yours."

Adah could not pray then, although she tried, but the fitting words would not come, and with her head still resting on his chair, she looked the terrible reality in the face, and saw just where she stood. Heretofore the one great hope, that she was really a wife, had buoyed her up when everything else was dark. Like a drowning person grasping at a straw, she had clung to that, even against her better judgment, but now it was swept away, and with it the semblance of a name. He had deceived her even there, and she had accepted the *Hastings* as something tangible. He was a greater villain than she had imagined a man could be, and again her white lips essayed to curse him, but the rash act was stayed by the low words whispered in her ear, "Forgive as ye would be forgiven."

"If it were not for Willie, I might, but oh! my boy, my boy disgraced," was the rebellious spirit's answer, when again the voice whispered, "And who art thou to contend against thy God? Know you not that I am the Father of the fatherless."

There were tears now in Adah's eyes, the first which she had shed.

"I'll try," she murmured, "try to forgive the wrong, but the strength must all be thine," and then, though there came no sound or motion; her heart went out in agonizing prayer, that she might forgive even as she hoped to be forgiven.

She did not ask that the dead love might ever return again. She had no desire for that, but she asked to feel kindly towards him, that the resentful feeling might be removed, that God would show her what to do and where to go, for she could not stay there now, in his home, whither he would bring his bride ere many days were gone. She must go away, not to Spring Bank, not anywhere where he or 'Lina could ever find her. She would far rather die. But Willie! what would she do with him, her tender, innocent boy?

"God tell me what to do with Willie?" she sobbed, starting suddenly as the answer to her prayer seemed to come at once. "Oh can I do that?" she moaned; "can I leave him here?"

At first her whole soul recoiled from it, but when she remembered Anna, and how much she loved the child, her feelings began to change. Anna would love him more when she knew he was poor Lily's and her own brother's. She would be kind to him for his father's sake, and for the sake of the girl she had professed to like. Willie should be bequeathed to Anna. It would break her heart to leave him, were it not already broken, but it was better so. It would be better in the end. He would forget her in time, unless sweet Anna told him of her, as perhaps she might. Dear Anna, how Adah longed to fold her arms about her once and call her sister, but she must not. It might not be well received, for Anna had some pride, as her waiting-maid had learned.

"A waiting-maid!" Adah repeated the name, smiling bitterly as she thought, "A waiting-maid in his own home! Who would have dreamed that I should ever come to this, when he painted the future so grandly? Be still, my heart, or I shall hate him yet, and I'm going to forgive him."

Then there came over her the wild, yearning desire to see his face once more, to know if he had changed, and why couldn't she? They supposed her gone to the office, and she would go there now, taking the depot on the way. She would go closely veiled, and none would suspect her errand. Rising mechanically, she donned her cloak and hood, and stealing down the stairs which led from Anna's room into the garden, she was soon out beneath the starry sky, inhaling the cool night air, so grateful to her heated brain.

Apart in the ladies' room at Snowdon depot, a veiled figure sat, waiting apparently for the cars, just as others were. She was the only female present, and no one had noticed her particularly when she came in, for the gentlemen walking up and down the room only glanced at her, and then gave her no further thought. And there she sat, Dr. Richards' deserted wife, waiting to look on his face once more ere she fled she knew not whither. He came at last, Jim's voice speaking to his horses heralding his approach. Adah could not see him yet, but she knew just when his feet struck the platform as he sprang from the carriage, and shivered as if it were a blow aimed at her heart.

The group of rough-looking men gathered about the office did not suit his mood, and so he came on to the ladies' apartment, just as Adah knew he would. Pausing for a moment on the threshold, he looked hastily in, his glance falling upon the veiled figure sitting there so lonely and motionless. She did not care for him, she would not object to his presence, so he came nearer to the stove, poising his patent leathers upon the hearth, thrusting both hands into his pockets, and even humming to himself snatches of a song, which Lily used to sing, up the three flights of stairs in that New York boarding-house.

Poor Adah! How white and cold she grew, listening to that air, and gazing upon the face she had loved so well. It was changed since the night when, with his kiss warm on her lips, he left her forever; changed, and for the worse. There was a harder, a more reckless, determined expression there, a look which better than words could have done, told that *self* alone was the god he worshipped. Adah doubted if he could have won her love with that look upon his face, and 'Lina Worthington was not envied the honor in store for her. It was a bitter struggle to sit there so quietly, to meet the eye before which she was wont to blush with happiness, to know that he was looking at her, wondering it might be, who she was, but never dreaming it was Lily.

Once, as he walked up and down the room, passing so near to her that she might have touched him with her hand, she felt an almost irresistible desire to thrust her thick brown veil aside, and confronting him to his face, claim from him what she had a right to claim, his name and a position as his wife. Only for Willie's sake, however for herself she did not wish it. He was not worthy, and forcing back the wild impulse, she sat with throbbing heart and bloodless lips watching him, as he still walked up and down, his brows knit together as if absorbed in some unpleasant thought.

It was a relief when at last the roll of the cars was heard, and buttoning his coat still closer around him, he went out upon the platform and stepped mechanically into the car.

Quickly Adah, too, passed through the rear door out into the street, and with a piteous moan for her ruined life, kept on her way till the post-office was reached.

There was a letter for Anna in the box, and thrusting it into her pocket Adah took her way back to Terrace Hill.

The family, including Anna, were spending the evening in the parlor, where there were callers, and thus none thought of or noticed Adah as she passed through the hall and crept up to her room.

Willie was asleep; and as Pamelia, who brought him up, had thoughtfully undressed and placed him in bed, there was nothing for Adah to do but think. She should go away, of course; she could not stay there longer; but how should she tell them why she went, and who would be her medium, for communication?

"Anna," she whispered; and lighting her little lamp, she sat down to write the letter which would tell Anna Richards who was the waiting-maid to whom she had been so kind.

Adah was very calm when she began that letter, and as it progressed, she seemed turning into stone, so insensible she was to what, without that rigidity of nerve, would have been a task more painful than she could well endure.

"Dear Anna," she wrote. "Forgive me for calling you so this once, for indeed I cannot help it. I am going away from you; and when, in the morning, you wait for me to come as usual, I shall not be here. I could not stay and meet your brother when he returns. Oh, Anna, Anna, how shall I begin to tell you what I know will grieve and shock your pure nature so dreadfully?

"I love to call you Anna now, for you seem near to me; and believe me, while I write this to you, I am conscious of no feeling of inferiority to any one bearing your proud name. I am, or should have been, *your sister*; and Willie!—oh, my boy, when I think of him, I seem to be going mad!

"Cannot you guess?—don't you know now who I am? God forgive your brother, as I asked him to do, kneeling there by the very chair where he sat an hour since, talking to you of *Lily*. I heard him, and the sound of his voice took power and strength away. I could not move to let you know I was there, and I lay upon the floor till consciousness forsook me; and then, when I woke again, you both were gone.

"I went to the depot, I saw him in his face to make assurance sure, and Anna, I,—oh I don't know what I am. The world would not call me a wife, though I believed I was; but they cannot deal thus cruelly by Willie, or wash from his veins his father's blood, for I—,who write this, I who have been a servant in the house where I should have been the mistress, am *Lily*— wronged, deserted Lily—and Willie is your brother's child! His father's looks are in his face. But when I came here I had no suspicion, for he won me as *George Hastings*; that was the name by which I knew him, and I was *Adah Gordon*. If you do not believe me, ask him when he comes back if ever in his wanderings he met with Adah Gordon, or her guardian, Mr. Redfield. Ask if he was ever present at a marriage where this Adah gave her heart to one for whom she would then have lost her life, erring in that she loved the *gift* more than the *giver*; but God punishes idolatry, and he has punished me, so sorely, oh so sorely, that sometimes my fainting soul cries out, ''tis more than I can bear.'"

Then followed more particulars so that there should be no doubt, and then the half crazed Adah took up the theme nearest to her heart, her boy, her beautiful Willie. She could not take him with her. She knew not where she was going, and Willie must not suffer. Would *Anna* take the child? Would she love him for his father's sake? Would she shield him from scorn, and when he was older would she sometimes tell him of the mother who went away that *he* might be spared shame?

"I do not ask that the new bride should ever call him hers," she wrote; "I'd rather she would not. I ask that you should give him a mother's care, and if his father will sometimes speak kindly to him for the sake of the olden time when he did love the mother, tell him—Willie's father, I mean—tell him, oh I know not what to bid you tell him, except that I forgive him, though at first it was so hard, and the words refused to come; I trusted him so much, loved him so much, and until I had it from his own lips, believed I was his wife. But that cured me; that killed the love, if any still existed, and now, if I could, I would not be his, unless it were for Willie's sake. Don't deem me too proud when I say, that to be his wife would be to me more terrible than any thing which I yet have borne, except it were for Willie. I say this because it's possible your kind heart would prompt you at once to bring back your erring brother, and persuade him at the last to do me justice. But I would not have it so. Shield Willie; nurture him tenderly; teach your mother to love him, and if you so desire it, I will never cross his path, never come near to him, though at a distance, if Heaven wills it, I shall watch my child.

"And now farewell. God deal with you, dear Anna, as you deal with my boy."

Calmly, steadily, Adah folded up the missive, and laying it with the other letter, busied herself next in making the necessary preparations for her flight. Anna had been very liberal with her in point of wages, paying her every week, and paying more than at first agreed upon; and as she had scarcely spent a penny during her three months' sojourn at Terrace Hill, she had, including what Alice had given to her, nearly forty dollars. She was trying so hard to make it a hundred, and so send it to Hugh some day; but she needed it most herself, and she placed it carefully in her little purse, sighing over the golden coin which Anna had paid her last, little dreaming for what purpose it would be used. She would not change her dress until Anna had retired, as that might excite suspicion; so with the same rigid apathy of manner she sat down by Willie's side and waited till Anna was heard moving in her room. The lamp was burning dimly on the bureau, and so Anna failed to see the frightful expression of Adah's face as she performed her accustomed duties, brushing Anna's hair, and letting her hands linger caressingly amid the locks she might never touch again.

It did strike Anna that something was the matter; for when Adah spoke to her, the voice was husky and unnatural. Still, she paid no attention, and the chapter was read as usual, after which Adah bade her good night and went to her own room. Anna slept very soundly, and when toward morning a light footstep glided across her threshold she did not hear it, neither did she know when two letters were laid softly on her pillow, where she could not fail to find them when she awoke, nor yet was she aware of the blessings breathed over her, as kneeling by her side Adah prayed out her farewell. Not wept. She could not do that, even when it came to leaving Willie. Her tears were frozen into stone, and the mighty throes of anguish which seemed forcing her heart from its natural position were of no avail to moisten the feverish lids, drooping so heavily over the swollen eyes. A convulsive prayer, in which her whole soul was embodied, a gasping sob of bitter, bitter pain, and then Adah put from her the little soft, warm, baby arm which Willie had unconsciously thrown across her neck when she laid her face by his. She dared not look at him again lest the sight should unnerve her, and with a decision born of desperation, she left her sleeping boy and hurried down the stairs into the gloomy hall, where not a sound was audible as her feet pressed the soft thick carpet on her passage to the outer door. The bolt was drawn, the key was turned, and just as the clock struck three, Adah stood outside the yard, leaning on the gate and gazing back at the huge building looming up so dark and grand beneath the starry sky. One more prayer for Willie and the mother-auntie to whose care she had left him, one more straining glance at the window of the little room where he lay sleeping, and she resolutely turned away, nor stopped again until the Danville depot was reached, the station where, in less than five minutes after her arrival, the night express stood for an instant, and then went thundering on, bearing with it another passenger, bound for—she knew not, cared not whither.

CHAPTER XXX
EXCITEMENT

They were not early risers at Terrace Hill, and the morning following Adah's flight Anna slept later than usual; nor was it until Willie's cry, calling for mamma, was heard, that she awoke, and thinking Adah had gone down for something, bade Willie come to her. Putting out her arms she lifted him carefully into her own bed, and in so doing brushed from her pillow the letters left for her. But it did not matter then, and for a full half hour she lay waiting for Adah's return. Growing impatient at last, she stepped upon the floor, her bare feet touching something cold, something which made her look down and find that she was stepping on a letter—not one, but two— and in wondering surprise she turned them to the light, half fainting with excitement, when on the back of the first one examined, she saw the old familiar handwriting, and knew that Charlie had written.

Anna had hardly been human had she waited an instant ere she tore open the envelope and learned that Charlie had returned from India and had not forgotten her. The love of his early manhood had increased with his maturer years, and he could not be satisfied until he heard from her that he was remembered and still beloved, that if this letter did not bring a reply he should come himself and brave the proud woman who guarded the entrance to Terrace Hill.

This was Charlie's letter, this what Anna read, and delicious tears of joy flowed over her beautiful face, as pressing the paper to her lips, she murmured,

"Dear Charlie! darling Charlie! I thank the kind Father for bringing him at last to me."

Hiding it in her bosom, Anna took the other letter, and throwing her shawl around her, sat down by the window and read it through—read it once, read it twice, read it thrice, and then— —Sure never were the inmates of Terrace Hill thrown into so much astonishment and alarm as they were that April morning, when, in her cambric night robe, her long hair falling unbound about her shoulders, and her bare feet, gleaming white and cold upon the floor, Miss Anna went screaming from room to room, demanding of the startled inmates if they had seen Adah Hastings—if they knew where she had gone—bidding Jim find her at his peril, telling Pamelia to join in the search, and asking her wonder-stricken mother and sisters "if they had any idea who it was that had been an inmate of their house for so many weeks."

"Come with me," she almost screamed, and dragging her mother to her room, where *Willie* sat up in bed, looking curiously about him and uncertain whether to cry or to laugh, she exclaimed, "Look at him, mother, and you, too, Asenath and Eudora!" turning to her sisters, who had followed. "Tell me who is he like?—Mother, surely you ought to know—ought to recognize your own son's offspring, for he is, he certainly is, John's child! and Adah was Lily, the young girl whom you forbade him to marry! Listen, mother, you shall listen to what your pride has done!" and grasping the bewildered Mrs. Richards by the arm, Anna held her fast while she read aloud the letter left by Adah.

Mrs. Richards fainted. It was the best thing under the circumstance which she could do, as it gave them all a little diversion from the exciting matter in hand. She soon recovered, however, and listened eagerly while Anna repeated all her brother had ever told her of Lily.

"I believe it is true," she said, and taking the letter she read it for herself, feeling an added respect for Adah, as she marked the flashes of pride gleaming out here and there, and showing themselves in the resentful manner with which she spurned the thought of now being the doctor's wife, except it were for Willie.

Poor Willie! He was there in the bed, looking curiously at the four women, none of whom seemed quite willing to own him, save Anna. Her heart took him in at once. He had been given to her. She would be faithful to the trust, and folding him in her arms, she cried softly over him, kissing his little face and calling him her darling.

"Anna, how can you fondle such as he?" Eudora asked, rather sharply, for her nature was the hardest, coldest of them all, and rebelled against the innocent boy.

"He is our brother's child. Our blood is in his veins, and that is why we all must love him. Mother, you will not turn from your grandson," and Anna held the boy toward her mother, who did not refuse to take him.

Asenath always went with her mother, and at once showed signs of relenting by laying her hand on Willie's head and calling him "poor boy." Eudora held out longer, but Anna knew she would yield in time, and satisfied with Willie's reception so far, went on to speak of Adah. Where was she, did they suppose, and what were the best means of finding her.

At this Mrs. Richards demurred, as did Asenath with her.

"Adah was gone, and they had better let her go quietly. She was nothing to them, and if they took Willie, it was all that could be required of them. Had Adah been John's wife, it would of course be different, but she was not, and his marriage with 'Lina must not now be prevented. Neither must any one save themselves and John ever know who Willie was. It was not necessary to bruit their affairs abroad. It was very wicked and bad in John, of course, but other young men were as bad."

This was Mrs. Richards' reasoning, but Anna's was different.

"John had distinctly said, 'I married Lily, and she died.' Adah was mistaken about the marriage being unlawful. It was a falsehood he told her. She was his wife, and he must not be permitted to commit bigamy, He loved Lily far better than he did 'Lina. He would move heaven and earth to find her, did he know that she was living. And he should know of it. She was going to Kentucky herself to tell him. She would not trust to the telegraph, and should start that very night. There would be no scene. She would only tell John in private. They need not try to dissuade her, for she should go."

This was what Anna said, and all in vain were her mother's entreaties to let matters take their course. Anna only replied by going deliberately on with the preparations for her sudden journey, pausing now and then to dream a moment over her own new happiness, taking the letter from her bosom and whispering, "Dear Charlie," and then as Willie cried for his mother, she essayed to quiet him, hugging him in her arms and mingling her own tears with his. The servants were told that Mrs. Hastings had run away, Eudora, the informer, hinting of insanity, and so this accounted for the sudden interest manifested for Willie by the other ladies, who had him in at their breakfast, and kept him with them in the parlor in spite of Pamelia's endeavors to coax him away. This accounted, too, for Anna's journey. She was going to find Adah, and blessing her for this kindness to one whom they had liked so much, Dixson and Pamelia helped to get her ready, both promising the best of care to Willie in her absence, both asking where she was going first, and both receiving the same answer, "To Albany."

Mrs. Richards was too much stunned clearly to comprehend what had happened or what would be the result; and in a kind of apathetic maze she bade Anna good-bye, and then went back to where Willie sat upon the sofa examining and occasionally tearing the costly book of foreign prints which had been given him to keep him still and make him cease his piteous wail for "mam-ma." It seemed like a dream to the three ladies sitting at home that night and talking about Anna; wondering that a person of her weak nerves and feeble health should suddenly become so active, so energetic, so decided, and of her own accord start off on a long journey alone and unprotected.

And Anna wondered at herself when the excitement of leaving was past, and the train was bearing her swiftly along on her mission of duty. She had written a few lines to Charlie Millbrook, telling him of her unaltered love, and bidding him come to her in three weeks time, when she would be ready to see him. She had unselfishly put the interview off thus long because she did not know what might occur in the interim, and when he came she wished to be quiet and free from all excitement. She had herself dropped the letter in the post-office as she came down to the depot. She knew it was safe, and leaning back in her seat in the car she felt a happy peace which nothing could disturb, not even thoughts of Adah—Lily she called her—wandering she knew not where.

It was very dark and rainy, and the passengers jostled each other rudely as they passed from the cars in Albany and hurried to the boat. It was new business to Anna, traveling alone and in the night, and a feeling akin to fear was creeping over her as she wondered *where* she *should* find the eastern train.

"Follow the crowd," seemed yelled out for her benefit, though it was really intended for a timid, deaf old lady, who had anxiously asked what to do of one whose laconic reply was, "Follow the crowd." And Anna did follow the crowd, which led her safely to the waiting cars. Snugly ensconced in a seat all to herself, she vainly imagined there was no more trouble until Cleveland, or Buffalo at least, was reached. How, then, was she disappointed when, alighting for a moment at Rochester, she found herself in a worse Babel, if possible, than had existed at Albany. Where were all these folks going, and which was the train. "I ought not to have alighted at all," she thought; "I might have known I never could find my way back." Never, sure, was a poor, little woman so confused and bewildered as Anna, and it is not strange that she stood directly upon the track, unmindful of the increasing din and roar as the train from Niagara Falls came thundering into the depot. It was in vain that the cabman nearest to her halloed to warn her of the impending danger. She never dreamed that they meant her, or suspected her great peril, until from out the group waiting to take that very train, a tall figure sprang, and grasping her light form round the waist, bore her to a place of safety—not because he guessed that it was *Annie*, but because it was a human being whom he would save from a fearful death.

"Excuse me, madam," he began, as with the long train between them and the people, they stood comparatively alone, but whatever she might have said was lost in the low, thrilling scream of joy with which Anna recognized him.

"Charlie, Charlie! oh, Charlie!" she cried, burying her face in his bosom and sobbing like a child.

There was no time to waste in explanations; scarcely time, indeed, for Charlie to ask where she was going, and if the necessity to go on were imperative. If her arrangements could not bend to his, why his must bend to hers, and unmindful of the audience away to the eastward who would that night wait in vain for the appearance of Mr. Millbrook, the returned missionary, Charlie wound his arm around the half fainting form, dearer than his own life, and carried rather than led her to a seat in the car just on the point of rolling from the depot.

"You won't leave me," Anna whispered, clinging closer to him, as she remembered how improbable it was that he was going the same way with herself.

"Leave you, darling? no," and pressing the little fingers twining so lovingly about his own, Charlie replied, "I shall not leave you again."

He needed no words to tell him of her unaltered love, and satisfied to have her at last, he drew her closely to him, and laying her tired head upon his bosom, gazed fondly at the face he had not seen in many years. That dear face he had once thought so beautiful and had dreamed about so often, even when another was sleeping at his side, was it changed? Yes, slightly. The fresh, girlish bloom of only eighteen summers was gone, but Anna wore her thirty-three years lightly, and if possible, the maturer face was more beautiful to Charlie than the laughing maiden's had been, for he traced on it unmistakable marks of that peace which Anna had found in her later life; and without questioning her at all, Charlie Millbrook knew his darling Anna had chosen the better part, and that in the next world she would be his, even as he hoped to call her his own for the remainder of his sojourn on earth. Curious, tittering maidens, of whom there are usually one or two in every car, looked at that couple near the door and whispered to their companions,

"Bride and groom. Just see how he hugs her. Some widower, I know, married to a young wife."

But neither Charlie nor Anna cared for the speculations to which they were giving rise. They had found each other, and the happiness enjoyed during the two hours which elapsed ere Buffalo was reached, more than made amends for all the lonely years of wretchedness they had spent apart from each other. Charlie had told Anna briefly of his life in India—had spoken feelingly, affectionately, of his gentle Hattie, who had died, blessing him with her last breath for the kindness he had ever shown to her; of baby Annie's grave, by the side of which he buried the young mother; of his loneliness after that, his failing health, his yearning for a sight of home, his embarkation for America, his hope through all that she might still be won; and his letter which she received. And then Anna told him where she was going, sparing her brother as much as possible, and dwelling long upon poor Lily's gentleness and beauty.

So it was settled that Charley should go with her, and his presence made her far less impatient than she would otherwise have been, when, owing to some accident, they were delayed so long that the Cleveland train was gone, and there was no alternative but to wait in Buffalo. At Cincinnati there was another detention, and it was not until the very day appointed for the wedding that, with Charlie still beside her, Anna entered the carriage hired at Lexington, and started for Spring Bank, whither for a little we will precede her, taking up the narrative prior to this day, and about the time when 'Lina first returned home from New York, laden with arrogance and airs.

CHAPTER XXXI
MATTERS AT STRING BANK

It had been a bright, pleasant day in March, when 'Lina was expected home, and in honor of her arrival the house at Spring Bank wore its most cheery aspect; not that any one was particularly pleased because she was coming, unless it were the mother; but it was still an event of some importance, and so the negroes cleaned and scrubbed and scoured, wondering if "Miss 'Lina done fotch 'em anything," while Alice arranged and re-arranged the plainly-furnished rooms, feeling beforehand how the contrast between them and the elegancies to which 'Lina had recently been accustomed, would affect her.

Hugh had thought of the same thing, and much as it hurt him to do it, he sold one of his pet colts, and giving the proceeds to Alice, bade her use it as she saw fit.

It was astonishing how far Alice made the hundred dollars go. Hugh had no idea it would buy so much, and in blissful ignorance that Alice herself had supplied many articles from her own funds, he assisted in nailing down carpets and oil-cloths, and putting up curtains, while he even ventured to try his hand at painting, succeeding admirably, but spoiling an entire suit of clothes, and leaving more than one mark of his brush on Alice's black dress. Spring Bank had never looked one-half so well before, and the negroes were positive there was no where to be found so handsome a room as the large airy parlor, with its new Brussels carpet and curtains of worsted brocatelle.

Even Hugh was somewhat of the same opinion, but then he only looked at the room with Alice standing in its centre, so it is not strange that he should judge it favorably. Ad would be pleased, he knew, and he gave orders that the carriage and harness should be thoroughly cleaned, and the horses well groomed, for he would make a good impression upon his sister.

Alas, she was not worth the trouble,—the proud, selfish creature, who, all the way from Lexington to the Big Spring station had been hoping *Hugh* would not take it into his head to meet her, or if he did, that he would not have on his homespun suit of grey, with his pants tucked in his boots, and so disgrace her in the eyes of Mr. and Mrs. Ford, her traveling companions, who would see him from the window. Yes, there he was, standing expectantly upon the platform, and she turned her head the other way, pretending not to see him until the train moved on, and Hugh compelled her notice by grasping her hand and calling her "sister 'Lina."

She had acquired a certain city air by her sojourn in New York, and in her fashionably made traveling dress and hat was far more stylish looking than when Hugh last parted from her. But nothing abashed he held her hand a moment while he inquired about her journey, and then playfully added,

"Upon my word, Ad, you have improved a heap, in looks I mean. Of course I don't know about the temper. Spunky as ever, eh?" and he tried to pinch her glowing cheek.

"Pray don't be foolish," was 'Lina's impatient reply, as she drew away from him, and turned, with her blandest smile, to a sprig of a lawyer from Frankfort, who chanced to be there too.

Chilled by her manner, Hugh ordered the carriage, and told her they were ready. Once alone with him, 'Lina's tongue was loosened, and she poured out numberless questions, the first of which was, "What they heard from Adah, and if it were true, as her mother had written, that no one at Terrace Hill knew of her acquaintance with Spring Bank."

"Yes, he supposed it was, and he did not like it either. Ad," and he turned his honest face full toward her, "does that doctor still believe you rich?"

"How do I know?" 'Lina replied, frowning gloomily. "I'm not to blame if he does. I never told him I was."

"But your actions implied as much, which amounts to the same thing. It's all wrong, Ad, all wrong. Even if he loves you, and it is to be hoped he does, he will respect you less when he knows how you deceived him."

"Hadn't you better interfere and set the matter right?" asked 'Lina, now really roused.

"I did think of doing so once," Hugh rejoined, but ere he could say more, 'Lina grasped his arm fiercely, her face dark with passion as she exclaimed, "Hugh, if you meddle, you'll rue the day. It's my own affair, and I know what I'm doing."

She was very angry, and her black eyes fairly blazed as they glanced at Hugh, who once would have returned her scorn for scorn. But Hugh was learning to govern his hot temper. The diamond was polishing; besides that, he would not quarrel with her on this first day of her return, so he answered in the same kind tone of voice he had assumed toward her.

"I do not intend to meddle, though I encouraged Adah in her wild plan of going to Terrace Hill, because I thought they would learn from her just how rich we are. But Adah foolishly says nothing of Spring Bank. I don't like it, neither does Miss Johnson. Indeed, I sometimes think she is more anxious than I am."

"Miss Johnson," and 'Lina spoke disdainfully, "I'd thank her to mind her own business. She's only jealous and wants the doctor herself."

Hugh made her no reply, and they proceeded on in silence, until they came in sight of Spring Bank, when 'Lina broke out afresh, "Such a tumble-down shanty as that! It was not fit for decent people to live in, and mercy knew she was glad her sojourn there was to be short."

"You are not alone in that feeling," came dryly from Hugh, who could not forbear that remark.

'Lina said he was a very affectionate brother; that she was glad there were those who appreciated her, even if he did not, and then the carriage stopped at Spring Bank, where the family stood waiting for her upon the long piazza. Mrs. Worthington was hearty in her welcome, for her mother heart went out warmly towards her daughter, who, as bride-elect of a Richards, was, in her estimation, a creature of more importance than plain 'Lina had been, with nothing in prospect. Oh, what airs 'Lina did put on, and what pains she took to appear *cityfied*, merely noticing the expectant negroes with a "how dye," offering the tips of her fingers to good Aunt Eunice, trying to patronize Alice herself, and only noticing Densie Densmore with a haughty stare.

"Upon my word," 'Lina began, as she entered the pleasant parlor, "this is better than I expected. Somebody has been very kind for my sake. Miss Johnson, I am sure it's you I have to thank," and with a little flush of gratitude she turned to Alice, who replied in a low tone, "Thank your brother. He made a sacrifice for the sake of surprising you."

Whether it was a desire to appear amiable in Alice's eyes, or because she really was touched with Hugh's generosity, 'Lina involuntarily threw her arm around his neck, and gave to him a kiss which he remembered for a long, long time.

Swiftly the days went by, bringing callers to see 'Lina, Ellen Tiffton, who received back her jewelry, and who was to be bridesmaid, inasmuch as

Alice preferred to be more at liberty, and see that matters went on properly. This brought Ellen often to Spring Bank, and as 'Lina was much with her, Alice was left more time to think. Adah's continued silence with regard to Dr. Richards had troubled her at first, but now she felt relieved. 'Lina had stated distinctly that ere coming to Kentucky he was going to Terrace Hill, and Adah's last letter had said the same. She would see him then, and— if he were George—alas, for the unsuspecting girl who fluttered gaily in the midst of her bridal finery, and wished the time would come when "she could escape from that hole, and go back to dear, delightful Fifth Avenue Hotel."

The time which hung so heavily upon her hands was flying rapidly, and at last only a week intervened ere the eventful day. Hugh had gone down to Frankfort on an errand to the dressmaker's for 'Lina, and finding that he must wait some time, it occurred to him to visit the Penitentiary, where he had not been for a long time. The keeper, a personal friend of Hugh's, expressed much pleasure at meeting him, and after a moment, said laughingly,

"We have no *lions* to show just now, unless it be Sullivan, the negro stealer. You have never seen him, I think, since he was sent to us. You know whom I mean, the man who ran off Uncle Sam."

Yes, Hugh knew, but he was not especially interested in him. Still he followed the keeper, who said that Sullivan's time expired in a few days.

"We'll find him on the rope-walk," he continued. "We put our hardest customers there. Not that he gives us trouble, for he does not, and I rather like the chap, but we have a spite against these Yankee negro-stealers," and he led the way to the long low room, where groups of men walked up and down—up and down—holding the long line of hemp, which, as far as they were concerned, would never come to an end until the day of their release.

"That's he," the keeper whispered to Hugh, "the one with that mark upon his forehead," and he pointed to one of the convicts advancing slowly towards them.

With a start and a shudder Hugh grew cold and sick, for it needed but a glance to assure him that he stood in the presence of Adah's guardian, whose sudden disappearance had been so mysterious. Hugh never knew how he kept himself from leaping into that walk and compelling him to tell if he knew anything of Willie Hastings' father. He did, indeed, take one forward step, but the next moment he controlled himself as he remembered where he was, and knew it was no place for a scene. "But I must see him," he thought, "I must talk with him and compel him to tell me what he knows of Adah Hastings."

Hastily quitting the spot, he explained to the keeper that there was a particular reason for his talking with Sullivan, and asked permission to do so. At first the keeper hesitated, but finally consented, and an hour later, when the convicts left their work, Hugh Worthington was confronting the famous negro-stealer, who gave him back glance for glance, and stood unflinchingly before him as if there were upon his conscience no Adah Hastings, who, by his connivance, had been so terribly wronged. At the mention of *her* name, however, his bold assurance left him. There was a quivering of the muscles about his mouth, a humid moisture upon his eyelids, and his whole manner was indicative of strong emotion as he asked if Hugh knew aught of her, and then listened while Hugh told what he knew, and where she had gone.

"To Terrace Hill—into the Richards family, this was no chance arrangement," and the convict spoke huskily asking next for the doctor, was he at home? had he met Adah yet? and still Hugh did not suspect the magnitude of the plot, and answered by telling how Dr. Richards was coming soon to make 'Lina his wife.

Hugh was not looking at his companion then, or he would have been appalled by the fearful expression which for an instant flashed on his face, and then quickly passed away, leaving there a look of terror and concern. Accustomed to conceal his feelings, the convict did so now, and asked calmly when the wedding would take place. Hugh named the day and hour, and then asked impatiently, if Sullivan knew aught of Adah's husband.

"Yes, everything," and the convict spoke vehemently, for he, too, saw the keeper consult his watch, and knew that he must hasten.

"Young man, I cannot tell you now—there is not time, but wait and you shall know the whole. You are interested in Adah. You have been kind to her. You never will be sorry. The wedding, you say, is Thursday night. My time expires on Wednesday.

"Don't say that you have seen me, or that I shall be present at that wedding. I shall only come for good, but I shall surely be there."

He wrung Hugh's hand and went to his lonely cell, while Hugh turned away, haunted by some presentiment of evil, and hearing continually the words, fraught with far more meaning than he supposed, "I shall surely be there."

CHAPTER XXXII
THE DAY OF THE WEDDING

Dr. Richards had arrived at Spring Bank. He, too, had been detained in Cincinnati, and did not reach his destination until late on Wednesday evening. Hugh was the first to meet him, for Alice had retired, and 'Lina had fled from the room at the first sound of the voice she had been so anxiously waiting for. For a moment Hugh scrutinized the stranger's face earnestly, and then asked if they had never met before.

"Not to my knowledge," the doctor replied in perfect good faith, for he had no suspicion that the man eyeing him so closely was the one witness of his marriage with Adah, the stranger whom he scarcely noticed, and whose name he had forgotten.

Once fully in the light, where Hugh could discern the features plainer, he began to be less sure of having met his guest before, for that immense mustache and those well-trimmed whiskers, had changed the doctor's physiognomy materially.

'Lina now came stealing in, affecting such a pretty coyness of manner, that Hugh felt like roaring with laughter and ere long hurried out where he could indulge his merriment.

'Lina was glad to see the doctor. She had even cried at his delay; and though no one knew it, had sat up nearly the whole preceding night, waiting and listening by her open window for any sound to herald his approach, and once she had stolen out with her thin slippers into the yard, standing on the damp ground a long time, and only returning to the house when she felt a chill creeping over her, and knew she was taking cold.

As the result of this long vigil, her head ached dreadfully the next day, and even the doctor noticed her burning cheeks and watery eyes, and feeling her rapid pulse asked if she were ill.

She was not, she said; she had only been troubled, because he did not come, and then for once in her life she did a womanly act. She laid her head in the doctor's lap and cried, just as she had done the previous night. He understood the cause of her tears at last, and touched with a greater degree of tenderness for her than he had ever before experienced, he smoothed her glossy black hair, and asked, "Would you be very sorry to lose me?"

Selfish and hard as she was, 'Lina loved the doctor, and with a shudder as she thought of the deception imposed on him, and a half regret that she had so deceived him, she replied, "I am not worthy of you, but I do love you very much, and it would kill me to lose you now. Promise that when you find, as you will, how bad I am, you will not hate me!"

It was an attempt at confession, but the doctor did not so construe it. Whatever her errors were, his, he knew, were tenfold greater, and so he continued smoothing her hair, while he tried to say the words of affection he knew she was waiting to hear.

It was very dark that night, and the doctor received only a vague idea of Spring Bank and its surroundings, and that did not impress him as grandly as he had thought it would. But then, he reflected that Southerners were not as noted for fine houses as Northerners were, and so felt secure as yet, wondering which of the negroes he had seen belonged to 'Lina, and which to Hugh. He knew Lulu was not to accompany his wife to Terrace Hill, for 'Lina had told him so, saying that in the present state of excited feeling she did not think it best to take a negro slave to New England. He knew, too, that nothing had been said about money or lands coming to him with his bride, but he took it all on trust, and looked rather complacently around the prettily furnished chamber to which, at a late hour, he was conducted by Hugh.

The bright sunlight of the next morning was very exhilarating, and though the doctor was disappointed in Spring Bank, he greeted his bride-elect kindly, noticing, when he did so, how her cheeks alternately paled, and then grew red, while she seemed to be chilly and cold. 'Lina had passed a wretched night, tossing from side to side, bathing her throbbing head and rubbing her aching limbs. The severe cold taken in the wet yard was making itself visible, and she came to the breakfast-table jaded wretched and sick, a striking contrast to Alice Johnson, who seemed to the doctor more beautiful than ever. She was unusually gay this morning, for while talking to Dr. Richards, whom she had met in the parlor, she had, among other things concerning Snowdon, said to him, casually, as it seemed, "Anna has a waiting-maid at last: You saw her of course?"

Somehow the doctor fancied Alice wished him to say yes, and as a falsehood was nothing for him, he replied at once, "Oh, yes, I saw her. Her little boy is splendid."

Alice was satisfied. The shadow lifted from her spirits. Dr. Richards was not George Hastings. He was not the villain she had feared, and 'Lina might have him now. Poor 'Lina! Alice felt almost as if she had done her a wrong by suspecting the doctor, and was very kind to her that day. Poor 'Lina! we say it again, for hard, and wicked, and treacherous, and unfilial, as she had ever been, she had need for pity on this her wedding day. Retribution terrible and crushing, was at hand, hurrying on in the carriage bringing Anna Richards to Spring Bank, and on the fleet-footed steed bearing the convict swiftly up the Frankfort 'pike.

Restless and impatient 'Lina wandered from room to room, stopping longest in the one where lay the bridal dress, at which she gazed wistfully, feeling almost as if it were her shroud. She could not tell what ailed her. She only knew that she felt wretchedly, as if some direful calamity were about to overtake her, and more than once her eyes filled with tears as she wished her path to Dr. Richards' name had been marked with no deception. He was now in his room, and it was almost time for her to dress. Lulu might begin to arrange her hair, and she called her just as the mud-bespattered vehicle containing Anna Richards drove up, Mr. Millbrook having purposely stopped in Versailles, thinking it better that Anna should go on alone.

It was Ellen Tiffton, who was to come early, 'Lina said, and so the dressing continued, and she was all unsuspicious of the scene enacting below, in the room where Anna met her brother alone. She had not given Hugh her name. She simply asked for Dr. Richards, and conducting her into the parlor, hung with bridal decorations, Hugh went for the doctor, saying, "a lady wished to see him."

"A lady! Who is it?" the doctor asked, visions of his aggrieved mother, in her black silk velvet, rising before his mind. "What could a lady and a stranger want of him?"

Mechanically he took his way to the parlor, while Hugh resumed his seat by the window, where for the last hour he had watched for the coming of one who had said, "I will be there."

Half an hour later, had he looked into the parlor, he would have seen a frightened, white-faced man, crouching at Anna Richards' side and whispering to her as if all life, all strength, all power to act for himself, were gone.

"What must I do? Tell me what to do."

She had given him no time for questioning, but handing him Adah's letter, had bidden him read it through, as that would explain her presence at Spring Bank. One glance at the handwriting, and the doctor turned white as marble. "Could it be? Had Lily come back to life?" he asked himself, and then eagerly, rapidly, he read the first two pages, every word burning into his heart and bewildering his brain. But when he came to the line, "*I am Lily, and Willie is your brother's child,*" sight and sense seemed failing him, and tottering to his sister, sternly regarding him, he gasped, "Oh, Anna, read for me. I can't see any more—it runs together, and I—I'm going to faint!"

"*No, you are not.* You must not faint; you shall not," Anna exclaimed, shaking him energetically and applying to his nostrils the bottle of strong hartshorn she had procured in Versailles for just such an emergency as this.

The odor half strangled him, but Anna's object was attained. He did not faint, but sat like an idiotic thing, listening while she read the letter through, and demanded if it were true. Was it Adah Gordon whom he deserted, and was it a mock marriage? She would have the truth, and he had no desire to conceal it.

"Yes, true—all true—but I thought she was dead. I did, Anna. Oh, Lily, where is she now? I'm going to——"

"Sit down," Anna said, imperatively; and with all the air of an imbecile he crouched at her feet, asking what he should do.

This was a puzzle to Anna, and she replied by asking him another question. "Do you love 'Lina Worthington?"

"I—I—no, I guess I don't; but she's rich, and——"

With a motion of disgust Anna cut him short, saying, "Don't make me despise you more than I do. Until your lips confessed it, I had faith that Lily was mistaken, that your marriage was honorable, at least, even if you tired of it afterward. You are worse than I supposed and now you speak of money. What shall you do? Get up, and not sit whining at my feet like a puppy. Find Lily, of course, and if she will stoop to listen a second time to your suit, make her your wife, working to support her until your hands are blistered, if need be."

Anna hardly knew herself in this phase of her character, and her brother certainly did not.

"Don't be hard on me, Anna," he said, "I'll do what you say, only don't be hard. It's come so sudden, that my head is like a whirlpool. Lily, Willie, Willie. The child I saw, you mean—yes, the child—I—saw—did it say he—was—*my*—boy?"

The words were thick and far apart. The head drooped lower and lower, the color all left the lips, and in spite of Anna's vigorous shakes, or still more vigorous hartshorn, overtaxed nature gave way, and the doctor fainted at last. It was Anna's turn now to wonder what she should do, and she was about summoning aid from some quarter when the door opened suddenly, and Hugh ushered in a stranger—the convict, who had kept his word, and came to tell what he knew of this complicated mystery. No one had seen him as he entered the house but Hugh, who was expecting him, and who, in reply to his inquiries for the doctor, told where he was, and that a stranger was with him. There was a low, hurried conversation between the two, a partial revelation of the business which had brought Sullivan there, and at its close Hugh's face was deadly white, for he knew now that he had met Dr. Richards before, and that 'Lina could not be his wife.

"The villain!" he muttered, involuntarily clenching his fist as if to smite the dastard as he followed Sullivan into the parlor, starting back when he saw the prostrate form upon the floor, and heard the lady say, "My brother, sir, has fainted."

She was Anna, then; and Hugh guessed rightly why she was there.

"Madame," he began, but ere another word was uttered there fell upon his ear a shriek which seemed to cleave the very air and made even the fainting man move in his unconsciousness.

It was Mrs. Worthington who, with hands outstretched as if to keep him off, stood upon the threshold, gazing in mute terror at the horror of her life, whispering incoherently, "What is it, Hugh? How came he here? Save me, save me from him!"

A look, half of sorrow, half of contempt, flitted across the stranger's face as he answered for Hugh kindly, gently, "Is the very sight of me so terrible to you, Eliza? Believe me, you have nothing to fear. I am only here to set matters right—to make amends for the past, so far as possible. Here for our daughter's sake."

He had drawn nearer to her as he said this last, but she intuitively turned to Hugh, who started suddenly, growing white and faint as a suspicion of the truth flashed upon him.

"Mother?" he began, interrogatively, winding his arm about her, for she was the weaker of the two.

She knew what he would ask, and with her eye still upon the man who fascinated her gaze, she answered, sadly, "Forgive me, Hugh, I thought he was dead. The paper said so, with all the particulars. Forgive me. He was— my husband; he is—'Lina's father, not yours, Hugh, oh, Heaven be praised, not yours!" and she clung closely to her boy, as if glad one child, at least, was not tainted with the Murdoch blood.

The convict smiled bitterly, and said to Hugh himself,

"Your mother is right. She was once my wife, but the law set her free from the galling chain. I have had a variety of names in my life; so many, indeed, that I hardly knew which is my real one."

He was perfectly cool, but his face showed the effort it was to be so, while his black eyes rolled restlessly from one object to another, and he was about to speak again when Alice came tripping down the stairs, and pausing at the parlor door, looked in.

"Anna Richards!" she exclaimed, but uttered no other sound for the terror of something terrible, which kept her silent.

It was no ordinary matter which had brought that group together, and she stood looking from one to the other, until the convict said,

"Young lady, you cannot be the bride, but will you call her, tell her she is wanted."

Alice never knew what she said to 'Lina. She was only conscious of following her down the stairs and into that dreadful room. Sullivan was watching for her, and the muscles about his mouth twitched convulsively, while a shadow of mingled pity and tenderness swept over his features as his eye fell on the girlish figure behind her, 'Lina, with the orange blossoms in her hair—'Lina almost ready for the bridal!

For an instant the convict regarded her intently, and there was something in his glance which brought Hugh at once to 'Lina, where, with his arm upon her chair, he stood as if he would protect her. Noble Hugh! 'Lina never knew one-half how good and generous he was until just as she was losing him.

Dr. Richards was restored by this time, and looked on those around him in utter astonishment; on Mrs. Worthington crouched in the farthest corner, her face as white as ashes, and her eyes riveted upon the figure of the man standing in the center of the room; on 'Lina, terrified at what she saw; on Anna, more perplexed, more astonished than himself, and on Hugh, towering up so commandingly above the whole, and demanding of the convict the explanation which he had come to make.

There was a moment's hesitancy, and his face flushed and paled alternately ere the convict could summon courage to begin.

"Take this seat, sir, you need it," Hugh said, bringing him a chair and then resuming his watch over 'Lina, who involuntarily leaned her throbbing head upon his arm, and with the others listened to that strange tale of sin.

CHAPTER XXXIII
THE CONVICT'S STORY

"It is not an easy task to confess how bad one has been," the stranger said, "and once no power could have tempted me to do it; but several years of prison life have taught me some wholesome lessons, and I am not the same man I was when I met you, Eliza, (bowing to Mrs. Worthington) and won your hand if not your heart. But previous to that time there was a passage of my life which I must now repeat. At my boarding-house in New York there was a young girl, a chamber-maid, whom I deceived with promises of marriage and then deserted, just when she needed me the most. I had found new prey, was on the eve of marriage with Mrs. Eliza Worthington. I—"

The story was interrupted at this point by a cry from 'Lina, who moaned,

"No, no, oh no! He is not *my* father; is he, Hugh? Tell me no. John, Dr. Richards, pray look at me and say it's all a dream, a dreadful dream! Oh, Hugh!" and to the brother, scorned so often, poor 'Lina turned for sympathy, while the stranger continued,

"It would be useless for me to say now that I loved the girl, for I did not; but I felt sorry for her, and when six months after my marriage I heard that I was a father I feigned an excuse and left my wife for a few weeks. Eliza, you remember I said I had business in New York, and so I had. I went to this young girl, finding her in a low, wretched garret, with her baby in her arms, and a look on her face which told me she had not long to live. I staid by her till she died, promising to care for her child and mine. I had a mother then, a woman, old and infirm, and good, even if I was her son. To her I went in my trouble, asking that she would care for the helpless thing to which I gave the name Matilda. Mother did not refuse, and leaving the baby in her charge I came back to my lawful wife.

"In course of time there was a daughter born to me and to Eliza; a sweet brown-haired, brown-eyed girl, whom we named *Adaline*."

Instinctively, every one in that room glanced at the black eyes and hair of 'Lina, marvelling at the change.

"I loved this little girl, as it was natural I should, more than I loved the other, and after she was born I tried to be a better man, but could not hold out long, and at last there came a separation. Eliza would not live with me and I went away, but pined so for my child, that I contrived to steal her, and carried her to my mother, where was the other one."

'Lina's eyes were dark as midnight, while she listened breathlessly to this mysterious page of her existence.

"My mother was very old and she died suddenly, leaving me alone with my two girls. I could not attend to them both, and so I sent one to Eliza, and kept the other myself, hiring a housekeeper, and because it suited my fancy, passing as Mr. Redfield, guardian to the little child, whom I loved so much."

"That was *Adah*," fell in a whisper from the doctor's lips, but caught the ear of no one.

All were too intent upon the story, which proceeded;

"She grew in beauty, and I was wondrous proud of her, giving her every advantage in my power. I sent her to the best of schools, and even looked forward to the day when she should take the position she was so well fitted to fill. After she was grown to girlhood we boarded, she as the ward, I as the guardian still, and then one unlucky day I stumbled upon *you, Dr. John*, but not until you first had stumbled on my daughter, and been charmed with her beauty, passing yourself as—as George Hastings,— lest your fashionable associates should know how the aristocratic Dr. Richards was in love with a poor, unknown orphan, boarding up two flights of stairs."

"Who is he talking about, Hugh? Does he mean me? My head throbs so, I don't quite understand," 'Lina said piteously, while Hugh held the poor aching head against his bosom, crushing the orange blossoms, and whispering softly,

"He means Adah."

"Yes, Adah," the convict rejoined. "John Richards fancied Adah Gordon, as she was called, but loved his pride and position more. I'll do you justice, though, young man, I believe at one time you really and truly loved my child, and but for your mother's letters might have married her honorably. But you were afraid of that mother. Your pride was stronger than your love; but I was determined that you should have my daughter, and proposed a mock marriage——"

"Monster! *You, her father,* planned that fiendish act!" and Alice's blue eyes flashed indignantly upon him, while Hugh, forgetting that the idea was not new to him, walked up before the "monster," as if to lay him at his feet.

"Listen, while I explain, and you will see the monster had an object," returned the stranger, speaking to Alice, instead of Hugh. "It was the great wish of my heart that my daughter should marry into a good family,—one which would give her position, and when I saw how much John Richards was pleased with her, I said *he* should be her husband, for the Richards were known to me by reputation.

"From what I knew of John I thought he would hardly dare marry my daughter outright, and so I cautiously suggested a mock marriage, saying, by way of excusing myself that as I was only Adah's guardian, I could not feel towards her as a near relative would feel,—that, as I had already expended large sums of money on her, I was getting tired of it, and would be glad to be released, hinting, by way of smoothing the fiendish proposition, my belief that, from constant association, he would come to love her so much that at last he would really and truly make her his wife. He seemed shocked, and if I remember rightly, called me a brute, and all that; but little by little I gained ground, until at last he consented, stipulating that she should not know his real name, which he knew I had discovered. It seems strange that a father should wish his child to marry one who would consent to act so base a part, but I knew there was nothing unkind in the doctor's nature, and I trusted that his fondness for Adah and her influence over him would bring it right at last.

"I had an acquaintance, I said, who lived a few miles from the city,—a man who, for money, would do any anything, and who, as a feigned justice of the peace, would go through with the ceremony, and ever after keep his own counsel. I wonder the doctor himself did not make some inquiries concerning this so called justice, but I think he is not remarkably clear-headed, and this weakness saved me much trouble. After a time I arranged the matter with my friend, who was a lawful justice, staying at the house of his brother, then absent in Europe. This being done, I decided upon *Hugh Worthington,* for a witness, as being the person of all the world, who should be present at the bridal. He had recently come to New York, and I had accidentally made his acquaintance, acquiring so strong an influence over him that when I invited him to the wedding of my *ward,* he went unsuspectingly, signing his name as witness and saluting the bride, who really was a bride, as lawful a one as any who ever turned from the altar where she had registered her vows."

"Oh, joy, joy!" and Alice sprang at once to her feet, and hastening to the doctor's side, said to him, authoritatively:

"You hear, you understand, Adah is your wife, your very own, and you must go back to her at once. You do understand me?" and Alice grew very earnest as the doctor failed to rouse up, as she thought he ought to do.

Appealing next to Anna, she continued:

"Pray, make him comprehend that his wife is at Terrace Hill."

Very gently Anna answered:

"She was there, but she has gone. He knows it; I came to tell him, but she fled immediately after recognizing my brother, and left a letter revealing the whole."

It had come to 'Lina by this time that Dr. Richards could never be her husband, and with a bitter cry, she covered her face with her hands, and went shivering to the corner where Mrs. Worthington sat, as if a mother's sympathy were needed now, and coveted as it had never been before.

"Oh, mother," she sobbed, laying her head in Mrs. Worthington's lap, "I wish I had never been born."

Sadly her wail of disappointment rang through the room, and then the convict went on with his interrupted narrative.

"When the marriage was over, *Mr. Hastings* took his wife to another part of the city, hiding her from his fashionable associates, staying with her most of the time, and appearing to love her so much that I thought it would not be long before I should venture to tell him the truth. It would be better to write it, I thought, and so I left her with him while I went South on—the very laudable business of stealing negroes from one State and selling them in another. At Cincinnati, I wrote to the doctor, confessing the whole, but it seems my letter never reached him, for, though I did not know it then, the car containing that mail was burned, and my letter was burned with it. Some of you know that I was caught in my traffic, and that the negro stealer, Sullivan, was safely lodged in prison, from which he was released but a day since. Fearing there might be some mistake, I wrote from my prison home to Adah herself, but suppose it did not reach New York till after she had left it."

A casual observer would have said that Mrs. Worthington had heard less of that strange story than anyone else, so motionless she sat, but not a word was missed by her in the entire narrative, and when the narrator concluded, she said anxiously,

"And that child, the lawful wife of this young man, was she mine, or was she the servant girl's?"

A little apart from the others, his arms folded tightly together, and his eyes fixed upon the convict, stood Hugh.

"Answer her," he said, gravely, as the convict did not reply. "Tell her if Adah be her child, or, — — 'Lina, — — which?"

Had a clap of thunder cleft the air around her, 'Lina could not have started up sooner than she did. It was the *very first suspicion* which had crossed her brain, and her life seemed dying out, as half way between Mrs. Worthington and the convict she stood with hands outstretched and livid lips, which tried to speak, but could only moan convulsively. The convict took his eyes away from *her*, pitying her so much, as he said, "*Adah* is my lawful child. I kept her, and sent the other back. It was a bold act, and I wonder it was not questioned, but Adaline's eyes were not so black then as they are now, and though five months older than the other, she was small for her age, and two years sometimes change a child materially; so Eliza took it for granted that the girl she received as Adaline, and whose real name was Matilda, was her own; but Adah Hastings is *her* daughter and Hugh's half sister while this young woman is—the child of myself and the servant girl."

Alice, Anna, and the doctor looked aghast, while Mrs. Worthington murmured audibly, "Adah, darling Adah, and Willie, precious Willie—oh, I want them here now!"

The mother had claimed her own, but alas, the fond cry of welcome to sweet Adah Hastings was a death knell to 'Lina, for it seemed to shut her out of that gentle woman's heart. There was no place for her, and in her terrible desolation she stood alone, her eyes wandering wistfully from one to another, but turning very quickly when they fell on the convict, her father. She would not have it so; she could not own a servant for her mother, that villain for her father, and worse—oh, infinitely worse than all—she had no right to be born! A child of sin and shame, disgraced, disowned, forsaken. It was a terrible blow, and the proud girl staggered beneath it.

"Will no one speak to me?" she said, at last; "no one break this dreadful silence? Has everybody forsaken me? Do you all loathe and hate the offspring of such parents? Won't somebody pity and care for me?"

"*Yes, 'Lina,*" and *Hugh*—the one from whom she had the least right to expect pity—Hugh came to her side; and winding his arm around her, said, with a choking voice, "*I* will not forsake you, 'Lina; I will care for you the same as ever, and so long as I have a home you shall have one too."

"Oh, Hugh, I don't deserve this from you!" was 'Lina's faint response, as she laid her head upon his bosom, whispering, "Take me away—from them all—up stairs—on the bed! I am so sick, and my head is bursting open!"

Hugh was strong as a young giant, and lifting gently the yielding form, he bore it from the room—the bridal room, which she would never enter again, until he brought her back—and laid her softly down beneath the windows, dropping tears upon her white, still face, and whispering,

"Poor 'Lina!"

As Hugh passed out with his burden in his arms, the bewildered company seemed to rally; but the convict was the first to act. Turning to Mrs. Worthington, still shivering in the corner, he said,

"Eliza, you see I did *not* die as that paper told you, but it suited me then to be *dead*, and so I wrote the paragraph myself, sending you the paper. For this you should thank me, as it made a few years of your life happier, thinking I was dead. I have come here to-night for my children's sake; and now that I have done what I came to do, I shall leave you, only asking that you continue to be a mother to the poor girl who is really the only sufferer. The rest have cause for joy; you in particular," turning to the doctor. "But tell me again what was that I heard of Adah's having fled?"

Anna repeated the story, and then conquering her repugnance of the man, asked if he would not immediately seek for her and bring her back if possible.

"My brother will help you," she said, "when he recovers himself," and she turned to the doctor, who suddenly seemed to break the spell which had bound him, and springing to his feet, exclaimed,

"Yes, Lily shall be found, but I must see my boy first. Anna, can't we go now, to-night?"

That was impossible; Anna was too tired, Alice said, and conducting her to her own room, she made her take the rest she so much needed.

When Alice returned again to the parlor, the convict had gone. There had been a short consultation between himself and the doctor, an engagement to meet in Cincinnati to arrange their plan of search; and then he had turned again to his once wife, still sitting in her corner, motionless, white, and paralyzed with nervous terror.

"You need not fear me, Eliza," he said, kindly; "I shall probably never trouble you again; and though you have no cause to believe my word, I tell you solemnly that I will never rest until I have found our daughter, and sent her back to you. Good-bye, Eliza, good-bye."

He did not offer her his hand; he knew she would not touch it; but with one farewell look of contrition and regret, he left her, and mounting the horse which had brought him there, dashed away from Spring Bank, just as Colonel Tiffton reined up to the gate.

It was Alice who met him in the hall, explaining to him as much as she thought necessary, and asking him, on his return, to wait a little by the field gate, and turn back other guests who might be on the road.

The Colonel promised compliance with her request, and as only a few had been invited, it was not a hard task imposed upon him. 'Lina had been taken very sick, was all the excuse the discreet Colonel would give to the people, who rather reluctantly turned their faces homeward, so that Spring Bank was not honored with wedding guests that night; and when the clock struck eight, the appointed hour for the bridal, only the bridegroom sat in the dreary parlor, his head bent down upon the sofa arm, and his chest heaving with the sobs he could not repress as he thought of all poor Lily had suffered since he left her so cruelly. Hugh had told him what he did not understand before. He had come into the room for his mother, whom 'Lina was pleading to see; and after leading her to the chamber of the half-delirious girl, he had returned to the doctor, and related to him all he knew of Adah, dwelling long upon her gentleness and beauty, which had won from him a brother's love, even though he knew not she was his sister.

"I was a wretch, a villain!" the doctor groaned. Then looking wistfully at Hugh, he said, "Do you think she loves me still? Listen to what she says in her farewell to Anna," and with faltering voice, he read: "That killed the love; and now, if I could, I would not be his except for Willie's sake. Do you think she meant it?"

"I have no doubt of it, sir. How could her love out live everything? Curses and blows might not have killed it, but when you thought to ruin her good name, to deny your child, she would be less than woman could she forgive. Why, I hate and despise you myself for the wrong you have done *my sister*," and Hugh's tall form seemed to take on an increased height as he abruptly left the room, lest his hot temper should get the mastery, and he knock-down his dastardly brother-in-law.

It was a sad house at Spring Bank that night, where 'Lina lay, tossing distractedly from side to side; now holding her throbbing head, and now thrusting out her hot, dry hands, as if to keep off some fancied form, who claimed to be her mother.

The shock had been a terrible one to 'Lina. She did love Dr. Richards; and the losing him was enough of itself to drive her mad; but worse even than this, and far more humiliating to her pride, was the discovery of her parentage, the knowing that a convict was her father, a common servant her mother, and that no marriage tie had hallowed her birth.

"Oh, I can't bear it!" she cried. "I can't. I wish I might die! Will nobody kill me? Hugh, you will, I know!"

But Hugh was away for the family physician, for he would not trust a gossipping servant to do the errand. Once before that doctor had stood by 'Lina's bedside, and felt her feverish pulse, but his face then was not as anxious as now, when he counted the rapidly increasing beats, and saw how fast the fever came on. There had been an exposure to cold, he said, sufficient of itself to induce a fever, but the whole had been aggravated a hundred fold by the late disastrous affair, of which Hugh had told him something. He did not speak of danger, but Hugh, who watched him narrowly, read it in his face, and following him down the stairs, asked to be told the truth.

"She is going to be very sick. She may get well, but I have little to hope from symptoms like hers."

That was the doctor's reply, and with a sigh Hugh went back to the sick girl, who had given him little else than sarcasm and scorn.

CHAPTER XXXIV
POOR 'LINA

Drearily the morning dawned, but there were no bridal slumbers to be broken, no bridal farewells said. There were indeed good-byes to be spoken, for Anna was impatient to be gone, and at an early hour she was ready to leave the house she had entered under so unpleasant circumstances.

"I would like to see 'Lina," she said to Alice, who carried the request to the sick room.

But 'Lina refused. "I can't," she said; "she hates, she despises me, and she had reason. Tell her I was not worthy to be her sister; tell her anything you like; but the doctor—oh, Alice, do you think he'll come, just for a minute, before he goes?"

It was not a pleasant thing for the doctor to meet 'Lina now face to face, for he thought she wished to reproach him for his treachery. But she did not—she thought only of herself; and when at last, urged on by Anna and Alice, he entered in to her presence, she only offered him her hand at first without a single word. He was shocked to find her so sick, for a few hours had worked a marvellous change in her, and he shrank from the bright eyes fixed so eagerly on his face.

"Oh, Dr. Richards," she began at last, "if I loved you less it would not be so hard to tell you what I must. I did love you, bad as I am, but I meant to deceive you. It was for me that Adah kept silence at Terrace Hill. Adah, I almost hate her for having crossed my path."

There was a fearfully vindictive gleam in the bright eyes now, and the doctor shudderingly looked away, while 'Lina, with a softer tone continued, "You believed me rich, and whether you loved me afterward or not, you sought me first for my money. I kept up the delusion, for in no other way could I have won you. Dr. Richards, if I die, as perhaps I may, I shall have one less sin for which to atone, if I confess to you that instead of the heiress you imagined me to be, I had scarcely money enough to pay my board at that hotel. Hugh, who himself is poor, furnished what means I had, and most of my jewelry was borrowed. Do you hear that? Do you know what you have escaped?"

She almost shrieked at the last, for she read his feelings in his face, and knew that he despised her.

"Go," she continued, "find your Adah. It's nothing but Adah now. I see her name in everything. Hugh thinks of nothing else, and why should he? She's his sister, and I—oh! I'm nobody but a beggarly servant's brat. I wish I was dead! I wish I was dead, and I will be pretty soon."

This was their parting, and the doctor left her room a sobered, sadder man than he had entered it. Half an hour later, and he, with Anna, was fast nearing Versailles, where they were joined by Mr. Millbrook, and together the three started on their homeward route.

Rapidly the tidings flew, told in a thousand different ways, and the neighborhood was all on fire with the strange gossip. But little cared they at Spring Bank for the storm outside. So fierce a one was beating at their doors, that even the fall of Sumter failed to elicit more than a casual remark from Hugh, who read without the slightest emotion the President's call for 75,000 men. At another time he might have been eager to join the fray and hasten to avenge the insult, for Kentucky held no truer patriot than he, but now all his thoughts were centered in that dark room where 'Lina raved in mad delirium, controlled only by his or Alice's voice, and quiet only when one of them was with her. Tenderer than a brother was Hugh to the raving creature, staying by her so patiently and uncomplainingly that none save Alice ever guessed how he longed to be free and join in the search for Adah, which had as yet proved fruitless. Night after night, day after day, 'Lina grew worse, until at last there was no hope, and the council of physicians summoned to her side, said that she would die. Still she lingered on, and the fever abated at last, the eyes were not so fearfully bright, while the wild ravings were hushed, and 'Lina lay quietly upon her pillow.

"Do you know me?" Alice asked, bending gently over her, while Hugh, from the other side of the bed, leaned eagerly forward for the reply.

"Yes, but where am I? This is not New York. Have I—am I sick, very sick?" and 'Lina's eyes took a terrified expression as she read the truth in Alice's face. "I am not going to *die*, am I?" she continued, casting upon Alice a look which would have wrung out the truth, even if Alice had been disposed to withhold it, which she was not.

"You are very sick," she answered, "and though we hope for the best, the doctor does not encourage us much. Are you willing to die, 'Lina?"

Neither Hugh nor Alice ever forgot the tone of 'Lina's voice as she replied,

"Willing? *No!*" or the expression of her face, as she turned it to the wall, and motioned them to leave her.

For two days after that she neither spoke nor gave other token of interest in any thing passing around her, but at the expiration of that time, as Alice sat by her, she suddenly exclaimed,

"Forgive us our trespasses as we forgive those who trespass against us. I wish he had said that some other way, for if that means we can not be forgiven until we forgive every body, there's no hope for me, for I cannot, *I will not* forgive that servant for being my mother, neither will I forgive Adah Hastings for having crossed my path. If she had never seen the doctor I should have been his wife, and never have know who or what I was. I hate them both, so you need not pray for me. I heard you last night, but it's no use. I can't forgive."

'Lina was very much excited—so much so, indeed, that Alice could not talk with her then; and for days this was the burden of her remarks. She could not forgive her mother nor Adah, and until she did, there was no use for her or any one else to pray. But the prayers she could not say for herself were said for her by others, while Alice omitted no proper occasion for talking with her personally on the subject she felt to be all important. Nor were these efforts without their effect, for the bitter tone ceased at last, and 'Lina became gentle as a child.

Taking Mrs. Worthington's hand one day, she said,

"I've given you little cause to love me, and I know how glad you must be that another, and not I, is your real daughter. I did not know what made me so bad, but I understand it now. I saw myself so plainly in that man's eyes; it was his nature in me which made me a second Satan—so bad to you, so hateful to Hugh. Oh, Hugh! the memory of what I've been to him is the hardest part of all, for I want him to think kindly of me when I'm gone!" and covering her face with the sheet, 'Lina wept bitterly; while Hugh, who was standing behind her laid his warm hand on her head, smoothing her hair caressingly, as he said,

"Never mind that, 'Lina; I, too, was bad to you—provoking you purposely many times, and exposing your weakness just to see how savage you would be. If 'Lina can forgive *me*, I surely can forgive 'Lina."

There was the sound of convulsive sobbing; and then, uncovering her face, 'Lina raised herself up, and laying her head on Hugh's bosom, answered through her tears,

"I wish I had always felt as I do now. We should have been happier together, and it would not be so great a relief to you'all to have me gone, never to come back again. Hugh, you don't know how bad I've been. You remember the money you sent to Adah last summer in mother's letter. I kept the whole. I burned the letter, and mother never saw it. I bought jewelry with Adah's money. I did so many things, I—I—it goes from me now. I can't remember all. Oh, must I confess the whole, everything, before I can say, 'Forgive us our trespasses?'"

"No, 'Lina. Unless you can repair some wrong, you are not bound to tell every little thing. Confession is due to God alone," Alice whispered to the agitated girl, who looked bewildered, as she answered back, "But God knows all now, and you do not; besides, I can't feel sorry towards Him as I do towards others. I try and try, but the feeling is not there—the sorry feeling, I mean, as sorry as I want to feel."

"God, who knows our feebleness, accepts our purpose to do better, and gives us strength to carry them out," Alice whispered, again bending over 'Lina, on whose pallid, distressed face a ray of hope for a moment shone.

"I have good purposes," she murmured, "but I can't, I can't. I don't know as they are real; may be, if I get well, they would not last, and it's all so dark, so desolate,—nothing to make life desirable,—no home, no name, no friends—and death is so terrible. Oh, Hugh, Hugh! don't let me go. You are strong; you can hold me back, even from Death himself, and I can be good to you; I can feel on that point, and I tell you truly that, standing as I am with the world behind and death before, I see nothing to make life desirable, but you, Hugh, my noble, my abused brother. To make you love me, as I hope I might, is worth living for. You would stand by me, Hugh,—you if no one else, and I wish I could tell you how fast the great throbs of love keep coming to my heart. Dear Hugh, brother Hugh, don't let me die,—hold me fast."

With an icy shiver, she clung closer to Hugh, as if he could indeed do battle with the king of terrors stealing slowly into that room.

"Somebody say 'Our Father,'" she whispered, "I can't remember how it goes."

"Do you forgive and love everybody?" Alice asked, sighing as she saw the bitter expression flash for an instant over the pinched features, while the white lips answered, "Not Adah, no, not Adah."

Alice could not pray after that, not aloud at least, and a deep silence fell upon the group assembled around the death-bed, while 'Lina slept quietly on Hugh's strong arm. Gradually the hard expression on the face relaxed, giving way to one of quiet peace, as they waited anxiously for the close of that long sleep. It was broken at last, but 'Lina seemed lost to all save the thoughts burning at her breast,—thoughts which brought a quiver to her lips, and forced out upon her brow great drops of sweat. The noonday sun of May was shining broadly into the room, but to 'Lina it was night, and she said to Alice, now kneeling at her side, "It's growing dark; they'll light the street lamps pretty soon, and the band will play in the yard, but I shall not hear them. New York and Saratoga are a great ways off, and so is Terrace Hill. Tell Adah I *do* forgive her, and I would like to see her, for she is my half sister. The bitter is all gone. I am in charity with everybody, everybody. May I say 'Our Father' now? It goes and comes, goes and comes, forgive our trespasses, my trespasses; how is it, Hugh? Say it with me once, and you, too, mother."

Mrs. Worthington, with a low cry began with Hugh the soothing prayer in which 'Lina joined feebly, throwing in ejaculatory sentences of her own. "Forgive my trespasses as I forgive those that trespass against me. Bless Hugh, dear Hugh, noble Hugh. Forgive us our trespasses, forgive us our trespasses, our trespasses, forgive *my* trespasses, *me*, forgive, forgive."

It was the last words which ever passed 'Lina's lips, "Forgive, forgive," and Hugh, with his ear close to the lips, heard the faint murmur even after the hands had fallen from his neck where, in the last struggle, they had been clasped, and after the look which comes but once to all had settled on her face. That was the last of 'Lina, with that cry for pardon she passed away, and though it was but a death-bed repentance, and she, the departed, had much need for pardon, Alice clung to it as to a ray of hope, knowing how tender and full of compassion was the blessed Saviour, even to those who turn not to him until the river of death is bearing them away. Very gently Hugh laid the dead girl back upon the pillow, and leaving one kiss on her white forehead, hurried away to his own room, where, unseen by mortal eye, he could ask for knowledge to give himself to the God who had come so near to them.

The next day was appointed for the funeral, and just as the sun was setting, a long procession wound across the fields, and out to the hillside, where the Spring Bank dead were buried, and where they laid 'Lina to rest, forgetting all her faults, and speaking only kindly words of her as they went slowly back to the house, from which she had gone forever.

CHAPTER XXXV
JOINING THE ARMY

Ten days after the burial, there came three letters to Spring Bank, one to Hugh, from Murdoch, as he now chose to be called, saying that though he had sought and was still searching for the missing Adah, he could only trace her, and that but vaguely, to the Greenbush depot, where he lost sight of her entirely, no one after that having seen a person bearing the least resemblance to her. After a consultation with the doctor, he had advertised for her, and he enclosed a copy of the advertisement, as it appeared in the different papers of Boston, Albany, and New York.

"If A— — H— — will let her whereabouts be known to her friends, she will hear of something to her advantage."

This was the purport of Murdoch's letter, if we except a kind enquiry after '*Lina*, of whose death he had not heard.

The second, for Alice, was from Anna Richards, who having heard of 'Lina's decease, spoke kindly of the unfortunate girl, and then wrote. "I have great hopes of my erring brother, now that I know how his whole heart goes out towards his beautiful boy, our darling Willie. I wish poor, dear Lily could have seen him when, on his arrival at Terrace Hill, he knelt by the crib of his sleeping child, waking him at once, and hugging him to his bosom, while his tears dropped like rain. I am sure she would have chosen to be his wife, for her own sake as well as Willie's.

"You knew how proud my mother and sisters are, and it would surprise you to see them pet, and spoil, and fondle Willie, who rules the entire household; mother even allowing him to bring wheel-barrow, drum, and trumpet into the parlor, declaring that she likes the noise, as it stirs up her blood. Willie has made a vast change in our once quiet home, and I fear I shall meet with much opposition when I take him away, as I expect to do next month, for Lily gave him to me, and brother John has said that I may have him until the mother is found, while Charlie is perfectly willing; and thus, you see, my cup of joy is full.

"Brother is away now, searching for Adah, and I am wicked enough not to miss him, so busy am I in the few preparations needed by the wife of a poor missionary."

Then, in a postscript, Anna added: "I forgot to tell you that Charlie and I are to be married some time in July, that the Presbyterian Society of Snowdon have given him a call to be their pastor, that he has accepted, and what is best of all, has actually rented your old home for us to live in. Oh, I am so happy; I do not feel like an old maid of thirty-three, and Charlie flatters me by saying I have certainly gone back in looks to twenty. Perhaps I have, but it all comes of happiness and a heart full of thankfulness to our good Father who has so greatly blessed me."

With a smile, Alice finished the childlike letter, so much like Anna. Then feeling that Mrs. Worthington would be glad to hear from Willie, she went in quest of her, finding her at the end of the long piazza, listening while Hugh read the sympathetic letter received from Irving Stanley.

From the doctor, whom he accidentally met on Broadway, Irving had heard of 'Lina's death, and he wrote at once to Mrs. Worthington, expressing his sympathy for her own and Hugh's bereavement; thus showing that the Dr. had only told him a part of the sad story, withholding all that concerned Adah, who was evidently a stranger to Irving Stanley. His sister, Mrs. Ellsworth, was well, he wrote, though very busy with her preparations for going to Europe, whither he intended accompanying her, adding "it was not so much pleasure which was taking her there, as the hope that by some of the Paris physicians her little deformed Jennie might be benefitted. She had secured a gem of a governess for her daughter, a young lady whom he had not yet seen, but over whose beauty and accomplishments his staid sister Carrie had really waxed eloquent." The letter closed by asking if Hugh were still at home or had he joined the army.

"Oh-h," and Alice's cheek grew pale at the very idea of Hugh's putting himself in so much danger, for Hugh was very dear to her now. His noble, unselfish devotion to 'Lina had finished the work begun on that memorable night when she had said to him, "I may learn to love you," and more than once as she watched with him by 'Lina's bedside, she had been tempted to wind her arm around his neck and whisper in his ear,

"Hugh, I love you now, I will be your wife."

But propriety had held her back and made her far more reserved towards him than she had ever been before. Terribly jealous where she was concerned, Hugh was quick to notice the change, and the gloomy shadow on his face was not caused wholly by 'Lina's sad death, as many had supposed. Hugh was very unhappy. Instead of learning to love him, as he had sometimes hoped she might, Alice had come to dislike him, shunning his society, and always making some pretense to get away if by chance they were left alone, or if compelled to talk with him, chatting rapidly on the most indifferent topics. She never would love him, Hugh thought, and feeling that the sooner he left home the better, he had decided to start at once in quest of Adah. This decision he had not yet communicated to his mother, but as the closing of Irving Stanley's letter seemed to open the way, he rather abruptly announced his intention of going immediately to New York. He did not however add that failing to find his sister, he might possibly join the Federal Army.

Ever since he had had time to think clearly upon the subject then agitating the public mind, Hugh had felt an intense desire to enroll himself with the patriotic men who would not sit idly down while their country was laying her dishonored head low in the dust. A Unionist to the heart's core, he had already won some notoriety by his bitter denunciations against those men who, with Harney at their head, were advocating secession from the union. But his first duty was to Adah, and so he only talked of her and the probabilities of his finding her. He should start to-morrow, if possible, he said. He had made his arrangements to do so, and there was no longer an excuse for tarrying. They would get on well enough without him; they would not miss him much, and he stole a glance at Alice, who, fearful lest she might betray herself, framed some excuse for leaving her seat upon the piazza, and stole up to her room where she could be alone, to think how desolate Spring Bank would be when Hugh was really gone.

Once she thought to tell him all, thinking that a perfect understanding would make her so much happier while he was away, but maidenly modesty kept her back, and so the words which would have brought so much comfort to Hugh were to the last unspoken. Gentler, kinder, tenderer than a sister's could have been, was her demeanor towards him during the whole of the next day, the last he spent at home. Once, emboldened by something she said, Hugh felt half tempted to sue again for the love so coveted, but depreciation of himself kept him silent, and when at last they parted, his manner towards her was so constrained and cold that even Mrs. Worthington observed it, wondering what had come between them. She wanted Alice to think well of Hugh, and by way of obliterating any unpleasant impression he might have left in her mind, she spent the morning after his departure in talking of him, telling how kind he had always been to her, and how kind he was to every body. Many acts were enumerated by the fond mother as proofs of his unselfishness, and among others she spoke of his heroic conduct years ago, when with his uncle he was on Lake Erie and the boat took fire. Had she never told Alice?

"No, never," Alice answered faintly, a new light breaking in upon her and showing her why it was that Hugh's face had so often puzzled her.

He was the boy to whose care she had entrusted her life, and *she* was the *Golden Haired*, remembered by him so long and so lovingly. There was one great throb of joy,—of perfect delight, and then an intense desire to tell Hugh of her discovery— —.

But Hugh was gone, and her only alternative now was to write. He was intending to stop two days in Cincinnati, and he had said to his mother, "If any thing happens you can write to me there," and something had happened, something which made her heart throb wildly, as alone in her room she knelt and thanked her God, asking that he would care for the Hugh so dear to her, and bring him safely back.

Two days later and Hugh, who had but an hour longer to remain in Cincinnati, sauntered to the post-office, with very little expectations that he should find any thing awaiting him. How then was he surprised when a clerk handed him Alice's letter, the sixth she had written ere at all satisfied with its wording. Hurrying back to his room at the hotel, he broke the seal, and read as follows.

"Dear Hugh:—I have at last discovered *who* you are, and why I have so often been puzzled with your face. You are the boy whom I met on the St. Helena, and who rescued me from drowning. Why have you never told me this?

"Dear Hugh, I wish I had known it earlier. It seems so cold, thanking you on paper, but I have no other opportunity, and must do it here.

"We were both unconscious when taken from the water, but you were holding fast to my arm, and so really was the means of my being saved, though a fisherman carried me to the shore. You must have been removed at once, for when we inquired for you we could only learn that you were gone. Heaven bless you, Hugh. My mother prayed often for the preserver of her child, and need I tell you that I, too, shall never forget to pray for you? The Lord keep you in all your ways, and lead you safely to your sister,

Alice."

Many times Hugh read this note, then pressing it to his lips thrust it into his bosom, but failed to see what Alice had hoped he might see, that the love he once asked for was his at last.

"If she loved me, she would have told me so," he thought, "for she promised me as much, but she does not, so that ends the drama. Oh, Golden Hair, why *did* I ever meet her, or why was I suffered to love her so devotedly, if I must lose her at the last!"

There were great drops of sweat about Hugh's lips, and on his forehead, as, burying his face in his hands, he laid both upon the table, and battled manfully with his love for Alice Johnson.

"God help me in my sorrow," was the prayer which fell from the quivering lips, but did not break the silence of that little room, where none, save God, witnessed the conflict, the last Hugh ever fought for Alice Johnson.

He *could* give her up at length; could think, without a shudder, of living all his life without her, and when, late that afternoon, he took the evening train for Cleveland, not one in the crowded car would have guessed how sore was the heart of the young man who plunged so energetically into the spirited war argument in progress between a Northern and Southern politician. It was a splendid escape-valve for his pent up feelings, and Hugh carried everything before him, taking by turns both sides of the question, and effectually silencing the two combatants, who said to each other in parting, "We shall hear from that Kentuckian again, though whether in Rebeldom or Yankee land we cannot tell."

Arrived at New York he wrote a reply to Alice's note, saying that what he had done for her was no more than he ought to have done for any one who had come to him for help, and that she need not expend her gratitude on him, though he was glad of any thing to keep him in her remembrance.

After this he wrote regularly, kind, friendly letters, and Alice was beginning to feel that they in some degree atoned for his absence, when there came one which wrung a wailing cry from Mrs. Worthington, and brought Alice at once to her side.

"What is it?" she asked in much alarm, and Mrs. Worthington replied, "Oh, Hugh, my boy! he's enlisted, joined the army! I shall never see him again!"

Could Hugh have seen Alice then, he would not for a moment have doubted the nature of her feelings towards himself. She did not cry out, nor faint, but her face turned white as the dress she wore, while her hands pressed so tightly together, that her nails left the impress in her flesh.

"God keep him from danger and death," she murmured; then, winding her arm around the stricken mother, she wiped her tears away; and to her moaning cry that she was left alone, replied, "Let me be your child till he returns, or, if he never does— —"

She could get no further, and sinking down beside Hugh's mother, she laid her head on her lap, and wept bitterly. Alas, that scenes like this should be so common in our once happy land, but so it is. Mothers start with terror, and grow faint over the boy just enlisted for the war; then follow him with prayers and yearning love to the distant battle field; then wait and watch for tidings from him; and then too often read with streaming eyes and hearts swelling with agony, the fatal message which says *their boy is dead*.

It was a sad day at Spring Bank when first the news of Hugh's enlistment came, for Hugh seemed as really dead as if they heard the hissing shell or whizzing ball which was to bear his young life away. It was nearly two months since he left home, and he could find no trace of Adah, though searching faithfully for her, in conjunction with Murdoch and Dr. Richards, both of whom had joined him in New York.

"If Murdoch cannot find her," he wrote, "I am convinced no one can, and I leave the matter now to him, feeling that another duty calls me, the duty of fighting for my country."

It was just after the disastrous battle of Bull Run, when people were wild with excitement, and Hugh was thus borne with the tide, until he found himself enrolled as a private in a regiment of cavalry, gathering in one of the Northern States. There had been an instant's hesitation, a clinging of the heart to the dear old home at Spring Bank, where his mother and Alice were; and then, with an eagerness which made his whole frame tremble, he had seized the pen, and written down his name, amid deafening cheers for the brave Kentuckian. This done, there was no turning back; nor did he desire it. It seemed as if he were made for war, so eagerly he longed to join the fray. Only one thing was wanting, and that was *Rocket*. He had tried the "Yankee horses," as he called them, but found them far inferior to his pet. Rocket, he must have, and in his letter to his mother, he made arrangements for her to send him northward by a Versailles merchant, who he knew, was coming to New York.

Hugh and Rocket, they would make a splendid match, and so Alice thought, as, on the day when Rocket was led away, she stood with her arms around his graceful neck, whispering to him the words of love she would fain have sent his master. She had recovered from the first shock of Hugh's enlistment. She could think of him now calmly as a soldier; could pray that God would keep him, and even feel a throb of pride that one who had lived so many years in Kentucky, then poising almost equally in the scale, should come out so bravely for the right, though by that act he called down curses on his head from those at home who favored Rebellion, and who, if they fought at all, would cast in their lot with the seceding States. She had written to Hugh telling him how proud she was of him, and how her sympathy and prayers would follow him everywhere. "And if," she had added, in concluding, "you are sick, or wounded, I will come to you as a sister might do. I will find you wherever you are."

She had sent this letter to him three weeks before, and now she stood caressing the beautiful Rocket, who sometimes proudly arched his long neck, and then looked wistfully at the sad group gathered round him, as if he knew it was no ordinary parting. Col. Tiffton, who had heard what was going on, had ridden over to expostulate with Mrs. Worthington against sending Rocket North. "Better keep him at home," he said, "and tell Hugh to come back, and let those who had raised the muss settle their own difficulty."

The old colonel, who was a native of Virginia, did not know exactly where he stood. "He was very patriotic," he said, "but hanged if he knew which side to take—both were wrong. He didn't go Nell's doctrine, for Nell was a *rabid Secesh*; neither did he swallow Abe Lincoln, and he'd advise Alice to keep a little more quiet, for there was no knowing what the hot heads would do; they might pounce on Spring Bank any night."

"Let them," and Alice's blue eyes flashed brightly while her girlish figure seemed to expand and grow higher as she continued; "they will find no cowards here. I never touched a revolver in my life. I am quite as much afraid of one that is not loaded as of one that is, but I'll conquer the weakness. I'll begin to-day. I'll learn to handle fire-arms. I'll practice shooting at a mark, and if Hugh is killed I'll——"

She could not tell what she would do, for the woman conquered all other feelings, and laying her face on Rocket's silken mane, she sobbed aloud.

"There's pluck, by George!" muttered the old colonel. "I most wish Nell was that way of thinking."

It was time now for Rocket to go, and 'mid the deafening howls of the negroes and the tears of Mrs. Worthington and Alice he was led away, the latter watching him until he was lost to sight beyond the distant hill, then falling on her knees she prayed, as many a one has done, that God would be with our brave soldiers, giving them the victory, and keeping *one* of them, at least, from falling.

Sadly, gloomily the autumn days came on, and the land was rife with war and rumors of war. In the vicinity of Spring Bank were many patriots, but there were hot Secessionists there also, and bitter contentions ensued. Old friends were estranged, families were divided, neighbors watched each other jealously, while all seemed waiting anxiously for the result.

Blacker, and darker, and thicker the war clouds gathered on our horizon, but our story has little to do with that first year of carnage, when human blood was poured as freely as water, from the Cumberland to the Potomac. Over all that we pass, and open the scene again in the summer of '62, when people were gradually waking to the fact that Richmond was *not* so easily taken, or the South so easily conquered.

CHAPTER XXXVI
THE DESERTER

There had been a desertion from a regiment on the Potomac. An officer of inferior rank, but whose position had been such as to make him the possessor of much valuable information, was missing from his command one morning, and under such circumstances as to leave little doubt that his intention was to reach the enemy's lines if possible. Long and loud were the invectives against the traitor, and none were deeper in their denunciations than Captain Hugh Worthington, as, seated on his fiery war-horse, Rocket, he heard from Irving Stanley the story of *Dr. Richards'* disgrace.

"He should be pursued, brought back, and shot!" he said, emphatically, feeling that he would like much to be one of the pursuers already on the track of the treacherous doctor, who skillfully eluded them all, and just at the close of a warm summer day, sat in the shadow of the Virginia woods, weary, foot-sore and faint with the pain caused from his ankle, sprained by a recent fall.

He had hunted for Adah until entirely discouraged, and partly as a panacea for the remorse preying so constantly upon him, and partly in compliance with Anna's entreaties, he had at last joined the Federal army, and been sworn in with the full expectation of some lucrative office. But his unlucky star was in the ascendant. Stories derogatory to his character were set afloat, and the final result of the whole was that he found himself enrolled in a company where he knew he was disliked, and under a captain whom he thoroughly detested, for the fraud practised upon himself. In this condition he was sent to the Potomac, and while on duty as a picket, grew to be on the most friendly terms with more than one of the enemy, planning at last to desert, and effecting his escape one stormy night, when the watch were off their guard. Owing to some mistake, the aid promised by his Rebel friends had not been extended, and as best he could he was making his way to Richmond, when, worn out with hunger and fatigue, he sank down to die, as he believed, at the entrance of some beautiful woods which skirted the borders of a well kept farm in Virginia. Before him, at the distance of nearly a quarter of a mile, a large, handsome house was visible, and by the wreath of smoke curling from the rear chimney, he knew it was inhabited, and thought once to go there, and beg for the food he craved so terribly.

But fear kept him back—the people might be Unionists, and might detain him a prisoner until the officers upon his track came up. Dr. Richards was cowardly, and so with a groan, he laid his head upon the grass, and half wished that he had died ere he came to be the miserable wretch he was. The pain in his ankle was by this time intolerable, and the limb was swelling so fast that to walk on the morrow was impossible, and if he found a shelter at all, it must be found that night.

Midway between himself and the house was a comfortable looking barn, whither he resolved to go. But the journey was a tedious one, and brought to his flushed forehead great drops of sweat wrung out by the agony it caused him to step upon his foot. At last, when he could bear his weight upon it no longer, he sank upon the ground, and crawling slowly upon his hands and knees, reached the barn just as it was growing dark, and the shadows creeping into the corners made him half shrink with terror, lest they were the bayonets of those whose coming he was constantly expecting. He could not climb to the scaffolding, and so he sought a friendly pile of hay, and crouching down behind it, fell asleep for the first time in three long days and nights.

The early June sun was just shining through the cracks between the boards when he awoke: sore, stiff, feverish, burning with thirst, and utterly unable to use the poor, swollen foot, which lay so helplessly upon the hay.

"Oh, for Anna now," he moaned; "if she were only here; or Lily, she *would* pity and forgive, could she see me now."

But hark, what sound is it which falls upon his ear, making him quake with fear, and, in spite of his aching ankle, creep farther behind the hay! It is a footstep—a light, tripping step, and it comes that way, nearer, nearer, until a shadow falls between the open chinks and the bright sunshine without. Then it moves on, round the corner, pausing for a moment, while the hidden coward holds his breath and listens anxiously, hoping nothing is coming there. But there is, and it enters the same door through which he came the previous night—a girlish figure, with a basket on its arm—a basket in which she puts the eggs she knew just where to find. Not behind the hay, where a poor wretch was almost dead with terror. There was no nest there, and so she failed to see the ghastly face, pinched with hunger and pain, the glassy eyes, the uncombed hair, and soiled, tattered garments of him who once was known as one of fashion's most fastidious dandies.

She had secured her eggs for the morning meal, and the doctor hoped she was about to leave, when there was a rustling of the hay, and he almost uttered a scream of fear. But the sound died on his lips, as he heard the voice of prayer—heard that young girl as she prayed, and the words she uttered, stopped, for an instant, the pulsation of his heart, and partly took his senses away. First for her baby-boy she prayed, asking that God would be to him father and mother both, and keep him from temptation. Then for her *country*; and the doctor, listening to her, knew it was no Rebel tongue calling so earnestly on God to save the Union, praying so touchingly for the poor, suffering soldiers, and coming at last to him, the miserable outcast, whose bloodshot eyes grew blind, and whose brain grew giddy and wild, as he heard again *Lily's voice*, pleading for *George*, wherever he might be. She did not say, "God send him back to me, who loves him still." She only asked forgiveness for the father of her boy, but this was proof to the listener that she did not hate him, and forgetful of his pain he raised himself upon his elbow, and looking over the pile of hay, saw her where she knelt, Lily,—Adah,—his wife, her fair face covered by her hands, and her soft, brown hair cut short, and curling in her neck.

Twice he essayed to speak, but his tongue refused to move, and he sunk back exhausted, just as Adah rose from her knees and turned to leave the barn. He could not let her go. He should die before she came again; he was half dying now, and it would be so sweet to breathe out his life upon her bosom, with perhaps her forgiving kiss upon his lips.

"Adah!" he tried to say; but the quivering lips made no sound, and Adah passed out, leaving him there alone. "Adah, Lily, Anna," he gasped, hardly knowing himself whose name he called in his despair.

She heard that sound, and started suddenly, for she thought it was her old, familiar name, which no one knew there at Sunny Mead. For a moment she paused; but it came not again, and so she turned the corner, and her shadow fell a second time on the haggard face pressed against that crevice in the wall, the opening large enough to thrust the long fingers through, in the wild hope of detaining her as she passed.

"*Adah!*"

It was a gasping, bitter cry; but it reached her, and looking back, she saw the pale hand beckoning, the fingers motioning feebly, as if begging her to return. There was a moment's hesitation, and then conquering her timidity, Adah went back, shuddering as she passed the still beckoning hand, and caught a glimpse of the wild eyes peering at her through the crevice.

"*Adah!*"

She heard it distinctly now, and with it came thoughts of Hugh. It must be he; and her feet scarcely touched the ground in her eagerness to find him. Over the threshold, across the floor, and behind the hay she bounded; out stood aghast at the spectacle before her. He had struggled to his knees; and with his sprained limb coiled under him, his ashen lips apart, and his arms stretched out, he was waiting for her. But Adah did not spring into those trembling arms, as once she would have done. She would never willingly rest in their embrace again; and utter, overwhelming surprise, was the only emotion visible on her face as she recognized him, not so much by his looks as by the name he gave her.

"George, oh, George, how came you here?" she asked, drawing backward from the arm reached out to touch her.

He felt that he was repulsed, and, with a wail which smote painfully on Adah's heart, he fell forward on his face, sobbing, "Oh, Adah, Lily, pity me, pity me, if you can't forgive! I have slept for three nights in the woods, without once tasting food! My ankle is sprained, my strength is gone, and I wish that I were dead!"

She had drawn nearer to him while he spoke, near enough to recognize her country's uniform, all soiled and tattered though it was. He was a soldier then—Liberty's loyal son—and that fact awoke a throb of pity.

"George," she said, kneeling down beside him, and laying her hand upon his ragged coat, "tell me how came you here, and where is your company?"

He would not deceive her, though tempted to do so, and he answered her truthfully, "Lily, I am a deserter. I am trying to join the enemy!"

He did not see the indignant flash of her eyes, or the look of scorn upon her face, but he felt the reproach her silence implied, and dared not look up.

"George," she began at last, sternly, very sternly, "but for Him who bade us forgive seventy times seven, I should feel inclined to leave you here to die; but when I remember how much He is tried with me, I feel that I am to be no one's judge. Tell me, why you have deserted; and tell me, too—oh, George, in mercy—tell me if you know aught of *Willie*?"

The mother had forgotten all the wrongs heaped upon the wife, and Adah drew nearer to him now, *so* near indeed, that his arm encircled her at last, and held her close; but the ragged, dirty, fallen creature did not dare to kiss her, and could only press her convulsively to his breast, as he attempted an answer to her question.

"You must be quick," she said, suddenly remembering herself; "it is growing late, Mrs. Ellsworth will be waiting for her breakfast; and since the stampede of her servants, two old negroes and myself are all there are left to care for the house. Stay," she added, as a new thought seemed to strike her;

"I must go, or they will look for me; but after breakfast I will return, and do for you what I can. Lie down again upon the hay."

She spoke kindly to him, but he felt it was as she would have spoken to any one in distress, and not as once she had addressed him. But he knew that he deserved it; and he suffered her to leave him, watching her with streaming eyes as she hurried along the path, and counting the minutes, which seemed to him like hours, ere he saw her returning. She was very white when she came back and he noticed that she frequently glanced toward the house, as if haunted by some terror. Constantly expecting detection, he grasped her arm, as she bent to bathe his swollen foot, and whispered huskily, "Adah, there's something on your mind—some evil you fear. Tell me, is any one after me!"

Adah nodded; while, like a frightened child, the tall man clung to her neck, saying, piteously, "Don't give me up! Don't tell; they would hang me, perhaps!"

"They ought to do so," trembled on Adah's lips, but she suppressed the words, and went on bandaging up the ankle, and handling it as carefully as if it had not belonged to a deserter.

He did not feel pain now in his anxiety, as he asked, "Who is it, Adah? who's after me?" but he started when she replied, with downcast eyes and a flush upon her cheek, "Major Irving Stanley. You were in his regiment,—the N. Y. Volunteers."

Dr. Richards drew a relieved breath. "I'd rather it were he than Captain Worthington, who hates me so cordially. Adah, you must hide me; I have so much to tell. I know your parents, your brother, your husband; and I am he. It was not a mock marriage. It has been proved real. It was a genuine Justice who married us, and you are my lawful wife. Oh, pray, please don't hurt me so," and he uttered a scream of pain as Adah's hands pressed heavily upon the hard, purple flesh.

She scarcely knew what she was doing as she listened to his words, and heard that she was indeed his wife. Two years before, such news would have overwhelmed her with delight, but now for a single instant a fierce and almost resentful pang shot through her heart as she thought of being bound for life to one for whom she had no love, and whose very caresses made her loathe him more and more. But when she thought of Willie, and that the stain upon his birth was washed away, the hard look left her eyes, and her hot tears dropped upon the ankle she was bandaging.

"You are glad?" he asked, looking at her curiously, for her manner puzzled him.

"Yes, very glad for Willie," she replied, keeping her face bent down so he could not see its expression.

Then when her task was done, she seemed to nerve herself for some painful task, and sitting down upon the hay said to him,

"Tell me now all that has happened since I left Terrace Hill; but first of Willie. You say Anna has him?"

"Yes, Anna—Mrs. Millbrook," he replied, and was about to say more, when Adah interrupted him with,

"It may spare you some pain if I tell you first what I know of the tragedy at Spring Bank. I know that 'Lina is dead, and that the fact of my existence prevented the marriage. So much I heard Mrs. Ellsworth tell her brother. I had just come to her then. She was prouder toward me than she is now, and I dared not question her. Go on, you spoke of my parents, my brother. Who are they?"

Her manner perplexed him greatly, but he controlled himself, while he repeated rapidly the story known already to our readers, the story which made Adah reel, and turn so white that he attempted to reach her and so keep her from falling. But just the touch of his hand had power to rouse her, and drawing back she laid her face in the hay, and moaned.

"It's more than I ever hoped. Oh, Heavenly Father accept my thanks for this great happiness. A mother and a brother found."

"And husband, too," chimed in the doctor, eagerly, "thank him for me, Adah. You are glad to find me?"

There was a pleading in his tone—earnest pleading, for the terrible conviction was fastening itself upon him, that not as they once parted had he and Adah met. For full five minutes Adah lay upon the hay, her whole soul going out in a prayer of thankfulness for her great joy, and for strength to bear the bitterness mingling with her joy. Her face was very white when she lifted it up at last, but her manner was composed, and she questioned the doctor calmly of Spring Bank, of Alice, of Hugh, of Anna, but could not trust herself to say much to him of Willie, lest her calmness should give way, and a feeling spring up in her heart of something like affection for Willie's father. Alas, for the miserable man. He had found his wife, but there was between them a gulf which his own act had built, and which he never more might pass. He began to suspect it, and ere she had finished the story of her wanderings, which at his request she told, he knew there was no pulsation of her heart which beat for him. He asked her where she had been since she fled from Terrace Hill, and how she came to be in Mrs. Ellsworth's family.

There was a moment's hesitancy, as if she was deciding how much to tell him of the past, and then resolving to keep nothing back which he might know, she told him how, with a stunned heart and giddy brain, she had gone to Albany, and mingling with the crowd had mechanically followed them down to a boat just starting for New York. That, by some means, she found herself in the saloon, and seated next to a feeble, deformed little girl, who lay upon the sofa, and whose sweet, childish voice said to her pityingly,

"Does your head ache, lady, or what makes you so white?"

She had responded to that appeal, talking kindly to the little girl, between whom and herself the friendliest of relations were established, and whose name, she learned, was Jenny Ellsworth. The mother she did not then see, as during the journey down the river she was suffering from a nervous headache, and kept her room. From the child and child's nurse, however, she heard that Mrs. Ellsworth was going to Europe, and was anxious to secure some competent person to act in the capacity of Jenny's governess. Instantly Adah's decision was made. Once in New York she would by letter apply for the situation, for nothing then could so well suit her state of mind as a tour to Europe, where she would be far away from all she had ever known. Very adroitly she ascertained Mrs. Ellsworth's address, wrote her a note the day following her arrival in New York, and the day following that, found her in Mrs. Ellsworth's parlor at the Brevoort House, where for a few days she was stopping. It had troubled her somewhat to know what name to take, but she decided finally upon Adah Gordon as the one by which she was known ere George Hastings crossed her path, and in her note to Mrs. Ellsworth she signed herself "A Gordon." From her little girl Mrs. Ellsworth had heard much of the "sweet young lady, who was so kind to her on the boat," and was thus already prepossessed in her favor.

Adah did not tell Dr. Richards, and perhaps she did not herself know how surprised and delighted Mrs. Ellsworth was with the fair, girlish creature, announced to her as Miss Gordon, and who won her heart before five minutes were gone, making her think it of no consequence to inquire concerning her at Madam — —'s school, where she said she had once been a pupil.

Naturally very impulsive and unsuspecting, Mrs. Ellsworth usually acted upon her likes or dislikes, and Adah was soon installed as governess to the delighted little Jennie, who learned to love her gentle teacher with a love almost amounting to idolatry.

"You were in Europe, then, and that is the reason why we could not find you," Dr. Richards said, adding, after a moment, "And Irving Stanley went with you—was your companion all the while?"

"Yes, all the while," and Adah's cold fingers worked nervously at the wisp of hay she was twisting in her hand. "We came home sooner than we intended, as he was anxious to join the army. I had seen him before—he was in the cars when Willie and I were on our way to Terrace Hill. Willie had the ear-ache, and he was so kind to us both."

Adah looked fixedly now at the craven doctor, who could not meet her glance, for well he remembered the dastardly part he had played in that scene, where his own child was screaming with pain, and he sat selfishly idle.

"She don't know I was there, though," he thought, and that gave him some comfort.

But Adah did know, and she meant he should know she did. Keeping her eyes still fixed upon him, she continued,

"I heard Mr. Stanley talking of you once to his sister, and among other things he spoke of your dislike for children, and referred to an occasion in the cars, when a little boy, for whom his heart ached, was suffering acutely and for whom you evinced no interest, except to say that you *hated* children, and to push his feet from your lap. I never knew till then that you were so near to me."

"It's true, it's true," the doctor cried, tears rolling down his soiled face; "but I never guessed it was you. Lily, I supposed it some ordinary woman."

"So did Irving Stanley," was Adah's quiet, cutting answer; "but his heart was open to sympathy, even for an ordinary woman."

The doctor could only moan, with his face still hidden in his hands, until a sudden thought like a revelation flashed upon him, and forgetting his wounded foot, he sprang like a tiger to the spot where Adah sat, and winding his arm firmly around her, whispered hoarsely,

"Adah, you *love Irving Stanley*. My wife loves another than her husband."

Adah did not struggle to release herself from his grasp, but her whole soul loathed that close embrace, and the loathing expressed itself in the tone of her voice, as she replied,

"Until within an hour I did not suppose you were my husband. You said you were not in that letter; I have it yet; the one in which you told me it was a mock marriage, as, by your own confession, it seems you meant it should be."

"Oh, darling, you kill me, yet I deserve it all; but Adah, I have suffered enough to atone for the dreadful past; and I tried so hard to find you. Forgive me, Lily, forgive," and falling again on his knees, the wretched man poured forth a torrent of entreaties for her forgiveness, her love, without which he should die.

Holding fast her cold hands, he pleaded with all his eloquence, until, maddened by her silence, he even taunted her with loving another, while her own husband was living.

Then Adah started, and pushing him away, sprang to her feet, while the hot blood stained her face and neck, and a resentful fire gleamed from her brown eyes.

"It is not well for you to reproach me with faithlessness," she said, "you, who have dealt so treacherously by me; you, who deliberately planned my ruin, and would have effected it but for the deeper-laid scheme of one you say is my father. No thanks to you that I am a lawful wife. You did not make me so of your own free will. You did to me the greatest wrong a man can do a woman, then cruelly deserted me, and now you would chide me for respecting another more than I do you."

"Not respecting him, Adah, no, not for respecting him. You should do that. He's worthier than I; but, oh, Adah, Lily, wife, mother of my boy, do you love Irving Stanley?"

He was sobbing bitterly, and the words came between the sobs, while he tried to clutch her dress. Staggering backward against the wooden beam, Adah leaned there for support, while she replied,

"You would not understand if I should tell you the terrible struggle it was for me to be thrown each day in the society of one as noble, as good as Irving Stanley, and not come at last to feel for him as a poor governess ought never to feel for the handsome, gifted brother of her employer. Oh, George, I prayed against it so much, prayed to be kept from the sin, if it were a sin, to have Irving Stanley mingled with every thought. But the more I prayed, the more the temptation seemed thrust upon me. The kinder, gentler, more attentive, grew his manners toward me. He never treated me as a mere governess. It was more like an equal at first, and then like a younger sister, so that few strangers took me for a subordinate, so kind were both Mrs. Ellsworth and her brother."

"And he," the doctor gasped, looking wistfully in her face, "does he—do you think he loves *you*?"

Adah colored crimson, but answered frankly,

"He never told me so; never said to me a word which a husband should not hear; but—sometimes, I've left him abruptly lest he should speak, for that I knew would bring the crisis I so dreaded. I must tell him the whole then, and by my dread of doing this, I knew he was more than a friend to me. I was fearful at first that he might recognize me, but I was much thinner than when I saw him in the cars, while my hair, purposely worn short, and curling in my neck, changed my looks materially, so that he only wondered whom I was so much like, but never suspected the truth."

There was silence, a moment, and then the doctor asked, "How is all this to end?"

The question brought into Adah's eyes a fearful look of anguish, but she did not answer, and the doctor spoke again.

"Have I found Lily only to lose her?"

Still there was no reply, and the doctor continued, "You are my wife, Adah. No power can undo that, save death, and you are my child's mother. For Willie's sake, oh Adah, for Willie's sake, forgive."

When he appealed to her as his wife, Adah seemed turning into stone; but the mention of Willie, touched the mother, and the iceberg melted at once.

"For Willie, my boy," she gasped, "I could do almost anything; I could *die* so willingly, but—but—oh, George, that ever we should come to this. You a deserter, a traitor to your country—lame, disabled, wholly in my power, and begging of *me*, your outcast wife, for the love which surely is dead—dead. No, George, I do forgive, but never, never more can I be to you a wife."

There was a rising resentment now in the doctor's manner, as he answered reproachfully: "Then surrender me at once to the lover hunting for me. Let him take me back where I can be shot, and that will leave you free."

Adah raised her hand deprecatingly, and when he had finished, rejoined: "You mistake Maj. Stanley, if you think he would marry me, knowing what I should tell him. It's not for him that I refuse. It's for myself. I could not bear it. I—"

"Stay, Adah, Lily, don't say you should hate me;" and the doctor's voice was so full of anguish that Adah involuntarily advanced toward him, standing quite near, while he begged of her to say if the past could not be forgotten. His family were anxious to receive her. Sweet Anna Millbrook already loved her as a sister, while he, her husband, words could not tell his love for her. He would do whatever she required; go back to the Federal army if she said so; seek for the pardon he was sure to gain; fight for his country like a hero, periling life and limb, if she would only give him the shadow of a hope.

"I must have time to think. I cannot decide alone," Adah answered, while the doctor clutched her dress, half shrieking with terror,

"You surely will not consult Major Stanley?"

"No," and Adah spoke reverently, "there's a mightier friend than he. One who has never failed me in my need. He will tell me what to do."

The doctor knew now what she meant, and with a moan he laid his head again upon the hay, wishing, so much that the lessons taught him when in that little attic chamber, years ago, he knelt by Adah's side, and said with her, "Our Father," had not been all forgotten. When he lifted up his face again, Adah was gone, but he knew she would return, and waited patiently while just outside the door, with her fair face buried in the sweet Virginia grass, and the warm summer sunshine falling softly upon her, poor half-crazed Adah fought and won the fiercest battle *she* had ever known, coming off conqueror over self, and feeling sure that God had heard her earnest cry for help, and told her what to do. There was no wavering now; her step was firm; her voice steady, as she went back to the doctor's side, and bending over him, said,

"I will nurse you, till you are well; then you must go back whence you came, confess your fault, rejoin your regiment, and by your faithfulness wipe out the stain of desertion. Then, when the war is over, or you are honorably discharged, I will—be your wife. I may not love you at first as once I did, but I shall try, and He, who counsels me to tell you this will help me, I am sure."

It was almost pitiful now to see the doctor, as he crouched at Adah's feet, kissing her hands and blessing her 'mid his tears. "He would be worthy of her, and they should yet be so happy."

Adah suffered him to caress her for a moment, and then told him she must go, for Mrs. Ellsworth would wonder at her long absence, and possibly institute a search. Pressing one more kiss upon her hand the doctor crept back to his hiding place, while Adah went slowly back to the house where she knew Irving Stanley was anxiously waiting for her. She dared not meet him alone now, for latterly each time they had so met, she had kept at bay the declaration trembling on his lips, and which must never be listened to. So she staid away from the pleasant parlor where all the morning he sat chatting with his sister, who guessed how much he loved the beautiful and accomplished girl, her daughter's governess.

Right-minded and high-principled, Mrs. Ellsworth had conquered any pride she might at first have felt—any reluctance to her brother's marrying her governess, and now like him was anxious to have it settled. But Adah gave him no chance that day, and late in the afternoon he rode back to his regiment wondering at the change in Miss Gordon, and why her face was so deadly white, and her voice so husky, as she bade him good-bye.

Poor Adah! Hers was now a path of suffering, such as she had never known before. But she did her duty to the doctor, nursing him with the utmost care; but never expressing to him the affection she did not feel. It was impossible to keep his presence there a secret from the two old negroes, and knowing she could trust them, she told them of the wounded Union soldier, enlisting their sympathies for him, and thus procuring for him the care of older and more experienced people than herself.

He was able at length to return, and one pleasant summer night, just three weeks after his arrival at Sunnymead, Adah walked with him to the woods, and kneeling with him by a running stream, whose waters farther away would yet be crimson with the blood of our slaughtered brothers, she commended him to God. Through the leafy branches the moon-beams were shining, and they showed to Adah the expression of the doctor's wasted face, as he said to her at parting, "I have kissed you many times, my darling, but you have never returned it. Please do so once, for the sake of the olden time. It will make me a better soldier."

She kissed him once for the sake of the olden time, and when he whispered, "Again for Willie's sake," she kissed him twice, and then she bade him leave her, herself buttoning about him the soldier coat which her own hands had cleaned and mended and made respectable. She was glad afterward that she had done so; glad, too, that she had kissed him and waited by the tree, where, looking backward, he could see the flutter of her white dress until a turn in the forest path hid her from his view.

CHAPTER XXXVII
THE SECOND BATTLE OF BULL RUN

The second disastrous battle of Bull Run was over, and the shadow of a summer night wrapped the field of carnage in darkness. Thickly upon the battle field lay the dead and dying, the sharp, bitter cries of the latter rising on the night wind, and adding tenfold to the horror of the scene. In the woods, not very far away, more than one brave soldier was weltering in his life-blood, just where, in his rapid flight, he had fallen, the grass his pillow, and the leafy branches of the forest trees his only covering.

Near to a running brook one wounded man was supporting another and trying to staunch the purple gore, pouring darkly from a fearful bullet wound in the region of the heart. The stronger of the two, he who wore a major's uniform, had come accidentally upon the other, writhing in agony, and muttering at intervals snatches of the prayer with which he once had been familiar, and which seemed to bring *Lily* back to him again, just as she was when in the attic chamber she made him kneel by her, and say "Our Father." He tried to say it now, and the whispered words caught the ear of Irving Stanley, arresting his steps at once.

"Poor fellow! it's gone hard with you," he said, kneeling by the sufferer, whom he recognized as the deserter *Dr. Richards,* who had returned to his allegiance, had craved forgiveness for his sins, and been restored to the ranks, discharging his duties faithfully, and fighting that day with a zeal and energy which did much in reinstating him in the good opinion of those who witnessed his daring bravery.

But the doctor's work was done, and never from his lips would Lily know how well his promise had been kept. Giddy with pain and weak from the loss of blood, he had groped his way through the woods, fighting back the horrid certainty that to-morrow's sun would not rise for him, and sinking at length exhausted upon the grass, whose freshness was now defaced by the blood which poured so freely from his wound.

It was thus that Irving Stanley found him, starting at first as from a hissing shell, and involuntarily clasping his hand over the place where lay a little note, received a few days before, a reply to the earnest declaration of love he had at last written to his sister's governess. There was but one alternative, and Adah met it resolutely, though every fibre of her heart throbbed with keen agony as she told to Irving Stanley the story of her life. She was a wife, a mother, the sister of Hugh Worthington, they said, *the Adah* for whom Dr. Richards had sought so long in vain, and for whom Murdoch, the wicked father, was seeking still for aught she knew to the contrary. Even the story of the doctor's secretion in the barn at Sunnymead was confessed. Nothing was withheld except the fact that even as he professed to love her, so she in turn loved him, or had done so before she knew it was a sin. Surprise had, for a few moments stifled every other emotion, and Irving Stanley sat like one suddenly bereft of life, when he read who Adah was. Then came the bitter thought that he had lost her, mingled with a deep feeling of resentment towards the man who had so cruelly wronged the gentle girl, and who alone stood between him and happiness. For Irving Stanley could overlook all the rest. His great warm heart, so full of kindly sympathy and generous charity for all mankind could take to its embrace the fair sweet woman he had learned to love so much, and be a father to her little boy, as if it had been his own. But this might not be. There was a mighty obstacle in the way, and feeling that it mattered little now whether he ever came from the field alive, Irving Stanley, with a whispered prayer for strength to bear and do right, had hidden the letter in his bosom, and then, when the hour of conflict came, plunged into the thickest of the fight with a fearlessness born of keen and recent disappointment, which made life less valuable than it had been before.

It is not strange, then, that he should start and stagger backward when he came so suddenly upon the doctor, or that the first impulse of weak human nature was to leave the fallen man; but the second, the Christian impulse, bade him stay, and forgetting his own slight but painful wound, he bent over Adah's husband, and did what he could to alleviate the anguish he saw was so hard to bear. At the sound of his voice, a spasm of pain passed over the doctor's pallid face, and the flash of a sudden fire gleamed for a moment in his eye, as he, too, remembered *Adah*, and thought of what might be when the grass was growing over his untimely grave.

The doctor knew that he was dying, and yet his first question was—

"Do you think I can live? Did any one ever recover with such a wound as this?"

Eagerly the dim eyes sought the face above them, the kind, good face of one who would not deceive him. Irving shook his head as he felt the pulse, and answered frankly,

"I believe you will die."

There was a bitter moan, as all his misspent life came up before him, followed closely by the dark future, where there shone no ray of hope, and then with the desperate thought, "It's too late now for regrets. I'll meet it like a man," he said.

"It may as well be I as any one, though it's hard even for me to die; harder than you imagine;" then, growing excited as he talked, he raised himself upon his elbow, and continued, "Major Stanley, tell me truly, do you love the woman you know as Adah Gordon?"

"I did love her before I knew I must not—but now—I—yes, Dr. Richards, my heart tells me that never was she so dear to me as now when her husband lies dying at my side."

Irving Stanley hardly knew what he was saying, but the doctor understood, and almost shrieked out the words,

"You know then that she is Adah, a wife, a mother and that I am her lawful husband?"

"I know the whole," was the reply, as with his hand Irving dipped water from the brook and laved the feverish brow of the dying man, who went on to speak of Adah as she was when he first knew her, and of the few happy months spent with her in those humble lodgings.

"You don't know my darling," he whispered. "She's an angel, and I might have been so happy with her. Oh, if I *could* only live, but that can't be now, and it is well. Come close to me, Major Stanley, and listen while I tell you that Adah promised if I would do my duty to my country faithfully, she would live with me again, and all the while she promised, her heart was breaking, for she did not love me. It had all died out for me. It had been given to another; can you guess to whom?"

Irving made no reply, except to chafe the hands which clasped his so tightly, and the doctor continued,

"I am surely dying—I shall never see her more, or my beautiful boy. I was a brute in the cars; you remember the time. That was Adah, and those little feet resting on my lap were Willie's, baby Willie's, Adah's baby."

The doctor's mind was wandering now, and he kept on disconnectedly,

"She's been to Europe with him. She's changed from the shy girl into a queenly woman. Even the Richards line might be proud of her bearing, and when I'm gone, tell her I said you might have Willie, and—and—it grows very dark; the noise of the battle drowns my voice, but come nearer to me, nearer—tell her—tell Adah, you may have her. She needn't mourn, nor wait; but carry me back to Snowdon. There's no soldier's grave there yet. I never thought mine would be the first. Anna will cry, and mother and Asenath and Eudora; but Adah, oh Lily, darling. She's coming to me now. Don't you hear that rustle in the grass?" and the doctor listened intently to a sound which also caught Irving's ear, a sound of a horse's neigh in the distance, followed by a tramp of feet.

"Hush-sh," he whispered. "It may be the enemy," but his words were not regarded, or understood.

The doctor was in Lily's presence, and in fancy it was *her* hand, not Irving's which wiped the death-sweat from his brow, and he murmured words of love and fond endearment, as to a living, breathing form. Fainter and fainter grew the pulse, weaker and weaker grew the trembling voice, until at last Irving could only comprehend that some one was bidden to pray—to say "Our Father."

Reverently, as for a departing brother, he prayed over the dying man, asking that all the past might be forgiven, and that the erring might rest at last in peace.

"Say Amen for me, I'm too weak," the doctor whispered; then, as reason asserted her sway again, he continued "I see it now; Lily's gone, and I am dying here in the woods, in the dark, in the night, on the ground; cared for by you who will be Lily's husband. You may, you may, tell her I said so; tell her kiss my boy; love him, Major Stanley; love him as your own, even though others shall call you father. Tell her—I tried—to pray—"

He never spoke again; and when next the thick, black, clotted blood oozed up from the gaping wound, it brought with it all there was of life; and there in those Virginia woods, in the darkness of the night, Irving Stanley sat alone with the dead. And yet not alone, for away to his right, and where the neigh of a horse had been heard, another wounded soldier lay—his soft, brown locks moist with dew, and his captain's uniform wet with the blood which dripped from the terrible gash in the fleshy part of the neck, where a murderous ball had been. One arm, the right one, was broken, and lay disabled upon the grass; while the hand of the other clutched occasionally at the damp grass, and then lifting itself, stroked caressingly the powerful limbs of the faithful creature standing guard over the prostrate form of his master.

Hugh and Rocket! They had been in many battles, and neither shot nor shell had harmed them until to-day, when Hugh had received the charge which sent him reeling from his horse, breaking his arm in the fall, and scarcely conscious that two of his comrades were leading him from the field. How or by what means he afterwards reached the woods, he did not know, but reached them he had, and unable to travel further, he had fallen to the ground, where he lay, until Rocket came galloping near, riderless, frightened, and looking for his master. With a cry of joy the noble brute answered that master's faint whistle, bounding at once to his side, and by many mute but meaning signs, signifying his desire that Hugh should mount as heretofore.

But Hugh was too weak for that, and after several ineffectual efforts to rise, fell back half fainting on the turf; while Rocket took his stand directly over him, a powerful and efficient guard until help from some quarter should arrive. Patiently, faithfully he stood, waiting as quietly as if he knew that aid was coming, not far away, in the form of an old man, whose hair was white as snow, and whose steps were feeble with age, but who had the advantage of knowing every inch of that ground, for he had trodden it many a time, with a homesick heart which pined for "old Kentuck," whence he had been stolen.

Uncle Sam! He it was whose uncertain steps made Rocket prick up his ears and listen, neighing at last a neigh of welcome, by which he, too, was recognized.

"De dear Father be praised if that be'nt Rocket hisself. I've found him, I've found my Massah Hugh. I tole Miss Ellis I should, 'case I knows all de way. Dear Massah Hugh, I'se *Sam,* I is," and with a convulsive sob the old negro knelt beside the white-faced man who, but for this timely aid, could hardly have survived that fearful night.

CHAPTER XXXVIII
HUGH AND SAM

It is more than a year now since last we looked in upon the inmates of Spring Bank, and during that time Kentucky had been the scene of violence, murder, and bloodshed. The roar of artillery had been heard upon its hills. Soldiers wearing the Federal uniform had marched up and down its beaten paths, encamping for a brief season in its capital, and then departing to other points where their services were needed more.

Morgan, with his fierce band of guerillas, had carried terror, dismay, and sometimes death, to many a peaceful home; while *Harney*, too, disdaining open, honorable warfare, had joined himself, it was said, to a horde of savage marauders, gathered, some from Texas, some from Mississippi, and a few from Tennessee; but none, to her credit be it said, none from Kentucky, save their chief, the *Rebel Harney*, who, despised and dreaded almost equally by Unionists and Confederates, kept the country between Louisville and Lexington in a constant state of excitement.

As the storm grew blacker, it had seemed necessary for Colonel Tiffton openly to avow his sentiments, and not "sneak between two fires, for fear of being burned," as Harney wolfishly told him one day, taunting him with being a "villainous Yankee," and hinting darkly of the punishment preparing for all such.

The colonel was not cowardly, but, as was natural, he *did* lean to the Confederacy. "Peaceful separation, if possible," was his creed; and fully believing the South destined to triumph, he took that side at last, greatly to the delight of his high-spirited Nell, who had been a Rebel from the first. With a look of reproach which the Colonel never forgot, Alice Johnson listened to his reasons for joining himself with the Secessionists, but when at the close of his arguments he kindly advised her to be a little more careful in expressing her opinions, saying there was no knowing what Harney, who was known to be bitterly prejudiced against Spring Bank, might be tempted to do, her blue eyes flashed proudly as she replied, "I should be unworthy of the state which gave me birth, were I afraid to say what I think. No, I am not afraid; and should Harney, with his whole band of marauders, attack our house, he will find at least one who is not a coward. I would not deny my country to save my life. Still, I do not think it right to expose myself unnecessarily to danger, and as Mrs. Worthington is very timid, and very anxious to go North, where there is safety, I too have concluded that it is best to leave Spring Bank for a time. Aunt Eunice, who is afraid of nothing, will remain in charge of the house, while you, we hope, will have a care for the negroes until we return, or Hugh, if that time ever comes," and Alice's voice trembled as she thought how long it was since they had heard from Hugh, three months having elapsed since a word had come to them from him.

Col. Tiffton was glad Alice was going North, for in those excited times he knew not what harm might befall her, alone and unprotected as she was at Spring Bank. He would willingly take charge of the negroes, he said, and he kindly offered to do whatever he could to expedite her departure. Alice would not confess to him that the great object of her going North was the hope she had of being nearer Hugh, for it was arranged between herself and Mrs. Worthington that, after stopping for a few days in Snowdon they should go on to Washington where some tidings might be received of the soldier, and where they might perhaps hear from Adah, who had not yet been found. This was Alice's plan, and after receiving the Colonel's approbation, she communicated it to the negroes, telling it first to Sam, who begged earnestly to go with her.

"Don't leave me, Miss Ellis. Take me 'long, please take me to Massah Hugh. I'se quite peart now, and kin look after Miss Ellis a heap."

Alice could not promise till she had talked with Mrs. Worthington, who offered no objection, and it was arranged that with Densie, Sam, and Lulu, they should start at once for Snowdon. Accordingly, one week after Alice's conversation with Col. Tiffton she bade adieu to Spring Bank and was on her way to the North, where there was safety and quiet.

Anna Millbrook's eyes were dim with tears, and her heart was sore with pain, when told that Alice Johnson was waiting for her in the parlor below. Only the day before had she heard of her brother's disgrace, feeling as she heard it, how much rather she would that he had died ere there were so many stains upon his name. But *Alice* would comfort her, and she hastened to meet her. Sitting down beside her, she talked with her long of all that had transpired since last they met; talked of Adah, and then of Willie, who at

Alice's request, was taken by her to the hotel, where Mrs. Worthington was stopping. He had grown to be a most beautiful and engaging child, and Mrs. Worthington justly felt a thrill of pride as she clasped him to her bosom, weeping over him passionately. She could scarcely bear to lose him from her sight, and when later in the day Anna came down for him, she begged hard for him to stay. But Willie preferred returning with Mrs. Millbrook, who promised that he should come every day so long as Mrs. Worthington remained at the hotel.

As soon as Mrs. Richards learned that Mrs. Worthington and Alice were in town, she insisted upon their coming to Terrace Hill. There were the pleasant chambers fitted up for 'Lina, they had never been occupied, and Mrs. Worthington could have them as well as not; or better yet—could take Anna's old chamber, with the little room adjoining, where Adah used to sleep. Mrs. Worthington preferred the latter, and removed with Alice to Terrace Hill, while at Anna's request Densie went to Riverside Cottage, where she used to live, and where she was much happier than she would have been with strangers.

Not long however could Mrs. Worthington remain contentedly at Snowdon, and after a time Alice started with her and Lulu for Washington, taking with them Sam, who seemed a perfect child in his delight at the prospect of seeing "Massah Hugh." From a soldier returning home on furlough they heard that he was with his Regiment but to see him was not so easy a matter. Indeed, he seemed farther off at Washington than he had done at Spring Bank, and Alice sometimes questioned the propriety of having left Kentucky at all. They were not very comfortable at Washington, and as Mrs. Worthington pined for the pure country air, Alice managed at last to procure board at the house of a friend whose acquaintance she had made at the time of her visits to Virginia. It was some distance from Washington, and so near to Bull Run that when at last the second battle was fought in that vicinity, the roar of the artillery was distinctly heard, and they who listened to the noise of that bloody conflict knew just when the battle ceased, and thought with tearful anguish of the poor, maimed, suffering wretches left to bleed and die alone. They knew *Hugh* must have been in the battle, and Mrs. Worthington's anxiety amounted almost to insanity, while Alice, with blanched cheek and compressed lip, could only pray silently that he might be spared. Only Sam thought of acting.

"Now is my time," he said to Alice, as they stood talking together of Hugh, and wondering if he were safe. "Something tell me Massah Hugh is hurted somewhar, and I'se gwine to find him. I knows all de way, an' every tree round dat place. I can hide from de 'Federacy. Dem Rebels let ole white-har'd nigger look for young massah, and I'se gwine. P'raps I not find him, but I does somebody some good. I helps somebody's Massah Hugh."

It seemed a crazy project, letting that old man start off on so strange an errand, but Sam was determined.

"He had a 'sentiment," as he said, "that Hugh was wounded, and he must go to him."

In his presentiment Alice had no faith; but she did not oppose him, and at parting she said to him hesitatingly,

"Sam,—did you,—do you,—has it ever occurred to you that your master cared particularly for me;—that is,—cared,—you know how," and Alice blushed scarlet while Sam replied eagerly, "Yes, Miss, Sam got mizzable memory, but he knows dat ar, and it passes him what Massah Hugh done jine de army for, when he might stay home and haved Miss Ellis just as Sam pray he might so long. Massah Hugh and Miss Ellis make good span. I tell Massah. Shall I?"

"Not unless you find him wounded and believe him dying, then, you may tell him,—tell him—that I said—I loved him; and had he ever come back, I would have been his wife."

"I tells him," was Sam's reply, as he departed on his errand of mercy, which proved not to be a fruitless one, for he *did* find his master, and falling on his knees beside him, uttered the joyful words we have before repeated.

To the faint, half-dying Hugh that familiar voice from home and that dusky form bending over him so pityingly, seemed more like a dream than a reality. He could not comprehend how Sam came there, or what he was saying to him. Something he heard of ole Miss and Snow-down, and Washington; but nothing was real until he caught the name of *Alice*, and thought Sam said she was there.

"Where, Sam—where?" he asked, trying to raise himself upon his elbow. "Is Alice here, did you say?"

"No, massah; not 'zactly here—but on de road. If massah could ride, Sam hold him on, like massah oncet held on ole Sam, and we'll get to her directly. They's kind o' Secesh folks whar she is, but mighty good to her. She knowed 'em 'fore, 'case way down here is whar Sam was sold dat time Miss Ellis comed and show him de road to *Can'an*. Miss Ellis tell me somethin' nice for Massah Hugh, ef he's dyin' —suffin make him so glad. Is you dyin', massah?"

"I hardly think I am as bad as that. Can't you tell unless I am near to death?" Hugh said; and Sam replied,

"No, massah; dem's my orders. 'Ef he's dyin', Sam tell him I' —dat's what she say. Maybe you *is* dyin', massah. Feel and see!"

"It's possible," and something like his old mischievous smile played round Hugh's white lips as he asked how a chap felt when he was dying.

"I'se got mizzable mem'ry, and I don't justly 'member," was Sam's answer; "but I reckons he feel berry queer and choky—berry."

"That's exactly my case, so you may venture to tell," Hugh said; and getting his face close to that of the young man, Sam whispered "She say, 'Tell massah Hugh—I—I' —you's *sure* you's dyin'?"

"I'm sure I feel as you said I must," Hugh replied, and Sam went on. "'Tell him I loves him; and ef he lives I'll be his wife.' Dem's her very words, nigh as I can 'member—but what is massah goin' to do" he continued, in some surprise, as Hugh attempted to rise.

"Do, I'm going to Alice," was Hugh's reply, as with a moan he sank back again, too weak to rise alone.

"Then you be'nt dyin', after all," was Sam's rueful comment, as he suggested, "Ef massah only clamber onto Rocket."

This was easier proposed than done, but after several trials Hugh succeeded; and, with Sam steadying him while he half lay on Rocket's neck, he proceeded slowly and safely through the woods, meeting at last with some Unionists, who gave him what aid they could, and did not leave him until they saw him safely deposited in an ambulance, which, in spite of his entreaties, took him direct to Georgetown. It was a bitter disappointment to Hugh, so bitter, indeed, that he scarcely felt the pain when his broken arm was set; and when, at last, he was left alone in his narrow hospital bed, he turned his face to the wall, and cried, just as many a poor, homesick soldier had done before him, and will do again.

Twenty-four hours had passed, and in Hugh's room it was growing dark again. All the day he had watched anxiously the door through which visitors would enter, asking repeatedly if no one had called for him; but just as the sun was going down he fell away to sleep, dreaming at last that *Golden*

Hair was there—that her soft, white hands were on his brow, her sweet lips pressed to his, while her dear voice murmured softly, "Darling Hugh!"

There was a cry of pain from a distant corner, and Hugh awoke to know it was no dream—the soft hands on his brow, the kiss upon his lips—for *Golden Hair was* there; and by the tears she dropped upon his face, and the caresses she gave him, he knew that Sam had told him truly. For several minutes there was silence between them, while the eyes looked into each other with a deeper meaning than words could have expressed; then smoothing back his damp brown hair, and letting her fingers still rest upon his forehead, Alice whispered to him, "I loved you, Hugh, when you left home, and I hoped that first note would have told you so. I wish it had, for then we need not have been separated so long."

Winding his well arm round her neck, and drawing her nearer to him, Hugh answered,

"It was best just as it is. Had I been sure of your love, I should have found it harder to leave home. My country needed me. I am glad I have done what I could to defend it. Glad that I joined the army, for Alice, darling, Golden Hair, in my lonely tent reading that little Bible you gave me so long ago, the Saviour found me, and now, whether I live or not, it is well, for if I die, I am sure you will be mine in Heaven; and if I live——"

Alice finished the sentence for him,

"If you live, God willing, I shall be your wife. Dear Hugh, I bless the Good Father, first for bringing you to Himself, and then restoring you to me."

CHAPTER XXXIX
GOING HOME

The village hearse was waiting at Snowdon depot, and close beside it stood the carriage from Terrace Hill; the one sent there for Adah, the other for her husband, whose life-blood, so freely shed, had wiped away all stains upon his memory, and enshrined him in the hearts of Snowdon's people as a martyr. He was the first dead soldier returned to them, his the first soldier's grave in their churchyard; and so a goodly throng were there, with plaintive fife and muffled drum, to do him honor. His major was coming with him, it was said—Major Stanley, who had himself been found in a half-fainting condition watching by the dead—Major Stanley, who had seen that the body was embalmed, had written to the wife, and had attended to everything, even to coming on himself by way of showing his respect. Death is a great softener of errors; and the village people, who could not remember a time when they had not disliked John Richards, forgot his faults now that he was dead.

It seemed a long time waiting for the train, but it came at last, and the crowd involuntarily made a movement forward, and then drew back as a tall figure appeared up on the platform, his uniform betokening an officer of rank, and his manner showing plainly that he was master of ceremonies.

"Major Stanley," ran in a whisper through the crowd, whose wonder increased when another, and, if possible, a finer-looking man, emerged into view, his right arm in a sling, and his face pale and worn, from the effects of recent illness. He had not been expected, and many curious glances were cast at him as, slowly descending the steps, he gave his hand to Mrs. Worthington following close behind. They knew her, and recognized also the two young ladies, Alice and Adah, as they sprang from the car. Poor Adah! how she shrank from the public gaze, shuddering as, on her way to the carriage, she passed the long box the men were handling so carefully.

Summoned by Irving Stanley, she had come on to Washington, and while there, had learned that Mrs. Worthington, Hugh, and Alice were all in Georgetown, whither she hastened at once. Immediately after the discovery of her parentage, she had written to Kentucky, but the letter had not reached its destination, consequently no one but Hugh knew how near she was; and he had only learned it a few days before the battle, when he had, by accident, a few moments' conversation with Dr. Richards, whom he had purposely avoided. He was talking of Adah, and the practicability of sending for her, when she arrived at the private boarding-house to which he had been removed.

The particulars of that interview between the mother and her daughter we cannot describe, as no one witnessed it save God; but Adah's face was radiant with happiness and her eyes beaming with joy when it was ended, and she went next to where Hugh was waiting for her.

"Oh, Hugh, my noble brother!" was all she could say, as she wound her arms around his neck and pressed her cheek against his own, forgetting, in those moments of perfect bliss, all the sorrow, and anguish of the past.

Nor was it until Hugh said to her, "The doctor was in that battle, did he escape unharmed?" that a shadow dimmed the sunshine flooding her pathway that autumn morning.

At the mention of *him*, the muscles about her mouth grew rigid, and a look of pain flitted across her face showing that there was yet much of bitterness mingled in her cup of joy. Composing herself as soon as possible she told Hugh that she was a widow, but uttered no word of complaint against the dead, and Hugh, knowing that she could not sorrow as other women have sorrowed over the loved ones slain in battle, drew her nearer to him, and kissing her tenderly, said, "Your home shall be with me and Golden Hair—who has promised to be my wife."

Then he asked what Major Stanley's plan was concerning the body of her husband, and upon learning that it was to bury the doctor at home, he announced his determination to accompany them, as he knew he should be able to do so.

It was a great trial to Adah to face the crowd they found assembled at the depot, but Irving, Hugh, and Alice all helped to screen her from observation, and almost before she was aware of it she found herself safe in the carriage, which effectually hid her from view. Slowly the procession moved through the village, the foot passengers keeping time to the muffled drum, whose solemn beats had never till that morning been heard in the quiet streets. The wide gate which led into the grounds of Terrace Hill was opened wide, and the black hearse passed in, followed by the other carriages, which wound round the hill and up to the huge building where badges of mourning were hung out for the only son, the youngest born, the once pride and pet of the stately woman who watched the coming of that group with tear-dim eyes, holding upon her lap the little boy whose father they were bringing in, dead, coffined for the grave. Not for the world would that high-bred woman have been guilty of an impropriety, and so she sat in her own room, while Charlie Millbrook met the bearers in the hall and told them where to deposit their burden.

In the same room where we first saw him on the night of his return from Europe they left him, and went their way, while to Dixon and Pamelia was accorded the honor of first welcoming Adah, whom they treated with as much deference as if she had never been with them in any capacity save that of mistress. She had changed since they last saw her—was wonderfully improved, they said to each other as they left her at the door of the room, where Mrs. Richards, with her two older daughters, was waiting to receive her. But if the servants were struck with the air of dignity and cultivation which Adah acquired during her tour in Europe, how much more did this same air impress the haughty ladies who had felt a little uncertain as to *how* they should receive her. Any doubts, however, which they had upon this subject were dispelled the moment she entered the room, and they saw at a glance that it was not the timid, shrinking Adah Gordon with whom they had to deal, but a woman as wholly self-possessed as themselves, and one with whose bearing even their critical eyes would find no fault. She would not suffer them to *patronize* her; they must treat her fully as an equal or as nothing, and with a new-born feeling of pride in her late son's widow, Mrs. Richards arose, and putting Willie from her lap, advanced to meet her, cordially extending her hand, but uttering no word of welcome. Adah took the hand, but her eyes never sought the face of her lady mother. They were riveted with a hungry, wistful, longing look on *Willie*, who, clinging to his grandmother's skirts, peered curiously at her, holding back at first, when, unmindful of Asenath and Eudora, who had not yet been greeted, she tried to take him in her arms.

"Oh, Willie, darling, don't you know me! I am poor mam-ma," and Adah's voice was choked with sobs at this unlooked for reception from her child.

He had been sent for from Anna's home to meet his mother, because it was proper; but no one at Terrace Hill had said to him that the mamma for whom Anna taught him daily to pray, was coming. *She* was not in his mind; and as eighteen months had obliterated all memories of the girlish creature he once knew as mother, he could not immediately identify that mother with the lady before him.

It was a sad disappointment to Adah, and without knowing what she was doing, she sank down upon the sofa, and involuntarily laying her head in Mrs. Richards lap, cried bitterly, her tears bringing answering ones from the eyes of all three of the ladies, for they half believed her grief, in part, was for the lifeless form in the room below.

"Poor child, you are tired and worn. It is hard to lose him just as there was a prospect of perfect reconciliation with us all," Mrs. Richards said, softly smoothing the brown tresses lying on her lap, and thinking even then that *curls* were more becoming to her daughter-in-law than braids had been, but wondering why, now she was in mourning, Adah had persisted in wearing them.

"Pretty girl, pretty *turls*, is you *tyin?*" and won by her distress, Willie drew near, and laid his baby hand upon the curls he thought so pretty.

"That's mamma, Willie," Asenath said; "the mamma Aunt Anna said would come some time—Willie's mamma. Can't he kiss her?"

The child could not resist the face which, lifting itself up, looked eagerly at him, and he put up his little hands for Adah to take him, returning the kisses she showered upon him, and clinging to her neck, while he said, "Is you mam-ma sure? I prays for mam-ma—God take care of her, and pa-pa too. He's dead. They brought him back with a *dum*. Poor pa-pa, Willie don't want him dead;" and the little lip began to quiver.

Never since she knew she was a widow had Adah felt so vivid a sensation of something akin to affection for the dead, as when her child mourned so plaintively for papa; and the tears which now fell like rain were not for Willie alone.

"Mrs. Richards has not yet greeted us," Asenath said; and turning to her at once, Adah apologized for her seeming neglect, pressing both her and Eudora's hands more cordially than she would have done a few moments before.

"Where is Anna?" she asked; and Mrs. Richards replied,

"She's sick. She regretted much that she could not come up here to-day;" while Willie, standing in Adah's lap, with his chubby arm around her neck, chimed in,

"You don't know what we've dot. We've dot 'ittle baby, we has."

Adah knew now why Anna was absent, and why Charlie Millbrook looked so happy when at last he came in to see her, delivering sundry messages from his Anna, who, he said, could scarcely wait to see her *dear sister*. There was something genuine in Charlie's greeting, something which made Adah feel as if she were indeed at home, and she wondered much how even the Richards race could ever have objected to him, as she watched his movements and heard him talking with his stately mother.

"Yes, Major Stanley came," he said, in reply to her question, and Adah was glad it was put to *him*, for the blushes dyed her cheek at once, and she bent over Willie to hide them, while Charlie continued, "Captain Worthington came, too. He was in the same battle with the doctor, was wounded rather seriously, and has been discharged, I believe."

"Oh," and Mrs. Richards seemed quite interested, asking where the young men were, and appearing disappointed when told that, after waiting a few moments in hopes of seeing the ladies, they had returned to the hotel, where Mrs. Worthington and Alice were stopping.

"I fully expected the ladies here; pray, send for them at once," she said, but Adah interposed.

"Her mother would not willingly be separated from Hugh, and as he of course would remain at the hotel, it would be useless to think of persuading Mrs. Worthington to come to Terrace Hill."

"But Miss Johnson surely will come," persisted Mrs. Richards.

Adah could not explain then that Alice was less likely to leave Hugh than her mother, but she said, "Miss Johnson, will not leave mother alone," and so the matter was settled.

It was a terribly long day to Adah, and she was glad when towards its close Alice was announced as being in the reception room. She had driven round, to call on Mrs. Richards, and after that take Adah with her to the cottage, where Anna, she knew, was anxious to receive her. At first Mrs. Richards demurred, fearing it would be improper, but saying, "My late son's wife is of course her own mistress, and can do as she likes."

Very adroitly Alice waived all objections, and bore Adah off in triumph.

"I knew you must be lonely up there," she said, as they drove slowly along, "and there can be no harm in visiting one's sick sister."

Anna surely did not think there was, as her warm, welcoming kisses fully testified.

"I wanted so much to see you to-day," she said, "that I have worked myself into quite a fever; but knowing mother as I do, I feared she might not sanction your coming;" then proudly turning down the blanket, she disclosed the red-faced baby, who, just one week ago, had come to the Riverside Cottage.

"Isn't he a beauty?" she asked, pressing her lips upon the wrinkled forehead. "A boy, too, and looks so much like Charlie, but—" and her soft, blue eyes seemed more beautiful than ever with the maternal love shining from them. "I shall not call him Charles, nor yet *John*, though mother's heart is set on the latter name. I can't. I loved my brother dearly, and never so much as now that he is dead, but my baby-boy must not bear his name, and so I have chosen *Hugh, Hugh Richards*. I know it will please you both," and she glanced archly at Alice, who blushingly kissed the little boy named for her promised husband.

They talked of Hugh awhile, and then Anna spoke of Irving Stanley, expressing her fears that she could not see him to thank him for his kindness and forbearance to her erring brother.

"He must be noble and good," she said, then turning to Adah, she continued. "You know him well. Do you like him?"

"Yes," and Adah's face was all ablaze, as the simple answer dropped from her lips.

For a moment Anna regarded her intently, then her eyes were withdrawn and her white hand beat the counterpane softly, but nothing more was said of Irving Stanley.

The next day near the sun-setting, they buried the dead soldier, Mrs. Richards and Adah standing side by side as the body was lowered to its last resting place, the older leaning upon the younger for support, and feeling as she went back to her lonely home and heard the merry laugh of little Willie in the hall that she was glad her son had married the young girl, who, now that John was gone forever, began to be very dear to her as his wife, the Lily whom he had loved so much. In the dusky twilight of that night when alone with Adah, she told her as much, speaking sadly of the past, which she regretted, and wishing she had never objected to receiving the girl about whom John wrote so lovingly.

"Had I done differently he might have been living now, and you have been spared much pain, but you'll forgive me. I'm an old woman. I am breaking fast, and soon shall follow my boy, but while I live I wish for peace, and you must love me, Lily, because I was his mother," and the hand of her who had conceded so much, rested entreatingly upon the bowed head of the young girl beside her. There was no acting there, Adah knew, and clasping the trembling hand she involuntarily whispered,

"I will love you, my *mother*."

"And stay with me, too?" Mrs. Richards continued, her voice choked with the sobs she could not repress, when she heard herself called mother by the girl she had so wronged. "Anna is gone, my other daughters are old. We are lonely in this great house. We need somebody young to cheer our solitude, and you will stay, as *mistress*, if you choose, or as a petted youngest daughter."

This was an unlooked for trial to Adah. She had not dreamed of living at Terrace Hill. But Adah had never consulted her own happiness, and as she listened to the pleading tones of the woman who surely had *some heart,* some noble qualities, she felt that 'twas her duty to remain there for a time at least, and so she replied at last,

"I expected to live with my own mother, but for the present my home shall be here with you."

"God bless you, darling," and the proud woman's lips touched the fair cheek, while the proud woman's hand smoothed again the soft short curls, pushing them back from the white brow, as she murmured, "You are very beautiful, my child, just as John said you were."

It was hard for Adah to tell Mrs. Worthington that *she* could not make one of the circle who would gather around the home fireside, but she did at last, standing firmly by her decision, and saying in reply to her mother's entreaties, "It is my duty. They need me more than you, who have both Hugh and Alice."

Adah was right, so Hugh said, and Alice, too, while Irving Stanley said nothing. He must have found much that was attractive about the little town of Snowdon, for he lingered there long after there was not the least excuse for staying. He did not go often to Terrace Hill, and when he did, he never asked for Adah, but so long as he could see her on Sundays when, with the Richards' family, she walked quietly up the aisle, her cheek flushing as she passed him, and so long as he occasionally met her at Mrs. Worthington's rooms, or saw her riding in the Richards carriage, so long was he content to stay. But there came a time when he must go, and then he asked for Adah, and in the presence of her mother-in-law invited her to go with him to her husband's grave. She went, taking Willie with her, and there, with that fresh mound between them, Irving Stanley told her what the dying soldier had said, and asked if it should be so.

"Not now, not yet," he continued, as Adah's eyes were bent upon that grave, "but by and by, will you do your husband's bidding and be my wife?"

"I will," and taking Willie's hand Adah put it with hers into the broad, warm palm which clasped them both, as Irving whispered, "Your child shall be mine, and never need to know that I am not his father."

It was arranged that Alice should tell Mrs. Richards, as Adah would have no concealments. Accordingly, Alice asked a private interview with the lady, to whom she told everything as she understood it. And Mrs. Richards, though weeping bitterly, generously exonerated Adah from all blame, commended her as having acted wisely, and then added, with a flush of pride:

"Many a woman would be glad to marry Irving Stanley, and it gives me pleasure to know that to my son's widow the honor is accorded. He is worthy to take John's place, and she, I believe, is worthy of him. I love her already as my daughter, and shall look upon him as a son. You say they are in the garden. Let them both come to me."

They came, and listened quietly, while Mrs. Richards sanctioned their engagement, and then, with a little eulogy upon her departed son, said to Adah, "You will wait a year, of course. It will not be proper before."

Irving had hoped for only six months' probation, but Adah was satisfied with the year, and they went from Mrs. Richards' presence with the feeling that Providence was indeed smiling upon their pathway, and flooding it with sunshine.

The next day Major Stanley left Snowdon, but not until there had come to Hugh a letter, whose handwriting made Mrs. Worthington turn pale, it brought back so vividly the terror of the olden time. It was from Murdoch, and it enclosed for Mrs. Worthington the sum of five hundred dollars, "I have no reason for thinking you rich," he wrote, "and should she need more I will try to send it as some atonement for the past."

Then, after speaking of his fruitless search for Adah, and his hearing at last that she was found and Dr. Richards dead, he added, "As there is nothing left for me to do, and as I am sure to be playing mischief if idle, I have joined the army, and am training a band of contrabands to fight as soon as the government comes to its senses, and is willing for the negroes to bear their part in the battle."

The letter ended with saying that he should never come out of the war alive, simply because it would last until he was too old to live any longer.

It was a relief for Mrs. Worthington to hear from him, and know that he probably would not trouble her again, while Adah, whose memories of him were pleasanter, expressed a strong desire to see him.

"We will find him by and by, when you are mine," Irving said playfully and drawing her into an adjoining room, where they could be alone, he said his parting words, and then with Hugh went to meet the train which took him away from Snowdon.

CHAPTER XL
CONCLUSION

The New England hills were tinged with that peculiar purplish haze, so common to the Indian summer time, and the warm sunlight of November fell softly upon Snowdon, whose streets were full of eager, expectant people— all hurrying on to the old brick church, and quickening their steps with every stroke of the merry bell, pealing so joyfully from the tall, dark tower. The Richards' carriage was out, and waiting before the door of the Riverside cottage, for the appearance of Anna, who was this morning to venture out for a short time, leaving her baby Hugh alone. Another, and handsomer carriage, was standing before the hotel, where Hugh and his mother were stopping, and where, in a pleasant private room, Adah Richards helped Alice Johnson make her tasteful toilet, smoothing lovingly the rich folds of greyish colored silk, arranging the snowy cuffs and collar, and then bringing the hat of brown Neapolitan, with its pretty face trimmings of blue, and declaring it a shame to cover up the curls of hair falling so luxuriously about the face and neck of the blushing bride. For it was Alice's wedding day, and in the room adjoining, Hugh Worthington stood, waiting impatiently the opening of the mysterious door which Adah had shut against him, and wondering if, after all, it were not a dream that the time was coming fast when neither bolts nor locks would have a right to keep him from his wife.

It seemed too great a joy to be true, and by way of reassuring himself he had to look often at the crowds of people hurrying by, and down upon old Sam, who, in full dress, with white cotton gloves drawn awkwardly up on his cramped distorted fingers, stood by the carriage, bowing to all who passed, himself the very personification of perfect bliss.

"Massah Hugh the perfectest massah," he said, "and Miss Ellis a little more so;" adding that though "Canaan was a mighty nice place, he 'sumed, he'd rather not go thar jist yet, but live a leetle longer to see them 'joy themselves. Thar they comes—dat's Miss in grey. She knows how't orange posies and silks and satins is proper for weddin' nights; but she's gwine travelin', and dat's why she comed out in dat *stun-color*, Sam'll be blamed if he fancies." And having thus explained Alice's choice of dress, the old negro held the carriage door himself, while Hugh, handing in his mother, sister, and his bride, took his seat beside them, and was driven to the church.

Twenty minutes passed, and then the streets were filled again; but now the people were going home, talking as they went of the beauty of the bride, and of the splendid-looking bridegroom, who looked so fondly at her as she murmured her responses, kissing her first himself when the ceremony was over, and letting his arm rest for a moment around her slender form. No one doubted its being a genuine love-match, and all rejoiced in the happiness of the newly married pair, who, at the village depot were waiting for the train which would take them on their way to Kentucky, for that was their destination.

In the distracted condition of the country Hugh's presence was needed there; for, taking advantage of his absence, and the thousand rumors afloat touching the Proclamation one of his negroes had already ran away in company with some half-dozen of the Colonel's, who, in a terrible state of excitement, talked seriously of emigrating to Canada. Hugh's timely arrival, however, quieted him somewhat, though he listened in sorrow, and almost with tears, to Hugh's plan of selling the Spring Bank farm and removing with his negroes to some New England town, where Alice, he knew, would be happier than she had been in Kentucky. But a purchaser for Spring Bank was not so easily found in those dark days; and so, doing with his land the best he could, he called about him his negroes, and giving to each his freedom, proposed that they stay quietly where they were until Spring, when he hoped to find them all employment on the farm he was to buy in New England.

Aunt Eunice who understood managing blacks better than his mother or his inexperienced wife, was to be his housekeeper in that new home of his, where the Colonel and his family would always be welcome; and having thus provided for those for whom it was his duty to care, he returned to Snowdon in time to join the Christmas party at Terrace Hill, where Irving Stanley was a guest, and where, in spite of the war clouds darkening our land, and in spite of the sad, haunting memories of the dead, there was much of hilarity and joy—reminding the villagers of the olden time when Terrace Hill was filled with gay revelers. Anna Millbrook was there, more beautiful than in her girlhood, and excessively fond of her missionary Charlie, who she laughingly declared was perfectly incorrigible on the subject of surplice and gown, adding that as "the mountain would not go to Mahomet, Mahomet must go to the mountain;" and so she was fast becoming an out-and-out Presbyterian of the very bluest stripe.

Sweet Anna! None who looked into her truthful, loving face, or knew the consistency of her daily life, could doubt that whether Presbyterian or Episcopal in sentiment, the heart was right and the feet were treading the narrow path which leadeth unto life eternal.

It was a happy week spent at Terrace Hill; but one heart ached to its very core when, at its close, Irving Stanley went back to where duty called him, trusting that the God who had succored him thus far, would shield him from future harm, and keep him safely till the coming autumn, when, with the first falling of the leaf, he would gather to his embrace his darling beautiful Adah.

On the white walls of a handsome country seat just on the banks of the Connecticut, the light of the April sunset falls, and the soft April wind kisses the fair cheek and lifts the golden curls of the young mistress of Spring Bank—for so, in memory of the olden time, Hugh and Alice have named their new home. Arm in arm they walk up and down the terraced garden, talking softly of the way they have been led, and gratefully ascribing all praise to Him who rules and overrules, but doeth nought save good to those who love Him.

Down in the meadow-land and at the rear of the building, dusky forms are seen—the negroes, who have come to their Northern home, and with them the runaway. Ashamed of his desertion he has returned to his former master, resenting the name of *contraband*, and denouncing the ultra-abolitionist as humbugs, who deserved putting in the front of every battle. Hugh knows it will be hard accustoming these blacks to Northern usages but as he has their good in view, he feels sure that in time he will succeed, and cares but little for the opinion of those who wonder what he "expects to do with that lazy lot of niggers."

On a rustic seat, near a rear door, white-haired old Sam is sitting, listening intently, while dusky Mug, reads to him from the book of books, the one he prizes above all else, stopping occasionally to expound, in his own way, some point which he fancies may not be clear to her, likening every good man to "Massah Hugh," and every bad one to the leader of the "Suddern Federacy," whose *horse* he declares he held once in "ole Virginny," telling Mug, in an aside, "how, if 'twant wicked, not agin de scripter, he should most wish he'd put beech-nuts under Massah Jeffres' saddle, and so broke his fetch-ed neck, 'fore he raise sich a muss, runnin' calico so high that Miss Ellis 'clar she couldn't 'ford it, and axin' fifteen cents for a paltry spool of cotton."

In the stable-yard, Claib, his good-humored face all aglow with pride, is exercising Rocket, who arches his neck as proudly as of old, and dances mincingly around, while Lulu leans over the gate, watching not so much him as the individual who holds him. And now that it grows darker, and the ripple of the river sounds more like eventide, lights gleam from the pleasant parlor where Mrs. Worthington and Aunt Eunice are sitting by the cheerful fire, just kindled on the marble hearth. Thither Hugh and Alice repair, while one by one the negroes come quietly in, and kneeling side by side, follow with stammering tongues, but honest hearts, their beloved master as he says first the prayer our Saviour taught, and then with words of thankful praise asks God to bless and keep him and his in the days to come, even as he has blessed and kept them in the days gone by.